UNCOMMON
REASON

Books by the same author

The Meeting,
Words of the shaman, Joshua. (A novel)

Like a large immovable rock,
A Festschrift in appreciation of Ramesh S. Balsekar.

Something To Ponder,
A contemporary version of Lao Tzu's Tao Te Ching.

Reviews of
"Uncommon Reason"

"This novel, (*Uncommon Reason*) does something unusual—it presents an imaginary situation which can give us hope because it indicates what is necessary and even suggests it is possible...and in these desperate times we need to imagine good things happening and to hear the arguments in the mouth of David Tremaine."

Howard Zinn, Professor Emeritus, Boston University, Boston, Massachusetts, USA

. . .

"Throughout this suspense filled, spiritual, political thriller Mallard weaves threads of wisdom. Entering a world of political intrigue, corruption, war and terror the reader finds his heart warmed by love, courage, peace and a sense of hope and optimism for humanity."

Madhukar Thompson, author of *The Odyssey Of Enlightenment, Rare Interviews With Enlightened Teachers Of Our Time*, Maui, Hi

. . .

Uncommon Reason is one of the most thought provoking books I have read...a wake up call... will [it] take another terrorist attack on US soil to bring us back to the question, "Why do the terrorists hate us?"...Ending our ignorance is a means to the solution. Thank you Colin Mallard, for having the audacity to begin the inquiry.

Felicia M. Barlow, MA, Producer & Writer, Annapolis, MD

. . .

"What is dangerous in Mallard's book is that his words ring true... *Uncommon Reason* is not fashionable literary entertainment it is instead something to ponder, something that challenges us in a passionate, powerful and straight-forward manner."

Manuel Fernandez, Courtenay, BC Canada

. . .

"In this book, the principles of love, mutual respect, and selfless service are applied to... the Middle East conflict, the attacks of 9/11 and the

current War on Terror. *Uncommon Reason* is a must read for those who are truly desirous of a more peaceful way of living in the world."
John Higgenbottom, Courtenay, BC Canada

. . .

"In his intriguing book, *Uncommon Reason*, Mallard breathes life and newfound wisdom into our understanding of hope for peace on earth... His message is one that is both clear and prophetic in nature."
Christine Welch, Courtenay, BC Canada

. . .

"With power and immediacy, Mallard shows how the teachings of the great masters are as necessary today as they have ever been."
Joyce Tinney, Qualicum Beach, BC, Canada

. . .

"The warlords response to 9/11 has clearly shown that the war on terror isn't working. Violence begets violence. This refreshing novel offers an uncommon response to violence. It shows there is hope for peace."
Sharone Elizabeth. RN. O.R. BA. Ayurvedic Medicine, Victoria, Canada

. . .

"*Uncommon Reason* gets to the root of conflict, and the remedy for healing...Local, provincial, national and international leaders can learn from this book...Once I started reading it I couldn't put it down."
Alvin "Bear" Scow, Campbell River, BC, Canada

. . .

*"Mallard crafts a message for today. Penetrating gradual unfolding of the secrets of life."
The Book Reader, San Francisco, CA

. . .

"The doors opened by the *Celestine Prophecy* are swung wide open by Mallard."
Vision Magazine, San Diego, CA

*"A real page turner that is sure to make the best seller list."
Aquarian Age Bookstore, Huntington Beach, CA

. . .

*"A thought provoking story...touches on the deeply spiritual and existential...Recommend [it] to your patrons who are interested in politics, social reform, and spiritual growth...I enjoyed the book tremendously."
Sandy Anastasi Starchild, New Age Retailer

. . .

*"...politically incorrect, religiously troubling and thought provoking... Mallard has provided the reader with something to ponder [it] is not a quick read. Don't expect to be simply entertained. Expect to be challenged. I was."
Ginger Cody, Ramona Sentinel, Ramona, CA

. . .

*"A stimulating piece of storytelling ... highly engaging, the ideas presented   very fresh. I recommend it."
NAPRA Re View ABA

. . .

*"A riveting book of our times that makes you think even in war there is hope, idealism and love. Read it and grow."
Leona Mayers, Camille Publications, Arlington, Texas

. . .

*"This book has everything; its philosophical yet has adventure, intrigue, pathos and romance...the reader is drawn into the story and finds subtle changes occurring in his/her own thinking."
Rev. Lavona Stillman, Universal Church of the Master, Santa Clara, CA

. . .

*"...a book to be read and discussed by all who govern or aspire to, from Presidents and Prime Ministers to Municipal Councilors and Non-government community leaders."
Derrick Mallard, National award winning environmentalist, Victoria, British Columbia, Canada

*"The time is now. Your imagination is my inspiration."
David Tarnas, State Representative, State Capital, Honolulu, Hawaii

. . .

*"It took me from skepticism, to hope, to commitment. It is a book that lingers in the mind, invites you to read it again, and compels you to pass it on to friends."
Ana Bergin, Ancient Wisdoms, Kailua, Kona, Hawaii

These reviews were of an earlier edition of Uncommon Reason entitled, Mr. President.

REVIEWS OF "THE MEETING."

"Not just another story, it's a new way of looking at things, a message here for all of us written in a poetic and gentle way."
B. C. Boggs. Kamuela, Hawaii, USA

. . .

"a great book that purveys wisdom and truth in an easy to understand format, a suspenseful and captivating story of a family's struggle to survive."
J. Banslaben, Long Island, New York, USA

. . .

"The search for truth and understanding can be an elusive one, especially if you are looking in all the wrong places. *The Meeting,* thankfully, offers no formula solutions to the complicated problems of relationship. It offers an opportunity to see more clearly how the telling of the truth about your situation can set you free."
Karl O. Hynes, D.C., Kona, Hawaii, USA

. . .

"I couldn't put it down. At times I cried so hard I couldn't see to read anymore. When I finished reading, I felt better than I had in a long time.

I felt uplifted, more at peace in myself and with the world."
Shanti, Honolulu, Hawaii, USA

. . .

"We sat at the beach in front of my condo with big tears running down our cheeks, me choking over the next few sentences, [C], saying: "Don't stop, keep reading." And then the laughing and crying at the same time. We had touched our own joy through the sorrow."
V. Bright, Kona, Hawaii, USA

. . .

"I found myself shocked, fiercely enraged and silently screaming. For the first time I heard the wisdom and counsel of Joshua and read and re-read the insights that have universal application."
K. Chickite, Campbell River, B.C., Canada

. . .

"*The Meeting* helped me gain insight into underlying, deeper issues that I never thought of previously. What dramatic change can result by gaining insight into why we behave the way we do."
Mina Morehouse, Courtenay, B.C., Canada

REVIEWS OF "SOMETHING TO PONDER."

"Like the happy, peaceful murmur of a healing stream, the wisdom and truth in the verses of *Something To Ponder* cascade effortlessly and ever so gently into the heart; there to remain in the silence, the truth of direct understanding. If you yearn for instant peace, this is the book to read."
Madhukar Thompson, author of *The Odyssey Of Enlightenment, Rare Interviews With Enlightened Teachers Of Our Time*, Maui, USA

. . .

"Intrinsic to resolving conflict within, thus promoting peace without"
Dave Dalton, Courtenay, B.C., Canada

Quotes on War and Peace

"This is the way of peace: Overcome evil with good, falsehood with truth, and hatred with love."
Peace Pilgrim

* * *

"War visits destruction on both the vanquished and the victor alike."
General Omar Bradley

* * *

"Observe good faith and justice toward all nations. Cultivate peace and harmony with all."
George Washington

* * *

"To kill in war is not one whit purer than committing any other murder."
Albert Einstein

* * *

"Selfishness, ambition, envy, anger, and pride; if these were banished, we would enjoy perpetual peace."
Petrarch (14th century)

* * *

"Men closely acquainted with the reality of the battlefield will not be found among the ignorant numbers who glibly pursue another war."
34th President of the United States, General Dwight D. Eisenhower

* * *

"What difference does it make to the dead, the maimed, the insane, the orphaned, the homeless, whether war's mad destruction is wrought in the name of tyranny or the holy name of "liberty" and "democracy"?
Mahatma Gandhi

* * *

"My first wish is to see this plague of war banished from the earth, and the people of this world employed in more innocent, pleasing and productive pastimes rather than producing and exercising implements and strategies for human destruction."
George Washington

* * *

"Youth is the first victim of war; the first fruit of peace. It takes 20 years or more of peace to make a man; it takes only 20 seconds of war to destroy him."
King Baudouin I, King of Belgium

"War is falsehood, fear and folly paraded as purpose, courage and glory."
General William Westmoreland

* * *

"Ours is a world of nuclear giants and ethical infants. We know more about war than we know about peace, more about killing than we know about living."
General Omar Bradley

* * *

"When you give food to the poor, they call you a saint. When you ask why the poor have no food, they call you a communist."
Archbishop Helder Camara, Brazilian Liberation Theologist

* * *

"Every gun that is made, every warship launched, every rocket fired signifies, in the final sense, a theft from those who hunger and are not fed, those who are cold and are not clothed."
Dwight D. Eisenhower (1890-1969)

* * *

"I hope...that mankind will at length, as they call themselves reasonable creatures, have reason and sense enough to settle their differences without cutting throats; for in my opinion there never was a good war, or a bad peace."
Benjamin Franklin

* * *

"While seeking revenge, dig two graves - one for yourself."
Doug Horton

* * *

"Nonviolence means avoiding not only external physical violence but also internal violence of spirit. You not only refuse to shoot a man, but you refuse to hate him."
Martin Luther King, Jr.

* * *

"It is clear that the way to heal society of its violence . . . and lack of love is to replace the pyramid of domination with the circle of equality and respect."
Manitonquat

"Whoever fights monsters should see to it that in the process he does not become a monster himself."
Friedrich Nietzche

* * *

"We must have research for peace ... It would embrace the outstanding problems of morality. The time has come for man's intellect, his scientific method, to win over the immoral brutality and irrationality of war and militarism ... Now we are forced to eliminate from the world forever this vestige of prehistoric barbarism, this curse to the human race."
Linus Pauling

* * *

"When will our consciences grow so tender that we will act to prevent human misery rather than avenge it?"
Eleanor Roosevelt

* * *

"When the rich make war, it's the poor that die."
Jean-Paul Sartre

* * *

"The story of the human race is characterized by efforts to get along much more than by violent disputes, although it's the latter that make the history books. Violence is actually exceptional. The human race has survived because of cooperation, not aggression."
Gerard Vanderhaar

* * *

"Always forgive your enemies. Nothing annoys them more."
Oscar Wilde

* * *

"God help those that bear the unfathomable sorrow of battle."
Unknown (Courtesy of Walt Cronin)

Uncommon Reason

A novel of peace in time of conflict,
turmoil and terror.

Colin D. Mallard, Ph.D.

Wild Duck Publishing

Uncommon Reason

A novel of peace in time of conflict,
turmoil and terror.

Colin D. Mallard, Ph.D.

Published by
Advaita Gems
Wild Duck Publishing
British Columbia, Canada
4th Edition, September 2005

cdm@advaita-advaita.com

Cover design & book layout by David Dalton of
onedesign, Courtenay, British Columbia, Canada
onedesignca@yahoo.ca

ISBN 1-59109-889-0

LET THERE BE JUSTICE FOR ALL.
LET THERE BE PEACE FOR ALL.
LET THERE BE WORK, BREAD AND SALT FOR ALL.
LET EACH KNOW THAT FOR EACH
THE BODY, THE MIND AND THE SOUL
HAVE BEEN FREED TO FULFILL THEMSELVES.

From Nelson Mandela's 1994 Inaugural Address

In appreciation for Nelson Mandela who showed us what we are capable of.

Ah Ramesh, the wily one

The light

The moth could not escape

TABLE OF CONTENTS

Acknowledgements

With love and deep appreciation for Ramesh, who directed my attention to the light and the peace that comes with understanding.

To the Advaita master Dr. Jean Klein, light on the way.

To Dr. Ronald Gray, who helped me see the obvious, Dr Wilbur Mullen who through his unusual questions opened my mind to the realm of philosophy and to Dr. Cecil Paul whose love of truth was stronger than the narrow minds of the ignorant.

To Lillian who showed me the power of love through example.

To my good friend and fellow traveler, Madhukar Thompson, who from the first moment fell in love with the book in all its incarnations. The gods granted us the same vision having burned us with the same fire.

To Stephanie, my beloved wife, friend, gadfly and merciless critic, who's editing and input were invaluable and without whom this project would not have come to fruition.

To Mac, who has since returned to the Source, who gave of his encouragement, time and resources before his death.

To Fran, without doubt, a mother-in-law par excellence!

To those who were the first to read the book and thereby demonstrate its appeal to the public at large.

To Jennay, Norman and Anne, Karl and Channing, who supported the book and contributed of their resources in ways unique to each.

To Joyce for her editing and her love of language; someone after my own heart.

To David, who understood what it means to combine simplicity and elegance and did so in the layout of the book and the design of the covers.

Thank you Christine for your invaluable input.

And Brian, thank you for clearing up the historical inaccuracies.

PREFACE

Why do people care so little about death?

When life becomes intolerable
Death is welcomed
And he who has embraced his death
Lives without fear.

A man like this makes a formidable enemy.

Lao Tzu

From space the earth appears like a spinning blue pearl of incomparable beauty. The first astronauts to see it experienced a profound shift in awareness. Instead of an awareness of nation states and their artificial boundaries, they became aware of the planetary whole, how fragile it seemed suspended in the blackness of space. That beautiful blue spinning place we call home is at risk, threatened not by natural catastrophe but by the distortions in men's minds.

Today's events are profoundly unsettling. Hardly a day passes without a suicide bomber striking somewhere in the world. Not too long ago such occurrences were non-existent but are now commonplace! Since 9/11 some nations, and in particular the United States, are attempting to wage war on terrorism. This has done nothing to alleviate the underlying causes. It has instead made the world less safe by fanning flames of division and hatred with an arrogant self-righteous zeal. Even a foolish man doesn't take a stick and poke at a hornet's nest and expect not to be stung. Yet this is exactly the action many of the world's most powerful leaders are intent on pursuing.

The Chinese sage, Lao Tzu, had this to say some twenty-five hundred years ago.

*In victory, after the slaughter of men
How can anyone rejoice?*

*That is why the wise enter a battle gravely
With sorrow and compassion in their hearts
Like those attending a funeral.*

When the President of the United States stood on an aircraft carrier arms upraised and rejoiced in victory at the end of the Iraq war, he displayed the ignorance of a man with little comprehension of the suffering and death he had brought to tens of thousands of human beings.

Uncommon Reason, is a novel, based on the following premise:

What might happen if a man of wisdom, a sage, someone of the stature of Lao Tzu, the Buddha or the Christ, became leader of one of the world's most powerful nations?

It is easy to criticize what doesn't work and much harder to suggest alternatives. *Uncommon Reason* is a critique of contemporary society. But, more than that it points to alternatives, not in a dry abstract way but through the use of storytelling.

In the light of world events it is time for a thorough discussion of terrorism and its causes: issues of wealth, poverty, hunger, power and powerlessness, on a global basis. These are things we must address or we will be forced to pay a horrendous price as 9/11 has already given us intimations of.

Uncommon Reason, seeks to examine some of these issues and in so doing contribute to a much needed global dialogue. The basic ideas in the book are not new—they can be found in all the world's major spiritual traditions.

This unfolding conflict of terrorism and counter terrorism, threatens to become global and should that happen we would discover we were engulfed in World War Three. But this war would be unlike any other war that has gone before it. Instead of nations clashing with nations, citizens of the wealthy nations would find themselves subject to death and injury at the hands of men and women called "terrorists." In most cases these men and women, these terrorists, are heroes to millions of poor people on this planet, people who have nothing left to lose.

If you and those you know and love are going to die of starvation and your neighbor has far more than he needs, and he offers you nothing, unless of course he can make a buck at it, how will you feel, what will you think, what will you do?

How dare we blame others for our insensitivity? It is we who have given rise to terrorism; it did not spring full blown out of nothing.

I believe that we, the inhabitants of this planet, are facing a crisis unlike anything we've ever faced before. The Chinese oracle, the I Ching, points out that crisis always provides opportunity: Since the crisis is great and the danger immense, the opportunity for transformation is also immense. We are either at the brink of catastrophe or the brink of global peace and what we do will determine which it is to be.

To get a sense of what is ahead if we continue to wage this war, just look at the microcosm of the Middle East. Israel with all its power cannot defeat those who have nothing left to lose. On the other hand when we look at the microcosm of South Africa we see another alternative. We are at a fork in the road. One way leads to death and suffering, the other to life. By life what I mean is not life without difficulties and suffering, but life in which the creative power of the human mind and the loving heart is free to express itself in harmony.

As a writer and one who loves this planet and the creatures who inhabit it, I have felt a tremendous sense of urgency to give voice to the dangers and opportunities I see before us.

This war upon which we've embarked can be stopped before it is too late but time is short. People already feel a great deal of anxiety and insecurity and as the war on terrorism escalates we are witness to the erosion of the rights and liberties of all men and women, everywhere.

Can we put an end to terrorism? I say we can, but only by understanding the root causes and taking appropriate action. It is light that dispels the shadows and light is understanding.

As to the root causes, what can be said?

It is not all right with me that a small proportion of the worlds population controls the vast majority of the world's wealth. It is not all right with me that people are starving while those of us in the West are fat and satiated.

It is not all right with me that those held at Guantanamo Bay in Cuba and other prisons around the world, have been held in violation of international law, their rights as human beings, suspended, by a nation that was once a champion of human rights and freedom.

It is not all right with me that children are being taught at school to hate others and emulate suicide bombers. It is not all right with me that we continue to engage in acts of genocide.

I am not alone in this. This is not what the vast majority of people on this planet want. We want a chance to live life fully, to have a roof over our heads, and raise our families in safety.

In a real democracy, people are the power; it is government that is subject to the will of its people, not the other way round. We are the people and we have said we want to live in peace. This was the message the Spanish people sent to the government in their recent national election.

As long as we see ourselves as citizens of one nation or another, followers of one religion or another we will perpetuate our difficulties. The truth is, we are human beings, citizens of one planet, all of us, along with all living beings, creatures of one Creator. The idea of a Christian God, a Jewish God, a Muslim God, a Hindu God and so on, is false.

What can we do?

Consider this. When a large ocean liner is passing through the water the momentum makes it difficult to turn the rudder and thus the ship. On the edge of the rudder, however, is a small flap, a kind of miniature rudder known as the "trim tab." Moving the trim tab creates a low-pressure area that pulls the rudder around with very little effort. The idea behind it is that something very small used in the right way can change the direction or course of events.

Studies show that shifts in perception, insight and attitude take place across a population and become permanent when only ten percent of them experience the shift.

What follows is a story, a novel; it is not the truth, simply a fiction permeated with uncommon reason. Consider if you will, another way to approach life, another way to live. Come with me to another world, one that is not so far away, one that can be accessed by a change in attitude, a shift in perspective, which brings with it, understanding.

Colin D. Mallard, Ph.D.
Comox, BC, Canada.
June 2004

FOREWORD

Can you imagine a sage in the White House? I know it's a bit of a stretch, but think about it; how might things be different given the events of today? Imagine a Sufi seer in the mountains of south Lebanon, a former guerilla leader. Imagine these men drawn inexorably together, these men of different cultures and one profound insight, men of wisdom, leaders of men.

Imagine two men who speak truthfully, do not mislead or misrepresent, men who have come to terms with themselves, men with no desire for self-importance, power or a place in history. Imagine two men whose only desire is to serve the well being of their people, and thereby the well being of all. Imagine these men with checkered pasts, men like you and me, who have done things we and others might find unacceptable. Imagine them in the world of today, imagine them bringing peace, poise and harmony to a time of conflict, turmoil and terror.

Imagine too, the utter simplicity of the mystery of life, and the event called enlightenment. All this and more you'll find in what follows, a book that has been called a political spiritual thriller. But, it is far more than that; it is a book of hope, inspiration and acute insight that points a way to the freedom and peace for which we all long. The author has done this in language that is simple and easy to understand and by means of an engaging and cordial story that touches our hearts.

· · · · · · · ·

I first met Colin ten years ago in South East India. At the time I had been living in India for seven years. Both of us were writers, both of us seeking the illusive pearl of great price, enlightenment. Over the ensuing years we stayed in touch. Whenever Colin came to India we would visit and talk of our spiritual quest and world events. It was obvious to me that he was a deeply spiritual person with tremendous compassion for the suffering of others. I am sure there are those who will want to know what qualifies him to write a book such as this. Let me tell you what I know of him and some of the key events that make him what he is today.

Colin was born in England during the Second World War. He immigrated to Canada with his parents in the mid fifties. In 1961 he moved to Boston to attend university and study psychology and philosophy. During the Vietnam War at a large demonstration on the Boston Common he came close to killing a man. In that moment he saw in himself what he abhorred in others, violence. From then on he felt a deep need to understand himself, what it was that takes a human being to the brink of death, and more importantly, beyond it to peace and harmony.

As a student he was involved in the Civil Rights and Anti War movements. He was one of five theological students at Boston University to grant sanctuary to a soldier who declined "Uncle Sam's" invitation to kill Vietnamese.

Later as a Unitarian minister in a large American city, he was targeted by the police for his work in the black community, arrested, beaten, thrown in jail and his church fire-bombed and destroyed.

In January 1990, his inquiry led him to India. Shortly afterward, he met two Advaita teachers, Jean Klein, and his final teacher, Ramesh S. Balsekar of Bombay India. Colin is the author of several books including a beautiful contemporary version of Lao Tzu's Tao Te Ching, called *Something To Ponder*, which provides much of the philosophical background for this book.

. . . .

I encourage you to think deeply on what follows. *Uncommon Reason*, is a modern parable, designed to uplift and shed light where shadows linger. Allow the story to wash over you and through you, ponder what is being said, and like John Lennon, imagine.

Imagine there's no heaven,
It's easy if you try,
No hell below us,
Above us only sky,
Imagine all the people
Living for today...

Imagine there's no countries,
It isn't hard to do,
Nothing to kill or die for,
No religion too,
Imagine all the people
Living life in peace...

Imagine no possessions,
I wonder if you can,
No need for greed or hunger,
A brotherhood of man,
Imagine all the people
Sharing all the world...

You may say I'm a dreamer,
But I'm not the only one,
I hope some day you'll join us,
And the world will live as one.

Madhukar B. Thompson
Maui, HI
March 4, 2004

Back in the sixties, I traveled south from Canada to attend university in Boston. In the years, 1961–1971, I found myself intensely involved in the Civil Rights and Anti-War Movements. The deep underlying concern I had for peace and equality at that time remains with me to this day.

I grew up in England during the Second World War and experienced first hand the suffering and destruction that results from bombing. In 1990, on the verge of the Gulf War, I felt a profound sense of despair and a feeling of impending catastrophe. I knew that the Iraqi people had no idea as to the destruction about to be visited upon them by the American military. It was clear to me that we were about to embark on a path from which it would be difficult to extricate ourselves.

During my travels I have seen the poverty and disease so prevalent in non-Western countries. It profoundly disturbs me that a small proportion of the world's population controls the vast majority of its resources and has been willing to maintain that imbalance through foreign policy and force of arms. In particular, I'm referring to the United States and Britain.

For more than forty years I have been keen to understand the cause of conflict and violence. The teachings of the ancient Chinese sage, Lao Tzu, seem to shed more light on the subject than anyone I have come across to date. The university I attended in Boston was the alma mater for Martin Luther King, Jr., who was a student of Gandhi's work and his approach to power. These two men understood some of the basic insights found in the teachings of Lao Tzu, albeit the source for their inspiration was different.

It seems to me that the dilemma we face globally can be

found in the following questions: *When we are unaware, how do we become aware? When we are ignorant how do we become aware of our ignorance?* This is a dilemma that has been with us, I suspect, since the dawn of human kind. But given our current problems, as evidenced in the global conflict between terrorism and its counter force, it is important we find an answer.

A Zen master tells a story of a man who was fishing. He caught a fish but the fish being small, he threw it back in the water. For the first time in its life, the fish realized it had been swimming in something. What the Zen master understood was that we are swimming in a sea of beliefs—cultural, national and religious beliefs; beliefs we take for granted and assume to be true and about which we are largely unaware. This is a kind of living sleep and is, I believe, extremely dangerous.

To discover the peace that most on this planet desire, we must awaken from the sleep of ignorance. Obviously for the fish, being out of the water is not the most pleasant experience. And, for us human beings, when our beliefs are challenged and we look honestly at what we are doing and our motives, it can be profoundly disturbing as well. But from what I have found this is an essential pre cursor to peace. Awakening to our ignorance is the place from which each of us must start.

My concern is that if we fail to address the underlying ignorance and cause of our collective distress, we will find ourselves enveloped in a violent conflict of truly global proportions. To avoid this, we must become aware of that about which we are unaware.

As a result of this book, I have been accused of being "anti Christian," "anti Semitic," "anti Muslim," and "anti American." No small accomplishment I assure you. It is not my intention, however, to needlessly upset people or generate anger. My sole purpose is to shake us into wakefulness that we may become aware of our ignorance.

Although I was born in England, I am a Canadian citizen who

has lived as many years in the United States as in Canada. Over the years, I have come to see the absurdity of national identity and, hence, now consider myself simply a human being born and raised on this planet we share.

I know I am not alone in my desire for peace and like many, I am sickened by the ignorance that continues to give rise to the bloody acts of terrorism on a global basis—be they the actions of fundamentalists or the state sponsored actions of multi-national corporations and governments. Each time this happens, I find myself wanting to shake us from our troubled sleep so that the vision of peace that resides within the hearts of all human beings will find lasting and permanent expression.

Given the time in which we live—a time of increasing violence, of increasing disparity between the rich and the poor, and a population growth that is beginning to strain both the space and resources of our planet during a time of unprecedented destruction and degradation of our land, air and water—it can be argued that we face a global crisis unlike any the world has known.

To that end, the book you are about to read is intended as a wake up call, to pull you out of the water in which you swim. You will encounter a number of perspectives, some of which you will agree with and some you will not; some could make you angry, some could make you sad, some I hope will bring joy to your heart. Be warned it may not be a comfortable read. I do hope, however, that it will cause you to question those things you've taken for granted, those things you've assumed to be true.

In closing, I have been told the book has certain shortcomings, that it is not like other novels and so on. The shortcomings, whatever they are, are mine. And, be that as it may, the content still stands and it is that to which I wish to draw attention. Although the book is a critique of contemporary society, I attempt to suggest alternatives. In doing so, I suppose it might be argued, tongue-in-cheek, that a more accurate classification would be that of "fantasy." Without dreams, however, I think we would all be lost and the sun would not shine so brightly.

For those of you who are interested in exploring these matters further, may I suggest you locate and read my book, *Something To Ponder,* a contemporary version of Lao Tzu's Tao Te Ching.

Peace be with you, Namaste, Inshalla, Shalom.

Colin D. Mallard.
Comox, BC, Canada
September 11, 2005

WHEN LEADERS

LIVE IN HARMONY WITH THE TAO

THE WINDS OF THE UNIVERSE DANCE BETWEEN THEM

AND THE EARTH LIES RESPLENDENT

LIKE THE DEW OF EARLY MORN

SPARKLING IN SUNLIGHT.

LAO TZU

1

The price of rigid ideas

It was Tuesday morning, the day after Christmas. Above the mountains to the east, a fiery sun burned in a cloudless sky. The street, cast in the shadow of tall buildings, was a hive of activity. Local merchants opened their stores, sliding back the iron grates, removing shutters, and wheeling out display carts loaded with produce. Along the street, traffic was heavy, impeded by trucks unloading fruit and vegetables from the kibbutz. Haggling was a way of life in most Mediterranean cities and Tel Aviv was no exception. Another busy day had begun.

The bus, filled with passengers on their way to work, pulled onto the street and joined the rush of traffic. Its klaxon horns added to the din of early morning. Through an open window a young girl watched, mesmerized by the activity of the shopkeepers, red hair blowing in the wind from the moving bus.

Above the cacophony of sounds, doves tumbled in play. Then, with a thunderous roar, the bus blew apart. A bright sheet of orange flame shot upward, sending metal fragments and body parts in every direction. The force of the blast shattered windows up and down the street.

A dreadful silence ensued, followed by moans and bloodcurdling screams that riveted the attention of onlookers. Lurid yellow flames and black smoke flickered in the twisted shell of the bus. Nearby, several cars lay on their sides, one spun slowly on its roof. Next to the destroyed bus, a large truck leaned at an odd angle, crushing the car beside it. The driver was dead, his head bloody on his chest.

People in the street ran in every direction. Some ran toward the bus. A woman got there first, climbed up the side and pulled herself into the burning wreckage to check for survivors. Within moments others joined her, and as quickly and carefully as possible they removed the injured before the flames could reach them.

The red-haired girl lay pinned beneath the twisted seats, a shard of metal protruding from a bloody shoulder beneath a shattered collarbone. Two men carefully lifted the twisted seat. Another man bent down and together he and the woman lifted the girl off the metal spike. She groaned and passed out as they lifted her over the side to waiting hands and safety. Climbing out of the bus, the woman knelt beside the injured girl. Blood was pumping from the wound and she knew it would have to be stopped quickly. Ripping pieces from his shirt, a man on the other side of the girl handed them to the woman. She glanced up and found herself looking into the green eyes of her husband.

Bunching up the pieces of shirt, she stuffed them into the bloody wound and quickly bound them tight. In the distance, sirens wailed. Once the girl was taken care of the woman looked around to see where else she could be of help.

....

That evening, just before sunset, a well-dressed man went to a phone booth on a busy street. Like any other businessman in that section of the city, he went unnoticed.

However, what he said did not. With the phone to his ear he waited. He heard a click, and a woman's voice came on the line. "Good evening," she said, "can I help you?"

"Yes. Listen closely. That bus this morning—it was the work of Hamas. We will never allow a dishonorable peace. We are not afraid to die. Allah is great!" The man hung up the phone, turned and hurried away. Joining a crowd in front of the synagogue, he adjusted his yarmulke and entered the building.

2

"Ask not what your country can do for you"

David Tremaine, President of the United States, had agreed to speak at his alma mater. He arrived in Boston in the late afternoon. Other than the Secret Service agents, he was alone. Sandra had remained in Washington. It had been hectic around the funeral and she'd decided to stay behind.

Half an hour before the speech, Tremaine and two Secret Service agents drove to the university and entered the chapel from the rear. An arched corridor joined it to the School of Theology on one side and the School of Philosophy on the other. A most appropriate arrangement, he thought.

The chapel itself stood back from the large trees that lined Commonwealth Avenue, making a spacious quadrangle in front. Behind it, the Charles River slipped quietly to the sea. The building was designed in the tradition of a European church with sandstone, stained glass windows, high Gothic arches and flying buttresses.

Sitting back, Tremaine looked over the expectant faces that stretched to the back of the chapel. Dr. Menzies, the President of the University, stood at the podium introducing him. Floodlights lit the stained glass in brilliant colors and gave the building an almost festive air. He'd not been here for three decades; he'd been a graduate student at the time, living in an apartment on Commonwealth Avenue, several hundred yards from where he now sat.

On October 7th 1968 at 5:15 in the morning, he had awakened to the tolling of the chapel bells. It was a prearranged signal. In less than a minute he flew down the stairs and into the cool night. For days he'd slept in his clothes, anticipating what he hoped would not come. As he raced from the apartment, he saw police cars lining the deserted avenue in front of the chapel. In the open quadrangle more than a dozen unmarked cars were parked haphazardly, some with doors still open. His heart pounded and his mouth was dry.

A small crowd gathered at the entrance to the chapel. He raced across the empty street and pushed his way to the top of the steps. Light spilled through the open doors into the darkness. Blocking the entrance were members of 'Boston's Finest.'

The chapel was packed; the quiet sobbing of a woman hung in the tense silence. The center aisle was clear, but at the end of each pew a marshal blocked the way, preventing anyone from leaving. As Tremaine watched, three federal agents emerged from the stairs behind the altar. They half-lifted and half-dragged a young man down the aisle toward the open doors where Tremaine stood.

It was Stephen, the young soldier to whom Tremaine and four other students had offered the sanctuary of the church. Stephen's shirt was torn and he was missing a shoe. One of the marshals held him by the hair, pulling his head back. Two others flanked him, holding his arms pinioned, the fingers forced back as if they would break. The men's faces were flushed, not used to such exertion.

Stephen was white, deathly white. His black, neatly cropped mustache and hair accentuated the pallor of his face. His dark eyes were large and frightened. He was obviously in pain. As he was pushed, lifted and dragged down the aisle, the refrain "We shall overcome..." burst from a thousand throats. The members of the Marsh Chapel Community swayed from side to side, their hands crossed and joined in front.

Efficiently and forcefully, police officers cleared a path

down which Stephen was quickly propelled. Reaching the bottom of the steps, they dragged the young soldier across the courtyard and forced him through the open door of a waiting car. Quickly, marshals and police filed from the chapel and entered the remaining cars. With roaring engines and screeching tires, they sped into the night.

It was over in a matter of minutes. The refrain of the song filled the air, and the tolling of the chapel bells signaled an end to the Marsh Chapel Community. For five days Stephen had sought sanctuary in the church, refusing to join his unit scheduled to leave for Vietnam. He believed the war was wrong and he wanted no part of the killing. To this end, Tremaine and four fellow students, in the tradition of the medieval church, had taken it upon themselves to grant Stephen sanctuary in the university chapel.

Dr. Menzies turned and with a smile gestured Tremaine to the podium. "Please welcome Dr. David Tremaine, President of the United States." Thunderous applause filled the chapel.

With a jolt Tremaine returned to the present. He stood, shook the outstretched hand, and waited at the podium for silence, glad of the few moments to collect his wits. Setting aside his notes, he gazed into the young, earnest faces before him. When silence returned he began to speak.

"One day in Bombay I was riding in a taxi when a friend of mine asked, 'what did the yogi say to the vendor at the hot dog stand?' I looked at him and laughed, but couldn't think of an answer. 'Make me one with everything,' he said."

Tremaine waited for the laughter to subside. "Sitting here, I found myself remembering the last time I was in this chapel. It was more than thirty years ago and our country was engaged in a war that many believed was wrong, a war that cost the lives of Americans and Vietnamese alike. Those who went to war and those who opposed it were, by and large, interested in the well-being of their nation. Each group saw their actions as the best way to serve the highest interests of the country. This is obvious to anyone with an open mind. But, to this day, that view has yet to be appreciated. Convinced the war was a terrible and costly mistake, I found myself in active opposition to it.

"After graduate school, I watched with a certain sadness what I considered to be the demise of the idea of true service within our system of government. The resignation of Richard Nixon signaled the beginning; Iran Contra continued the legacy. It seemed to me the idea of service had been perverted by selfish interests. I found myself wondering how we'd drifted so far from what the founding fathers had envisioned. Though I turned my back on government, I watched with interest the process of governing. What fascinated me most were the attempts to create and implement constructive social policy. To actively participate in government, however, was not something I'd ever really considered. But then the 'gods' intervened and presented me with the unexpected. And now I stand before you as the President of this vast country.

"Since the Republicans held the White House for twelve years straight, it was assumed their hold on power was strong enough to preclude any change in the governing party. As a result, no Democratic contender was enthusiastic to risk the expense, and his good reputation, on what seemed like certain defeat.

"When Emerson was persuaded to stand as the Democratic candidate, it was generally looked upon as a token gesture to provide a voice of opposition to the Republicans. A small cog in a meaningless ritual called the Presidential Race. However, that was not how he saw himself. He was a good man who spoke truthfully about what he saw in the country and its role in the world. I had known him for many years and had a great respect for him. When he asked me to accept his nomination, as Vice

President I felt sure we would not, indeed could not, be elected.

"It crossed my mind at the time, that Emerson might have regretted his choice of a running-mate, because of the firestorm of controversy over my stand on Vietnam, which greeted the nomination. I was surprised by the vehemence in the headlines and editorials that described me as a traitor. I offered to withdraw from the ticket, but Emerson said something that made a lot of sense to me. 'You and I signify the healing of old wounds,' he said, 'wounds brought about by differences of opinion concerning the Vietnam War. You represent those opposed to it while I, on the other hand, represent those who fought in it. Unquestionably both of us were interested in the well-being of our country and could not be faulted for our views and actions.'

"We were surprised during the campaign by the level of disgust toward the Republican Administration, which tried hard to deflect public attention from the Iran Contra scandal. However, as more and more details became known, the administration's election campaign faltered. For the first time we heard whispers of a possible Republican defeat. Some of the early Democratic Presidential hopefuls, those who'd held back, were berating themselves for not having entered the race after all.

"When the Japanese government collapsed in scandal two weeks before the election, few thought much of it, engrossed as we were in what had become a quixotic tilt at the windmills of power. But as revelations from Japan spilled into the papers and dominated the news, the administration's duplicity and betrayal of public trust was a shock. As we now know, the cost to the country was enormous in both jobs and finances. It was, in my opinion, these events that determined the election and took the Republicans down in defeat.

"Though some might believe otherwise, I do not think we were elected because of what we were about or the programs we espoused or, for that matter, because we were Democrats.

We were elected because, at the time, anything seemed better than the Republicans and their twelve years in power. But the truth is, we did stand for something. Emerson had, in his own unique way, injected the simple values of common sense, decency and accountability into the campaign. For the three years of his presidency, he worked to restore the integrity of government and the nation as a whole. In the beginning, he was faced with constant criticism and ridicule from a cynical press and a disgraced opposition. Through it all, however, he neither lost sight of his goals nor his sense of humor.

"During those years he sought to educate the American people. He saw education as an important part of his job. He knew that the hearts and minds of the people had to be weaned away from petty thinking and selfish actions. Neither the House nor the Senate would pass constructive legislation without the collective will of the people behind it. To that end, he spoke often with the American people, explaining what he was doing and the decisions he was taking. With great care he prepared people for the changes to come.

"Not once did he avoid issues; never did he gloss over the difficulties. He said, 'I'd rather we anticipate the worst and be pleasantly surprised than anticipate the best only to suffer disappointment. People are tired of being told things aren't so bad, only to discover they're worse than anyone expected. We must be honest with people. In the end it is the only way to restore the nation's health. We cannot afford to put off what must be done today.'

"I know that many of you came to respect and appreciate Emerson, even though you didn't always agree with everything he had to say. One thing you knew was that he spoke truthfully whether you liked it or not. There was a stirring in the population, a sense of hope and even an eager anticipation that, from my perspective, showed a willingness to wake up and face reality.

"With one year left of his first term he found he was dying. Nothing the doctors did was able to save him. For two months we had lengthy discussions about the country and the direction we had charted. He wanted me to continue what we had started. I agreed. We were a good team and I knew I would miss his understanding of the political process.

"Even on his death bed, his strength gone, he still insisted I come and see him. At three in the morning he gathered his wife and two daughters to his side and said good-bye to them. When the sun lit the eastern horizon, he slipped into unconsciousness and died several hours later. When I left his side I was determined to do my best to carry out the work we'd begun.

"In this chapel, in 1968, five students took it upon themselves to grant 'sanctuary' to a young soldier who refused to follow the orders of his commander-in-chief. He was, like you, a young man with hopes and dreams. He said, 'I cannot in good conscience take up a gun to kill those called my enemy in a cause I consider terribly wrong.' I don't know what happened to him. I only know his sincerity and clarity left an indelible impression on me.

"As a nation, and as citizens of the world, we can combine our creative abilities to resolve the difficulties that lie before us. Despite the progress we've made during the past three years, our nation is beset with violence and crime and, generally speaking, there is little appreciation of its cause. Despite being one of the most technologically advanced nations in the world, too many of our citizens lack adequate medical coverage. There are problems of poverty, racial inequality, violence and crime. Only by understanding the root of these problems can we do anything about solving them. The willingness to face facts and to look at ourselves with dispassion is essential to this undertaking. This must also be accompanied by patience and persistence, for the problems we face now were not created in a day.

"We live in a democracy. From an early age we've come to believe it's the best form of government the world has ever known. But let me ask you a question. Does this democracy, in the form in which we practice it today, really help all of us to live full and productive lives? Think about it for a moment. Isn't 'no' the answer for too many of us? Keeping that in mind, I propose that we as a nation engage in a great undertaking, in which we look honestly at our problems, seek the deepest possible understanding and apply the creative genius of the human mind to the problems before us. Let us transform our difficulties into opportunities. I urge you to take up President Kennedy's challenge: 'Ask not what your country can do for you; ask instead, what you can do for your country.' The invitation he extended was an invitation to know the joy and fulfillment that comes with true service. That invitation still stands. Let us accept it anew, but this time on a broader basis. Not just as citizens of this country but as citizens of the world.

"We, the people who make up the nations of the world, are all brothers and sisters. It is not acceptable that we in North America, who comprise such a small proportion of the population of the planet, take for ourselves a disproportionate amount of the world's resources and do so at the expense of others. It is time we ask ourselves how we contribute to the destruction of the world's rainforests for instance, and more importantly, what can we do about it? What we take for granted, our standard of living, our homes, food, cars and jobs, is not secure and will never be secure as long as the vast majority of the world is poor and hungry. We cannot escape the fact that modern technology has created a global village to which we all belong.

"Modern communication brings with it a greater awareness of different cultures, and yet beneath our differences, the human heart remains forever the same. The truth is that human beings, regardless of nationality, religion or culture, consist of one single family, the family of man. When members of a family are sick or in need, we reach out and offer whatever comfort and assistance we can. And since our resources are great, we have a great deal to offer. Thank you."

The students were on their feet and filled the chapel with applause. Tremaine stood quietly, waiting until they sat down. "Are there any questions?" Hands waved in the air. Tremaine pointed to a well-dressed young man with brown curly hair.

"You mentioned the young man who refused to go to Vietnam and follow the orders of his commander-in-chief. Now you are the commander-in-chief. What would you do if a young man refused to follow your orders to go to war?"

"I can't say for sure, but I'll share with you some thoughts that arise in response to your question. First of all, I'd have to be convinced that war was the only way left to us. At the moment, that possibility seems remote. But if events arose as they did with Hitler, I'd do my best to convey my opinion to the country at large and enlist the support of its citizens. For those who could not support such an undertaking, I would request their assistance in some other way, perhaps in national service to the sick and poor of our own country."

"What other thoughts do you have?"

"In the mid-sixties, I took a philosophy course. We'd just passed through the McCarthy era of 'red-bating' and purges of those who were thought to be communist sympathizers. In a way, it was a milder version of the Inquisition. It was the height of the cold war, and tensions between the U.S. and the Soviet Union ran high. One morning, the discussion came down to what might we do if we were threatened with invasion from the Soviets. Most of the students argued long and hard for a forceful and violent response. Dr. Mullen, the philosophy professor, suggested an approach I found most intriguing. 'What if we did not oppose such an invasion?' he asked. The students were aghast at such an 'unpatriotic' thought. What would happen if they just took

over? Think about it. How would they run the government and
the bureaucracies? How would they provide services? How would
they communicate with the population? How could they run two
countries located so far away? Would not the resources of the
Soviet Union be taxed to the breaking point in such a venture?
Those were intriguing questions that held a great deal of appeal."

A young man dressed in faded jeans and a jacket stood up.
"The United States has long been looked upon with great respect
and admiration for what is known as the 'American Dream.' Can
you give your thoughts on this?"

"Yes. What was that dream? Essentially, it held that those
who worked hard would realize a reward commensurate with their
efforts. If the quality of their work was excellent, if they were
honest, accountable and hard working, they could expect to live
reasonably well, free of economic deprivation within a society
that safeguarded the various freedoms we take for granted.

"Although as a society we still lay claim to this dream, we've
parlayed it into a nightmare. At a deep and fundamental level
we've lost the vision and replaced it with the idea of something
for nothing.

"From a psychological perspective, this represents a failure
to deal with reality. Because of this, we've elected politicians
who are afraid to tell us the truth. Most householders understand
you cannot spend what you don't have. Of course, from time
to time, we can and do borrow money to pay for the things we
need. But we promise to repay what we borrow in a reasonable
time. If we keep borrowing, we eventually lose the capacity to
repay the loan.

"We want and expect many things from our society. We
want insurance, medical services, jobs, welfare, unemployment
insurance and social security. Every time there's a flood or a
hurricane we expect government help; when crops fail we
expect help too. It's all well and good to expect such things,

but we must not forget that it costs money and the money the government spends is money it collects from its people. It seems to me that we've been unwilling to pay for all the things we want. If a politician tells us it will cost "X" amount of dollars and suggests it be raised by taxes we vote him out of office. If we attempt to downsize government, members of the affected bureaucracies backed by the unions find ways to prevent it.

"Government administrations overcame this problem by borrowing money. They bought the support of the people by giving them what they wanted while postponing payment to a later time. Their children would repay the debt.

"Who's responsible for this? It's fashionable to blame the Republican administrations, but they fed us what *we* wanted. The truth of the matter is that *we* the people are responsible! All of us! We're the ones who've coerced our politicians into borrowing money by threatening to vote them out of office should they increase our taxes and tell the truth we do not wish to hear.

"We want something for nothing. It cannot work. Sooner or later we must grow up; it's time we stopped seeing the government as a sugar daddy on one hand and the enemy on the other. We are the government. And in a representative government such as ours, the representatives reflect the collective will of the people.

"Lincoln said that democracy is government *of* the people *by* the people and *for* the people. In other words we govern ourselves in the interest of all people. Recently perhaps, we've not done such a good job."

Tremaine pointed to a student in the front row. A young woman with short brown hair and granny glasses stood up. "You say we must come to understand our problems. Can you say more about what you mean by the term 'understanding?'"

"Real understanding comes about by facing facts. By that I mean seeing things as they are, not the way we want them to be, or according to a particular social or political theory. The good scientist takes into account what lies before him. He does not discard that which fails to fit his preconceived notions. Sometimes he's forced to allow apparent contradictions to coexist. In time, the mind resolves the contradictions by bringing about a new level of understanding.

"As a nation we could stop blaming others and take a close and honest look at ourselves. In so doing, the solutions will make themselves known. Those of us called upon to represent this nation through its government must be willing to transcend party lines and party prejudices. If a man is the best in his field for a job, he should be chosen without regard to his political affiliations. When other political parties have good ideas we must use them."

"Can you give an example of seeing things as they are?"

"In the Middle East we have a conflict that's been going on since the founding of the State of Israel. That conflict has caused a great deal of death and suffering for all involved. The tendency of participants and observers alike is to take sides. When that happens, information is selectively used. Information that supports the side *I* support is highlighted, and information that supports the opposing side is minimized. When people engage in this kind of process, the factual occurrence of events becomes skewed. The skewed perception of events creates a solidification of opposing points of view.

"On the Israeli side, we see a spectrum of positions that range from the hard line fundamentalist on one end to those interested in peace on the other. On the Palestinian side the same spectrum exists. But those who wield the power on both sides, and have done so increasingly over the past fifty years, are those who are the most rigid in their beliefs. They have successfully dominated the political landscape and have justified their extremism with the extremism of the opposing side. Violence begets violence; it does not end it. These extremists believe in right and wrong and are prepared to use force to get their way.

"The Taoist Masters were keen observers of life and understood certain basic principles. For instance, they knew that force used against force only leads to injury and death on both sides. What they also observed was that force could be absorbed by softness. Now, softness is not to be mistaken for weakness. The softness they spoke of was the softness of absorbing and deflecting. This required great discipline, patience and timing. This same principle was understood as well by Christ when he said, 'resist not evil,' and 'turn the other cheek.' It became a strategy when he said, 'Do good to those who despitefully use you and in so doing you will heap coals of fire upon their head.' In modern times, this understanding and the same strategy found expression in the life and work of Mahatma Gandhi and Martin Luther King."

"Do you think it is possible to devise a system of government that will eliminate corruption?"

"No matter what kind of system we have, we'll never remove corruption completely. Corruption is found wherever human beings are found. It is rooted in selfishness. I suspect selfishness will continue to exist no matter what. Perhaps there is something that can be offered as an alternative. We might consider ways to help people re-discover the joy of service. In the East this is known as Karma Yoga."

"Would you mind explaining what you mean by Karma Yoga?"

"Essentially, yoga means path and karma means action. To put it simply, Karma Yoga is the path of action or service. An artist finds the greatest satisfaction in the creative expression to which he is best suited. Albert Einstein found great satisfaction when he applied his mind in the area of its greatest ability. For Bertrand Russell, this took place through his exploration and expression of philosophy. For a healer, it takes place through the expression of healing. In a way, all of these can be considered aspects of service.

"A person may serve because it is a way to make a living. In that case it becomes an exchange, and there is nothing wrong with that. Some people seek to serve because they want recognition. They want their name on a park bench or a hospital wing named after them. They contribute from their wealth. That marks the beginning of the path. Toward the end of the path, there comes the realization that the act of service is the place where the greatest satisfaction lies, and that satisfaction is so great that the person will serve without any recognition. This is much like the basketball player who so loves the game he cares little about who wins and who loses. The highest form of Karma Yoga takes place when the egoic structure dissolves and what takes place is *selfless service.* It is here that the deepest satisfaction is found.

"In a culture like ours, materialistic and self centered, the premise, albeit a false one, is that the accumulation of material objects, wealth, etc., will bring deep and lasting satisfaction. This is not true. A great deal of advertising is spent supporting this idea. 'Buy this or that and you'll be happy and satisfied with life.' Consequently the basic idea of Karma Yoga, and the satisfaction that comes from it, is not well known. It is interesting, however, to look back at our founding fathers. The principle of selfless service was much more present then than it is today. To me, government is a place where Karma Yoga makes a great deal of sense."

"Would mother Teresa be an example of a Karma Yogi?

"Yes, she would be an example."

"Are you suggesting all people should try and practice this path?" The question came from a gray-haired lady with sparkling blue eyes in the front row.

"No, I'm not suggesting that at all. Only those with a particular temperament are best suited to that path. Others find themselves attracted to other things such as business, inventions, or race car driving to name a few. What I am suggesting is that the joy and satisfaction that comes from service for service's sake is something we seem to have lost in Western society. I would like to draw people's attention to it again.

"I know some of you still have questions but it's getting late and I have to get back to Washington tonight. Thank you for being here this evening, I've enjoyed our dialogue and look forward to more of the same." With that, Tremaine turned, shook Dr. Menzies' outstretched hand, walked quickly down the steps, and exited from the rear of the chapel, discreetly accompanied by the Secret Service Agents.

3

Meeting at Whistler

It was late when David arrived at the White House. It felt strange to think that this was now his home, albeit temporarily. He went straight to the bedroom. Sandra lay propped against the pillows, reading. She greeted him with a smile. Sitting beside her on the bed, she took his hand and kissed it affectionately.

"How did it go?" She asked.

"Pretty good. You'd think I'd know better than to take notes; I never use them. Anyway, it was enjoyable. I like the university setting. I enjoy the give and take of students; they seem less 'jaundiced' and more open to the exploration of ideas."

"How long is it since you were last there? It must have been the early seventies, wasn't it?"

"It was. The talk was in the chapel, which brought back a flood of memories. Anyway, it was a break from the country's mourning and a good place to pick up where Emerson left off." He looked at Sandra, glad to be home and in her presence again. "How was your day?"

"We finished the living quarters the way I want them. I had lots of help, of course. I find the lack of privacy quite annoying. We've got to do something about it."

"I agree!"

"Lacy was back in Washington to tie up loose ends so she came by this afternoon. We had tea and talked for several hours."

"How is she?"

"As well as can be expected. She said she's glad to be back on the farm again, glad to be out of the White House and the city."

"How's she handling Emerson's death?"

"She cries easily, she keeps looking for him, expecting him to show up. She said it's especially hard when she finds herself in places they had frequented. It's sinking in that he's dead and not coming back. That was one of the hard things about being back at the farm, she said it was a place where she could still feel the comfort of his presence."

"How are the girls doing?"

"She says they're well. They cry a lot. Sometimes they all cry! They talk about Emerson and the things they did together. They've been going through his personal effects. Did you know he kept a journal filled with the poems he wrote?"

"I didn't, but I'm not surprised."

"He began writing in the early sixties when he was an undergraduate student, and the last poem he wrote was the evening before he died. Lacy said it's like a journal of his life. Over the years he read some of the poems to her, but she never realized how much he'd written. Each evening for the past week, she and the girls have taken turns reading the poems. There are lots of tears, but I think it's good for them."

"I think so."

"Anyway, she was very helpful. She said she and Emerson had some difficulty getting used to the White House, and she thought we might too. She said she felt like she was living in a museum. She was afraid to sit on the furniture. The only way she could handle it was by making it into a home."

"How did they do that?"

"They insisted on more privacy and changed some of the procedures. She said they met stiff resistance. The argument they kept hearing was, 'This is the way we do things here.' Breaking that kind of thinking was hard, but they did have some success. She thought it would soon revert to its old form and we'd have to begin all over again."

"It already seems that way. I think we'll have to be equally firm."

"So, that was my day. Are you coming to bed?"

"Not yet. I'm going to take a shower and read for a while. I've a meeting with the chairman of the Joint Chiefs in the morning."

He squeezed her hand and, getting up, went into the bathroom.

David luxuriated in the shower, as though washing off the accumulation from his first two weeks as President. He read for a couple of hours before going to bed. Coming back to the bedroom he found Sandra asleep, the book she was reading open on her chest. Gently, he put the book away and slid in beside her. She stirred and snuggled close to him.

He found his mind drifting back to their first meeting. He'd loved her from the start, although he'd not realized it at the time.

....

David had been invited to Vancouver to speak on a book he'd written. Because of the proximity of Whistler and Blackcombe, he rented a car and drove inland to the ski resort. He had the use of a friend's condo for a week. Situated in the village of Whistler, it was in easy walking distance of the lifts. He loved skiing. At the end of the first day, he was, as usual, one of the last off the slopes. The mountain had obscured the sun by the time he reached the bottom of the run.

Later, he wandered through the village. It had been several years since he'd been there, and he'd had to familiarize himself with it again. The village was crowded with the bright-colored clothes and the red, wind-burned faces of the skiers. Laughter, the murmur of voices and music filled the crisp air. It was one of the things he loved about skiing: it put people in a happy mood.

He entered a small English-style pub and ordered a McEwans. He sipped his beer slowly; glad to take the weight off his feet. His body tingled and his face felt flushed and hot. He relaxed and enjoyed the pleasing effect of the beer as he listened to the friendly conversations and laughter that surrounded him. The pub was packed and yet, despite the crush of people, he felt alone and happy to be so.

She came out of nowhere and asked to sit with him. "No more empty chairs," she explained. She was tall, standing by his table, her head bent toward him. Light from the ceiling framed her dark hair with an aura of reflected gold. She wore a red ski jacket over a navy blue sweater that accentuated her unusually dark eyes, eyes that were large, open and quiet. A hint of mischief lurked at the corner of her mouth, but it was the eyes that drew his attention. They seemed to sparkle from the light in the room, while beneath the surface he sensed a quality of utter stillness. There was an ease about her that he liked at once.

They talked of skiing and the different areas on the mountain about which he was unfamiliar. He learned she was a nurse working for a home health agency on Vancouver Island.

Before long their conversation drifted to a recent trip she'd made to India and Nepal. She'd gone to study Buddhism and art and had offered her services as a nurse. She spent nine months there.

"It helped me get a better perspective on life," she said. "I traveled in the north and spent a month in Benares, which is where those who are ill go to bathe in the Ganges before they die."

"Why did you go there?"

"Benares or India?" She asked with a smile.

"India."

"I think I wanted to get a perspective on Canada and my life here. I also felt drawn there. I had the idea I might be of help. Now I see what a condescending attitude I had. How arrogant we are, how arrogant were our forefathers who settled North America."

"What do you mean?"

"I went to India thinking that as a Westerner I had something special to bring to the suffering people of this poor country. I think Christian missionaries have much the same attitude wherever they go, even today. As a result, like me, they fail to see what lies before them. In some cases, I'm sure, they stand in the presence of enlightened masters with no awareness of who it is that stands before them. The Greeks had a term for this; they called it *hubris,* which means, 'overweening pride.'

"I mistakenly believed that when people are poor and suffering, they can't be happy. I hoped to bring them a measure of happiness. So it was a shock for me when one day I realized that most of the people I met seemed quite happy, despite appalling circumstances and diseases."

"One day in Nepal I watched some children playing. One of them, a little girl of about six, must have had polio or some other crippling disease. Her legs were shriveled and distorted. She played with the other children who included her in their activities. She got around by using her hands and scooting her legs along after her. All the children were having a good time; I could hear their joyful laughter. The place where they played had an irrigation ditch running beside it. Every now and then they'd go in the ditch to cool down.

"I thought of how it would be if the little crippled girl lived in Canada. She'd be sitting in a wheel chair, watching the other children play. It made me realize that the joy of life is not dependent on what we have, on wealth or even a strong healthy body. And here, I'd been thinking I had something to offer. I had indeed, but not what I thought in my condescension."

"Was it hard to adjust to Western life when you came back to Canada?"

"It was. The last two months I spent in India, six weeks of

which were spent in a Buddhist convent in silent meditation. The village was small and so was the population. When I came out, there were people everywhere. What had been a sleepy little village was now teeming and overcrowded.

"The Dalai Lama was to arrive the next day and thousands of Tibetans, Nepalese and Indians had come to the village to be with him. That was the first shock. When he came, I joined the others and listened to his discourses.

"Shortly afterward, I was on a plane to New York for a connection to Vancouver. When I arrived in New York I found my father had changed my ticket. He wanted me to spend time with my sister who was having a rough time. She lived in Toronto. So there I was, one day in Nepal, and two days later walking down Yonge Street with a sister who was bored with life and upset that she couldn't have everything she wanted, yesterday! That was another shock. Life seemed completely unreal; I felt like I was living in a dream.

"India and Nepal affected me a lot. I came to realize that what was important had nothing to do with wealth or power or our position in society, who we knew or who we didn't. For the first time in my life I felt overwhelmed by the sheer waste in our society, particularly in our cities. It seems to me we're cut off from nature and have lost the sense of our own mortality.

"What struck me was that for many Westerners there is a deep and disturbing emptiness, untouched by anything we have. It became clear to me that nothing in our culture could ever satisfy this hunger, not even the religious practices and beliefs found in our churches."

"Are you feeling pessimistic?" David interjected.

"No, I don't feel that way. I think this hunger, this emptiness, is necessary because it turns many of us away from Western thinking and Western values."

"How do you mean?"

"Well, the Beatles, with their music, long hair, irreverent ways and drugs, spoke to many of us about what we sensed was the hypocrisy of our society. We listened to them. When they introduced us to the Maharishi, a window to India was opened."

"What makes you think that was important?"

"I think India has for a long time been the spiritual heart of the planet. The strange paradox is that among a large number of the Indians I met, there was a strong desire to live in the West and, failing that, to emulate Western values. They wanted to bring India into the fold of Western technology, hoping affluence would follow."

"Why do you think that is?"

"I would say that in both India and Nepal the culture as a whole is deeply religious, but that religiousness tends to be superficial in the sense that it represents a literal adherence to thousands of beliefs and spiritual practices. These beliefs, and the practices that go with them, obscure the great spiritual truths. In India there's a constant preoccupation with the outward observances of religious practice.

"I think an increasing number of Indians are beginning to sense the emptiness of such a way of life. So what do they turn to in their search? Images of America. They believe materialism and technological sophistication can fill that emptiness.

"In the West, on the other hand, we've already tasted this fruit and found it does not bring lasting satisfaction. And no matter how we attempt to repackage the rituals and religious beliefs of modern Christianity, they do not fill the emptiness we feel. The world-view of Christianity, to my way of thinking, is too limited. The result is that more and more are turning to India, and some are finding what they seek.

"If there's so much superficiality of belief, why would anyone want to turn to another superficial system?" David asked.

Sandra thought for a moment. "The answer, I think, lies in

the fact that despite the prevalence of religious superficiality, there are probably more enlightened men and women in India than in any other country in the world. I know of very few enlightened masters in the Americas. Now, why is that? Perhaps the lack stems from the fact that in the West we have social and cultural freedom, accompanied by a kind of restriction in the realm of ideas and spiritual understanding.

"In India, on the other hand, the opposite is true. The power of the caste system is strong; there's little social freedom. Whereas in the realm of ideas and spiritual understanding, the mind is free to soar, and it does."

"What makes you say that we in the West are restricted in the realm of ideas and spiritual understanding?"

"There's still fear in our society when it comes to exploring spiritual and philosophical ideas. Christianity is one religion among many. It arose as a direct result of the life and teaching of the enlightened Jewish master, Jesus. Before the time of Jesus there had been other enlightened masters, such as Buddha, Lao Tzu, Ashtavakra and so on. All of these masters, including Jesus, spoke of the truth and attempted to instill in their listeners the direct understanding they'd realized themselves.

"The further removed the followers were from the master, the more the teachings assumed the characteristics of belief. Christians and Muslims were unique in a certain disturbing way.

"They each assumed their beliefs to be the one true description of the way. The corollary to this assumption is that all other teachings are false. Such thinking denied them access to living masters because, according to them, the last great masters were Jesus and Mohammed.

"The results of such narrow-minded thinking led these two great religious bodies into a dead end. They could no longer recognize enlightenment when it happened. Even the idea of it was largely unknown. This was more so in Christianity I think. Anyway, it is this kind of rigid thinking that led to the bloodshed of the Crusades and the current conflict in the Middle East.

"Such rigid religious thinking has led, sooner or later, to religious warfare. The inquisitions that spread across Europe cost the lives of millions of people and were the direct result of intolerance for anything but accepted doctrines. Freedom of thought was prohibited on pain of death.

"People believed it was better for others to die at the stake than to be eternally lost in the fires of hell. Such thinking had a profound effect upon our European forebears.

"In your country, it gave rise to the separation of church and state. In fact, your Declaration of Independence, even the founding of your nation and the formulation of its constitution, was a direct result of a deeply held desire for freedom of thought in the pursuit of happiness. But even so, eighteenth and nineteenth century Christianity has left an indelible impression on the collective psyche of the Americas, North and South."

They'd finished their beer and David invited her to dinner. She accepted, and they left the pub and walked to a quiet, secluded Italian restaurant he knew. Once they were seated, the conversation continued.

"You say there's freedom of ideas and religious thinking in India which is not present in the West, and yet it seems to me there's been a rise of conflict between Hindus and Muslims." David said.

"That's true, but the fact is that in India as a whole there's a freedom of thought concerning religious matters not found anywhere else in the world. I would say that the religious conflict between the Hindus and Muslims has basically two causes. One is nationalism, and the other is religious fundamentalism.

"When the British conquered India, they conquered other countries as well. So, for instance, Kashmir, which is now considered a state in Northern India, was at one time a separate Muslim country more closely associated with Muslim Pakistan than Hindu India. When India received its independence, Kashmir was invited to be part of this process. The promise made to Kashmir was that Indian independence would bring Kashmir independence.

"The Indian government, to this day, has refused to honor its promise. So what is occurring is less a conflict between religious ideas than a war to gain independence. Kashmir is not the only trouble spot in India that, on the surface, looks like a battle between religious ideologies."

"I see. You said the other cause had to do with religious fundamentalism. What do you mean?"

"Religious fundamentalism is a rigid adherence to a literal interpretation of beliefs. There's a tendency to define reality in terms of right and wrong, good and bad, black and white. Even today, when there's a rise of religious fundamentalism, conflict and warfare seem inevitable by-products. A recent example would be the excesses of Khomeini, and his followers in Iran.

"Even in your own country, the religious right is becoming more strident. The killing of abortion doctors and bombing of clinics are examples of the same religious intolerance. In India, religious intolerance is small by comparison. Freedom of religious thought in India is appreciated.

"From a larger perspective, what I think is underway is an evolutionary process that will, in the end, bring together the social and cultural freedom of the West with the religious and spiritual freedom of the East."

After dinner, David walked Sandra to her condo, which turned out to be near his. For a week they skied the mountain together and in lengthy conversations explored a wide range of subjects. The conversations seemed to stem from a deep commonly held interest in philosophical inquiry. David was delighted to find the conversations with Sandra had none of the superficial and argumentative speculations he'd sometimes encountered with university students. Her thinking seemed, instead, to be the result of inquiry and reflection. In her he found a wisdom and serenity he'd rarely encountered before.

She seemed unaffected by power, prestige, or the opinions of others. He watched her, fascinated, and saw how easily people gravitated to her. It was as if they didn't know why they were being drawn to her, they just wanted to be in her presence. In those sunlit lovely days on the mountain, they became good friends.

Friday was David's last day at Whistler. He and Sandra met for an early breakfast and were on the slopes as soon as the lifts opened. They skied all day, exploring the places they'd visited in six days of skiing on the mountain, stopping only briefly for lunch.

In the late afternoon, they came over the crest of a hill and paused. Far below, the valley lay in shadow. They leaned on their poles and drank in the magnificence before them. They'd spoken little all day, just enjoying the thrill and exhilaration of a full day skiing.

"Let's sit a while" Sandra said, then turned and skied slowly to the lee of some nearby firs. David followed. She trampled a spot with her skis, and then removed them and drove them into the snow for a backrest. She sat on her hat and gloves. David did the same.

In silence, they watched the shadows reach farther and farther up the valley. In the distance, they could see Whistler Village. Blue wood-smoke lay curled in layers around the tops of the trees, and the lights of evening twinkled through the gathering dusk.

The remaining rays of sunlight winked out as a golden sun slid below the ridge behind them. Already they could feel the coming cold of night. Sandra turned and reached for David's hands. She looked at him and smiled.

"Thank you so much for an enjoyable day," she said.

That was the first time he'd known he loved her. But he wouldn't allow himself to believe it. I hardly know her, he thought, and in the morning we'll go separate ways and never see each other again.

He helped her to her feet, and she stood before him, pulling on her gloves. He caught a hint of the fragrance she wore. Her face was flushed from the wind and sun, her eyes bright and still. He leaned over and kissed her gently. She responded in kind. He wanted to tell her he loved her but couldn't bring himself to say the words. Then the ski patrol came over the hill on their last sweep of the day and the intimacy was suddenly interrupted.

"We must go," she said. Turning, she launched herself down the hill. He followed. David reached the bottom before her and was stepping out of his skis when she came racing down the last slope. She came straight for him, flipped her skis, and sprayed him with snow.

They stopped for a beer in the pub where they'd first met. Both felt the impending separation; both were aware their time together was all but over. After finishing their drinks, they went to their respective condos to shower and dress.

When David knocked on her door an hour later, Sandra was almost ready. She wore a long, full denim dress with a red sash about the waist. While he watched, she pulled on thick, woolen navy socks and lambskin boots, then threw her parka over her head and slid her arms into the sleeves. Grabbing a scarf, she wrapped it around her neck. They stepped into the cold night and then, arm in arm, walked the short distance to the Hokkaido, a Japanese restaurant they'd picked out earlier.

Alone in the small elegant room of rice paper walls and tatami mats, they sat across from each other on small cushions. David picked up on the conversation they'd had the night they first met.

"I've been thinking about this idea of religious fundamentalism," he said. "It seems to have less to do with religion and more to do with narrow-minded beliefs held firmly. I've seen people in politics with the same kind of fanaticism. I've seen it on the left and on the right. As you said, there's a tendency to define things in terms of right and wrong, good and bad."

"What do you think gives rise to it, David?"

"I think it has to do with the nature of belief itself."

"What do you mean?"

"What would you say is at the heart of all belief?" he asked.

Sandra thought for a moment then shook her head, "I don't know."

"Think about it. What's implicit to all belief?"

Again she couldn't see what he was getting at. "I don't know."

"Suppose we'd never met and a friend of yours said there's a psychologist she knows called David Tremaine and that he can help you with a problem you have. Would you believe your friend?"

"If my friend was noted for her honesty, yes."

"Okay. Now suppose on your way to see me you stop for a cup of tea and a close friend, who's always told you the truth, comes into the restaurant. You talk, and in the course of the conversation mention you're going to see a man called David Tremaine. Your friend looks at you oddly and says, 'There's no such person as David Tremaine.' What happens in your mind?"

"Doubt enters. I doubt the friend who first told me about you."

"Right. Now let's try another scenario. Your first friend tells you of David; you come, and we meet and we spend some time together. You leave, and on your way home, you stop for tea. The same friend comes in and you strike up a conversation. She says the same thing. 'David Tremaine doesn't exist.'" David, observing her closely, saw the hint of a smile on her face.

"What happens in the mind? The smile gives it away, doesn't it?"

"I think my friend has gone over the edge."

"Is there any doubt this time?"

"No."

"Why not?"

"Because having met you, I know you exist."

"Then returning to my earlier question, what would you say is implicit to all belief?"

"Uncertainty or doubt."

"Yes, uncertainty or doubt. Belief is not the truth. It represents instead, *not* knowing. Belief might correspond to the truth, but for the believer there's no certainty. He simply doesn't know. That's an important distinction."

"I agree. So you're saying uncertainty produces insecurity.

"Yes, and in order to overcome insecurity, we try to get others to agree with us in the vain and largely unconscious hope that if enough people believe in something, it must be true."

"That's interesting. I've never thought of it in that way. I've always felt that truth is self-evident."

"How do you mean?"

"We recognize it. So obviously it is not something we learn but something we already know."

"Yes, and in the realm of belief, the believer has identified so closely with his belief that any challenge to it is felt as a threat to his identity."

"That explains why some people become fanatical and, in extreme cases, dangerous." She smiled at him, and the smile took his breath away, he loved talking with her. In fact, he'd enjoyed everything he'd done with her. She was a remarkable woman.

They drank sake and savored the delights of Japanese cuisine. It was a precious time for both of them. The shadow of the next day's parting lent exquisite richness to the moment.

David watched her across the table. She was radiant. The waves of her dark hair shone in the light. She looked up, and their eyes met. Her eyes were almost black. They were so dark that the pupil and the iris seemed to be one. A quiet serenity was always there, even when she laughed or cried. Perhaps this is what people feel drawn to, he thought.

"Do you mind my looking at you?" he asked, suddenly aware that his eyes were taking her in completely.

"No, not as long as you grant me the same enjoyment."

He smiled. She sat before him straight and strong, a light dusting of freckles covering her arms. The neck of her dress was unbuttoned at the top and formed a V that revealed the gentle curve of her breasts. She reached across the table and took both of his hands in hers, kissing them.

"Let's go back to the condo," she said. "I've a hot tub, and we can ease these aching muscles."

David smiled and nodded.

Walking slowly, hand in hand beneath the old-fashioned street lamps, they wended their way along the crowded sidewalk, absorbed in each other's presence.

At the condo, Sandra stamped the snow from her boots, unlocked the door and went inside.

"Come in," she said. She bent down, removed her boots and socks, and then stood and hung her coat. David did the same. She led him through the living room to an outside deck. Sliding the doors back, they stepped outside. The deck faced the mountain. A dark ridge of peaks stood against the brilliant stars glittering in the sky. A crescent moon delicately tipped the ridge to the east. On either side, the silent firs stood unmoving in the cold night. She pointed toward a small bench against the wall. "You can put your clothes there," she said. "I'll get some towels."

David undressed and slipped into the tub. It took a few moments to get used to the hot water. Sandra returned, draped in a large towel secured above her breasts. She put extra towels on the bench and reached up to switch off the lights. By the light of the stars and the bright snow, he watched as she slipped the towel from around her. For a moment she paused, and he could see the lovely curves of her body silhouetted against the sky. Bending, she slid into the water. Her breasts hung full and round before they disappeared below the water. She sat facing him. A breeze stirred the nearby branches.

"Oh my, this feels sooo... good," she said.

"It does indeed."

They soaked in the warmth and their tired muscles relaxed. Suspended in the still, warm water, they rested easy in the cold mountain night. Several times they emerged, then slipped with tingling bodies back into the enveloping warmth. That night they stayed together, their lovemaking strong and tender.

....

It had been seventeen years since then, seventeen years of loving her deeply. David kissed her while she slept. Funny, he thought, I had no doubts about her from the start. He switched off the light. In the darkness he gently caressed her nipples. She stirred. "Good night darling," he said. "Thank you for being my wife."

4

One world, another reality

Shamir adjusted the yoke across her shoulders and set out along the path. The fierce heat of day had subsided. She loved the walk to the watering hole; it was always a welcome break from caring for her brothers and sister. While she was gone, her mother would prepare the evening meal and her father would be home by the time she returned.

She followed the trail as it wound along the shore and over the low-lying hills. The ocean sparkled in the sunlight. Beneath the bending palms, small waves brushed the shoreline. The trail turned and followed a shallow valley that led to the foothills. Already the grasses were brown and parched from lack of rain. Clumps of sycamore and poplars dotted the hillsides offering sharp contrast to the barren terrain.

Shamir climbed steadily until she reached a curve where the trail turned south. She walked though a series of low hills before ascending a steep incline. She crested the hill and paused. Below, the trail sloped gently to the well, its pool of water shimmering in the light. Around the water's edge, a sea of green grass created a startling contrast to the parched land. A cluster of palms stood at the abrupt end of a ridge that extended from the mountain. Beside the palms, a steep canyon cut into the hillside and vanished from sight.

She could see him sitting on the rocks at the edge of the pool, his sheep gathered at the entrance to the canyon. He'd been there every evening for two weeks. She first saw him one afternoon when she'd come to the well for water, as she did each day.

At first she was afraid of him, but as she got to know him her fear subsided. Each evening he drew water and filled her pots. He wore the traditional clothes of a herdsman, and his hair and close-cropped beard were white. Black bushy eyebrows were a sharp contrast to his white hair. His skin was dark, like hers, but weathered. His eyes seemed to sparkle and emanated great strength and gentleness. She'd been taught to avoid the eyes of men, but she could not avoid this man's. When he spoke, his voice was soft and rich and soothing. He said his name was Nassir, and he'd lived in the hills all his life. His ancestors, who'd built this well and others, had taken care of it for generations. He'd told her that as the seasons came, he moved the flock from place to place, visiting different wells. For the past two weeks she'd talked with him when she'd gone for water. After their talks, she would hurry home before darkness swallowed her surroundings.

The evening before, she'd told her parents of meeting the shepherd at the well. Her mother stopped eating and looked quickly at her father. Shamir caught the look and asked, "Do you know him?"

"What does he look like?" her father asked.

She described him. "Do you know him?" she persisted.

"Yes," her father answered. "Eighteen years ago, just before you were born, Nassir arrived one evening at sunset. He'd been traveling hard and seemed exhausted. We gave him water and shared a meal. After we'd eaten, we sat around the table relaxing. He looked at me and asked if I trusted him. I thought it a strange question, but I realized I did. I couldn't explain why. Later, your mother told me she felt the same way about him. Then Nassir looked at us and, taking both our hands in his, told us we were in great danger and must leave for several days until the danger passed. We asked him to explain, but he wouldn't.

"We packed some food and a few belongings and he took us, that night, into the hills. We walked until dawn. Just as light crept up the eastern sky, he helped us through an opening into a deep cave. Water skins hung on wooden pegs and sheepskins surrounded the charcoal remains of a cooking fire and woven mats.

"For three nights we remained in the cave. In the middle of the fourth we returned home. We arrived at first light and could see at once that something was terribly wrong. Only the almond and sycamore trees remained, and one small shed. Everything else was a pile of rubble, one white wall and an empty doorway marked the place where our house once stood. Several craters gouged the earth, and a strange smell hung in the air.

"Nassir assured us we would now be safe. We asked him if he knew what had happened. 'Israeli Air Force' was all he would say. For seven days he helped us rebuild our home, and before he left he brought us a pair of goats.

"I was furious over the destruction of our home. We'd done nothing to deserve it. For the first time, I felt an urge to join the guerrillas. I wanted to strike back; I wanted the Israelis destroyed. I wanted things to be the way my father and his father had described them, before the Israelis had taken the land and formed their own nation. A long-standing hatred had simmered inside me all those years. Now it boiled over, a silent controlled rage. I wanted to leave right away, wanted to kill. Your mother begged me not to go, but I wouldn't listen.

"That evening, Nassir went with me to gather water at the well. We filled the pots and then he told me to sit down. He sat opposite me. For what seemed like a long time he fixed his eyes on mine. At first I was impatient and didn't want to sit, but I couldn't break the hold of his eyes. After what seemed like an hour or so I found myself filled with a strange peacefulness. I think Nassir had been waiting for this, for only then did he speak.

"'It's not your destiny to go to war. Your wife is pregnant, 'though she doesn't know it yet. Your first-born will be a girl, a lovely girl. She'll bring you great joy and, like all of us, she has a destiny to fulfill. You'll have three more children, and it's imperative you take care of your family. Not only must you take care of their physical needs; but you must also nurture them with a loving heart. That love is the gift required of you in this lifetime. Like a pure well, you must not allow it to be contaminated with bitterness and hatred. Do you understand?'

"He'd spoken quietly, and, in the silence, his words touched my heart. I did understand. In that moment I saw that only love and understanding could put an end to hatred and the terrible bloodshed of war. As if reading my mind, he said softly, 'we're all brothers, all the children of the Exalted One. There are no exceptions.'

"The next evening he left. We gathered together as we had the first night he came. 'Much suffering comes from wanting something to be other than it is," he said. "It is Allah, the Exalted One, who gave us birth; it is He who brought us together. Each of us is part of a great cosmic dance about which we know very little. Everything unfolds, as it should. There are no mistakes, only insufficient understanding.

"'For this lack there can be no blame. As you come to accept the all-pervasive harmony of things, you'll notice the twin snakes of good and evil have vanished. Never again will their poison infect you. Then will come the realization that all actions are appropriate. Then perhaps you'll come to know yourself as the all-encompassing silence, the peace within which all universes, all things and all events take place.' He paused and looked at each of us separately.

"Then he said, 'I'll not see you again, but will one day meet your daughter by the well. When she tells you of our meeting, as she will, you must tell her of these events. Shortly after we meet, a new stage in your lives will come to pass. No matter what happens, never forget that you are deeply loved by some who walk the earth today and some who are yet to come.' Then Nassir stood and embraced us. I walked with him as far as the well and watched him disappear into the hills. We haven't seen him since."

Now, as Shamir approached the well, her mind was suddenly in turmoil. She felt as if the very stability of the world she'd known was threatened. How could Nassir know the things he knew? She looked up and saw him walking to meet her. Reaching her, he took her hands and looked into her eyes. The turmoil subsided.

"They've told you, haven't they?"

She nodded.

"Come and sit down," he said, then led her to the edge of the well.

They sat across from each other, and once more she felt the peacefulness in his eyes.

"Who are you?" she asked.

He smiled slowly, a radiant smile, and his eyes sparkled. "Just a friend," he said. "Shamir, before long, things will change drastically. Life as you've known it will be swept away, and you'll enter the unknown. You'll need courage to overcome the fear that will hold you in its grip. When the changes come, there'll be many twists and turns. In time you'll leave the shores of your homeland and come to a new one. There your surroundings will reflect the peace you've found in yourself. At that time you'll meet a man who will help you.

"You must never regret the past, only enjoy the present. For the past be thankful as the tree is thankful for the seed that brought it into existence, for the winds that caressed it and the waters that quenched its thirst."

"What do you mean, Nassir?"

"I'm sorry, Shamir, but I can't explain. My task is merely to inform you and be a friend to you and your family when the time comes."

"Are you a prophet?"

"No, little one, I'm what is known as a 'seer'. I have the gift of sight. I know what is to come and the parts we play. I follow the impulse of the heart and never go astray. That's all for now; let's fill the pots so you can make it back by dark."

When they finished, he walked with her to the top of the hill, carrying her yoke. Carefully he set the pots down and stood looking at her.

"One day soon you'll see a stranger dressed in black. When you do, you must run and hide. Make your way to the well. I'll be waiting for you. Under no circumstances must you go home, nor can you do anything to help. Just come here, and I will help you. You must go now." He lifted the yoke and placed it gently across her shoulders.

"Nassir, I'm frightened by what you say."

"I know, but it had to be spoken. I'll see you tomorrow. Have a good evening and give my greetings to your parents. Tell them all is well and not to worry."

When she got home, Shamir gave her parents Nassir's message. She felt disinclined to tell them what else he'd said. She hugged her brothers and her sister as she put them to bed and told them how much she loved them.

She sat for a long time with her parents at the table that night. The light from the lamp cast a warm glow and helped ease the fear lodged in the back of her mind. She kissed her parents good night and went to bed. Outside the window, a bright moon cast a tapestry of shadows across the uneven ground. In the silence, she could hear the sound of the poplars, their leaves stirred by a vagrant breeze. She'd grown up here, and she loved the isolation.

In the morning, she got up early and helped prepare breakfast. Her father arrived with milk from the goats just as breakfast was ready.

By mid-afternoon the heat was intense, and they napped.

When Shamir awoke, it was already late. Her mother was baking bread for supper. Shamir splashed water on her face and emptied the water pots, ready to go to the well.

Kissing her mother, she set out, the pots swaying as she walked. As she turned away from the shore and headed into the hills, she looked back. She loved her home with its whitewashed walls and orange, tiled roof. It was like a precious gem nestled in the convergence of low hills, surrounded by stands of trees, gardens, and the sparkling blue ocean.

Suddenly she caught a movement on the hill behind and above her home. Something stirred a cloud of dust. As she listened, she heard the sound of a high revving engine. Whatever it was, was moving fast.

Then she saw it: a military jeep with four men inside. With a squeal of brakes, it pulled up beside the house. The men jumped out and quickly ran inside. To her horror, she saw one of the men emerge with her two brothers. He was dressed in black. Her stomach knotted, her heart jumped in her chest. She couldn't catch her breath. Nassir's words rang in her mind. Her family, she must help them. She heard a scream from the house, and the sound of a shot cut it short.

Above the ocean, two jets screamed directly inland. They came in low, guns blazing. She saw flashes of flame from their wings. In horror she watched her father racing up the shallow valley from the fishing boat. She saw the puff of bullets hit the dirt and watched helplessly as they reached him and cut him down, his body jerking with the impact.

As if in slow motion, she saw a rocket detach from the belly of the lead jet. On a tail of fire, it slammed into her home with a loud explosion and burst of flame. The roar was deafening; the concussion from the explosion knocked her down. Her ears were ringing as she pulled herself to the edge of a large rock and looked down. The warplanes were gone. All that was left was the thunderous roar from their engines and the smoldering rubble where her home once stood.

As she watched, more trails of dust came down the hill toward the smoldering ruins. As they reached the bottom, men jumped from jeeps and quickly fanned out beneath the trees. She watched for a few minutes, terrified. Then, with a deafening rush, small rockets lifted into the air. Streaming flame behind them, they came toward her, passed overhead, and vanished beyond the hills.

She picked herself up and ran as fast as she could. As she rounded the trail and started up the steep incline, she saw Nassir running toward her. She flung herself into his arms, sobbing uncontrollably.

"Are you unharmed?" he asked, looking her over. Satisfied she was all right, he held her tightly.

....

Yigall and Joseph found their places at the table. Standing behind their chairs, they waited for the Rabbi's blessing. The families had gathered to celebrate the boy's bar mitzvah. It was a big event, and all the members of the settlement joined in. Days had been spent preparing the hall; the food had taken a week. The boys spent the afternoon listening in fascination to the older men who congregated at the end of the hall, smoking their pipes and telling stories. The women had put the finishing touches to the food and all was now ready.

The murmur of voices and sounds of laughter subsided. The boys listened to the familiar words of the blessing. When it was finished, they seated themselves to the accompanying scrape of chairs. In that same instant, two rockets slammed into the hall. With an ear-shattering roar, bricks, mortar, wood, metal, tiles, and bodies hurtled in every direction. Flames flickered among the ruins. Groans and cries of pain mingled with the sound of falling rubble. Smoke and dust were everywhere – choking, gagging.

Yigall knew he was hurt but felt no pain. He squeezed his friend's hand; there was no response. He looked over to see if Joseph was all right. A deep cry of revulsion and fear burst from his lips. In the light from the flames, he saw the stump of Joseph's arm, the hand still holding his in its death grip.

☰ 5

Travis' first meeting with Tremaine

General J. P. Travis left the room. He was smiling and confident. The meeting had gone well. Since Emerson's death, he'd held several meetings with the Joint Chiefs. He'd not wasted time, feeling it imperative to strike before the new President got his bearings. All of them supported keeping gays out of the military, he thought. These limp-wristed fairies must not corrupt the military. The military is really a man's world, and as far as he was concerned, it would stay that way.

Although there'd been unanimous agreement in opposing gays in the military, not all of the Joint Chiefs felt as he did regarding the new President. Most of them held a respect for the office, if not for the man. Travis had an implacable distaste for the man. He considered him a draft dodger because he'd actively opposed the Vietnam War and then, years later, through a quirk of fate, he'd become the President of the country—a country he'd long held to be the greatest in the world. It was his duty to prevent any man who'd not served in the military from exercising control over the collective might of the military forces of the country he loved.

He was prepared to offer his services in that capacity, distasteful as it might be. He was willing to advise the President, to make decisions for him on military matters. He would be the real power, while the President would defer to his knowledge and expertise. Of course, he'd maintain the fiction that the President was actually the one in command.

McManus had warned him to be careful, that Tremaine was not to be taken lightly. McManus was a fool.

Travis was hungry. He glanced at his watch. He had time for a quick breakfast. From there he'd go to the White House for his appointment at ten. As he came down the steps, his aide opened the car door and held it while he got in. He gave the name of the restaurant and sat back complacently. It was a lovely morning. Trees were still in full, fresh foliage, while the grass in the parks was lush and green, accompanied by the smell of moist earth. A brisk wind had swept the pollution from the city, and visibility was good.

After breakfast, he was driven to the White House, arriving precisely thirty seconds before the meeting. Tremaine arose from the desk and approached Travis with a smile, his hand extended in greeting.

Travis had forgotten how striking the man was. He was six feet tall and weighed about a hundred and seventy pounds. He appeared slim and athletic, with brown wavy hair and the most unusual green eyes he'd ever seen, Travis guessed he was in his late fifties.

They shook hands, and Travis felt the man's strength. Two chairs sat in front of the desk and Tremaine signaled Travis to take one while he took the other. They sat comfortably and faced each other over a small elegant coffee table. On the table stood a silver coffeepot, creamer, sugar bowl, two mugs and spoons.

The two men presented a strange contrast. Travis was in dress uniform, ribbons and medals prominent on a broad chest. His creases were sharp, his shoes like polished ebony. A big man, over six feet tall, he weighed two hundred and twenty pounds. He had a short, iron gray, military haircut and the solid strength of a very fit sixty-year-old man who'd seen his share of life.

Tremaine was dressed casually in a pair of light brown cotton slacks, sandals and socks, and a white cotton shirt open at the neck. "Care for some coffee, General?" he asked.

"Yes, that would be fine."

Tremaine reached over and poured coffee into the mugs. "Help yourself," he said as he poured a touch of milk. He settled back in the firm comfortable chair and waited.

Travis spooned in sugar and stirred brusquely. He savored his coffee, eyes momentarily closed. Suddenly, he realized Tremaine was waiting for him.

"Travis, I'm not one to beat around the bush. We must address this issue of gays in the military. It was something Emerson was committed to, and I feel the same as he did. Before he died, there wasn't much support for this policy among the Joint Chiefs. I need to know your thoughts on the matter."

"It's our feeling—" began Travis.

"No, I want to know *your* thoughts on the matter," said Tremaine, interrupting him.

"My thoughts?" Travis was taken aback.

"Yes, your thoughts."

"I think the military is no place for gays."

"Why?"

"Because I think it will affect the morale of the men."

"How do you see that?"

"I think it's uncomfortable for most men to have other men look at them with sexual interest. Since you've not served in the military yourself, it might be difficult for you to understand how men feel when they live in close proximity and have little privacy. This is compounded during time of war. In time of war the men must have as few distractions as possible. They don't need the extra discomfort of other men being sexually interested in them, or being sexually attracted themselves. The same goes for female personnel."

"That was the argument against women serving in combat?"

"Yes, it was, and as far as I'm concerned, the argument

still holds. Women in the service are a distraction for men who must be about the business of war. Besides, women are not suited to combat. And even less suited are men who, apart from having a penis, are in most respects women themselves. We've had to create separate quarters and segregate the sexes. It would require even further segregation to meet the needs of most normal men with regard to gays. I doubt there's a single heterosexual man who would feel comfortable taking a shower with a homosexual. Not one!"

"So you're suggesting that if gays were allowed to serve openly in the military they'd have to be segregated much as women are today."

"Yes. But I would not recommend them being allowed to serve in the first place!"

"I understand. Our present policy is to refuse entrance into the military of those who openly declare their homosexuality. We also discharge those who are found to be gay. Yet it seems obvious that there have always been, still is, and will continue to be, gays in the military who remain undetected. How does this affect your argument concerning the discomfort of men being looked upon as sexual objects by other men?"

"The men feel supported by their government and commanding officers if they know there's an active policy forbidding gays in the military. By denying gays access to military service, we don't encourage them to join. So the number of gays actually serving is less than in an open system."

"I understand your point." Tremaine sipped his coffee and seemed lost in thought.

Travis picked up his mug and took several swallows. It was good coffee. He watched Tremaine closely without being obvious. It was the first face-to-face conversation he'd had with the man. Before today, his conversations had been with Emerson; Tremaine, though present, had always remained quiet, not speaking a word.

For that reason, he'd concluded that Tremaine would be easy to deal with. He wasn't so sure anymore.

"General, what do *you* think of gays yourself? What are your personal views?"

"I don't think my views have anything to do with this," he said carefully.

"I disagree. Our personal views deeply affect how we conduct ourselves professionally. Some men, knowing their bias, may bend the other way to compensate, while for others, professional and personal opinions are the same. I'd like to know your personal views on the matter."

"Well, gays make me uncomfortable. I don't like the idea of men looking at me with sexual interest."

"Why not?"

"I'm not sure... I feel uncomfortable, and I find myself getting angry. I think homosexuality is wrong and unnatural. It's obvious to me that from a physiological standpoint, men and women were made different sexually in order to continue the species through the act of procreation. Homosexual acts cannot do that, and I find them unnatural and repugnant."

"You said you felt it was wrong. Is that from a religious perspective?"

"No, I don't consider myself a religious man. I do believe in God, but I don't attend church and haven't for a long time. I think things that are natural are largely right and things that are unnatural are largely wrong. There may be exceptions, but that's the way I see it."

"It's interesting to me that the dialogue going on in the country as a whole is similar to this one. Most of the conversations take place from the perspective of gay and heterosexual men and not from the perspective of the women who also serve. Do you have any thoughts about why that is?"

"From what I hear, it is the men who feel the most

uncomfortable with it."

"Some have suggested that masculine gay females make good soldiers because they're more aggressive, more masculine in their manner of being. What do you think?"

"I really don't know, but it does seem to be true. There are women serving in the military who exhibit more masculine characteristics than their counterparts in the civilian population. Maybe that has to do with the fact that the military has, until recently, been an institution dominated and run by men. It could be they instill certain characteristics and women assume them. I doubt it, though."

"Some contend that gay men are not aggressive enough to make good soldiers. What do you think?"

"It seems to me that a soldier needs to be aggressive. Most of the gay men I've met do not exhibit those characteristics. My honest opinion is that gay men do not make good soldiers, period."

"I understand your point of view, but I believe it bears scrutiny. It seems to me that some very fine soldiers were gay. Lawrence of Arabia is one of them. He was a pioneer in the art of modern guerrilla warfare. His sexual preference didn't seem to inhibit his ability to instill allegiance in his men and didn't appear to interfere with his abilities as a soldier."

"I know there are exceptions," said Travis, "but I think they are few. Those exceptions don't change my opinion, the opinions of the other Joint Chiefs of Staff or, for that matter, the opinions of the vast majority of men in uniform who serve their country today."

"Emerson considered the ban of gays a violation of their constitutional rights."

"Most of us who serve in the military feel that the military does not fall within the jurisdiction of civilian courts and is not subject to the guaranteed rights of civilians. Military law and civilian law are two distinctly separate systems and must remain so."

"Why?"

"Why? Because the military is inherently an authoritarian system with a chain of command that works from the top down. If civil law was applicable, a soldier might refuse to carry out a direct order on the grounds that it could jeopardize his life or the lives of those under him. Civil law can never be tolerated in a military establishment. Like oil and water, they don't mix."

"What are your thoughts on allowing women to fly combat missions?"

"I oppose it!"

"Again, may I ask why?"

"For the same reasons that I oppose women being in the military in the first place. First of all, I don't think that by nature women are aggressive fighters. Second, they put other men at risk should they be captured. And, if captured they can easily suffer rape and sexual torture at the hands of enemy soldiers. This gives opposing military forces a great deal of leverage against a nation such as ours where women are respected, valued highly and must be protected. Ultimately, we'd be more likely to sacrifice a man to an enemy than we would a woman." Travis picked up his mug and took a long swallow.

"General Travis, I appreciate your forthrightness. Now I wish to talk to you on another matter."

Good, Travis thought. He disliked having to deal with this issue. It was distasteful to him, and he wanted to get on with more important matters.

"More coffee?"

"Please."

"Before we move on, I want to know one more thing on this matter. If I issued an executive order banning discrimination against gays, would you support it?"

Travis was annoyed by the question but tried not to let his feelings show. Tremaine sat casually in his chair, but his eyes were fixed firmly on the general's.

"No, I would not!" he said gruffly.

"Would you actively oppose it?"

"I would!"

"And what is your assessment of the other Joint Chiefs? Would they also actively oppose it?"

Here it was at last, he thought, the beginning moves of the showdown. Travis was glad he'd taken the time earlier in the week to gain the Joints Chiefs' undivided support.

"They would actively oppose it as well."

"How?"

"I don't really know at this time."

"Might it involve resignations?"

"It might."

"Once more, I appreciate your honesty."

For a few moments, they sat quietly. Tremaine appeared thoughtful, and then putting his coffee down said, "It's no secret that I did not serve in the military, so there's been speculation as to my fitness to be Commander in Chief."

"Yes."

"I will need the assistance of men like yourself for as long as I hold this office. I will need your knowledge, your expertise and the benefit of your informed opinion. But it must be clearly understood, *I* will make the decisions and you will have to follow them whether they contradict your informed opinions or the judgment of the other Joint Chiefs. I will expect you to follow the orders I issue. There'll be no hindrance or sabotage of those orders. If there is, I will not hesitate to fire whoever engages in such behavior. Is that understood?"

Travis was taken aback by the directness of Tremaine's statement. He'd felt the force behind the words even though it had been spoken quietly. Tremaine's eyes had not wavered and Travis had been unable to avoid them. He had the uneasy feeling that Tremaine was reading his mind, or at least assessing him, and doing so accurately. Travis felt off-balance, almost trapped. All his scheming would come to nothing if he could not dominate this man. From the conversation so far, he was beginning to feel he might not be able to do so.

"Yes, I think I understand," Travis finally responded.

"I don't mean to be rude, Travis, but I'm not interested in what you think. I will issue the orders and expect you and the other Joint Chiefs to carry them out, to do so faithfully and in no way obstruct them. Is that clearly understood?"

"Yes!"

"Now you must understand something else. I have no interest in having anyone advise me by giving me what he or she thinks I want to hear. I'm open to all points of view, all input. Each of us has a job to do, and we must do it well. We must speak the truth, as we understand it. Nothing less will be accepted. If you can't give me what I ask for, then you must consider whether you can serve me in this capacity or not. If you cannot, you must resign. I will understand. I do not ask of anyone what he is not prepared to give. Do I make myself clear?"

"You do."

"What is your response?"

"I will think about what you've said."

"That's fair enough. You have one week. I want you to convey to the Joint Chiefs the substance of our conversation today. We'll meet next week at the same time." With that Tremaine stood, and Travis followed suit. The President saw him to the door. The two men shook hands. "Thank you for your time, General, I appreciate your candor. I think we understand each other now. I'll see you next week."

Travis stepped into the hall and the door closed behind him. He made his way to the entrance where the driver waited. He felt dazed by what had just transpired. Thoughts tumbled through his mind. He ordered his aide to drive back to his office. On the way, he changed his mind.

"Take me to the Lincoln Memorial," he said.

"Yes sir."

A few minutes later, they stopped in front of the immense statue of the seated Civil War President. Travis got out and instructed the driver through the window. "I'll walk back," he said. "Be ready for me at three. I have a meeting at the Senate."

"Yes sir."

The wind blew stiffly. Turning his back to the Lincoln Memorial, Travis walked toward the Washington Monument. On the way, he took a detour and slowly made his way toward the Vietnam Wall. From a distance he could see a small crowd of visitors, Vietnam Vets and their families. There was something powerful about this place. At first he'd disliked the monument, preferring the more traditional statues of war. But it had grown on him, and it was a place where many Vietnam Vets gathered. He himself had looked for names inscribed on the black marble, names of men he'd known during three tours of duty in Vietnam.

He knew men who'd not returned, more than he cared to count. It had been a vicious war, one not easily forgotten by those who'd been there. He sat on a bench and watched the memorial through the trees. Somehow the presence of the wall reminded him that he must not forget the men who'd fought with him so many years ago.

To support a President who had actively opposed the war was anathema to him, nothing less than a betrayal of the young men who'd given their lives and the thousands who'd returned maimed in body and soul. No, he'd not support this man. He couldn't! Nor would he quietly go away. He'd oppose him in every way he could, of that he was certain.

He stood and straightened his shoulders. His mind was calm again, his direction clear. As he started to walk, a man in a wheelchair, dressed in army fatigues, came along the path toward the memorial. Unshaven and dirty, his eyes were wild and uneasy. A battered hat was stuffed on his head. He saw Travis and recognized the uniform. Taking his hand from the wheel, he saluted smartly. Travis returned the salute. In that brief moment the man lost control of his chair, which quickly gathered speed as it headed down the steep path. Several times he tried to slow the wheels with his bare hands. Travis jumped for the wayward chair, grabbed it by the handles, slowed it down and brought it to a stop.

"Are you all right?" he asked.

"Yeah," came the breathless reply. "Thanks for yer help."

"Can I help you to the bottom of the hill?" Travis asked.

"Yeah, if ya don't mind. Name's Luke."

"Mine's Travis." He held the handles and slowed the chair with his weight as they descended. "Serve in 'Nam?" he asked Luke.

"Yeah, you?"

"Yeah, sixty-six through sixty-nine."

"Holy jeez, ya must've been fuckin' crazy. What are ya, a super patriot or somethin'?"

Travis was stung.

"If ya spent three years there, ya must have been brass, high muck-a-muck. Bastards like you sent the likes of me into that living hell. Follow orders, or be shot for disobedience. So what the fuck, what choice did we have? We followed yer fuckin' orders and a lot of us died.

"We were smart mother-fuckers then. Remember when a newsman asked that asshole general why they'd destroyed the hamlet? Remember what he said?"

Travis shook his head.

"'We had to destroy it in order to save it.' Well, wasn't that the goddamned truth? I was there in that god-forsaken Iron

Triangle; I lost my legs there, one hell of a gift for being a patriot, serving this godforsaken country and following the orders of men like you. And when I got back stateside, what the fuck did I get? Five years in a V.A. hospital getting shafted."

Travis' face flushed and his neck puffed up. He couldn't believe what he heard. Boiling, he looked at the top of Luke's head. He had the urge to tip Luke out of the chair. They reached the bottom of the hill, and Travis stopped.

"You're on your own," he said, and, without a backward glance, turned on his heel and headed back up the hill.

6

The long reach of hatred

We must leave quickly," Nassir said. "Come with me." He turned and headed back along the trail. Shamir followed. She felt dazed, unable to comprehend what had happened. As they came to the top of the incline, she heard the frightening sound of rockets passing overhead.

"There are guerillas in these hills. We must not attract their attention." Nassir turned toward her, making sure she heard him above the noise. She nodded. For half an hour she followed him. They passed the well from which she'd drawn water. She noted absently that the flock was gone.

Nassir was moving fast, and she struggled to keep up with him. Finally, they came to a valley leading toward the rocky peaks of the mountains to the northeast. Nassir headed up its slope. The going was rough, and she could tell by the lengthening shadows it was almost evening. For an hour they climbed steadily.

Above her labored breathing, she heard the sound of gunfire somewhere behind them. She turned to look, but Nassir grabbed her by the hand and pulled her toward an outcropping of rocks and stunted oak. She scrambled as fast as she could. At last they reached the protection of the rocks.

Out of breath and lying flat, she pulled herself to the edge of the outcropping and looked over just in time to see two jets far below lifting out of the valley. Hugging the hills, the jets streaked toward them. In the failing light she saw flashes of fire from the guns on their wings.

The jets were firing at someone who was following the same path she and Nassir were taking. As they watched, one of the jets exploded in a huge ball of flame. A moment later they heard the explosion and watched pieces of flaming wreckage tumble lazily through the air. The remaining warplane peeled off, and at high speed turned back on its prey. Guns blazed long beads of brightness in the sudden darkness. Then, as quickly as they'd come, the remaining aircraft was gone. Only a hushed silence remained.

Shamir and Nassir looked in the direction from which the jets had come. In the distance to the west, a light winked on and off. Above them, a ridge of mountains formed a black silhouette against a carpet of stars. Suddenly, to the south, three bright lights lifted out of the darkness and arched across the night sky to disappear over a ridge to the south.

"What's that?" Shamir whispered.

"Rockets being fired into Israel. Come," he said and reached down to pull her to her feet. "We must be far away by morning. If the planes catch us in the open we won't stand a chance."

....

By ten o'clock that night, they were climbing along a ridge Shamir had seen before the light faded.

"We'll rest here." Nassir sat with his back to a rock. Shamir sat beside him. A cool breeze was blowing and brought with it the familiar scents of the high country. They heard a loud hoarse braying from a donkey somewhere to the north. For a while they sat quietly. Shamir caught her breath; the cool breeze on her skin was refreshing. Turning to the east, she saw a huge moon rise from behind the serrated peaks above.

As Shamir beheld the beauty all around a profound peace enveloped her. She sat absorbed in her surroundings until her mind recalled the day's events and she was once more plunged into sorrow. She found herself re-living the morning. The moon lifted into the sky before her sightless eyes and her mind shifted back to the night before her family was killed. She sat with her parents around the table as they discussed the day's events. Feeling tired she kissed them goodnight and before lying down her lips had brushed her brothers and sister while they slept. All dead! She couldn't believe it. Last night was a world away. Her life would never be the same. Tears flowed down her cheeks. Nassir put his arm about her shoulders and let her cry.

....

Shamir was exhausted when at last she became aware of the approaching dawn. She was following Nassir down a steep ravine into a dark valley. They were no longer following a trail. She slipped in loose shale. Nassir stopped her slide before she went over the edge. She found herself trembling.

"Not much further," he promised.

She looked at him in the subdued light and saw the exhaustion in his face. She got to her feet, and they continued. When they reached the valley floor, the going was easier. Eventually, they came to a steep rock face.

Carefully, Nassir climbed a narrow goat trail that angled up the side of the wall. Shamir looked up to see where it went. In the faint light of dawn, she saw that it disappeared into a sharply inclined ravine a hundred meters above where she stood.

She worked her way up the trail until she reached the intersecting ravine. Nassir was waiting for her. She stopped to catch her breath. The valley floor below was lost in shadow, while the rim above was bathed in the light of the rising sun. Rocks and boulders stood in stark relief and the grasses shone golden, waving in the early morning breeze.

Shamir turned to follow Nassir, but he was nowhere in sight. She looked up the ravine toward a cluster of giant boulders that had fallen from the rocky wall. She walked toward them. As she approached, she saw Nassir sitting in the shadow, his back against the cliff.

"We've made it," he said.

"Where will we stay?" asked Shamir.

"Up there. " He pointed.

All she could see were more boulders protruding from the rocky wall and rising thirty meters from where she now stood, nearly twenty five meters from the top of the wall.

"Come," he said, and climbed directly up the tumbled boulders. She followed, careful not to fall into the cracks. At last she reached the top; she was shaking from exhaustion.

Nassir lowered himself through an opening and signaled her to follow. She climbed down a sharply inclined tunnel that gave access to a large cave. Light entered indirectly from several sources at the back. The cave was lived in. Sheepskins were spread on the floor around a circle of firestones. Leather water skins hung on poles, and she noted cooking utensils and a variety of foods on ledges. On one side were two sleeping pallets with woven blankets covering them. At the back, she could hear the sound of trickling water.

"Welcome to my summer home." Nassir smiled at her. "We're safe here; it's not easy to find. There's a spring of water over there," he said, pointing in the direction of the trickling water. "If you want, you can wash. I'll get something to eat, and then you can rest."

They ate in silence. When they finished, Nassir pointed toward one of the sleeping pallets.

"You can take that one over there. I must go and check on the flock. My brother's watching them and is expecting me."

"Don't you need to rest?" she asked.

"Once I make it to the flock I'll get some rest, but I need to be off before it's too hot. I'll be back at dusk. Be careful not to be seen; stay in the shadows as much as possible. Help yourself to food and water."

She watched him as he gathered dried fruit and picked up a water skin. "I'm sorry to leave you. Sleep well. You'll be perfectly safe here. I'll see you when I get back."

Slinging the water skin over his shoulder, he disappeared through the opening. She walked over to the pallet and lay down. Before long, she fell into an exhausted sleep filled with frightening dreams.

....

She watched helplessly as an Israeli warplane came directly at her, guns blazing. She awoke with a scream. For a moment, she didn't know where she was. Then the memories of the preceding night flooded in and she shook with great sobs of grief. She missed her family. Vividly etched in her mind was the convulsive movement of her father's body as bullets from the low-flying aircraft struck him. She wanted to kill those who'd killed her family. Sorrow and rage alternated in an endless cycle with the images and thoughts in her mind.

Finally, she got up and looked around. It was already afternoon. She drank some water, found some dried fruit and took it with her through the entrance. Sitting in the shade against the rocky face, she had a clear view of all approaches. Hidden in the shadow, she would be difficult to see.

What could she do? Where would she go? What was to become of her? There were no answers to these questions. After a while, her eye caught movement far below. She watched as a tiny figure crossed the valley and disappeared from sight. She saw Nassir emerge at the lower end of the ravine. She stood and went to greet him.

"I'm glad you're back," she said.

He looked at her closely, aware of the sorrow in her voice. He noticed her cheeks still wet with tears, her eyes swollen and red. Opening his arms, he let her head rest on his shoulder and held her as she cried.

....

Once more, Shamir followed Nassir along a narrow trail leading to the rim above the valley. He helped her up and they climbed higher into the mountain. Darkness had fallen by the time they stopped.

From where they sat, they'd be aware of any movements beneath them. A warm breeze brought again the fragrance of old cedar. Overhead, the great dome was studded with millions of winking lights.

Nassir spread a blanket on a smooth rock and they sat back to back. An hour passed without a word before Nassir finally spoke.

"Talk to me, little one," he said softly.

Immediately her eyes filled with tears. After they subsided, she told him of her day and the thoughts that bedeviled her mind.

"Let the thoughts come," he said. "They cannot be stopped; just let them come. You are not the author of the thoughts; they simply come by themselves. Let them come and let them go. If you can observe them, see how they have a life of their own, coming and going like clouds drifting across the emptiness of the sky."

"I want to kill those who killed my family, but I don't know where to begin or how to go about it."

Nassir felt her anguish and understood.

"In the morning, you'll meet my brother. When you do, you'll see there's something wrong with him; he's simple."

"Was he born that way?" she asked.

"No, he was struck in the head with a gun by an Israeli

soldier. It left him brain-damaged. He knows sheep though, and that knowledge is unaffected. He's been a great help to me. He no longer has much need to be around people. The silence and the mountains are home to him."

"What happened to the soldier who hurt your brother?"

"My father killed him."

"When did this happen?"

"Almost fifty years ago."

"Nassir, what happened? Can you tell me?"

"I will tell you. I've never told this story before, but I think it has bearing on your own. I once told your parents their gift to life was the love they gave their children. It's their legacy to you. They've nurtured you with love and given you an inner strength. In this way, they have molded you for what destiny has in store."

Shamir's eyes filled with tears again. She was puzzled by his statement but said nothing.

Nassir sat quietly for a few minutes, collecting his thoughts. "My family had been shepherds for generations, and the land on which they raised sheep lay in both southern Lebanon and what is now northern Israel. When the State of Israel came into existence, we had no idea of the changes about to take place. The British had broken the hold of the Turks and established their own rule. But none of it really affected the lives of the people who lived on the land for generations. My mother and father had three children, my two older brothers and myself. Father worked the flocks with my uncle, who also lived with us. My mother ran the home and, as my brothers and I became old enough, we helped my father and uncle tend the sheep. We were sometimes away for days at a time. My mother spent time carding, spinning and weaving, and she had charge over the household. We lived in a small valley that sloped from the hills and gave way to the Mediterranean, much like the valley where you lived. We had almond trees, sycamore, and a tall, beautiful stand of poplar. It was a place of great but simple beauty.

"We didn't understand at the time that our home was just inside the northern border of the new Jewish state. One morning I was to leave early with my father, uncle, and two brothers. We were moving the flock higher into the mountains. I wasn't feeling well. I felt light-headed and couldn't keep food down. I was disappointed when I had to stay behind. I was ill for two days, but by the end of the second day I was feeling better. We expected the men to return at any time.

"My mother and I were sitting at the table. We'd finished supper and were talking by the light of the lamp. I loved my mother. She must have been thirty-seven at the time. Her name was Fatah. She was a striking and beautiful woman, with a lovely warmth about her, dark almond eyes and jet-black hair. We heard a sound outside and were about to get up, thinking the men had returned. The door burst open and four soldiers glared at us, rifles leveled. They were Israeli soldiers. They tied my hands with cord and pushed me into a chair. I was shaking with fear. I looked at my mother. She was shaking too. Then two of the soldiers grabbed her. The third started tearing her clothes off. They raped her in front of me right there on the kitchen floor. When they finished, they dragged us both outside. Twenty meters away stood a military truck and a jeep with more Israeli soldiers waiting nearby.

"We were dragged toward the jeep and watched as men poured gasoline and torched the house and surrounding buildings. The fire lit up the sky. Above the roar of flames we heard shouts coming from the hills. I knew it was the men returning home. The Israelis heard the shouts too. All but the four soldiers who'd entered the house jumped in the truck and drove away. The soldier holding my mother pulled his gun and, before I realized what was happening, he held it to her head and killed her. I managed to loosen the cord around my wrists, and when he turned toward me

I charged, knocking him down. The gun spun out of his hand. I dove on it and turned it toward him. He drew his knife and came straight for me. I leveled the gun and fired.

"I'll never forget the surprised look on his face as he fell in the dirt. Shots rang out, and I felt something strike my arm. It burned and spun me around. Lying on the ground, I saw the remaining soldiers crouched beside the jeep, their rifles leveled at me. My father and uncle came racing into the light of the fire. The soldiers were so concentrated on me; they were unaware of anyone behind them. My father and uncle swung their staves at the heads of two of the soldiers. They went down before they could get off a shot. The third man fired, but my older brother, who charged him from behind, spoiled his aim. The rifle jerked out of his grasp. He grabbed it by the barrel and swung it at my brother, hitting him in the head. He hit him several times before my father killed him."

"Nassir, I'm so sorry."

"After we nursed my brother back to health, he and my uncle looked after the sheep. My other brother, my father and I joined one of the guerrilla groups defending the land against the Israelis. We started attacking them wherever we could. For five years we raided, killing the men and destroying their property. We knew the hills and mountains far better than they, and in the beginning they were no match for us.

"One evening, we attacked a convoy delivering industrial equipment to a new factory. We ambushed the trucks in a narrow valley and blew several of them up. Most of their men were killed in the initial ambush. Several, however, managed to escape and dug in against a low cliff. Each time we tried to overrun them, we got hit with fire from a machine gun.

"We got close enough to lob grenades. We couldn't tell whether we'd killed them all. We withdrew carefully and waited for morning. We moved in, only to get caught in a hail of bullets.

One of our men was wounded, and we withdrew.

"We were unable to attack head on so we took cover behind the wrecked trucks and devised a plan. Since I knew the terrain well, I was to work my way into the cliff behind them while the other men kept them distracted. I was in position by late afternoon.

"For some reason, the Israelis had not contacted their base. Maybe their radios had been destroyed. As the sun sank, the shadows lengthened, and I was able to crawl to a place above the enemy position. All firing had stopped, and stillness descended with the approaching night.

"Looking down, I could see the Israelis dug into the sand behind some rocks. I counted ten of them. There was no movement. They seemed at odd angles, and it was then that I realized they were dead. There'd been no firing from them since mid-afternoon. Carefully, I climbed to where they were. As I got closer, I saw that some of them were severely dismembered from the grenades we'd lobbed earlier.

"I climbed over the parapet for a closer look, and carefully checked each one of them. There was a sound behind me and I whirled around in time to see one of the Israelis getting to his feet. I saw something glint in his hand as he moved toward me. We were so close; I couldn't get my rifle up. I felt his weight on me, and in that moment I drew my knife and drove it deep in his gut. His mouth was beside my ear, his chin on my shoulder. I could hear the agony.

"As he slid to the ground, I rolled him over. He was a young man, no more than eighteen, with brown hair and blue eyes. Blood oozed from a wound in his belly, and the side of his face was badly disfigured and covered with dry blood. He looked at me, and I looked at him. He tried to say something and lifted his hand. I jumped back. Then I saw in his hand a silver pen and a piece of folded paper. With his eyes he pleaded

for me to take it. I reached down and opened his hand. The pen
fell out and I took the paper. It was a letter.

Dear Mama,

*We were ambushed yesterday and most of the men were
killed. Some of us were able to escape but were soon pinned down
by enemy fire. About an hour before the sun came up grenades hit
us. All of us were wounded, and in the heat of this awful day my
comrades died. I know I'll not live to see another day.*

*I love you and thought of you and papa at the end. Give Benjamin
a hug for me. Tell him to take care of you, and when the time comes,
may he be as good a man as he has been a brother to me.*

*Please tell my lovely Sarah that I love her and I'm sorry
to cause her this grief. I wanted to bring her happiness and joy
and now that will never be. One day, when the sorrow has gone
from her heart, may she find love and happiness with someone
who loves her as I do.*

*It is getting harder to write. I watch the sun sink behind these
hills in a beautiful glow and know that I am going with it too. I
hope this letter finds its way to you. Peace be with you.*

Your loving son,
Josef.

"I looked down at the dying soldier. His eyes pleaded and his
lips gurgled blood. I knelt beside him and gently took his head in
my lap. Leaning over, I whispered in his ear, 'I'll make sure your
family gets the letter.'

"I straightened up and, looking in his eyes, so blue and so
innocent now, I told him how sorry I was. I wasn't sure he had
understood what I'd said, but there was a deep peacefulness that
seemed to come from him. Despite our differences, in the face
of death we were brothers who shared the same life force. I sat
with him in the silence, a comfort in his dying. Then he gripped

my arm, his body shuddered, and his breath went out and did not return. I removed his identification tag and later sent it along with the letter to his parents."

Shamir was crying softly. Nassir let her cry.

"I left the group of men with whom I'd fought and went into the mountains. I thought a lot about what had happened, the events of the past five years. I saw that hatred and the thirst for revenge had poisoned my very being. The young soldier had somehow set something in motion. I saw that hatred begets hatred, and in the process it twists a human being into a monster. I spent forty days in the mountains, and then one day I had the distinct feeling I had to find someone. It was a strange feeling that stayed with me for months.

"I climbed high into the mountains. From there I had an unobstructed view to the west. In the distance, the Mediterranean stretched to the horizon. The lower slopes of hills showed green and lush and vineyards draped the undulating hills like little patches. Small settlements, whitewashed houses with their red slate roofs and clumps of trees dotted the landscape.

"As I wandered along a ridge, I noticed a grove of cedars nestled in a small ravine below. I climbed down and walked into the grove. The smell of cedar permeated the warm air, and a breeze stirred the upper limbs of the ancient trees. It was late afternoon, and birds called back and forth in anticipation of day's end. I sat beneath a tree and leaning against the trunk, looked up into the mountain.

"Beyond the ridge I'd just descended, the jagged sand and orange-colored peaks pushed into the blue sky. Some of the higher peaks trailed long wisps of thin cloud. I sat and observed the changing colors and lengthening shadows. As I watched, I caught a movement above me and saw an old man come into view, ascending from the other side of the ridge.

"He stood on the top for a few moments, as though getting

his bearings, and then he started down the ravine toward the cedars. He wore white cotton pants gathered below the knees. On his feet was a pair of old sandals. He wore a white, loose-fitting shirt, and around his shoulders hung a robe, like a thick, cotton blanket in which a pale red and gray pattern had been woven. His skin showed the effects of long exposure to the sun. His hair was white and long. He had a white mustache, and on his face was the stubble of several days' growth.

"I watched him as he came to the trees. He entered the glade and then stopped. He paused, waiting and listening as though expecting someone. After a few moments he approached my hiding place. I pulled back out of sight and continued to watch. He stopped ten meters in front of me. Although the light would soon fade, I saw his face clearly. There was something about him I really liked. His movements, I realized, were graceful and effortless, despite his advanced years.

"In his hand he carried a stout walking staff, which he leaned against a tree. Taking the blanket from around his shoulders, he spread it on the ground and on it placed a small carrying bag. He sat down and crossed his legs and closed his eyes. His back was straight, relaxed. Dusk fell upon the mountain, and the birds became suddenly quiet. I made myself as comfortable as I could and waited to see what would happen next.

"I must have fallen asleep, for when I awoke, a shaft of moonlight came through the trees, illuminating the glade in which he sat. He was as still as I'd last seen him, except that his eyes were open and he was looking in my direction.

"He said, 'Come and sit with me, Nassir.'

"I couldn't tell if I'd really heard the words, for they seemed to originate in my head. I waited.

"'Come and sit with me, Nassir. I've been looking for you. The Exalted One sent me to find you.'

"Again I couldn't tell where the sound of his voice was

coming from, and I remained still and hidden, or so I thought.

"'Yes, I'm speaking to you. You cannot hide from me. I know what happened. I know of your beloved mother's cruel death and of the young Israeli soldier. Come and sit with me. I've been looking for you.'

"I got up and stepped into the clearing. He patted the blanket in front of him, 'Sit here,' he said.

"I sat in front of him and felt a strange wave of relief passing through me. I found myself crying. It was as though I'd been lost for a long time and had finally found my way home. When the tears subsided, I sat quietly, suspended in a deep and infinite peace.

"'It is time for you to awaken, Nassir, awaken from this living dream. It is my task to show you the way. Now that hatred has drained from you, the flame of Allah's knowledge can make itself known. Soon it will burn full and bright of its own accord, illuminating your way. When the time is right, the Exalted One will send those on the edge of wakefulness across your path. You are the Divine instrument of Allah's peace, Allah's wisdom. This encompasses both the beginning and the end. What lies between is yet to be revealed.'

"What do you mean?' I asked.

"'I've come to burn that which is dead and dry. It is fuel for the light of understanding that will dawn in you. When it's finished, you'll understand the unspeakable simplicity of life and wonder how you could have missed something so obvious.

"'This is not something unique. Understanding is passed down from generation to generation, from the beginning to the end of time. It has ever been this way, although the vast majority of men are ignorant of it, which is as it is. The dance of life spins out and is a wonder to behold. For those within whom the flame of truth is kindled, suffering has ended, and the heart overflows with compassion.'

"We spent two years together. I had many questions at first. At last they were exhausted, and no more arose in the mind. One day he sent me to find my uncle and brother, saying they needed my help. We worked together from that time forth.

"One day, word came to us that my father and my other brother had been killed. For the next six years, I tended the flocks and went to see the Master whenever I felt the need. One night, I had a dream. The Master came toward me, his eyes radiating a deep love that I received and gave back. He put his hands on my shoulders kissing me on both cheeks. Then, without a word, he turned and walked away. I knew I would never see him again. I never did.

Shamir sat in the silence. Tears rolled down her face.

"Who was he?" she asked eventually.

"He was a Sufi sage. I knew him as Bokhari."

"Was he able to heal the sorrow in your heart?" Shamir asked.

"He was," Nassir answered simply.

"Will you help me too, Nassir?"

"If it is the desire of your heart."

"It is the desire of my heart," she answered.

Tears flowed and took with them the poison that had filled her with hatred. When the moon reached its zenith, they returned by its light to the cave.

7

Manipulation

Travis had a busy week, twice meeting with the Joint Chiefs. At the first meeting he told them of the conversation with Tremaine. They agreed to enlist the support of pro-military congressmen and senators. Under Travis' guidance, they were determined to prevent the President from opening the military to gays.

For a week they walked the halls of congress, from early morning until late evening. Travis was successful in getting the chairman of the Senate Armed Services Committee, Sam Jackson, firmly behind him. Jackson was a tough man, probably the most powerful of the southern senators; his influence was legendary. Jackson shared Travis' distaste for the new President for many of the same reasons.

The day after his meeting with Jackson, Travis met with Senator Bill Cole, who'd assumed the mantle of opposition leader. Travis felt the Senator would readily support him in his opposition to gays in the military. He was not disappointed. To his surprise, he found Cole disturbing to deal with. He was more cunning than any politician Travis had ever met. Travis was left with the impression that the man was not entirely honest. He had a way with words; he could twist them to suit his purpose and make those who opposed him look like fools.

Travis was in the Senator's office when Senator Dixon came in. Cole excused himself. "Did you get it?" he demanded.

"No, I couldn't get..."

"Don't give me excuses Senator," Cole said, cutting him off. "I expect you back here at five this evening." With that, he ushered the hapless Dixon from his office.

Travis felt sorry for Dixon; he was no match for Cole. When Travis left the office he had Cole's support and an uneasy feeling. The man was not to be trusted.

By week's end, the Joint Chiefs were pleased with the support they'd marshaled. Things looked good and Travis was confident they'd hand the President his first defeat. McManus had spoken with Bill Jamieson, the Secretary of Defense, who'd listened carefully and politely but refused to support what they were about.

"We never expected his support anyway," Travis explained defensively to the Joint Chiefs. "We don't need it."

"You may be right, but it concerns me that we haven't changed anyone's mind. We've been preaching to the converted."

"McManus, you worry over nothing. Tremaine wouldn't dare oppose us. What's he going to do, fire us? I doubt that."

"Don't be so sure. You said yourself he gave you a warning and told you he expects his orders followed whether you agree with them or not."

"That's what he said, but he can't function without our help and he knows it."

"I think we need to be cautious," said Frank Williams. "Tremaine's no fool. He needs our help all right, but we mustn't forget, whether we like it or not, he is the Commander in Chief."

Travis was getting angry. "How can you call him the Commander in Chief? He's that in name only. We all know it! He knows nothing about the military; he's not competent to tell us how to do our job."

"Presidents don't tell us how to do our job," said Williams, "but they do make policy decisions. It'll be the same with this President whether he served in the military or not."

"We'll see, we'll see," Travis said, calming himself down. He preferred not to pursue this further. As long as they stayed on the topic of gays in the military, they were united; as soon as they strayed to the powers of the presidency, their harmony vanished.

After the meeting, Travis went home. Entering the house, he yanked off his tie, grabbed a beer and flung himself in a chair. Clicking through the channels, he found a football game and watched the final thirty minutes. Through the window, he saw his wife, Mildred, working in the garden. The game ended, and he went upstairs and took a shower. When he came back, Mildred was washing her hands at the sink. He kissed her on the neck and she smiled.

"Don't forget, we've got dinner this evening at the convention center. We have to leave by five thirty," he reminded her.

"I hadn't forgotten," she said. "As soon as I'm done putting things away, I'll get ready."

. . . .

They left promptly at five thirty. At precisely six forty-five, they entered the hall. The convention was the largest annual gathering of veterans anywhere in the country. More than two thousand had descended on the city. Travis was the keynote speaker. Dinner was at seven thirty, preceded by cocktails. He and Mildred circulated, looking for friends and associates. Travis saw McManus, Frank Williams and Vince Bradford, all accompanied by their wives.

In some ways, Travis disliked being the speaker. He had to be careful how much he drank. He didn't want to make a fool of himself. By the time they sat down for the meal, he was already feeling the effects of the alcohol. He was glad for some food.

After dinner he was introduced, with emphasis on his three tours of duty in Vietnam. The hall erupted with applause, everyone standing.

Travis, eager to get on with it, spoke into the microphone.

"I'm glad to be here tonight, glad to be among friends and those who've served our nation in its armed services," he began. "I don't have to tell you our military is second to none. It is the finest fighting machine in the world and has at its disposal the most sophisticated weaponry on the face of the earth. Largely because of its might, we've been able to live in peace. Because of its power, the threat of communism was held in abeyance until it collapsed of its own accord. Most of us never dreamed we'd see the changes we have. Who'd have guessed the Berlin Wall would be gone and the once mighty Soviet Union would no longer exist? The world has changed, and the military must change with it.

"We must downsize, and that's not easy. We've all served, so we know how important it is to be alert and ready for anything. To show weakness is to give our enemies an advantage. As chairman of the Joint Chiefs I promise to do my best to prevent that happening.

"Given the changing times, we cannot justify keeping two armies capable of fighting on two fronts simultaneously. We will instead keep one large standing army, capable of great mobility and of responding to the threat of hostile forces, much as we did in the Gulf War. The new Army will be more mobile and more sophisticated than any the world has ever known. Combined with the Air Force it will, in a matter of days, be capable of deployment anywhere in the world.

"Our Air Force has demonstrated the unsurpassed capability of our fliers, support personnel and the aircraft and weaponry at our disposal. With increasing technology, that high standard will be pushed even higher. In the Navy, as in the Air Force, we're moving more into the area of stealth technology. Modern weaponry will engender less danger for our personnel, while inflicting higher and higher casualties on those who might oppose us with force.

"But we're faced with a problem; one that threatens to undermine the strength of our military forces. No matter how well trained or how sophisticated our weaponry, the heart of any fighting force is its morale. When morale is low, battles are lost and defeat is inevitable. In the last election, candidate Emerson promised gays and lesbians he'd allow them to serve. He said he wouldn't allow discrimination on the basis of sexual orientation. These ideas worried most of us in the military.

"After Emerson's election, commanders reported that some young men under their command talked of refusing to re-enlist if gays were admitted. Others threatened to quit regardless of the consequences they might face. Induction centers over the past three years have reported a decline in enlistees. A soldier in Japan beat a gay soldier to death. There's no doubt in my mind that such action is an outward expression of how disturbing this policy will be, if implemented.

"Nothing will do more to undermine the morale of our military than to allow homosexuals to serve freely. Just because gays have organized themselves into pressure groups we can't allow them to dictate policy on such an important matter as this. Under no circumstances can national security be compromised.

"Make no mistake, that's precisely the issue here. What we face is a threat to our national security through the undermining of the morale of the greatest fighting machine the world has ever known."

The hall erupted in applause and a standing ovation. When the applause subsided Travis continued.

"If you love your country, you must help. Call your senators and congressmen. Write letters to them. Let them know how you stand on this matter. The President is considering issuing an executive order to implement this policy. We must do our best to stop him. If it is issued, we must be able to override it. We of the Joint Chiefs will do our part, but it will be easier with your support. Organize your fellow veterans. We cannot allow the implementation of this policy. We need you to do your part. Thank you."

Once more, the hall was filled with applause. Travis made his way from the stage back to the table. All around him veterans stood clapping, cheering, patting him on the back and offering words of encouragement. He felt good. While he was speaking, he noticed members of the press at the back of the hall and along the sides. His speech would be in the morning papers.

He and Mildred left the gathering at midnight. As they came out of the hotel, they were met by a crush of reporters, cameras, microphones and flashbulbs. Already his speech had signaled the beginning of a war between the military and the new President. The members of the press, smelling blood, were ready.

"What will you do if the President issues an executive order? Will you obey it?"

"I think he knows he cannot sustain it, so I don't think he'll issue it," Travis responded.

"Do you speak for the Joint Chiefs? Do they feel the same way?"

"Yes, to both questions."

"Is this a clash between the military and a civilian President?"

"No, this has to do with our national security. Under no circumstances can we undermine the morale of our troops."

"Is it not the task of the President to determine national security?"

"When it comes to military matters, it's up to the military to determine national security."

"But the President is the Commander in Chief, surely he's the one with the final say."

"That would be the case when a President understands military affairs and how they work. Due to lack of experience, this

President can't be expected to function with competence in such matters. Therefore, I'm sure he'll consider carefully the advice of his military advisors."

"Is this a slap at the President because of his lack of military service?"

"Draw your own conclusions."

"What's it like to be under the direct authority of a man who never served in the military and who was opposed to the country's involvement in Vietnam?"

Travis, realizing he was being drawn into quicksand, brought things to an end.

"Goodnight, ladies and gentlemen," he said with a salute.

With the help of his military aides, he made his way to the waiting car through the blinding flashes of the cameras. Nearing the bottom of the steps he tripped and, but for one of his aides, would have fallen. Quickly he helped Mildred into the car, got in himself and closed the door. He was glad of the sudden quiet.

"Take us home!" he ordered.

....

The following morning Tremaine was in the Oval office at dawn. At eight o'clock he returned to their private quarters; Sandra was sitting at the table in her gown, reading the paper and drinking coffee.

"Would you like some breakfast?" she asked.

"That would be nice." He loved being with her, sharing breakfast with her in the mornings. It was a time for both of them to touch base before going about their day. Evenings, too, were enjoyed, the time before going to bed when they sat quietly and caught each other up on the day's events.

"Travis made front page headlines this morning," she said, bringing him a cup of tea.

"How's that?"

"He gave a speech last night at the veterans' convention." She handed him the paper and went to butter the toast. "I don't think he likes you very much."

"Could be. I think he finds it difficult taking direction from a non-military man."

David unfolded the paper. The headlines read, "PRESIDENT INCOMPETENT!" David read the comments of the reporter who'd written the article, and the questions and answers that followed Travis' speech. On the second page, he read the text of the speech itself.

Sandra watched her husband. Absorbed in his reading, his breakfast was getting cold.

"You know what I find disturbing about something like this?" he asked. "I don't mind Travis speaking his mind; he has a right to. But the press has an obligation to speak the truth, to report the facts and they don't. They get carried away with their self-serving and pompous analysis. They interpret the facts according to their own petty notions. They've become a problem in and of themselves; they love conflict more than they love the truth. Such reporting is an abuse of the people. The press have lost touch with their purpose, to report the facts and allow people to form their own opinions.

David put the paper aside and ate his breakfast. Looking at Sandra, he smiled "I'm glad you're here. With you, at least there's some sanity to life. You see through the illusion of it all. Words are such a web. They create realities that don't exist. We even go to war over words. So much suffering results from words. And, as if that isn't enough, we seek to imprison each other with the labels we attach. We're so clever in our use of language that it's become an abuse, difficult to recognize, and even more difficult to put a stop to. We're suckers; words easily confuse fact with fiction.

"It's something that needs to be addressed. The press is important because it's the vehicle of communication as well as a watchdog. It's important to talk with people, to educate and awaken them to other possibilities. It's difficult to do so when the press distorts what is being said."

"Why don't you address the Press Club? Why not beard the lion in his den? Talk with the members of the press."

"That's an interesting idea."

"I agree with you that the press has forgotten its mandate, and I don't expect they'll wake up to it quickly. I do believe it's something you can begin at the Press Club, although I'm sure it will require far more than one talk."

"That's a great idea, Sandra. I'll ask Jonathan to look into it."

8

Opening mind

Travis was on time. At precisely ten o'clock, the secretary ushered him into the Oval Office. Tremaine was at the desk, writing. He looked up.

"Have a seat, Travis. I'll be with you in a moment. Help yourself to coffee."

Travis walked over and sat down. He poured coffee, stirred in sugar and looked around. He noticed the newspapers on the desk. His heart gave a start and, despite himself, he began to sweat. Damn the reporters, he thought.

Tremaine finished writing and, pushing the chair back, walked around to join Travis. Travis stood and the two men shook hands. Tremaine looked at the general and felt the uneasiness in the man. Then he sat and poured himself a cup of coffee.

"I like coming here if for no other reason than for the coffee," Travis joked.

Tremaine smiled, appreciating the good humor. He hoped to keep Travis on board. Maybe the man is just testing the limits, he thought.

"What's the word from the other Joint Chiefs? Will they support a change in policy regarding gays?"

"No, they will not!"

"I trust you conveyed to them the gist of our conversation last week."

"I did, but it didn't change their minds."

"From what I've heard, you and the other Joint Chiefs have

been on the hill gathering support for your position."

Travis once more felt himself off balance with Tremaine's directness.

"Yes, we have. We cannot support your proposed change, and we intend to do all we can to stop it."

"Fair enough."

"I think we have enough strength to override an executive order."

"I think you may be right."

"So what will you do?"

"I'll issue one anyway."

"Why?"

"Because I believe it's the right thing to do."

"But you can't win!"

"Well, General, you should know that a war is rarely won by the first battle."

"I get your point. But then what?"

"If the executive order is overridden, then the issue will go before the Supreme Court. I'm confident the Court will support my position. If it doesn't, then so be it. The matter will end there."

"That process will take a long time. In the meantime, gays will be excluded."

"Emerson made a promise during the campaign and he wanted it kept. I agree with him on this point. I gave my word too. There's too much prejudice in the world. Are we not all brothers and sisters in the great family of humanity? What divides us is the intransigence of our ideas."

"But with these people, it's not just ideas. What they practice under the guise of sexual preference is immoral; it's not natural."

"I understand your opinion on the matter. It is opinions themselves that divide. If we do away with ideas of right and wrong, moral and immoral, all that remains is action taking place."

"How can you say that there's no such thing as right and wrong, moral and immoral?"

"Is it not obvious to you that these are just words. Words are labels, concepts. They create divisions where none exist. Look, Travis, right and wrong change over time and between people. The idea of morality changes too. For some people, it's immoral to dance or go to movies. For others it's immoral to engage in violent acts or serve in the military. For others, the opposite is true."

"There must be some sense of morality that most people agree upon."

"I don't know what it is. Perhaps the closest thing we come to is the idea of the sacredness of life. But who wants to live ninety years if you have to spend the last fifteen in bed suffering from bed sores, with tubes down your throat, your heart monitored by a machine and unable to take care of yourself?"

"I wouldn't."

"Yet some consider it immoral to allow people to die without taking extraordinary measures to save them. There comes a time when the quality of life is such that death is welcome."

"I understand your point, but I still don't see how we can live without morality or a sense of right and wrong."

Tremaine smiled. "Trees do, and, as far as I can tell, so do dogs, cows, bears, lions and tigers. So it seems obvious that it is possible to live quite well without the need to define everything in these terms."

Travis was uncertain how to take Tremaine. "I don't follow."

"Trees make no judgment about the wind. They don't call gentle breezes good and limb-breaking winds bad. When a cougar stalks a deer, the deer doesn't think the cougar is immoral, it simply tries to escape. And, when a bear chases a human being, just like the deer, he doesn't think the bear is immoral, he simply tries to escape. Life goes on without regard for human judgments of right or wrong, moral or immoral. Actions take place, that's all. If we see the various actions as they are without making judgments about them, we'll find we're drawn to act in a particular way regarding them. Such action is spontaneous and appropriate."

"But there are bound to be others who respond in different ways."

"That's true, of course, and their actions will be appropriate for them."

"What about such people as Hitler? He thought he was right but what he did was wrong."

"Hitler and his supporters believed they were ridding the world of a scourge. Others believed otherwise and opposed him, and fortunately that perspective won out. I say fortunately, because I could not have supported him either, and that would have been my point of view. Despite the different points of view, all sides involved in the Second World War believed God was on their side and that their enemies were wrong. Good and bad are judgments we make and are not absolute but relative."

"I see what you're getting at. But surely we couldn't have just sat still and let Hitler do what he did?"

"No, you and I couldn't have, we'd have taken whatever actions we could to try and stop him. That, however, was not a question of right and wrong. It was simply actions and reactions happening, which make up the events taking place."

"But surely there must be some guidelines concerning right and wrong."

"I've not found any, Travis. When we look down from a tall building in New York, we see traffic flowing in an orderly manner according to certain predetermined rules, signal lights, dividing lines and so on. When we look down at traffic in the city of Bombay, however, we might at first think that there is utter chaos. But if we watch for a while, we would see patterns that were not at first apparent. Such patterns are unfamiliar to us here in the West. Once the person lets go of his preconceived notions on how it should occur, he discovers there's another way of driving that's also relatively safe.

"Driving in India is like driving without regard for right

and wrong. Someone comes at you in a certain way, and you spontaneously respond, usually with the steering wheel and horn and, as a last resort, the brake. Your action precipitates a chain of responses amongst other drivers, and all those responses precipitate further responses in others and so on. Taken as a whole these myriad responses merge, becoming one whole and beautifully orchestrated event with no one conducting any of it."

"What you're describing reminds me of a flock of birds swooping up and down."

"That's the idea. Perhaps your analogy is a better one."

"I'll have to think about what you say. One thing still puzzles me though."

"What's that?"

"You want to implement this new policy that others oppose. You think your idea is right and we think ours is. How can something like this be resolved?"

"I don't think my point of view is right and yours wrong. I do feel that my point of view will, in the end, prevail. Now that's my point of view. I'll do my best to argue that point of view and give the reasons I think it's better. The truth is, it might not be better. On the other hand, the idea may be ahead of its time. New ideas are not always welcomed at first, because there are vested interests which hold the old ideas in place. Change begins with the introduction of ideas. The church for a long time resisted the idea that the earth was not the center of the universe. Openness to the idea had to occur first. Only then was the truth perceived. If we're interested in discovering the truth, we must be open to possibilities. We must become aware when fear causes us to be closed to ideas other than our own.

"In the case of gays in the military, I feel the need to articulate this position and remove all the false and unexamined assumptions upon which the former policy is based. I welcome you to do the same. I don't mind differences; I welcome them. Let there be openness and honesty. Truth may not fit our preconceived ideas."

"I'll have to give it some thought."

"Good."

Tremaine offered Travis more coffee, but he declined. He seemed to be thinking about something. Tremaine didn't interrupt him. He waited until he saw the General become wholly present again. "I'd like to change the topic if you don't mind."

Travis nodded, "Go ahead."

"I read the reports on your speech last night and the comments to the press afterward. I want to talk with you about it."

Travis felt himself beginning to sweat.

"There are certain things I find distasteful in what you said, things I find inaccurate and provocative. Your continuing as Chairman of the Joint Chiefs is contingent on your following my instructions in this matter."

Travis had trouble dealing with Tremaine. His words were potent, the tone of his voice was calm but firm. He couldn't read the man. There was no animosity from him, and yet Travis felt a great discomfort in the pit of his stomach. An unpleasant image entered his mind; he saw himself as a strutting rooster with ruffled feathers.

Tremaine watched Travis closely. He saw the General's discomfort, the small beads of perspiration collecting above his lip and knew the Chairman was off balance.

"What I object to is the constant reference to the 'greatest this' and the 'greatest that.' It's your opinion that we have the greatest Army, Navy and Air Force, isn't it?"

"Yes."

"Is it a fact?"

"Yes."

"Be careful Travis. Are you sure?"

"I think it is."

"Whether you think it is or not doesn't make it so does it?"

"No."

"How do you think the British, the Italians, the Russians, the French and the Israelis feel about their military capabilities?"

"They probably feel they're very good."

"Wouldn't some, if not all, claim to be the best?'

"You may be right," Travis said with a wry smile.

"In this country, we have a tendency to think of ourselves as the best in everything we do. The Japanese gave us a stiff dose of reality that contradicted that idea with regard to cars, cameras and other sophisticated technologies. We didn't like it, and we resort to wild claims and bragging rather than making the necessary improvements. Do you follow?"

"Yes."

"Talk is cheap. It alienates both our friends and those who already dislike us. I've traveled a fair bit, and I know how people of other countries feel about Americans. We're considered bullies and braggarts, dishonest in our selective support of UN resolutions, uneven and unfair in our support of various policies throughout the world. We jump in and enforce our will against a weak neighbor and refuse to do so with a strong one. We're more than willing to use our aircraft, missiles and bombs on those we consider our enemies. We have little genuine concern for others, and we are motivated almost entirely by self-interest. We are not well liked. Even our allies don't like us much. Why is that do you think?"

"I don't know. I hadn't thought of it before."

"It's because we look upon ourselves as special. Our actions are governed by our 'national interest.' If a plane crashes somewhere in the world, what gets reported? Not how many people are killed but how many *Americans* are killed. It's this kind of arrogance, our lack of concern for our fellow human beings, that contributes to our poor reputation and the hostility aimed at us.

"I think you're right."

"Are you familiar with the Chinese sage, Lao Tzu?"

"No."

"He lived about twenty-five hundred years ago and was a contemporary of the reformer Confucius. Lao Tzu was wise. He said, 'The wise ruler of a strong country does not parade his weapons in public nor make boastful remarks.' Why? Because he knows that whoever sets himself above others will in the end be brought low by his pride. The history of civilizations bears out his observations."

"I don't see how we bring ourselves down by pride."

"By pride I'm referring to arrogance. When arrogance is present, there are those around who take it upon themselves to topple the arrogant in the dust. It becomes their mission in life."

"Yes, I understand."

"Lao Tzu said, 'There are three great treasures in life. Mercy, economy and daring not to be ahead of others.' "

"What did he mean?"

"He said, 'Courage arises from mercy, generosity from economy and leadership from humility.' Lao Tzu must have lived in a time much like our own for he went on to say. 'Today, men have little mercy and try hard to be generous, they tell others how humble they are and always find a way to be first.'"

Travis thought about Tremaine's remarks. They had a certain unpleasant truth about them. His conversation with Tremaine was both unsettling and exhilarating. This man is unlike any I've known, he thought. He's certainly no fool.

Tremaine sat and watched Travis. Travis looked up to find a pair of green eyes smiling at him.

"Travis, I have no objection to you speaking your mind on anything, but I want you to learn to do so with honesty, simplicity and humility. As the Chairman of the Joint Chiefs, you represent the government. I want you to represent it in such a way as to not alienate others deliberately. Do you have a problem with this?"

"No, I don't. I appreciate what you've said. It makes sense. Travis could hardly believe the words he'd spoken. What's happening to me, he wondered.

"Good. That's what I'm asking of you." Just then, the sound of a dove came mellow through the french doors. Tremaine looked up and saw by the sun it was almost noon.

"Last week when I spoke with you I asked if you were prepared to serve me, to follow my orders and direction, to speak the truth as you saw fit and in no way sabotage the orders and instructions once given. What is your answer?"

Travis thought for a moment.

"May I speak frankly, sir?"

"I expect it. Go ahead."

"I've not liked you at all. I have detested what I thought you stood for. To serve under a man who actively opposed a war in which I fought and in which so many lives were lost was, in my mind, some kind of sour joke. I could not support you because I felt I was betraying the young men I knew in Vietnam. I disliked you intensely and was prepared to do whatever I could to bring you down, to make visible to others what I thought you to be, a weak and traitorous man unfit to be President. When I walked in here this morning, I felt that way. I'm ashamed to admit that much of my opposition to your policies and the support I put together to oppose them came from this perspective. I no longer feel that way. I'm surprised at myself; it's hard to believe I'm saying these things. What you say makes sense; I can see how petty and vindictive I've been. I still cannot say I'll support your policy regarding gays but I will oppose it cleanly."

Tremaine felt a deep appreciation for the man before him. He liked him a lot. He watched and sensed a peacefulness he'd not noticed before in those tired eyes.

"Thank you. I appreciate your honesty," he said, smiling at Travis. "I still need to know the answer to my question, however."

"I will give you the benefit of my experience. I will advise you to the best of my ability. I will speak the truth as I see it, whether you agree or not. I will accept and respect your decisions and policies once they're made. I may oppose them when they're being formulated, but once that's done I'll support you. If I find I can no longer support you in this manner, I'll let you know and offer my resignation. Does that answer your question?"

"It does. Thank you. That's the kind of support I need!"

Tremaine stood and Travis followed suit. Tremaine extended his hand, shaking Travis' firmly.

"Welcome aboard," he said, smiling, and clapped Travis on the shoulder.

....

Late in the afternoon, word came that Tremaine's nominee for Vice President had been approved. Fifty-year-old Senator William G. Morgan of Maine would be sworn in early next week.

Emerson's Proposal

I want to go back to work."

"I was wondering about that." Sandra and David had just sat down to breakfast. "What do you have in mind?"

"There's a health clinic in Anacostia that is looking for nurses. I'd like to see what I can do."

David began to chuckle. "I think it's a great idea. I can imagine it will throw the Secret Service into cardiac arrest, though."

"Yes, I've wondered about that. Anyway, I'm going to do it and I wanted to let you know."

"Sandra, my dear, you have my blessing. Let me know how I can help."

"I will."

David poured himself juice and spooned porridge into his bowl. "Are you going to the clinic today?"

"I thought I would. I want it to be as quiet as possible. I don't want to make things difficult for the Secret Service, or the clinic. I know the agents are concerned for my safety and are doing their best."

"Yes."

David got up, washed his dishes and put them in the drain board. Then he walked over and held Sandra in his arms.

"I've got to go. I'll see you this evening. Have a good day, love."

....

Sandra stormed from the office, furious. How dare

they restrict her freedom? She was not an employee of the government; her husband held the job, not her. But Phillips had been adamant. He would not let her go to the clinic. She felt completely frustrated, angrier than she could remember being in a long time. She called the Women's Clinic in Anacostia and asked to speak with the director. Briefly she explained the situation, saying she'd resolve things within the next couple of days but, until then, she'd not be able to come. The director understood and said she'd await Sandra's call.

Putting the phone down, Sandra went upstairs to the living quarters and made herself a cup of tea. She tried calling David, but his secretary said he was in a meeting and not to be disturbed.

She'd never liked formality, and especially disliked restrictions on her personal freedom. She'd lit into Phillips in no uncertain terms. Her tongue could be sharp when she was angry. Through her rage she'd watched the blood drain from his face with the impact of her words. Thinking back on their conversation brought a smile to her face. He'd been completely taken aback by her explosion. His condescending manners had been like gasoline on a fire. He was not used to being opposed by a woman. But when he recovered, he'd stood his ground. Grudgingly, she admired him.

Sandra poured another cup of tea. David had warned her things wouldn't be easy living in Washington. She remembered the day he'd first spoken to her of that possibility.

She'd arrived home one evening at eight following a visit to a patient's home. David had supper ready, and they'd eaten at once. He'd seemed unusually quiet. She'd asked him if he was all right.

"I'm fine, but I need to talk with you about something. Let's go for a walk."

Wrapped in warm clothes, they went out, accompanied by Murphy, their black lab, and walked slowly through the leaves of autumn. On that rare cloudless night, the stars stretched full across an inky sky.

"I received a call from Emerson this evening. He's been persuaded to run for President."

"He has?"

"Yes. With the stranglehold the Republicans have on the White House, no Democrat is enthusiastic about launching a run against them."

"Why?"

"Well, for one thing, no one wants to spend money on something that looks as though it will fail. Emerson thinks that since the odds of defeating an incumbent President are slim, those who do have aspirations for the White House don't want their names associated with a losing cause. They'd rather wait until the next election."

"Is he really going to run?"

"Yes, he's already accepted, and no other Democrat will run against him. So he is, by default, the only Democratic candidate for President."

"He doesn't stand a chance, does he?"

"I don't think he does. Anyway, we talked by phone this evening. He said it was time someone injected a sense of reality into the coming race. He said the economic, social and political health of the country isn't good. We talked about why and what could be done. He's a good thinker with an enormous heart. Being from Maine, he has that dry, down-to-earth, common sense approach. It's unacceptable that the deficit is so high, that the elections are largely bought by mortgaging the country's future. He makes a lot of sense, and I like his ideas. As he said, 'I couldn't find a good reason not to run. I've nothing to lose, so from that perspective I can afford to speak the truth as I see it.'

"We talked for a couple of hours. He explained his thinking and posed many questions. The conversation was a lengthy exploration of how we see things. You know me, I love exercises like that, and Emerson is a good man to have that kind of discussion with. Anyway, the crux of the matter is that he wants me for his running mate."

"What?" She stopped abruptly. "You mean he wants you for his Vice President?"

"Yes."

"What did you tell him?"

"That I had to talk with you."

They walked in silence for several minutes. Murphy rummaged through the leaves not far away. Above them, through the bare trees, Orion glittered in the cold night sky.

"What do you think, David? Is it something you want to do?"

"I'm not sure. Running would mean giving up my practice; I'd have to take a leave of absence from the university. I've cut back so much to write that I could probably do it. Writing would go on the back burner for a while, though. What do you think?"

"I don't know. I'll have to think about it. Campaigning would mean you'd be gone a lot, wouldn't it?"

"It would."

"There's not much chance you guys could really get elected, is there?"

"No, I think our chances of that are one in a million. But, Sandra, if I should accept Emerson's offer, we will both be in it to win."

"But you just said you didn't think you can win."

"I don't, but I can't enter the race from that perspective. Don't get me wrong, I'm a realist when it comes to things like this, but I would only accept Emerson's invitation if I was prepared for the possibility that you and I would live in Washington, even the possibility that we'd live someday in the White House."

"The White House!"

"Yes. That is one of the eventualities a Vice President must consider. As I said, I'm not expecting anything, but the possibility exists. I'll not enter the race in a halfhearted manner. Am I prepared for the eventuality of winning and all that it would entail? I don't want second thoughts when it's too late. It's not too smart to jump off the high board only to regret it on the way down."

"I understand."

"Like Emerson, I think my countrymen deserve more than a halfhearted undertaking. That's one of the reasons I'm thinking seriously about running. Those who are afraid to run are more interested in themselves and their image than they are in the contribution they can make. I care nothing for the image; I care only about service."

"When the campaign is over, will you come back here?"

"Of course. But Sandra, you must consider this for yourself. Don't assume we won't win."

"Why?"

"Because when opportunities present themselves it seems to me we must look at them and feel which way we are drawn. Life requires we make our gifts available in one way or another and when a door opens, we must be prepared to go through it."

Sandra realized that she, like her husband, had to consider the possibility that he and Emerson might win. Although highly unlikely, it was a possibility. Murphy nuzzled her hand with his cold nose and disappeared into the woods again. Winning would mean moving to Washington and the curtailment of their privacy and freedom. They'd have to leave their home and she, the home-health agency for which she worked.

She liked nursing and was not willing to give it up. I'd find a way to continue, she thought. She'd be a long way from her parents, and her beloved Vancouver Island. That would be hard. Washington was an alien place to her. She didn't like cities, and for this city, the seat of the American government, she had considerable antipathy. She was a Canadian country girl. Living across the border in the Pacific Northwest was a lot like being home, but living in a foreign city a continent away would be another thing altogether.

"You'll have to give me some time to think about it, David."

"Yes, of course."

"How long before you must let Emerson know?"

"A week."

"Okay."

They talked often over the ensuing week, and in the end David had called Emerson and accepted his invitation. Without reservation, Sandra had supported him. Then, for a year, she'd watched the events unfold. She'd ached inside for him when an affair he'd had during his first marriage became public. She felt angry over the cruel comments by some members of the press regarding his stand on Vietnam and the questions concerning his drug experiences. She had loved, however, the honesty and openness with which he faced the crises as they came. She would never forget his talk to the students at Yale three weeks into the campaign.

10

The campaign address at Yale

Early in the campaign, Tremaine was asked to speak at Yale University. He was a guest lecturer of the Philosophy Department and was to give a talk and answer questions concerning the coming election. Members of the press were invited. The place in which they met was a small ivy-covered hall situated beneath towering beech trees and surrounded by manicured lawns.

Emerson, as a distinguished alumnus of Yale, was asked to introduce Tremaine. "I chose Dr. Tremaine as my running mate," Emerson said, "because I think he's the best man for the job. I've known him for a long time. He has one of the most creative minds I've ever known. He is also a meticulously honest man, as I know many of you are aware. He accepted my invitation to run because of a deep desire to serve. I support him, and I urge you to listen with an open mind to what he has to say."

Tremaine stepped to the podium. "Thank you Emerson," he said and turned to the students and members of the press.

"When Emerson asked me to join him on the ticket it was a surprise. In the three weeks since then there has been a great deal of discussion in the press as to whether I am a suitable candidate, given the fact that I opposed the Vietnam War, took LSD, smoked pot, had an affair and went through a divorce. I'd rather deal with these issues at the outset of the campaign. Perhaps then we can put them behind us, move on to address the difficulties and possibilities facing our nation and thereby determine the directions in which we will move. Those of you who are familiar with me know that my primary interest is in the philosophical background from which ideas and action emerge. Another area of interest has to do with public policy and the well-being of people.

"I've been accused of lecturing but I assure you I come by it honestly." Tremaine smiled. "When you've taught at university for the past thirty years it could be considered an occupational hazard." A murmur of laughter passed through the hall. "For those unfamiliar with me, may I suggest that a little patience is in order, and you'll soon discover that dialogue and the mutual exploration of ideas are important to me. You'll have ample opportunity to engage in this process and ask whatever questions you wish.

"As a student I was enthralled when my philosophy professor introduced me to Socrates. I read all I could about the sage of Athens. At the time I was struck by the similarities between his death and the death of Christ. When I read the dialogues of Socrates I saw how clear and logical he was. Compared to the fuzzy thinking of his contemporaries his reasoning had an unusual quality about it, it was an uncommon form of reason, that is, it was not the common reasoning of consensus. Needless to say I have a great appreciation for the Socratic method. Socrates was the doorway through which I entered the hall of philosophy, a place where I have always felt at home. The journey that commenced in university did not end there, it continues to this day. I think I will always be a student at heart. Since those early days however, I have ventured into the field of Western and Eastern psychology, as well as the study of Eastern philosophy

"As a young man there were times when I had regrets about some of the things I did or didn't do, even regrets about my lot in life. Fortunately, over time I came to accept those experiences, those so-called mistakes. It is obvious to me now how those events brought me to this place in life, so the idea of making mistakes is misleading. The truth is I have no regrets. Life is full, and the events of the past were, as it turns out, stepping-stones along the way, and mistakes simply a name I gave to a process of learning, an educational process.

"To begin with, let me define what I mean by education. The word is derived from the Latin and to understand it is to understand education as I use it. Educate when it is broken down into its component parts means to bring forth, to elicit, by facilitating a process. But what is to be brought forth, elicited, facilitated? In philosophy one of the definitions of 'truth' is that it is self-evident. If it is self-evident, then it follows we must already be aware of it and somehow or other forgotten it. Therefore the real purpose of education, as I see it, is to bring forth that which is already known, that which we recognize as being true. This to me is the heart of the Socratic method. So without further ado let's have your questions and let them take us where they will."

Hands shot up all over the hall. Tremaine pointed.

"In a sense you are saying there are no mistakes, only lessons being learned. Could this not be used as justification for dishonesty?"

"It could. Do I detect a note of skepticism?"

"You do."

"I can understand your skepticism. But what has given rise to it?"

"I suppose being lied to and misled."

"Yes, and therein lies the problem. Let's say you've been lied to by politicians for instance. What happens? It may cause you to draw the conclusion that politicians can't be trusted. Then when a politician does speak the truth it is difficult for you to be aware of it because your conclusion, which is now your belief, makes it more difficult for you to recognize the truth when it is present."

"Why is that?"

"I would suggest it's because you've become invested in your belief, your point of view."

"You had an affair with another woman during your first marriage. That was dishonest on your part. How can we be sure you'll be honest when you speak to us now, or in governing us, should you be elected?"

"You can't be sure. There's no way I can make you sure. All you can really do is to see, over time, if my words match my actions. I did have an affair and that was dishonest on my part. The result of it was that I hurt myself, my wife and the woman with whom I had the affair."

"Did you learn from it?"

"I did."

"What did you learn?"

"Several things. One is that lying really did not sit well with me. I didn't feel good about myself. I also learned that attachment to what I wanted was the source of those lies, and that attachment is not love."

"What do you mean by attachment?"

"Attachment is derived from what *I* want. Its origin is selfish. When I love someone I'm interested in his or her well-being. The origin is selfless. Selfishness has a certain unsettling quality about it, which brings about a kind of dis-ease."

"Thank you, Dr. Tremaine."

"Yes, over here," Tremaine pointed to a well-dressed young woman to his left.

"There are those who say you're a poor role model. Having an affair and going through a divorce is hardly a ringing example. After all, the President and Vice President, whether we like it or not, are people we look up to in our society."

"There are plenty of people who are divorced and live honorable, creative lives of service; there are also those who don't. There are those who stay in marriages and are unhappy, living with sadness, hopelessness, bitterness, and sometimes even violence. Still others are married and find it a loving and supportive experience; a place of companionship, friendship, respect and love, something they wouldn't exchange for the world.

"I think we must take our attention off external things and see into the heart of a man and a woman. The heart is what matters; it is the source of love and inspiration. To see someone openly confess what he's done, and undergo the transformation that comes from it, is inspiring. Life is not easy, it is full of suffering."

"It's been reported that you used various forms of drugs. I'd like to know if it's true?"

"It's true. I have."

"Why? Don't you think it sets a bad example to others, particularly the young, many of whom are caught up in drugs like crystal meth, cocaine and heroin?"

"This is not a topic to be brushed over lightly, so it may take some time to answer your question. To begin with, I have not taken the drugs you mentioned. I'll do my best to explain what happened and my thoughts on it. In the early '60's, Timothy Leary and Richard Alpert were engaged in LSD research at Harvard. At the time, many believed LSD created a kind of induced psychosis. It was their hope that if they studied the effects of LSD they would first of all better understand psychosis, and through understanding, be closer to finding a cure for it. Their research was based upon the work of two Swiss chemists, Stoll and Hoffman, who first discovered LSD in 1938.

"Leary was fired from the university for using LSD himself, and with his students. Both Leary and Alpert believed that the best way for them to understand the effects of the drug was to take it themselves. Their experiences had a profound affect on them. I won't go into their experiences, you can read about them for yourself. I'd gone to University with a strong desire to serve, and for a while I pursued pre-med. As it turned out, I was better suited to philosophy than chemistry. I still had a desire to serve, however, and at the time I was deeply involved in the Civil Rights Movement and vehemently opposed to the Vietnam War. My mind was exceptionally rational; I believed everything could be figured out, that the problems of society could be resolved when we put our minds to the task.

"As I mentioned, I delved into the philosophers, wondered about life and the world in which we lived. Philosophy was not just an intellectual exercise for me; it was something with which I examined life deeply. While in graduate school, I took LSD several times. I took it alone, or with a close friend in a safe environment. Later I took peyote and mescaline, often in the mountains. What I discovered had a profound affect on me and how I viewed the world.

"Imagine if you will, being blind from birth. Those with whom you live are also blind. Consequently, blindness is normal for all of you. No one knows what is missing. Then one day, someone is able to see. No matter how he tries to tell others what he sees through his eyes, they simply cannot comprehend because they have no shared frame of reference. If he persists in his attempts to tell them about it, they'll get tired of him and think he's crazy. Why? Because he speaks of things that, from their perspective, are impossible to know. Now if he should ever go blind again, he could not forget the reality he'd seen. He would also have a great desire to recover his sight. That desire would give birth to a search that might eventually lead to the permanent restoration of his sight.

"Seeing, as used in this metaphor, represents a deep understanding. That understanding can come about naturally, sometimes through illness, or the social and psychological shocks of life itself. In cases where the understanding is only temporary, the search will invariably continue because the nectar of understanding is so sweet one cannot live without it. Sometimes a person will turn to drugs to help open the eyes of understanding again. However, to glimpse those realities only to have them vanish as the effect of the drug wears off, leads to disappointment. So the search continues and moves beyond the use of drugs to something else.

"During the experiences I had on LSD, I came to know the interrelatedness of everything. Although I had rejected the organized aspects of Christianity as practiced by the various churches, I had studied in considerable depth the Old and New Testaments and particularly the teachings of Christ. The teachings of Christ I found to be simple, profound and beautiful. I also studied the teachings of Lao Tzu, the Buddha, and read the Bhagavad-Gita. I was curious; I wanted to know what they meant. At the same time, the horrors of the Vietnam War deeply disturbed me. Under the effect of those drugs, I began to understand many things.

"My experiences on LSD showed me a world held together by subtle agreements, agreements that were usually unquestioned. In psychological terms these agreements comprise what is known as 'consensual validation.' Consensual validation pertains to certain basic or fundamental assumptions about life which are subscribed to by the culture within which the human being is raised. Once in place, these assumptions, these agreements, remain hidden while exercising considerable control over human perceptual and conceptual processes.

"Such agreements remain unquestioned as long as we're not aware of them. All perceptions, the simple seeing of the reality around us, even our perceptions of ourselves, are filtered through those beliefs in such a way that it is exceedingly difficult to see anything outside them. In the Hindu tradition this is known as 'Maya,' which can be translated as illusion, or not real. The Buddhists refer to the learning of these culturally shared beliefs as the 'endarkenment' process. The Christians refer to it as the 'fall from grace.' All these traditions say that the reversal of this process is possible and has existed since the beginning of time. The Buddhists and other non-Christian religions have maintained that enlightened masters have always been present and still are; to shed light on the spiritual path for those ready to see. The Buddhists refer to the process as one of awakening or enlightenment.

"During those LSD experiences, the concept of God fell away, and an intuitive understanding replaced it. I understood why the Jewish philosophers removed the vowels from 'Yahweh,' rendering it unspeakable. The Buddhists refer to the same reality and call it the 'Void,' the Taoists refer to it as the 'Tao', while in philosophical terms it is known as the 'Noumenal.'"

"Could you explain what you mean by the term Noumenal?"

"It means that which gives rise to and sustains the phenomenal world and is not separate from it. The Noumenal, the indefinable, becomes defined, becomes the phenomenal world with which we're all familiar. Another way of describing it is that the Noumenal is potential energy, energy at rest, which spontaneously activates itself and gives rise to the world of phenomena. In other words, the Noumenal refers to both the potential energy and the manifestation of it in the form of the phenomenal world with which we are all familiar."

"Dr. Tremaine, you use the term 'sage' and 'enlightened masters'. Are they the same?" The question came from the back of the hall.

"To me the sage and enlightened masters are one and the same. The idea of the sage is someone who has great wisdom."

"I would like to know what you mean by the term enlightenment? I also wonder if you would be willing to share how you came to this understanding?" Again the question came from the same earnest young man at the back of the hall.

"Enlightenment, is the permanent dissolution of the

personal or ego-centered consciousness and the recovery of the impersonal consciousness with which we are born. For me the process that led to this understanding was a lengthy one. I grew up in a family in which there was considerable emotional suffering. My family was poor, and the distress caused by my parents' attempt to save their failing marriage disturbed me a great deal. The sense of helplessness I felt over my mother's suffering was a major impetus leading me to find the cause of suffering and to alleviate it wherever I could. For years I struggled with the issue of suffering. Nowhere could I find an answer that satisfied me.

"One day, I happened to smoke some marijuana. I sat alone in my study at home, looking out the window. I was a professor at a small college at the time. My mind turned back to the question of suffering. As I looked outside, the clouds cleared and I saw the huge ridge of a glacier caught in a shaft of sunlight. Above it, a patch of blue sky contrasted with the surrounding gray mists. At that moment, everything quavered as though seen through intense heat. Something shifted, the normal certainty with which I was familiar, the veneer of reality, slipped. In that moment I knew the answer to what I'd been seeking all those years. At the same time, I remembered I had always been, and always would be; I was eternal. Once again, I cannot explain this event with language; words seem inadequate. All I can say is that, from that time forth, I felt a deep sense of peacefulness. I saw clearly that all suffering comes solely from attachment—attachment to the expectations and objects of our desires. I saw distinctly and unforgettably the intrinsic harmony of all things.

"I began to share with a few friends what I'd realized. I even offered courses. Then one day it dawned on me that this profound state of awareness had slipped away, gone, become a memory. I stopped teaching and withdrew. The withdrawal lasted about fifteen years, but during that time I read everything I could get my hands on that had to do with enlightenment. In the meantime I sought out several teachers, but as I got to know them I realized they had a theoretical knowledge. It was not derived from experience. I needed to find someone who knew, first hand.

"The search led me to India, and shortly afterwards I found two men who 'knew,' one of whom became my teacher. I was with him for about fifteen years, but in our first meeting he dismantled the whole theoretical edifice I had built over the preceding twenty-five years. In its place emerged the reality I'd been looking for.

"You asked me what is enlightenment. Let me ask you a question. What would you say is the one thing you know for sure? What is it you know beyond all belief or theoretical considerations? Take a few moments to think about it." Tremaine paused and sipped quietly from a glass of water. The hall was silent. "Do you know what it is?"

"That I exist."

"Yes, that you exist. It is the only first hand knowledge you have, is it not?"

"It is."

"What does it mean when you say, I exist?"

"It is hard to point to."

"Yes, it is hard to point to. In fact it is impossible to point to, because, when you think about it, the awareness of existing is not an object. Objects can be perceived whereas the perceiving subject is the sense of presence, of 'I am,' and it cannot be perceived. This can be understood as follows. In the absence of reflection, the eye that sees cannot see itself."

"When I think about it, there appears to be a difference between the awareness of 'I am,' and the awareness that, 'I am Robert.' Is that correct?"

"It is correct. The fact that 'I am' is very different from the statement 'I am Robert.' The I am Robert is personal and involves your personal history; it comprises your personal consciousness. But, in truth that personal consciousness is secondary. The primary consciousness is 'a priori,' it is the sense of being, the sense of, 'I am,' which is, impersonal.

"It is this to which Christ spoke when he said, '*I am* the way, the truth and the light, no man cometh unto the Father but by me.' This is to be understood as follows. 'It is the *I am* that is real, it is the only truth you have, and it is the way to God. No one can come to God except through the awareness of the *I am;*' which of course signals the demise of the ego or personal centered consciousness.

"So in a sense it can be said that when enlightenment takes place, nothing really happens, nothing has changed. The impersonal consciousness has never not been there. The shadow, the personal consciousness, has dissolved in the light of understanding. I hope this is clear."

"I followed what you said closely. It is clear. Thank you. It is something which I have wondered about. I have been a diligent seeker for a long time. What you've said has been very helpful, thank you, again."

"You're most welcome." Tremaine smiled at the young man. The power of love that flowed from him was palpable. "Over here," Tremaine pointed to a woman in her mid-forties.

"You mentioned that you had repudiated Christianity and yet you speak with considerable affection of Christ and his teachings. I find this somewhat confusing."

"Suppose you climbed to a mountain top and from there you saw a sea of white peaks. That view, for someone like myself living in the valley, is unknown. You can describe it to me but I'm forced to believe it, or not, until I've climbed the mountain for myself. Once I've climbed it I have the same direct first hand knowledge that you have. It could be that your description inspired me to make the climb, and if that was the case I would have a profound appreciation for you."

"So, are you suggesting that masters, such as Christ, have

climbed to the mountain top, spiritually speaking?"

"Yes. What Christ or any master speaks of is a direct understanding of the underlying reality. Those who have not had the experience are forced to believe or not believe what is described. The early church fathers did not have that direct first-hand experience, although some of the disciples did. As a result the church, over the years, developed various forms of theology to explain Christ's words. This eventually formed the basis for Christian Doctrine.

"It can be said that what Christ taught was simply a description of what he'd understood. What the church taught was second hand and comprises the teachings of Christianity. These teachings have changed Christ's *description* into a *prescription*, a prescription for behavior. I have no interest in the teachings of Christianity. What Christ said I recognize for the truth it is. Why would I have any interest in second-hand knowledge?"

"Thank you Dr. Tremaine."

....

Tremaine's conversation with the students at Yale was an important turning point in the campaign. It became the subject of radio talk shows and TV news pundits. The religious right was incensed by his remarks. But those who took time to think about what he said realized it made a lot of sense.

The Republicans subjected Emerson and Tremaine to scathing attacks attempting to portray them as men bent on undermining family and religious values. The press, for its part, became less hostile and more curious. More and more they enjoyed the engagements with the Democratic contenders. There was something refreshing about them. Although they seemed to have little hope of being elected, they addressed things other politicians were afraid to touch. They spoke to the concerns of all segments of the population. But the general consensus was that they couldn't be elected, so why throw away votes?

Ten months later, the Republicans were caught up in the "Japan scandal," and lost the election. The unlikely had become reality.

11

Fear

Eight o'clock the next morning, Phillips walked into the Oval Office. Tremaine extended his hand and offered a warm greeting and friendly smile. He and Phillips had, over the months, come to know each other well. The Director of the Secret Service was a veteran of the agency; he'd worked hard to arrive at his current position. Gray-haired and distinguished, he was widely considered the best in his field.

In twenty-five years Phillips had served a variety of Presidents, some he liked and some he didn't. This President he found difficult to deal with, but he didn't dislike him. In fact, he respected him. The same things that had driven his predecessors didn't drive Tremaine. He didn't appear to fear death, and he assumed control over the agency right from the start. He did what he saw fit and expected the agency to do its job. He didn't allow the agency to dictate his movements based solely on what was best for security. Phillips disagreed with Tremaine on some things, yet found his ideas and his observations astute.

"Phillips, I know you're doing the best to make sure my wife and I are safe. We greatly appreciate your efforts. I'm sure you understand that we cannot allow you to determine what we can and cannot do. I will not prevent Sandra from going to Anacostia if that's what she wants. Nor will you."

"But this is an unusual request," Phillips protested. "Anacostia is not a safe place for the President's wife. We can't guarantee her safety."

"You can't guarantee our safety here either, can you?"

"Well... no, I can't, but protecting you is a lot easier here than it would be in Anacostia."

"Granted, but we've gone over this before. My job description requires I govern myself in ways appropriate to the job entrusted me. Your job is to safeguard my family and me while I do that job. Your job is made more difficult because you must afford us a certain level of privacy. For that reason, we've asked for less intrusive protection. I hope we can lessen the need for that protection even further as time goes on.

"We can't safeguard against everything, which is what we've been trying to do in our society as a whole. By trying too hard to protect ourselves, life becomes more and more circumscribed; we buy more and more insurance; we safeguard against this and safeguard against that. We're so busy safeguarding ourselves that we don't have time to live. The fear of what *might* happen contaminates the enjoyment of the moment. It doesn't make for good living. I believe, the process can be reversed and one way is by living life fully, despite threats and fears. I realize Sandra and I don't make your job easy, but that's the way it is. I'm open to your *suggestions* on how to do things, not on whether we can or cannot do them."

"But Mr. President, this is dangerous for all concerned. She could be exposed to threats against her life."

"I understand your point, but the presidency cannot be a prison. Neither Sandra nor I find that acceptable. We'll not live our lives out of fear. We all die sooner or later; no one knows when. "

"You have to consider the potential threat to the country should either of you be kidnapped," Phillips insisted.

"Look, Phillips, I appreciate your concern and your persistence. I've left instructions that are to be carried out if such an eventuality should occur."

"I don't understand."

"I will not go into the details, but suffice it to say that Sandra and I have talked about this. If something should happen, there will be no extraordinary measures made to save us. We're not afraid to die. Don't get me wrong—we're not seeking death. And, by the same token, there's no desire to create unnecessary worry or difficulties for those like yourself who have a particularly difficult job to do."

Tremaine looked at Phillips. He could see the man was not happy.

"Look, Phillips, life is dangerous. If we allow fear to run our lives, the freedom we enjoy will vanish. Fear has brought about much of the sorry state we as a nation find ourselves in today."

"I get what you're saying, but you have a responsibility to the people who elected you. You must not put yourself or your family at undue risk. Going to Anacostia is, in my opinion, undue risk."

"Let's look at the problem from another perspective. Clearly, you put yourself at risk on our behalf. I imagine neither your wife nor your family are particularly thrilled over what you do. Their attitude doesn't stop you from doing your job, does it?"

"No, it doesn't."

"Like you, we must all take risks in life and one day we will die. We can never safeguard against everything. Even when we attempt to safeguard ourselves, we really can't.

"I heard of a man who went to unusual lengths to preserve his life. He hired guards and put in the most sophisticated security system possible. He had a doctor and surgeon on call twenty-four hours a day. His home and his vehicles were bulletproof. He never married, for fear of blackmail. He lived life out of fear. In his early forties, he had minor surgery that proved successful, and he recovered well.

"Then one day, he slipped getting out of the bath, struck his head and died. Such is life. It was his destiny to die that way. He could not have escaped it."

"Okay, I get your point."

Tremaine smiled. "Then Sandra will be going to work in Anacostia as soon as you've made the best arrangements possible. Let us know when you're ready."

"I will."

Tremaine and Phillips stood and shook hands.

"I'll expect to hear from you soon."

12

Historical antecedents of an unjust God

Day after day, night after night, the Israelis flew into Lebanon, destroying everything that moved within twenty miles of their northern border. Troops, tanks and guns crossed the border and pounded villages into rubble. Gunboats patrolled the western shoreline, destroying fishing settlements and sinking every boat they found. Within days, a flood of refugees streamed north toward the war-torn city of Beirut.

Squads of Hizballah guerrillas fired hand-launched missiles across the border into Northern Israel. They moved quickly, never staying in one place, sometimes taking cover in the tide of humanity flowing north. Syrian and Jordanian troops mobilized along the borders with Israel. Lebanon appealed to the UN Security Council for help.

David spent the day in the briefing room being apprised of the fighting that raged in Lebanon. He solicited and received suggestions and options from foreign policy experts and National Security advisors, Doug Kersey, the Secretary of State; and Jonathan Makarios, his personal advisor. At five o'clock, he pushed his chair back. "I need a break."

The briefing had been thorough, the suggestions helpful. Now he must be alone with the information and ideas. When it was time, he'd know what action to take. David stretched. "Doug, I'll meet you back here in an hour." He pushed his chair in, and walked out into the fresh air. He set out at a brisk walk.

When he returned to the briefing room, David found Doug

waiting for him. "Let's walk a little," he said.

They walked in silence for a while. The intense heat of the day had subsided, and a full-bodied warmth bore upon it the fragrance of roses.

"Now, concerning this crisis in the Middle East, it's time to implement the new policy we discussed previously."

"I agree," Doug said.

"You'll go to Israel tomorrow. After you meet with Prime Minister Levin, we'll talk further. I'll brief you this evening at nine. Come to the Oval Office."

"I'll be there."

David put his arm around Doug's shoulders and gave them a squeeze. "I'll see you this evening at nine. Now go home to your wife."

....

A week later, Michael Levin and his Foreign Secretary, Joseph Goldstein, entered the Oval Office. Doug Kersey and Jonathan Makarios stood with Tremaine. They shook hands all around and made the introductions.

"Have a seat." Tremaine nodded toward the chairs around the coffee table where fresh coffee and fresh-baked pastries had been placed. "Coffee, gentlemen?"

They accepted. Tremaine poured coffee and Doug passed the pastries. Tremaine sat back and waited. He'd never met the Israeli Prime Minister or his Foreign Secretary before. They looked tired.

Looking out the window, Tremaine noticed a red rose hanging from a trellis. Caught in a shaft of sunlight, it bobbed back and forth, nuzzled by a soft breeze. Tremaine returned his attention to the Israelis. They'd been watching him, gripping their mugs tightly. They seemed uneasy.

"Well gentlemen, let's get under way." Tremaine turned

toward Levin. "Mr. Prime Minister, you requested this meeting so please begin."

"Mr. President, we cannot accept your proposals. In fact, as a nation we are insulted by the suggestions conveyed earlier this week through your Secretary of State, Mr. Kersey."

"I'm sorry to hear that, gentlemen. There was no insult intended. What specifically do you object to?"

"First of all, we object to your interference in our political affairs. We have a right to defend ourselves in any way we see fit. We're a country at war, a country that's been at war since its birth.

"Since the very beginning we've been forced to defend ourselves from hostile neighbors. We live under constant threat of death and are subject to terrorist attacks all over the world. During the Gulf War, under pressure from Mr. Bush, we withheld our response to the Iraqi Scud attacks. But this latest attack by Hizballah cannot go unpunished. We will not stop our bombardment of Lebanon until the Lebanese government pressures the Syrians to call off the rocket attacks. The only thing our neighbors understand is strength. They're afraid of our strength, and that keeps us safe. If we appear weak, then we're no longer safe."

"I'm sorry, Mr. Levin but I do not accept your reasoning. You and your countrymen seem to think you must retaliate for every attack that comes your way. But this constant warfare is a symptom of something else. It will continue until there's a willingness on both sides to address the problems that underlie the hostilities..."

Angrily the Prime Minister interrupted. "Rockets slamming into a hall filled with innocent people are not a symptom, no matter how you look at it!"

"I'm sorry, but I see it differently. I'll do my best to explain. So far you've lived by the gun. I'm not saying it's unwarranted. But violence hasn't solved the problem, merely perpetuated it. This violence now jeopardizes the safety of the world.

"The mass of armaments in your region beggars the mind. And because of your power, some of your neighbors feel they must develop nuclear weapons as well. That is a frightening prospect for the rest of the world. Your war with your neighbors threatens the well-being of every person on the planet."

"We're not the threat; we merely respond to the threats of those who would destroy us."

"I understand, but it sounds too much like spoiled children pointing fingers at each other, each accusing the other of starting it first."

Levin exploded. "What the hell gives you the right to call us spoiled children?"

"Look," Tremaine continued, "Israel was established as a nation by the displacement of Arabs from land they'd held for the last fourteen hundred years. I doubt whether Israel would have come into existence without the support and assistance of both the American and British governments. As I see it, there was little concern or consideration for those who inhabited the land before you, those who were forced to move and make way for the new nation state."

"That's not true. Israelis have always lived in Palestine. The Zionism of the 1800's was the precursor to modern Zionism and was proposed and thought out by Jews living in Palestine."

"I don't disagree with the fact that Jews were living in Palestine all along. But these people, apart from their religious affiliation, had more in common with their Arab neighbors than they did with European Jews.

"Like it or not, the fact of the matter is that, with the establishment of the Jewish State, large numbers of Jews immigrated from Europe and settled in Israel. By doing so, they displaced the people who'd lived there for more than a thousand years. This is the issue that's never been adequately addressed.

"Until now you've had to defend yourselves. In so doing,

you've established yourself in the region, and that is unlikely to change. Now it's time you address the legitimate needs of the people around you, those whom you displaced."

"Why should we address these so-called needs? Our neighbors have sworn to destroy us. It's either us or them."

"That kind of thinking fuels this whole conflict. The problems of the Middle East are like a weeping sore; the time has come to treat it so that it can heal. To do so requires that all of us face facts and do away with our ideologies and pet points of view."

"You've no idea what it's like to live under constant threat from your neighbors, so how can you presume to tell us what to do?" interjected Goldstein angrily.

"We don't presume to tell you what to do; we presume to tell you what we're going to do. Please understand I'm not pointing a finger at you while being oblivious to our own problems. As a nation, some of our policies have, in the past, been hypocritical. That is changing."

Levin looked at Tremaine. His whole demeanor was disconcerting. He, unlike his Israeli counterparts, was dressed casually. He'd kicked off his shoes. He seemed relaxed and at ease, but his green eyes missed nothing. The two men with him were also dressed casually.

Tremaine continued. "I don't feel that we as a nation have been any better than you. The white man came to the shores of the Americas and systematically destroyed the culture, religion and lives of millions of indigenous people, people who lived on these continents long before the white man ever set foot here.

"To this day, large numbers of indigenous people are treated as second-class citizens. They live in poverty and suffer from ill health, a high mortality rate and, amongst the young, a very high suicide rate. As far as I can tell, the same behavior occurred in Australia and New Zealand. What difference is there between the white man who came to the Americas and the white Europeans who settled Palestine?"

"I don't see how you can equate the two situations; they're quite different. We have a long-standing historical association with Palestine, which even your own Christian religion recognizes."

"The Christian religion does recognize the historical connection between the Jewish people and the area known as Palestine, but what are we really saying?"

"What do you mean?"

"First of all, as I understand it, the historical Jewish people stemmed from Esau and Jacob. Two of the tribes derived from Jacob constitute the lineage to which most Jews subscribe. Over time, many Diasporas occurred, and the Jewish people were scattered throughout the world. The majority spread into Europe. But who were they? Were they descendants of Esau and Jacob? No, they were only the descendants of Jacob. And what of the descendants of Esau? They also integrated with others over a long period of time.

"Many became Muslims, having lost the religious roots originally associated with their cultural heritage. So it could be argued that if anyone is to lay claim to the lands of the Middle East, it would appear to be the Arabs."

Levin was flabbergasted at the turn of the conversation. It was a far cry from his dealings with the American Presidents who'd preceded Emerson and Tremaine. He felt angry and exasperated. He couldn't believe what he was hearing. Was this new President serious? Was he mad? An anti-Semite?

Tremaine paused to give Levin a chance to speak. He knew his words had upset the Israelis, and he felt sorry for them. They weren't getting what they hoped for. Neither man spoke, so Tremaine continued. "From another perspective, it is easily seen that the two tribes from which modern Jewry traces its lineage have been a warlike people themselves. They've had a history of occupying land others once lived on and justifying their behavior with the argument that God gave them the land. That's good for those who subscribe to such a frame of reference, but what about those who don't? What of the people who are displaced?"

"Our history is a history of people chosen by God, people who were obedient to Yahweh and the Law."

"That's what I mean. It's internally consistent for traditional Jews—and meaningless and unacceptable for non-Jews.

"Many nations have made similar claims. The British colonial expansion was justified because the British were a Christian nation. Their missionaries set out to convert the people in the lands they conquered, with the best of intentions. They believed they were providing a service.

"Our own country has acted in a similar vein in its war with Mexico, and in its meddling in the affairs of Central and South America. We've forced our way on others under the auspices of 'Manifest Destiny' and the 'Monroe Doctrine.' The fact of the matter is that all people deserve to live and raise their families without regard to religious beliefs, and in comparative safety.

"As far as I can tell, there's been too much blood shed in the name of religions that lay claim to the 'one true God.' The Jew is no better than the Christian or the Muslim when it comes to such arrogance. Such reasoning carries little weight with me."

"What are you getting at?" Goldstein demanded.

"What I'm getting at is that you support your position with the idea of tradition and the authority of God. This only holds weight with those who accept the same basic assumptions as you."

"What do you mean?"

"One person might say 'the fourth of July was a wonderful day.' Another might say 'the fourth of July was a terrible day.' They disagree based upon a shared basic assumption, which is that the day was the fourth of July. Without agreement as to the basic assumption, the conversation becomes confusing and the source of considerable misunderstanding."

"I don't understand the point you're making."

"The British and the Americans, and perhaps most other Christian nations, accept the same basic assumption: that the Jews who moved to Palestine from Europe had a historical right to do so.

"They agree that such a right justified taking the land lived on and belonging to others. What I'm questioning is the very assumption itself. The Palestinians, the Lebanese, the Jordanians and so on, see all this from a much different perspective. We'll have difficulty seeing their point of view as long as we continue to subscribe only to our own perspective and are blind to others."

Tremaine watched Levin carefully. He saw that he'd made a crack in Levin's arguments; a slight opening had occurred. He doubted, however, that this conversation alone would suffice.

"I understand your point, but I'm not sure I can accept it," Levin said.

"Look at it from another perspective. The Buddhist and Hindu peoples believe in reincarnation. So from that perspective, what possible sense can be made of claims that argue a historical lineage?"

"What do you mean?"

"From the perspective of reincarnation, we've all taken our turn being men and women, black and white, Jew and Gentile, rich and poor, beggar and king. If such is the case, how can anyone claim he is descended from one tribe, one race, or from one sex?"

"You can't argue that we have no claim to the land we call Israel," Goldstein blurted out.

Tremaine looked at Goldstein. "Neither more nor less than others. The United States has, in the past, accepted the same basic assumption to which you subscribe. Our policies regarding Israel and its neighbors reflected this. As I said before, that assumption has now been questioned."

"So what are you proposing?" demanded Levin.

"I'm proposing that we will no longer blindly support your country's actions no matter what you do. We will support direct talks with the PLO and other Arab leaders."

"You'll what?" Levin snapped.

Tremaine looked carefully at Levin, giving him a moment to calm down. "Hassan has been the only representative for many displaced Palestinians. He speaks for them. You may not like what he has to say, but you cannot ignore him."

"We will never recognize him or the PLO."

"That's nothing more than political posturing. Insisting that you don't recognize someone doesn't make that person go away; it only leaves you ignorant concerning him. The fact of the matter is that he exists, and he does speak for many of the people that, by your own admission, hate you and wish to destroy you. That hatred comes from something. If these problems are to be resolved, they must first be understood. We must each be willing to listen to one another. We must find out what it is that bothers our so-called enemies. What do they believe from their point of view? What frustrations do they have, what hopes and aspirations? Without that understanding, little can occur that is beneficial."

"We'll never deal directly with Hassan. Both he and the PLO have, as their stated purpose, the destruction of Israel."

"Do you think a lifetime of war has no effect on a man? You've been at war now for fifty years and you're no closer to achieving peace than when you first began. I'm sure you've lost friends and loved ones to this incessant fighting. The same is true of Hassan. He's a human being like you and me. All of us have loved people, some of whom we've lost through death, some through violence and war. Only a few, the most hardened, remain untouched by such events.

"What is it like to near the end of one's life, to look back at what one has accomplished, and behold fifty years of bloodshed, untold suffering, and no end in sight? I suspect a man such as you, having lived more than seventy years, must have had such thoughts from time to time. Your own people, your neighbors and your allies are weary of this war. The time has come to bring it to an end. Talk with your enemies; talk with Hassan."

"This is not open for discussion," Levin said forcefully.

"I'm sorry to hear that."

"You said you wouldn't tell us what to do, so let's hear what you intend to do. We've heard only a little of that. You've subjected us to a history lesson that we don't accept. What's the rest?"

"You're right. I wanted you to be the first to know what lies behind our changing policies. We will sever all financial ties, curtail all trade, and cancel all military contracts with you. We'll no longer guarantee your loans. We'll support the enforcement of UN Resolution 242. We'll consider introducing our own troops into areas where you attack civilians of neighboring nations..."

Levin stood up, knocking the chair over. He was furious. "How dare you say such things? You'll not get the support of your congress and I doubt your Joint Chiefs will go along with such actions."

"We'll see," said Tremaine, his voice firm. "You asked what we are prepared to do and I'm answering you. I want you to understand our point of view on these matters and be prepared for the actions that follow."

Levin, his anger now under control, picked up his chair and sat down. "Go on," he said.

"What I'm explaining is a range of actions we're considering if things don't change."

"Yes, yes, get on with it," Levin snapped.

Tremaine chose to ignore Levin's tone of voice. "We'll actively support the resolutions passed by the UN after the 1967 war. No longer will we support and enforce sanctions against nations we disagree with while ignoring the sanctions against you. Our policies from now on will be more evenhanded.

"On the other hand, we're prepared to use our goodwill to bring a lasting settlement. We'll do our best to defuse this powder keg that threatens us all."

Tremaine looked at Goldstein. He could feel the anger in the man. "Speak your piece," he said.

"You remind me of the anti-Semites I know. A more sophisticated one, but an anti-Semite nevertheless. This is nothing more than blatant prejudice."

Tremaine looked at the two men and said in a quiet voice, "As I understand the term anti-Semite, it refers to hating or discriminating against Jewish people simply because they're Jewish. I don't hate Jews and I don't discriminate against them, in fact what I have to say is a mark of not discriminating. I find it abhorrent that the young people, even the very young, in some Palestinian schools are taught to hate Jews and emulate suicide bombers. Am I anti-Muslim for my views? When I decry what Christians have done to the native people in the America's does it make me anti-Christian? If I spoke out against those things while ignoring what your country is doing it would be a kind of reverse anti-semitism, which is just another form of prejudice and discrimination.

"When your countrymen don't wish to hear those who criticize policies and actions that are harmful to others, it becomes a convenient ploy to accuse them of being anti Semitic. This shifts the focus from the issues being raised and refocuses attention on a false issue. In my view, there are too many people who've become overly sensitive to the charge of being anti Semitic. As a result they remain quiet when in fact there is a great need to speak out. This is reverse anti-semitism.

"What I'm opposed to is man's inhumanity to man, regardless of who is responsible for it. I don't look at a person's color his nationality or his religious perspectives. Murder, theft and brutality, are still murder, theft and brutality regardless of who is the perpetrator. What you think of me is your business, not mine, you can call me by whatever label you wish and it will not prevent me from speaking out and taking the action I see fit when addressing such issues. My remarks today are directed to you from a place of respect, from one human being to another because I think that what you're doing is not helpful, It has nothing to do with the fact that you're Jewish."

"The state of Israel is here to stay," said Levin. "Your change in policy will not change that reality."

"We have no interest in changing that," responded Tremaine evenly. "We are simply interested in doing what we can to help end this conflict in the Middle East. For us, that means a shift in the way we look at the world, which means a shift in foreign policy as well. Since you are part of the world community, it will have a bearing on how we relate to you.

"Of one thing you can be certain. This administration will speak the truth as we see it. We'll do our best to express our views with clarity and make clear the reasoning behind them. We will actively seek to understand those who disagree with us. We are open to all points of view. Understanding does not occur when one is unwilling to listen or consider other points of view."

Levin was tired and wanted a break, something to eat and a good rest.

Tremaine sensed the exhaustion of his guests. "Why don't we take a break? Get some rest and then, please, share dinner with my wife and me. Dinner will be at eight if that's acceptable to you."

The invitation was accepted, and the Israelis left. Tremaine walked to the window and stood looking into the garden. Large black clouds hung threateningly over the city. Lightning flashed and thunder rumbled close by.

"What happened here today will send shock waves through

the Middle East," Doug said quietly.

Tremaine turned and looked at Doug and Jonathan.

"It strikes me," he said, "that what's being worked out in the Middle East today is the old conflict between the twin brothers, Esau and Jacob."

"I'm not familiar with the story," Doug said.

"Isaac had two sons, Esau, the elder, and Jacob, the younger. In those days, the father, as head of the household, bestowed his herds and certain belongings upon the eldest son. This was an expression of the father's blessing. It was not something undertaken lightly.

"Isaac decided the time had come for the ceremony to take place. Esau went out hunting to find the ingredients to make his father's favorite dish. Rehekah, the boy's mother, favored Jacob and schemed to have him receive the blessing instead.

"She prepared Isaac's favorite dish herself and, while Esau was out hunting, brought Jacob to receive the blessing. Isaac, getting on in years, could no longer see properly. Rehekah was thus able to fool Isaac into thinking Jacob was Esau."

"How did she do that?"

"Esau was peculiarly hairy, so Rehekah covered Jacob with goat skins. Isaac, surprised his son had returned so quickly and unable to see, reached out to touch his son. Feeling the hair, he was convinced that Jacob was Esau.

"Isaac bestowed the blessing and his herds upon Jacob. When Esau returned and entered his father's presence, they both learned of the deception. Esau begged his father to take back his blessing and bestow it on him instead. Although Isaac wanted to, he felt bound by his oath. He loved his son dearly and was angry over the deception. But he believed that once a man's word was given, it couldn't be rescinded.

"From that time forth, there was great animosity between the brothers. In fact, Jacob had to flee in order to escape his brother's murderous rage. As the story goes, God changed Jacob's name to Israel and told him he'd be the father of a special nation. It is from his lineage that the Jewish people of today are descended."

13

Dinner at the White House

Michael Levin and Joseph Goldstein, despite their initial trepidation, enjoyed dinner with the Tremaines. Once more they were surprised at the informality with which they were greeted. Their hosts were dressed casually and comfortably rather than in the semiformal attire they'd expected.

Only the four of them were present, Sandra and David having elected to serve the guests themselves. At first the experience was disconcerting for the Israelis, but after a while they loosened their ties, removed their jackets and felt more comfortable. After dinner they moved into the study.

"Coffee?" Tremaine asked.

"Please."

"I'll make some," he said. "I'll be back shortly."

With that he left the room.

"This is quite different from our last visit," commented Michael.

"It certainly is," agreed Joseph.

"How do you mean?" asked Sandra, looking at the two men.

"I suppose it's the informality," said Michael.

"Oh," Sandra smiled. "Since David became the President, we decided we would forego formality in the interest of comfort. Both of us enjoy cooking, which we do as often as time permits. It's been a fight though to get our way. Privacy is important to us, and it's difficult to have privacy in this position."

"I know what you mean," said Joseph.

"You know, Mrs. Tremaine, this whole day has been most disconcerting."

Sandra looked at Michael Levin and saw the confusion in his face. "Please call me Sandra—I like my name," she said with a mischievous smile.

"All right."

"What's disconcerting about it?" she asked.

"We came to your country after a most disturbing conversation with your Foreign Secretary, Doug Kersey. He conveyed a message from your husband that was not what we expected. We hoped in coming here to change his mind and restore support for our actions against the guerrillas in Lebanon."

"And how did you fare?" Sandra asked with a slight smile.

"He understood our position," Michael said. Joseph nodded. "But your husband's point of view didn't change. It's difficult for us to accept. We find ourselves in an awkward position."

"In what way?"

There was an uncomfortable silence and the two Israelis looked at each other.

Sandra laughed and her eyes twinkled, making the two men even more ill at ease. "I'll bet you wondered if he was an anti-Semite, crazy, or... ill-suited for the job of President. You wouldn't be the first to have such thoughts."

The two men looked at her with uneasy smiles.

Sandra laughed again. "On that last point, he'd be the first to agree. He might even agree on the one before it. On the first, however, he would have to disagree. He is in no way a bigot or racist. He has for a long time been deeply concerned for the well being of indigenous peoples all over the world. He gets upset over the unthinking and uncaring treatment they receive at the hands of government. Now that he's in a position to do something about it, he'll expend whatever effort he can to do so."

Just then the phone rang, and Sandra picked it up. She

listened for a moment and, putting it down, excused herself. She returned in a few moments with the coffee. Putting the tray down, she replaced the phone in its cradle.

"David has to take this call," she said. "He'll join us as soon as he can."

Sandra poured coffee for her guests and herself.

"David's an unusual thinker," she continued. "He's got a knack for seeing through what most people take for granted. He says that when things are locked up, it's because no understanding is present. In Tai Chi, 'he who yields breaks the deadlock of force.'"

"He used the word *understanding* earlier today, and I had the distinct feeling he meant something quite specific," Joseph interjected.

"Do you know what he means?" asked Michael.

"There was a time when it was believed that the earth was flat. Sailors were afraid to sail out of the sight of land. Once it was understood that the earth was not flat, behavior changed as a direct result of that understanding. Sailors began to sail all over the world even though, to begin with, fear of the unknown still remained."

"That's an interesting explanation," Michael said with a smile.

"Another area he often points to has to do with communication. When we talk with each other, particularly concerning things about which there is a disagreement, communication often fails. Why? Because of a misunderstanding. Take the coffee pot, for instance. There are three of us here in this room all looking at the coffee pot. There are three points of view."

"Yes, that's right."

"Can any of those points of view ever coincide?"

"Strictly speaking, no."

"So if we're interested in getting a rich picture, we must take into account all points of view. But what usually happens? I look at the object and I see it as I do. Let's say that the side I'm looking at is red, and the side you're looking at, Michael, is black. When you describe what you see, it is not what I see. I know that what I'm seeing is red, but what you're describing is black. The mistake comes when I assume that you are just not seeing things right, and I attempt to persuade you of the error of your ways.

"The same is true for you. If I'm successful in persuading you, then you must lie and tell me that the black you see is red. But that is not the truth, nor is the red I see the black you see. It is clear there are as many points of view as there are people. In order to create a greater understanding, it's obvious that all points of view have to be taken into account, and that all points of view are true. Now, this may create some confusion, even anxiety, but in the end it can only be beneficial. Although some points of view may appear to conflict, it is important for the mind to become aware of them all. Then, on an unconscious level, the mind works to resolve the apparent contradictions, taking it to a new level previously unseen. When that occurs, resolution is at hand, appropriate action follows, and the stalemate is broken."

"When you explain it that way," Michael said, "It makes a lot of sense. I can understand much better what your husband is talking about. Thank you." Joseph nodded his agreement.

The door opened and Tremaine entered.

"I'm sorry to be so long," he said.

Sandra poured his coffee and Michael extended his cup for a refill.

"I know you've had a long day, and the time is getting late," Tremaine said, "but, I'd like to know if you've given thought to our earlier conversation. If you've any questions please feel free to ask."

"We've given it a lot of thought," Michael responded. "We'll take your comments back and present them to our advisors and to the Knesset. You've placed us in an awkward position."

"I can imagine."

"It's been a shock to our way of thinking," Michael admitted. Joseph nodded in agreement. Michael paused for a moment as though debating with himself.

Tremaine waited, noticing that the two men appeared tired—tired with years and tired with war, he thought. Joseph had a reputation as a great general, usually credited with the defeat of Egypt, Syria and Jordan in the Six Day War.

"Are you really serious?" Michael asked. "Did you mean what you said this afternoon?"

"Yes, I'm completely serious. Please understand that behind my remarks there is only a deep desire to see a resolution to this endless conflict. I believe that reasonable men and women of goodwill can, with hard work, open minds and patience, bring forth a lasting peace that serves both the Palestinians and the Israelis. There's war weariness among all concerned. I'm convinced a resolution can be found to the problems before us. Don't get me wrong, I'm not naive enough to believe it will happen overnight."

"Do you think there's ever a time when force is warranted?" Michael asked.

"Yes. In this case, however, I feel understanding and firmness will bring the desired results. Talk with Hassan; talk with the Palestinian leaders, those who represent the different factions, in secret if necessary. Find out if they're serious. Find out what they need, what the needs are of the people they represent. See what you can do to help meet those needs. Communicate your own needs to them and be sure they understand. How can they help? Find out. If you do it quietly, you'll not arouse opposition, and you can work for the time being without distraction."

"The United States actively supported the founding of the State of Israel, as did many others at the time," Goldstein said. "All those who supported it recognized that the Jews had a right to a homeland in Palestine; there was unanimity on the matter."

"I don't think there was unanimity, but given what had happened to the European Jews in the Second World War, there was the sense that something needed to be done. The idea of forming a Jewish State was the one that was accepted."

There was silence for a moment. In the background could be heard the muted sounds of the city.

"We had a right to live in Palestine, and if we formed our own nation it would be the one place we could be safe." Joseph stated flatly.

"I know that was the thinking once, but the facts have proved otherwise have they not? It can hardly be said you've been safe since the country first came into being."

Joseph ignored Tremaine's question and continued with his train of thought. "We had a right to live as a Jewish State," he said, "there can be no argument about that, even from you."

"The right to live life in relative safety, free of persecution, free to think as you wish, able to look after and support your family in a reasonable manner, is the right of *all* human beings regardless of nationality. I support that for you *and* the Palestinians.

"What I do not support is your rights *over* the Palestinian people. Now, as to whether I would advocate the formation of a new State to do this, I'm not sure. If it was the best way to bring it about, then certainly. The only problem with that idea is that when it happened, it was at the expense of those who were living there in the first place. The Americas are certainly a recent example of that, are they not? When the Spanish, French, British and Portuguese came to the Americas, they destroyed and displaced the indigenous people in order to claim land for their respective nations."

"But as you pointed out, this is what history records. Why should we be any different? "Joseph persisted. "Even the native peoples went to war with each other, and nations conquered nations. This isn't new."

"I agree. This is what history tells us. I also know it is a way the conflict is perpetuated through the generations."

"So are you trying to change history?" Levin asked. "It seems to me this issue has more to do with human nature. If there wasn't greed, selfishness and inconsiderateness, the problem wouldn't exist."

"Let me pose a question. Because you have power, is it right to impose your will on your weaker neighbors?"

"You're posing the question, 'Does might make right?'" Levin suggested.

"Yes, you could say that."

"Look Tremaine, if human nature doesn't change, and I see no reason to think it will, then how can the patterns of history be changed? I don't think they can."

"I agree with you. What I am suggesting, however, is that there are certain basic human rights that are important for all human beings, regardless of their nationality, religion or skin color. All human beings are of equal value in the sight of the Supreme Creator. It makes no difference whether one is a Jew, a Muslim, or a Christian."

"I understand your point," Levin said.

"We know from statistics that there'll be a certain percentage of fatalities amongst the driving public," Joseph interjected. "Car accidents happen, they're a fact of life. In the same way, powerful nations have conquered and displaced others. Are you suggesting we can do something about it?"

"Yes and no. I think we can do *something* about it all right, but I do not think we can change the facts of human nature. Given human nature, there will always be those who are selfish and self-absorbed. There will also be those who seek to impose their will on their neighbors. As you've pointed out with your analogy, we know that people are always going to be killed in automobile accidents, that's true. But when we encounter a crash on the highway and people are badly injured, we stop and offer assistance.

"So here is the other side of human nature. In as much as we can be mean spirited, we can also be generous. Human selfishness and human compassion represent the poles between which human nature finds expression. The Taoists refer to this as the principle of balance and harmony, as depicted by the yin yang symbol. We Americans are largely a product of Christian Theology. We've been taught to hold on to the good and destroy the bad. But this is not possible because the idea of good and bad are complimentary opposites that do not exist alone. Reality simply is, and no beliefs to the contrary can change it."

"So you're suggesting that the idea of getting rid of one and elevating the other is not realistic?" Levin asked.

"That's right. Keeping that in mind concerning you and the Palestinians, what can be said? Within the two societies there are extremists with rigid ideas. These extremists are supported by a kind of theological thinking that perceives life in black and white, right and wrong; *their* ideas and *their* way is right and all others are wrong. On the other side we find opposing views which are equally extreme. To support these opposing positions both sides claim that God is on their side!"

"In a sense, they counteract one another," said Joseph.

"That's true, but when these opposing views clash in society, it can lead to bloodshed. Consequently, when the issues raised by different perspectives are not addressed, it leads to a hardening of positions and more extreme expressions and activities designed to get attention. When this gets out of hand, it tends to destabilize all aspects of life. A more balanced approach is needed, one in which the legitimate concerns of those involved are taken into account. Since it is more in harmony with reality it has, I think, a better chance of succeeding.

"What gives power to the extremists is the sense that the

needs of their constituents have not been taken into account. When we ignore or minimize the needs they represent, we only confirm their beliefs about us. Namely, that we don't care about them, that we are at best, insensitive, more interested in our own selfish ends."

"So when the concerns and needs of all people are looked at from the perspective of a larger and more comprehensive whole, there's a better chance of peace?"

"Yes, that's my point. "

"Are you also suggesting that our inability to listen to another point of view, in this instance, that of the Palestinians, tends to reinforce the extremist position?"

"Yes. To me this is the major contributing factor that leads to terrorism. The Chinese sage Lao Tzu, speaks of this when he says, 'Prevent trouble before it starts, put things in order before they exist. It is easier to maintain peace than bring it about when lost. It is easier to deal with difficulties before they get out of hand.'"

The Israelis sat quietly. The only sound in the room was the ticking of the clock on the mantel.

"Don't mistake what I said today as a personal attack on you or your countrymen. It's not. I have nothing but goodwill in my heart."

"Thank you." Levin said quietly.

"Are you suggesting that this is the basis of your foreign policy?" asked Joseph.

"It is some of the reasoning behind what informs it, the basic assumptions so to speak. But as times change, so will the expressions of it."

Michael looked puzzled. "I'm not sure I follow you."

"Sandra once told me that during one Canadian election, Robert Stanfield proposed wage and price controls. Pierre Trudeau, the Prime Minister at the time, opposed them. Stanfield lost the election and Trudeau was returned to power.

Later, Trudeau implemented Stanfield's ideas. A reporter asked Trudeau why he did so. He responded that at the time it was proposed, he didn't think it was a good idea. During the next year, however, the economy had taken a turn for the worse. 'I thought about Mr. Stanfield's ideas,' he said, 'and came to the conclusion they were worth trying.' The reporter pressed him further. Trudeau's response was that good ideas were not just the province of his own party or himself. He appreciated good and creative ideas without concern for the political persuasion of those who espoused them."

"What about consistency?" Michael asked.

"George Bernard Shaw once said that consistency was 'the hobgoblin of small minds.' Times change. If we advocate a particular policy, and that policy is good at the time, it may not be good a year later. I'm sure you understand what I'm saying."

"I do," said Levin. Joseph nodded agreement.

"Let's call it a night," Tremaine said.

All of them stood.

"You'll be heading back tomorrow?" Tremaine asked.

"Yes," Levin responded. "We leave in the morning."

"Thank you for joining us for dinner," Sandra said, shaking their hands warmly. "It was a pleasure to have you with us."

The Israelis smiled and thanked her. They'd enjoyed the evening and the chance to get to know her. Tremaine opened the door and escorted them down the hall to their car.

"I expect to hear from you," Tremaine said.

"You will."

....

The Israelis sat back in the leather seats, lost in thought, as the car cleared the White House checkpoints.

Joseph voiced the thoughts on his mind. "The more we talk

with Tremaine, the more sensible he seems."

"Yes, and it puts us in a quandary."

"I agree. What are your thoughts about all of this?"

"When we came here, I had one thing in mind: to get back the support we'd lost. I was frustrated and angry over Tremaine's comments. I took them as a personal affront. But, as he pointed out, there was nothing personal in his remarks. Then, on the way over this evening, I realized I *am* tired of this constant bloodshed. The thought of peace is appealing! Until today, it was just an idea, a hope that might come to pass sometime in the future. Not something here and now. Somehow these conversations have brought it into the present."

"Lets see what kind of a reception this will find in the Knesset."

The car entered the gates of the Israeli Embassy and stopped in front of the building. The two men left the car and walked through the guarded entrance.

14

Finding the guru

David always found Tai Chi restful and energizing. After completing Chi Gung, he slipped into the effortless grace of the form, which took him forty minutes more. Although his body moved, his mind was still. There was something so basic about Tai Chi; he always felt connected to the earth. It was an awareness that the body was from the earth and would return to the earth. He felt a sense of oneness with the ancient Taoist monks who'd developed the art so many years ago. They'd understood the nature of the Tao and, in some unfathomable way, had found the means of expressing it.

Earlier that morning, he'd received a letter from a friend who'd recently returned from Bombay and a visit with Avinash. His friend had mentioned what an impact the meeting had on him. David chuckled; he knew firsthand what it was like to be exposed to the intense light of the guru's understanding. His first meeting with Avinash had destroyed all his pre-conceived notions concerning who or what he was, and had left him suddenly adrift in life like a rudderless ship on the ocean.

For as long as he could remember, he'd been interested in spiritual matters. This had been the call of philosophy that he loved so much. For him, philosophy was an inquiry into the nature of reality, an inquiry into human nature and mankind's relationship to the universe. It asked the questions: Who am I? Where do I come from? What is this "I," I call myself? What is real? What is illusion? What is good and evil, moral and immoral?

This search had taken him into psychology, believing it was an application of the fundamental insights of philosophy. His studies eventually led him to the field of Transpersonal Psychology. Here, he found the perfect marriage between insight and application. While Western Psychology addressed the personal consciousness of the individual, what is commonly known as the ego, Transpersonal Psychology addressed both the personal and impersonal consciousness. The impersonal consciousness being that which lay beneath the ego and remained when it died; it was the sense of presence, of being alive, *I am,* or what the Hindu referred to as the 'Atman.' Transpersonal Psychology, informed by Eastern philosophy, embraced a more comprehensive description of human nature. These insights he came to through Advaita Vedanta, Taoism, and Zen.

Yet, despite his studies, he'd longed to know someone who understood, someone with more than just an intellectual comprehension. He knew that such knowledge had been available, since it was obviously present in historical figures like Jesus, the Buddha, and Lao Tzu. But surely there must be someone alive today within whom that sacred knowledge burned bright and intense. Where would he find such a person?

Years before he'd been involved in social action, believing that through it society could be changed, humanized. At a demonstration in Boston, he witnessed a policeman brutalize a helpless young man, breaking his back with a vicious blow from a nightstick. And David, the pacifist, went into a blind rage, solely intent on killing. In that moment, he discovered the beast, so readily apparent in others, resided within himself as well. He realized social action by itself was useless without a change of heart derived from a rigorous examination of oneself. A self-righteous arrogance had masked his ignorance and brought him to the brink of catastrophe, to the verge of killing another human being. That shock had intensified his search.

Early in life, he'd felt cradled by an implicit God, a God he came to know in nature. That God existed, gave him a deep sense of peace. But for a while, the twisted concept of a terrible God obscured the deep certainty he'd had as a child. As part of his Christian faith, he was told, by those who claimed to know, that God had created human beings flawed from the beginning with the stain of sin. As a result they would, as a natural consequence, end their days in the fiery pits of hell.

This same God, in his benevolence, gave birth through Mary to a miraculously conceived son. And then this benevolent God condemned his son to die a painful death on a cross for sins others were supposed to have committed. Jesus was the sacrifice required to save the likes of David from an eternity in hell. Pagans sacrificed animals, but this God demanded human sacrifice. And not just any human being, he demanded that his son pay the price. What kind of a monstrosity was this God?

These frightening thoughts had filled David's heart with fear. Eventually, he came to voice the unspeakable. This God, as far as he was concerned, was evil. It was a perversion of what he'd known, a perversion perpetrated by the clerics of the church throughout the centuries.

Briefly, he'd believed what the clerics taught. If what they said was true, then his chance of escaping the fires of hell were pretty slim. The clergy he came across taught it was a sin to doubt God's existence. The plea of ignorance, they argued, would be of no avail on the final judgment day. He felt trapped for the time being by their arguments.

Fortunately, good sense prevailed, and he was delivered from the snare of fear. Reason came to his rescue. If I say I doubt the existence of God, he thought, which would be the truth at the moment, how could a just God condemn me for telling the truth? If He did, He would not be worthy of respect. For if I, a mere mortal, can find it in my heart to forgive anyone anything, what kind of a God would not do the same for me? Such a God would obviously command neither my love nor respect. An eternity in hell was far more inviting than eternity in heaven with such a barbaric concept of God. This provided him with the final break from fundamentalist thinking.

It was thirty years since it happened, thirty years since he rejected the church and the religion of the clerics. He wanted no part of it. As the belief systems fell away, he remembered what he'd always known. He was a child of the universe, and the universe was an intrinsically friendly place. It was his home; it had given birth to him and nurtured him. The fires of hell portrayed by the preachers could no longer frighten him; they were nothing more than the figments of demented minds, and he knew it.

The ingestion of LSD and peyote broke the hold of his rational mind, which had, until that time, been like a steel trap. The mind, he'd believed, was all-important. A rational approach, he was convinced, was the avenue to truth. Despite its limitations, it had served him well. At this time he had a mechanistic understanding of the world. He saw objects as objects, and only intellectually understood the nature of energy.

But when he ingested those drugs, he came to know that objects with density, size and shape were in fact nothing more than vibrations of energy. He saw that everything was made of energy; everything vibrated at frequencies peculiar to them. Those vibrations were like signatures with specific characteristics that gave rise to the names by which they were called. He saw that the subtlest form of energy was thought. Light took time to travel, whereas thought was not subject to time.

In those altered states he recognized the truth; he understood life, how it had always been. He saw that what caused it to be hidden from normal awareness was the training human beings receive, the preconceived notions promulgated by society, the fundamental assumptions accepted as true. He saw how powerful this cultural agreement was, what psychology referred to as "consensual validation." It was as powerful as a black hole from which nothing could escape.

Everything was connected to everything else. There were even different energy systems with forms of life peculiar to them, whole universes within universes that, because of the sensory make-up of the human being, were largely inaccessible to him except through the special training found in some of the shamanic or yoga traditions.

It was during these years that he read the *Bhagavad-Gita* and the *Tao Te Ching*. Those teachings directed his attention deeper and deeper. He recognized things he'd always known and somehow forgotten. He knew and understood what Lao Tzu meant when he said, "When free of desire the mystery is revealed; when subject to desire, only the manifestation is seen."

The experiences under the influence of those drugs were like intimations of things to come. They opened him to the intuitive understanding of life itself.

Eventually, he came across the idea of enlightenment. Intellectually he understood it at once. It was what he'd been searching for all his life, but he'd never known what it was called. Now that he had a name for it, his search for it intensified. For years, he engaged in various spiritual practices and disciplines. In the end, he'd repudiated them all, being firmly convinced that life was utterly simple and that life itself was the great teacher. He found that no discipline could bridge the gulf between God and man. Instead, it seemed to take man further away from what he sought.

Then came the urge to go to India. It had always been there from the time he was a child. So he went. Sandra had accompanied him. He had been immensely glad of her presence. Without her, the shock of India would have been more intense.

Being a practical man, he wondered whom he should see. At the time, an acquaintance had introduced him to the teachings and stories of Sai Baba. David had read all he could, and he liked what he found. Here was a Master with a vast following, unafraid of performing miracles. He was reputed to be an Avatar who, like Jesus and the Buddha, was of such spiritual stature that through his teachings, he could set the tone for the coming age. Millions of people from all over the world came to see him; he was well respected and deeply loved.

One day, David arrived at the ashram in Puttapharti in time for the festival of Shivarati. That morning he caught a glimpse, through a vast throng, of the Master dressed in an orange robe.

Each morning and afternoon he'd gone and sat in the long lines in the dust and dirt, ready to enter the courtyard of the Mandir for darshan. Once inside, he found himself reading the works of Nisargadatta and only looked up when Sai Baba came into view.

He thought it strange; here he was in the presence of a guru and unable to set aside the book on Nisargadatta's teachings. They were like an elixir to the soul. At last he'd found the truth he'd craved, and he had found it in the words of a master now dead.

The night before reaching Puttapharti, he'd gone to the Vedanta Bookstore in Bangalore. It was dark when he arrived. Getting out of the taxi, he stepped onto the littered sidewalk and made his way toward a light coming from a doorway and two open windows. In the dark, he almost bumped into a bookstand upon which nine books were arranged. They had orange covers. In white letters the title read, *I Am That.* He felt something in his chest, like a blow, and he wondered where he'd seen the book before. There was a strange familiarity to it that he was never able to explain.

Later, he wondered how he could have seen the books on the stand. They had been lit from behind, with no light in front. Despite this, they had caught his attention. Being of an ornery temperament and unwilling to see the obvious, he walked around the bookstand and entered the store. An hour later, he came across the same book in the stacks. He opened it and knew at once he'd found what he'd been looking for. He felt his heart leap, and his whole being sang with joy. It was this that had brought him to India.

But what of Sai Baba, the living guru? One morning at darshan, Sai Baba stood before him and their eyes met. At that moment, he knew this was not the guru he'd been seeking.

He was not suited to be a disciple of a Bhakti Master. It was not in his nature to submit his life to the devotion, rituals and spiritual practices of any guru.

He'd heard an exquisite call, and the peculiarities of his mind were such as to draw him to it. It was the song of wisdom, the path of Jnana Yoga, also known as Advaita Vedanta.

Colloquially, the path was known as the "pathless path" to which access was granted through the "gateless gate." It employed the mind in the all-absorbing task of self-inquiry; ritual and spiritual practices played no part. It was utterly simple, in a sense, indistinguishable from life itself. This was what he'd been looking for.

At last he came into the presence of Avinash. Seven months after his return from India, he flew to Los Angeles with his friend Brian. Avinash had come from India and was to speak at Hermosa Beach. In a room above a restaurant on the strand, the meeting took place.

He and Brian climbed the stairs, found a seat and waited. Some twenty people had already gathered. More drifted in, some renewing old acquaintances, others sitting quietly with eyes closed. He noticed a short, elderly man enter, a man with white hair and thick-rimmed glasses. He stood quietly, watching. A few people engaged him briefly in conversation. He was exceptionally gracious to all who greeted him. David wondered if this was Avinash.

At four o'clock, the same man sat in a single chair on a low platform beside a bouquet of flowers on a small table. He waited for people to become quiet, and then he began to speak in a soft and compelling voice. With an Anglo-Indian accent, Avinash talked and took questions for about an hour that afternoon. He spoke of many things, but one thing in particular became firmly rooted in David and forever changed his life.

In response to a question he'd asked, Avinash looked at David and said, "The seeker is the obstacle to that which is sought." It was as though David had stepped off a cliff. In that moment, he understood Avinash completely. He knew that he who was seeking would never arrive at the destination. For entrance to be granted to that sacred place, the seeker, the separate identified consciousness, the ego, must be absent.

For twenty-five years, he'd actively sought enlightenment. He'd understood that enlightenment meant union with the Divine. At that moment, he knew that he, the one who was seeking, was the identified consciousness. The nature of that consciousness was its individuality, its separateness. Being individual, it could never enter the place of oneness without losing itself. Individuality was separation; enlightenment was union or oneness. Enlightenment was the absence of the one doing the seeking. With that realization, the journey was over, although it took six months before he realized what had happened.

He, the identified consciousness, had glimpsed the Promised Land and, like Moses of old, he could not enter. Nothing he could do would ever take him there. All that was left was to wait while the identity slowly disappeared. At first, he suffered a deep disappointment. His life, as he'd known it, came to an end. The search he'd engaged in all his life was over. For years, his last thought before going to sleep at night and the first thought upon awakening had been of enlightenment. Everything he'd done, every aspect of his life, had been submerged in this all-consuming search. In one sudden burst of understanding, it had all been swept away.

After living with the emptiness for six months, he had

occasion to speak with Dr. Klein, another Advaita Master. David had asked why he felt this strange kind of depression. The Master had looked at him and smiled. "Dispense with labels," he said. "Let go of the need to name everything and face the feelings without naming." Then he had fixed David with eyes that peered from beneath shaggy brows and in a rich French accent he had said, "The seeker _is_ the sought!"

David found unusual changes, subtle changes taking place over the next few months. No longer was he trying to fulfill any image, be it that of a psychologist or professor. No longer was he invested in the results of his clients. No longer did he worry what others thought of him. He accepted himself exactly as he was without concern for how he thought he should be.

Life became effortless. Nothing had really changed; it still went along as always and yet somehow, inexplicably, it was completely different. A year later, Avinash delivered a stunning blow. Someone had asked, "Are there any indications when enlightenment is close?" Avinash had responded, "Give up all hope. When it is finally accepted that enlightenment may or may not happen in this body-mind organism in this lifetime, the end is near." With this statement, David realized just how strong the desire for enlightenment was. He thought he'd dealt with it all, but that statement brought to the surface one great gush of despair. Then slowly, over time, a deep stillness settled in him. He engaged in the ordinary events of daily life. The all-consuming intensity of the spiritual search subsided, and at times he could even forget about it.

On the day of the first meeting with Avinash, David and Brian walked to the end of a pier that jutted into the ocean across from the building where the meeting had taken place. The sun sank, pink in the purple haze of autumn. Lovers strolled on the pier, roller skaters and rollerbladers rumbled by. David looked back and saw the pink clouds reflected in the windows of the upper room where the meeting had taken place. He was struck with the thought that in that room, the conduit of the eternal had been present while, all around them; the commerce of daily life had gone on. Only those present in the room had any understanding of what had taken place. He thought of another upper room, some two thousand years ago, and the disciples who'd been present then. Tears of joy rolled down his cheeks. He looked at his friend and smiled. They both sensed the momentousness of what had taken place that afternoon at Hermosa Beach.

15

Selfless service

enator William G. Morgan strolled leisurely through the grounds of his new home. It was the first time he'd done so since he and his wife Marianne had moved in the week before. Until today, he'd been busy finding his way around and learning what was expected of him.

Marianne found Washington a big adjustment. Thirty years in Camden, Maine was a long time, and she had good friends there. She'd gone to Washington with him on many occasions, but she was always happy to return to the old seaport she loved.

Morgan knew he would miss his fellow New Englanders and their down to earth practicality. They'd be less accessible to him now. Morgan knew that as Vice President, his time would be less his own than he was used to. He shook his head, still disbelieving. The sudden change from Senator to Vice President took some getting used to.

He hadn't known Emerson well, but years ago he'd taken political science courses from him at the University of Maine. He'd been impressed with the man then. He'd been impressed again when Emerson became president.

Morgan liked Tremaine, although he'd been unknown to him until the campaign. He sensed right away that Tremaine was straightforward and honest. Morgan had followed carefully what he had to say during the presidential race. Tremaine and Emerson had made a good team. Morgan's initial antipathy for those who'd opposed the Vietnam War had given way to a grudging respect for the man. He'd read the press reports and the speech Tremaine had given at Boston University the week after Emerson's death. Morgan found himself agreeing with what the new President had said. Tremaine articulated his views clearly and was a keen observer of life.

The interviews Morgan had with Tremaine had been lengthy and substantial, lasting more than a week. Overall, they'd been a delightful surprise. Morgan found Tremaine a relaxed and attentive person with a mind free of preconceptions. Tremaine's questions had been probing and far-reaching. He wanted to know Morgan's thoughts on foreign affairs. He had dug deeply into his views on the Middle East, asking the basis for his observations and conclusions. For four days they had explored the issues of crime, the courts, guns, violence, drugs, poverty, unemployment, the effects of the demilitarization of American industry, globalization, and foreign policy.

Tremaine wanted to know why Morgan thought the way he did, what he saw as key issues, what ideas he had concerning the resolution of the difficulties facing the country. At one point he had said, "Some accuse me of being a philosopher and not a practical man. My response is that philosophy sets the tone, expresses a fundamental way of seeing life and our role in it as human beings. Philosophical understanding is imbedded in all cultures and all ages. It is from this context that behavior springs forth. In order to truly understand behavior, it is necessary to understand the philosophical background from which it emerges."

Morgan found himself coming back to that statement over and over again. The more he thought about it, the more he sensed it was true. Under Tremaine's probing, Morgan was again reminded that public service was a high calling when it expressed the sincere unselfish desire to serve. He knew by the end of the interviews that he and the President were in complete accord in their understanding of service. Morgan found himself smiling. He was excited to be in this position. It was going to be challenging, but what an opportunity, an opportunity to serve.

Morgan climbed carefully onto a large rock partially imbedded in the ground, left by glaciers, thousands of years ago. He made himself comfortable. The rock was still warm from the sun. It was pleasant in the cool evening air. Birds gathered high in the trees, anticipating the end of day. All about him the cacophony of their cries was a pleasing welcome.

It was already dark when he saw the lights through the trees, warm and welcoming. As he approached the house, he could see Marianne through the window, working in the kitchen. He chuckled to himself. He could still see the pained look on the cook's face when Marianne had patiently explained that she enjoyed cooking and was not about to give up control of "her" kitchen, no matter where she lived, no matter what position her husband held.

For twenty-seven years they'd been married. Twenty-seven years of joys and sorrows, hopes and disappointments. Life had been rich and rewarding. He and Marianne had three children, two boys and a girl. Mary, the youngest, had married a fisherman and together they crewed their forty-foot fish boat off the rugged coast of northern Maine. Ross, the eldest, was an accountant for a firm in Cambridge. Ted, their middle boy, had entered medical school four years ago at the University of California in San Francisco.

The thought of his son Ted brought a rush of emotion. During a mid-semester break, Ted had gone with his friend Damien to his home in Los Angeles. The two of them had played basketball in a park near Damien's home. By all accounts, it had been an enjoyable reunion with some of Damien's high school buddies. They'd played for several hours. With slaps on the back and firm handshakes, they had parted. They went their separate ways, with light hearts and tired bodies.

Ted and Damien had walked five of the seven blocks home when they rounded a corner and found themselves caught in the crossfire between two rival gangs. Ted, mortally wounded, died before they could get him to hospital. Damien had received a gunshot wound to his thigh.

Ted's death had hit the family hard. It had been devastating to Marianne. She'd become severely depressed. Morgan had cut back his duties in the Senate, taken himself off several committees and reached out to his wife. The death of their son brought them closer together, further solidifying their friendship. Death made one realize what was really important, the intangibles such as love and appreciation, he thought.

His son's death had given rise to a fierce desire to bring an end to the needless violence that plagued so much of the nation. Somehow, he wanted to help. He loved this country: the vast diversity of its land, the aspirations of its founding fathers and the spirit of its people. This democracy, founded with so much hope and boundless enthusiasm, was in trouble. It seemed that too many of its citizens had abrogated their responsibility and now saw themselves as helpless victims. The price of being taken care of was the loss of one's autonomy. The government had taken over, stepped in where citizens had stepped out, and now they felt powerless.

In the years since Ted's death, Morgan and Marianne had found nothing that offered them the hope they sought. However, when Morgan had described his conversations with Tremaine, he was pleased to see the excitement and hope that had suddenly appeared in his wife's face. Her expression served to confirm what he sensed for himself. He had the feeling the country was on the verge of much needed change, a change that would not be heralded with great fanfare. No, this time it would be different.

It would be profound, perhaps linked to the philosophical understanding of the new President. Tremaine had rekindled in Morgan his own sense of inspiration and the wondrous anticipation of new possibilities and true service.

16

A Vision of Possibilities

"Good evening," Tremaine stood before the podium. He was to address the National League of Women Voters at their annual meeting in San Diego. "This evening I want to sketch out a comprehensive and holistic approach to health care that our administration will soon embark upon.

"There are three areas I wish to discuss under this heading. One has to do with theoretical considerations underlying present medical practice. The second has to do with food, and includes current agricultural practices; the third has to do with health care providers. I will present you with a vision of possibilities.

"You may wonder how we will accomplish this and I must admit that I don't know the details at the moment. When President Kennedy spoke of putting a man on the moon within ten years he created a context for that event. At the time he didn't know how it would happen he just knew it would. The vision I'll be sharing with you can be held in a similar fashion. Our goal is to have it in place within ten years.

"There are an estimated 250,000 deaths per year in this country's hospitals caused by Western allopathic medical practices. Compare this with 42,000 deaths last year from automobile accidents. Dr. Barbara Starfield, MD, MPH, of the Johns Hopkins School of Hygiene and Public Health reported the following facts. 12,000 deaths per year from unnecessary surgery; 7,000 deaths per year from medication errors in hospitals; 20,000 deaths per year from other errors in hospitals; 80,000 deaths from infections acquired while in hospitals and a 106,000 thousand deaths resulting from adverse reactions to correctly prescribed medications in those hospitals. These statistics do not reflect the deaths occurring from allopathic practices by physicians outside hospitals. According to the statistics cited it is safer to ride in a car than enter a hospital for treatment. This is not acceptable. To me, these statistics point to a major theoretical problem with Western medicine.

"It can be argued that Western medicine as practiced today with its emphasis on drug therapies is based on a premise that is at best questionable. Louise Pasteur a nineteenth century physician played an important role in the development of the germ theory, which stated that disease is caused by a variety of infectious organisms. Pasteur devoted most of his life to discovering substances that would kill these organisms one of which was penicillin. Another nineteenth century French scientist, a contemporary of Pasteur by the name of Claude Bernard suggested another approach to disease and its treatment. What Bernard proposed was that the health of the human organism was determined by the body's internal environment. His point was that if the internal environment maintained an optimum balance, it would resist infectious diseases and when the internal environment was out of balance, the body was susceptible to disease. A Russian scientist by the name of Elie Metchnikoff, the discoverer of white blood cells, was also a proponent of the internal harmony theory of the organism. Metchnikoff believed, like Bernard, that the best way for the human being to resist disease was to support its own natural defense systems. To prove his theory he and his research associates consumed millions of cholera bacteria and not one of them became ill. This would explain why some who are exposed to disease become infected and others don't. Those who have good immune systems are able to maintain health despite the presence of disease.

"During the latter part of their lives Pasteur and Bernard carried on a discussion on the scientific merits of the germ theory and the internal terrain theory. At the time of his death Pasteur stated, 'Bernard was right. The pathogen is nothing. The terrain is everything.' It is unfortunate that Western medicine had, by the time of Pasteur's death, accepted the germ theory and disregarded the terrain theory, which has since become virtually unknown. What this means is that the use of drug therapy is based on an inadequate premise. Infectious diseases are communicated by infectious agents but only when the immune system is not operating optimally. The ever-increasing reliance on drugs indicates we are moving further and further in the wrong direction. The problem is compounded by the power of the pharmaceutical industry, which reaps immense profit from the manufacture of drugs. As a result they are loath to accept any theory or research that would question the current belief in germ theory. As Barbara Starfield's statistics prove, even the use of correctly prescribed drugs are more lethal than driving a car.

"Now I wish to move to the second major area of focus. The late Dr. Max Gerson was a well-known German physician who successfully treated patients with a number of deadly illnesses including tuberculosis and all forms of cancer. Albert Schweitzer's wife was cured of lung tuberculosis and Schweitzer himself of diabetes. Gerson did this not through the use of drugs but through diet and a rigorous detoxification process. In 1946 he was invited to address the Pepper-Neely Congressional Subcommittee where he presented his findings from twenty-two years of meticulous research. At one point he was asked what was the key upon which health and disease turned. He responded that the most important source for our health or lack of it could be found in the soils that grow our food. If the soil is unhealthy so is our food and if our food is unhealthy the effect on the body over time is, the onset of disease. Obviously if we are to effectively shift our focus from allopathic medicine we must first restore the health of our agricultural practices and thus the fuel the body uses.

"My wife and I have a friend who is a physician in Canada, an intelligent woman. One day we were in conversation with her and found ourselves discussing the research of Doctor Barry Sears, which has a great deal to do with food and how the body processes it. She looked at me shaking her head and said, 'What you're talking about is beyond my expertise, I know nothing about diet and the effects on the body.' I was astounded. 'How come?' I asked. 'When I was in medical school there were no courses on diet, in fact diet is not taught in any of our medical schools as far as I know.' At the time she had only been out of medical school five years.

"Food is the fuel that keeps us alive. We know that if we use incorrect fuel in our vehicles they don't run properly. The same is true with the fuel put in the human body. We are facing an epidemic of obesity in our nation; you've all seen the figures. The young are particularly vulnerable. There is general consensus that there are two basic reasons for this, unhealthy food and lack of exercise. To resolve this problem and prevent major problems later in the lives of our young people we will introduce the most up to date and comprehensive educational programs on diet and the biological understanding of how food is used in the body. We will re-instate physical education programs in all schools in order for children to have a combination of daily physical activity along with their academic courses of study. The courses will be mandatory.

"To educate our children in these matters would be insufficient without also addressing food production. Agricultural practices have become increasingly centralized and what we see is the emergence of huge industrial factory-farms where large numbers of animals live in overcrowded conditions. This has taken place in the beef, pork, poultry and fish industries. There is a broad consensus of research that points to major problems when living beings of any kind are placed in confined and crowded spaces. Cancers, unusual growths and tumors are some of the results of these conditions. To counteract such problems the industries resort to the use of hormones to speed up growth so that animals come to market more quickly. By doing this it is hoped that the cancers will have less chance to develop. In addition, the animals are fed a wide range of antibiotics to help stave off infectious diseases until they can be slaughtered. The end result is that the public is being exposed to a food supply that puts them at risk, at risk from hormones that have been proven to create birth defects, at risk from diseased animals, and at risk from antibiotic contamination.

"Another problem arises from the amount of waste that factory-farms produce. In the summer of 2000 a large segment of the population of Walkerton, a town in Ontario, Canada, became ill followed by several deaths. Later investigation linked the illness to E-coli emanating from waste seeping into the water system from a local farm. Current farm practices increase the risk of drinking water contamination in many rural communities. Communities that once had excellent water are now finding that it has to be treated.

"These problems are not just taking place on land. They are happening in our oceans as well. Fish farms, for instance, in the Pacific Northwest are situated in protected waters where the tide is used to flush the accumulated waste. This in turn damages larger and larger segments of the ocean floor, disrupting the food chain of other species in the area. In addition the salmon grown in these overcrowded pens are a species of Atlantic salmon not found in the Pacific. Over the last several years hundreds of thousands have escaped into the wild and now compete with the native salmon of the area. The growth of fish farms have had a negative impact on fishing along the coast because restaurants prefer farmed salmon over wild salmon, largely for cosmetic reasons and because of year round availability; this despite the need to add food coloring and problems with antibiotic contamination.

"In the 1900s farms were generally small family-run operations. The food produced was sold and distributed in neighboring areas, nearby towns and cities. By the 1960's small farms were beginning to disappear and by the year 2000 had almost completely vanished, replaced by massive factory-farms. Whereas in the first half of the twentieth century, food distribution tended to be local and shipping costs comparatively low we now have very little local distribution and complex shipping and storage industries utilizing refrigerated warehouses, trucks, trains and planes. The cost of distribution, and refrigeration is inefficient by comparison and utilizes substantial energy resources. Two years ago we suffered a major power blackout that affected large portions of the southwest. We were fortunate it lasted only four days. But, in those four days we had massive food spoilage and the problem of what to do with the spoiled food afterwards.

"As we've moved away from small farms we've become increasingly reliant on chemical fertilizers and pesticides and the use of organic methods has declined. The result has been to deplete our soils, killing off the microbes and worms that aerate the soil which in turn has caused our foods to be less nutritious than they were seventy, fifty or twenty years ago.

"As a first step we will initiate measures that support greater agricultural diversity, a movement away from industrial farming as well as decentralizing the locus of our food production. This will make us less reliant on the large storage and distribution infrastructure currently being used; thereby reducing energy costs. At the same time we will move toward the restoration of our soils through increased emphasis on organic methods and crop rotation. This process will be comprehensive and long term. It will not come about overnight. We will encourage a return to the land and the establishment of smaller farms that utilize healthier agricultural practices for the growing of this most precious of commodities, our food.

"We will implement legislation that prevents overcrowding of animals in confined spaces and put a stop to the use of growth hormones and antibiotics in food production. We will make it a top priority to restore balance and health to our soils and oceans. We cannot afford to be focused on short-term profit. We must put our energies toward sustainable, efficient, and healthy food production. Our emphasis will shift from the accumulation of financial wealth amongst a few, to long term human health for all.

"Now I wish to move to the third major focus, that of health care providers. Today we find ourselves suffering from a worldwide shortage of nurses, which will only get worse as the baby boomers move along life's path. There is also a growing shortage of physicians and most of the physicians we do have are found in the larger population centers. Our healthcare costs are increasing at an alarming rate and are utilizing more and more of our resources. We cannot afford for this increase to be sustained for many more years. We must take steps to correct it now.

"Generally speaking the medicine practiced in North America is allopathic in nature. By and large we have not practiced preventive medicine. And in the long run preventive medicine is the most cost effective method known; far better to maintain health than try and restore it once lost.

"As soon as financial considerations enter into the health picture we have a conflict of interest. I'll give you two examples. We have an Aides pandemic that is impacting the population of many countries in Africa. Stephen Lewis, the Canadian special envoy to the UN on HIV/Aids has been calling upon countries to make drugs available to those who can't afford the high cost of treatment. The drug companies have resisted and put pressure on Western nations not to move to generic drugs; the argument being that if they cannot make a profit they cannot invest in the needed research and development for newer and better drugs. To date, only Canada has resisted the pressure and has expressed a willingness to help. What is the problem? The problem comes from competing objectives. The drug companies are large multi and trans national corporations; businesses whose primary objective is profit. This conflicts with the primary objective of medicine, which is to help restore health and prevent disease. Setting aside for the moment the questionable validity of pharmaceuticals it is obvious that for these companies profit is more important than the lives of people.

"As most of you are aware there are some health care systems, in the world, that provide physicians with a salary for their work instead of the cumbersome fee for service model we've employed. This enables a doctor to take whatever time is needed for his patient. He is not motivated by trying to see as many patients as he can in the shortest possible time, thereby increasing his income. To administer the fee for service model is more complex and more costly than the salary model, which is straightforward and more easily administered.

"Several years ago my wife attended a weekend gathering in Canada sponsored by the local nursing center. The purpose of the conference was to present more effective ways of providing health care delivery to meet the needs of the community. All the physicians in the town were invited, more than a hundred all told. One of the presenters was a salaried physician who worked in the north. When the local physicians learned he was one of the presenters they tried to have him removed from the agenda. When they were unsuccessful they boycotted the conference;

not one of them attended. We might well ask what was their priority, money or medicine?

"Several years ago I happened to be in Bombay. I'd been ill for several weeks. It was suggested I go to the Bombay hospital to see a particular physician. I took with me a friend, Prakash, who was dying from liver failure, a man of a lower caste without sufficient income to get himself to the hospital. When we arrived at the doctor's office I noticed the sign over the door. Beneath the doctors name was the following title: 'Chief of Pediatrics and Parapsychology.' I was a little taken aback, given my Western background.

"Upon entering his office we were welcomed by a man in his late sixties. I explained the nature of our visit. Prakash was told to sit in front of the doctor's large desk. Then the doctor reached over and took my friend's thumbs between the first and second fingers of his hands. He closed his eyes for a moment then letting go took a pen and drew a line vertically on a sheet of paper and proceeded to write something on either side of the line. Taking Prakash's thumbs again he repeated the procedure several more times until the paper was full. Afterward he repeated the same process with me. When he was finished he wrote a prescription of Ayurvedic herbs for both of us. He told me they would be sufficient for my friend's complete recovery. He then directed me to the chemist shop across from the hospital. Before I left the office I offered to pay him. He looked at me and with a smile said, 'I'm a physician, it's my calling in life, I'm paid by the hospital for my work, My job is to serve all who come to me no matter who they are or where they come from,' and with that he bowed to me, hands clasped over his heart in the traditional Indian greeting of namaste.

"In this new comprehensive policy of universal health care we will shift the emphasis from the treatment of illness to that of prevention of illness and the maintenance of health. We are going to open medical practice to include naturopaths. We will also make available Chiropractic treatment and, in addition seek to attract those who are trained in Chinese, Ayurvedic, Homeopathic and Energy medicine. All will become part of a new health care system. This will enable people to choose the method of treatment they wish. Eventually we will provide a broad and comprehensive approach to health and the treatment of illness; drawn from the best the world has to offer.

"What I've presented here is an overview of the direction in which this administration will be moving. We've already struck a committee headed by Vice-President Morgan the purpose of which is to provide a comprehensive and holistic approach to health and to create the necessary legislation and structures to implement it. This presentation commences a national discussion on this topic by providing the broad parameters of the program. We cannot bring this about in isolation it will only happen as a collective expression of the will of the people. To begin with the biggest undertaking is to create a broad understanding of the issues involved, issues all can come to understand. We can expect strong opposition from three areas in particular. One, the physicians themselves through the American Medical Association who have a vested interest in the status quo, a vested interest in fee for service medicine. I recognize that this is not the view of all physicians as there are many who still hold within their hearts the flame of the healer. Another source of opposition will come from the pharmaceutical companies and a third will come from the agribusiness industry. I would suggest that in all three cases opposition would ultimately be found to arise from the motive of money over medicine, profit over people.

"Three weeks ago we forwarded copies of this speech to the AMA to the major drug companies and representatives of agribusiness. We have since received strong opposition to the ideas expressed. We don't expect the opposition to diminish but I have faith in the intelligence and thoughtfulness of our people when presented with the facts. Thank you for your time."

....

Over the next month the Committee on Health Care formed several sub committees under the three main categories outlined in Tremaine's speech. Major universities were involved in the project and funding for research was already in place. Opposition to the "New Initiative In Health Care," as it was called was swift. But Tremaine and members of the committee continue to involve the general public in an ongoing discussion aimed at understanding the various aspects of the "Initiative." Tremaine and Morgan maintained that accomplishment of the objectives would indeed take place. What the Committee was charged with was to find the best possible way to bring it about.

17

Master of deception

I want a copy right away," Senator Cole said into the phone. "No, I don't give a damn how you get it, just get it. No, in my office by tomorrow morning.... What do you mean you can't get it by then? By when? Okay, have it on my desk by Tuesday morning at nine.... Yes.... Yes, I know. No, you don't need to be concerned, no one will know. No, we'll keep you out of it.... If your name comes up, we'll just deny it. No, you don't have anything to worry about.... Okay, Thanks! Good-bye."

As Senator Cole put the phone down, a cynical smile spread over his face. He picked up a cigar. Biting the end off, he spit it into his wastebasket, a skill he'd gained over years of practice. Flicking a lighter, he puffed until a cloud of smoke billowed above him. He pulled out the writing tray at his desk, put his feet up, leaned back in his expensive old leather chair and puffed contentedly. Life was good, and he was at the pinnacle of his power.

A man in his late fifties, Cole had greasy, thinning hair that gave him a seedy look. He was five foot ten and weighed two hundred pounds. He was a hard drinker with a sallow complexion. The cold gray of his eyes was ameliorated by a wateriness that sometimes gave an onlooker the unsettling feeling that he was crying. He had a reputation for getting his way and was known to be savvy and unscrupulous. He knew what he wanted, and was not easily swayed by the opinions of others. After the defeat of the Republican administration, he had assumed the de facto leadership of his party and had become the spokesman for their policies.

Despite the fall of the previous administration, Cole had somehow remained clear of scandal himself. There was talk that he'd been involved in the whole Japan affair, but no one could substantiate anything. As minority leader, he kept a tight rein on his fellow Republicans. Most of them stayed in line. Legislation that passed did so only because the Democrats had a majority. Even then, there were numerous riders attached.

He'd hated Emerson with a passion and had made it his mission to disrupt him in every way possible. When Tremaine assumed power, he had continued the same policy with one additional proviso. Tremaine didn't even possess the saving grace of having served in the military. Tremaine was a maverick, an unconventional thinker, more difficult to handle than Emerson.

It was Cole who had ordered his henchmen to dig into Tremaine's past. What he had found he leaked to the press. Several times, he was sure his revelations would ruin the man and force his resignation, but time after time, the President slipped away unscathed. The press has gone soft, he thought. Never mind, he was a patient man; sooner or later, Tremaine would slip up. No one could be that smart. Besides, he had a lead on something. If it proved true, Tremaine would have to step down.

The phone rang. Cole picked it up.

"Yes, Midge, put him through. Hello, Cole here.... Who?... Congressman Smythe. Thanks for getting back to me. I understand you want to look at the budget that's coming down... I know it's not down yet.... Yes, I know, but I don't want any surprises.... You know what I mean. We vote as a block, no breaking ranks.... I know how Emerson thinks. It was his budget until he died. Tremaine will follow his lead on this matter.... No, it's not a Republican budget.... I don't give a damn. If you break ranks with us, you'll not get your grain subsidy bill into committee.... No, Smythe, don't give me any of that liberal crap. We already know how this administration works.... Listen, son, I've been around the Hill for a long time. I know how things work. Tremaine's no different from any other Democratic president.... No, he doesn't make more sense. He's a con artist who's good with words, that's all.... I'm not going to argue with you.... Just keep in mind who your friends are.... Right, Right.... As soon as I get a copy of the budget I'll let you know.... Good.... Yes.... Next week.... Good .... Good.... Okay.... Yes, there's still an opening on that committee.... Good.... Then we understand each other.... I'll be in touch.... Bye."

Cole put the phone down and, leaning back, lit his cigar again and puffed hard. Through the clouds of smoke, a low shaft of sunlight struck a wilted bouquet of flowers and fallen petals on the corner of his desk. It had been another full day. Four days it had taken him. He'd been on the phone with every Republican on the Hill. He was satisfied now, certain he had them all in line. They'll follow my lead and there'll be no surprises, he thought. My troops are well disciplined. Pressing a button, he spoke into the intercom.

"Midge, did that memo get sent out to McClelland's?"

"Yes, it went out yesterday."

"Anonymously?"

"Yes."

"Good. I'm finished for the day. I'll be back in the morning at nine. Have a nice evening."

"I will. You too," came the disembodied voice.

....

Three days later, Mark Turner, the president of McClelland's, sat at his desk. He finished reading the letter and was angry. He buzzed for his secretary. An elderly woman with white hair and a pleasing smile pushed the door open.

"Mary, where's Angus?" he demanded.

The smile vanished from her face. "He went out to lunch with the Canadians. He said he'd be back by three. He should be here any moment." She looked at her watch.

"As soon as he gets back, send him in; I need to talk with him. Tell him if he's got something else going on, he'll have to put it on hold."

Mary nodded and left. She had known he'd be upset, but she hadn't expected such a strong reaction. Turner was not by nature an angry man. He tended to be quiet and self-contained. Fifteen minutes later, Angus walked breezily into the office. Mary gave him the message.

"What's it about?" he asked.

"He received a letter saying the president is about to issue an order that all paper used by the government must be recycled."

The news was a jolt to Angus too. He knocked on the door and pushed it open.

"Come in, come in," Turner muttered impatiently.

Angus walked to the desk. Turner indicated the letter.

"Read it," he said.

Angus picked up the letter and sat down. Quickly, he glanced it over and tossed it back on the desk.

"If it's true, it's bad news," he said.

"You're damned right it's bad news," Turner sputtered. "We've got to find out and quick. Who would know?"

"There are several people I can think of."

"Get on it right away. Find out all you can and get back to me. If it's true, we've got to put a stop to it."

"Right. I'll get on it at once. I'll have to fly to Washington though, I can't do it from here."

"I don't care how you do it, just get it done."

Angus knew by Turner's voice that he was dismissed. Outside

the inner office, he talked briefly with Mary, giving her instructions.

"Call me at home when you've booked the flight. I'm going to pack and let Julie know."

....

Turner swiveled in his chair and looked out over the city. In the distance, above the haze, he could see the mountains of the Olympic Peninsula. Damn, he thought, this couldn't come at a worse time. The Canadian Company, Crown McClelland, had just settled a contract dispute following a lengthy strike. On top of that, the Canadian government had increased the stump rate for Crown Lands. The advantage American companies had enjoyed as a result of the difference in currencies had almost been eroded by the increased prices. Only the steadily increasing purchase of paper by government bureaucracies in Washington had enabled them to afford such a high settlement in the Canadian operations.

If the government was going to use recycled paper, McClelland's mills were just not equipped for it. Existing contracts were due to be renegotiated in January. They could lose business to the smaller companies, some of which had already developed the capacity to use the recycled paper by mixing it with their existing pulp. Turner shook his head.

We can't let this happen, he thought. Angus is good; the people he knows are powerful. Damn it, we'll have to invest more money in the Political Action Committees. This is not something we expected. Our budget is set. Shit, this will take a lot of work and money and still we could lose it all.

Turner gazed through the window. The Olympic Mountains had assumed the purple haze of late afternoon. All his life he'd sought out the mountains when he was troubled. They calmed him. At this time of day there was a marvelous beauty to them. A niggling thought insinuated itself in his mind and he tried to put it aside. Perhaps we've been greedy and shortsighted. Perhaps we've taken the land and the trees for granted. Fifty years ago, when he first started out in the forestry industry, no one had ever thought that the vast wilderness of Canada would someday be unable to meet the demand for trees.

The same thing was happening now to the tropical rain forests. Have we abused the land and now the time has come to pay the piper? He didn't want to think about it. The problem was beyond him; it was not up to him to deal with it. Soon those matters would be in the hands of a new generation. He was a businessman entrusted with running a company. His stockholders expected him to make money for them in the shortest possible time. Besides, few of them would still be alive fifty years from now, so what did it matter?

He pushed the thought into the back of his mind. It wasn't up to him to set policy or resolve the world's difficulties. Business was business. Turning around, he reached for the desk lamp and switched on the light. Its opaque green glass shielded his eyes and its warm glow fell on the papers scattered across the highly polished wooden desk. Slowly, he sorted them and put them away. Standing, he pushed his chair neatly in place, took his coat from the rack and walked out of the office. "Good evening," He muttered.

Mary watched him go as the door swung shut behind him.

....

Friday evening, Angus left the Hill and caught a taxi back to his hotel. He sat back and relaxed, thinking of the events that had transpired since his arrival two weeks before. He'd mobilized the Political Action Committee and invaded the Hill. Not a congressman or senator had been missed. He was satisfied now that the company was safe. No president could resist the opposition he'd mobilized.

He looked out the window, watching the people pass by, not really seeing them. Tomorrow, he'd catch a plane. By evening, be home. Sunday he'd go fishing. He smiled in anticipation. He was glad to leave the city.

18

A plea for help

Michael Levin dispatched Joseph Goldstein, his Foreign Secretary, to meet with Tremaine and bring him up-to-date on events taking place in Israel. They met at the White House with the President and his top aides.

"We felt it was important to apprise you in person of what is happening," Goldstein said.

"Thank you." Tremaine responded.

"We've had indirect talks with the Syrians and Lebanese. If we stop attacking inside their borders and withdraw our troops, they'll do their best to rein in the guerrillas. They say they cannot promise anything, but they're willing to try. I think they mean what they say. Normally such assurances are insufficient, but we're willing to see what happens this time. In fact, we're willing to explore a wide range of options. We want your support."

"We'll be happy to play a part if we can, but it has to be a genuine undertaking on your part."

"We understand. There's been a lot of discussion between the Prime Minister and the Cabinet concerning the conversations we had with your Administration. Needless to say, there's been some stiff opposition. We don't know how far we'll get with the Knesset at the moment. The Prime Minister and I have given a lot of thought to the matter. As I've said before, we're in a very difficult position. In the past, we've felt the need to respond with considerable force when attacked.

"In the areas we occupied, we've built settlements and

the land has become productive. Our enemies want the land returned. We might consider returning it, but if we do, we'll meet fierce opposition from those who've settled there. They had the support of the past administrations that saw the settlements as a way of conveying to our enemies that, if they keep provoking us, we'll just take more and more land, and we'll keep it.

"It looks as if that strategy has painted us into a corner. Syria wants the return of the Golan Heights, Jordan wants the return of the West Bank, and we have serious problems in Gaza. Opposition to the return of these lands is also very strong. We find ourselves locked in a position from which it's difficult to extricate ourselves. We have our share of fundamentalist hard-liners who are unwilling to negotiate with the enemy, unwilling to swap captured land for peace. They see only a continued escalation of force until the countries along our borders are willing to sue for peace on our terms."

"Very unrealistic."

"Yes, unrealistic, we agree. But what do we do? As you know, going against the will of a large minority is difficult; against a majority, it is almost impossible."

"Surely your people must be tired of war," Tremaine said.

"They are."

"We won the election with a promise to explore ways to bring about peace. But the negotiations have not been fruitful, and many are skeptical. With a minority government such as ours, we would be hard pressed to survive a vote of non-confidence. The 'Intifada' continues unabated, and our people are still subject to attack wherever they go. We sense a softening in the stance of the PLO, but there's also been a proliferation in radical fundamentalists not accountable to any central authority. This is why Syria and Lebanon tell us they cannot guarantee the control of such groups."

"Our concern is that the PLO will lose control because of

so little progress in the peace process. These radical groups will increase in strength and become more intransigent, more difficult to deal with. That could derail the peace process in Israel, which is exactly what they want. If that happens, Israeli hardliners will form the next government, and the conflict will escalate even more."

"There's no doubt you've a difficult task ahead," Tremaine agreed.

"To bring about peace, the social and political problems must be resolved, particularly in such places as Gaza. We will grant Palestinian self-rule, but there can be no effective self-rule in an area where there are few jobs, no social structures, sewage treatment plants, housing, medical facilities, banks and so on.

"This requires a large financial undertaking. I'm not sure anything like this has been done before. However, until we deal with these issues, Israel's safety will remain at risk and peace will not be possible. Like it or not, we are inextricably bound to the Palestinians. No matter how distasteful, the fact is we need each other to survive."

"I think you're right."

"We need your help."

"What do you have in mind?" Tremaine asked.

"We're extending an invitation to you and your wife to visit Israel in the near future. We want you to see firsthand the country and the kind of situations we face. We want you to address the Knesset. Although the Prime Minister and I found your remarks provocative during our last meeting, upon further consideration we realized they made sense. For us to say some of those things to our countrymen would be to invite political suicide. For you to say such things could help us a great deal, and help further the peace process, with no risk to you. You offered your assistance. This is one of the ways we think you can help."

"I would be happy to be of assistance. I'll have to look at times that I have available. How soon do you need to know?"

"I fly back tomorrow. If you know by then, fine; if not, you can let us know through normal channels. There's no deadline, but the sooner the better."

"I'll let you know before you return; the details can be worked out later. If we have any questions, where can we reach you?"

"I'll be at the embassy; you can reach me there."

"Great," said Tremaine, standing. The four men shook hands and Tremaine saw Joseph to the door.

"I'll be in touch," Tremaine said. "Jonathan, get my schedule and go over it with Elsie."

"Are you going?" Jonathan asked, trying to hide a smile.

"Of course. I'll visit Jordan, Lebanon and Syria while I'm there. I want you to set up the trip and coordinate it with Elsie."

For two hours, they discussed the options, objectives, dangers and opportunities of such an undertaking.

....

Cole sat back in his favorite recliner. He was alone in the den, engrossed in a baseball game on TV. The bases were loaded. The Red Sox were up to bat in the last inning. He swished the ice and whisky in his glass and took a long swallow.

The phone rang in the hall and his wife picked it up. A line drive to center field held his attention, and the announcer's excited voice filled the room. He didn't hear his wife enter.

"It's for you," she said, tapping him on the shoulder.

"Just a minute, dear." The throw to home plate was fumbled and a run scored. The fans erupted, and the announcer went wild.

"Take a message, dear, I'll call back later."

"They insisted on speaking with you now."

"Iris, I told you I'm not available to take calls."

"I know, dear, but he was insistent. It's Williams."

Cole flicked the mute button, got up and crossed the room to his desk. "I'll take it here," he said. He waited for his wife to leave before he picked up the phone. He said nothing until he heard the click of the phone in the hall.

"Cole here." He listened intently. "Are you sure? What's the woman's name? Jennifer Ramirez.... And she has a daughter, you say? How old? Eighteen. And Tremaine's the father?... You're sure?... She's prepared to go public with this?... Can she take the pressure?... Good. Look, meet me at the Toledo tonight at ten? Bring everything you've got... Yes, I'll see you at ten."

Cole hung up the phone and smiled. "Gotcha, you bastard! Let's see you squirm out of this."

≡19

Dispeller of darkness

Nassir sat quietly waiting, his back against the trunk of an old cedar. He had a clear view across the undulating hills that fell away to the Mediterranean in the west. To the east, the hills gave way to the steep sides of the mountains with their rocky peaks. Six months had passed since he had taken Shamir into the mountains. They'd walked and talked, and many tears had fallen down her dark, pretty face.

Shamir took it upon herself to prepare meals that Nassir and his brother enjoyed. It was good to have the presence and skills of a woman in his life again. He'd forgotten the different perspective a woman can bring, and he appreciated her input. She was good with animals as well, and she soon learned to work with the sheep. His brother had readily accepted her, and, in his own simple way, showed his appreciation for her.

With the recent conflict between the guerrillas and the Israelis, Nassir moved further north away from the border. Under his guidance, they'd been careful not to draw attention to themselves. Some of the guerrillas that operated in Lebanon were men from outside the country and could be dangerous if encountered. He preferred caution to conflict.

Two days ago, he learned that Kahlil wanted to see him. They'd meet at the old cedar grove. Shamir wanted to know where he was going, but he preferred not to involve her. She packed his skins with nuts, dried fruits and meat and then he left, telling her he'd return in two days. She was afraid, he could see it in her face. She was brave though, and he knew she'd be fine.

....

More than twenty years had passed since he had first begun to meet the men and women who sought him out. The train of events had begun innocently enough one evening in Tyre. Several years after the death of his father and brother he'd gone to pick up supplies.

That evening he walked beside the ocean watching the activities of the fishermen around their boats. Suddenly, he saw his friend Hafaz coming toward him. Nassir hadn't seen him since they'd ambushed the Israeli convoy twenty years earlier. Hafaz had aged; he looked worn-out. Nassir watched his old friend approaching, and he sensed the bitterness and sorrow that seemed to ooze from him. When Hafaz was close, Nassir spoke.

"Hello, old friend."

Hafaz stopped and looked sharply at Nassir, who stood just a few feet away. Recognition lit up his face, along with the long lost joy of friendship regained. He flung his arms around Nassir, dancing and kissing him on the cheeks.

"Nassir, Nassir, I'm so glad to see you! I've thought about you often; I wondered if you were still alive! I was with your father and brother until they died. They told me you'd gone into the mountains."

"Yes, since the attack on the convoy, I've lived in the mountains. I've been tending sheep with my brother. I had enough fighting. It seemed endless and futile. I wanted no more of it."

"Nassir, do you have time? Can we sit and talk?"

They found a little place where they could sit quietly and drink the strong coffee both of them loved. Hafaz poured out the sorrow of his soul.

"Sometimes I think war is the ultimate folly. It costs so much, and when it ends you have to settle for less than when you started. In the meantime, you can't really live. In some ways, you become a brute bent on destruction. There's no room for enjoyment and love; raising a family is an impossibility. Most of those I've known are dead. And after all these years, the Israelis seem more firmly entrenched than ever. The harder we fight, the more powerful they seem to become. For so long, I've hated them and everything they represent. I've killed, mutilated and maimed hundreds of them.

"When I was younger, hatred was an all consuming fire that gave me strength. Now hatred has gutted my being and eats away at my soul. Joy is gone; death is a familiar companion. I find myself welcoming it, for life is increasingly futile."

"Hafaz, my dear friend, I know of what you speak. I hear the longing of your heart and I'm glad it's still open after all these years.

"When I went into the mountains I found myself with similar doubts to those you've expressed today. They nearly drove me crazy. I had to find an answer to them. But first I had to get away from the madness of war. Only then could I begin to get a perspective on what was going on. Like you, I was a child of loving parents and beloved brothers. And what I'd become was a vicious and capricious killer, taking insult at the slightest thing, I was a danger to myself and to all I met."

"What happened? How did you get away from it?"

"Growing up and tending the sheep with members of my family gave me familiarity with the mountains. Though I didn't realize it at the time, the mountains were a place of solace for me, a place where I could feel their stillness and their age. At night, I looked at the stars and wondered at my role in this vast unfathomable universe. For months I wandered alone except for occasional meetings with my brother and uncle, who tended the sheep. I felt the poison and the horrors of war slowly seeping out of me, as though absorbed by the mountains themselves. I had not, for a long time, thought of the God of our forefathers, yet one day I found myself pondering this mystery again. I didn't welcome such thoughts because the idea of God created problems I didn't want to face."

"What do you mean?"

"With the idea of God comes the idea of some kind of justice. When I looked around, there seemed to be very little of it. Then came the questions. If there really is a God, how can there be so much suffering, so much hatred and so much death? What about right and wrong? Why does my enemy prosper after stealing our land, the land of our forefathers passed down for generations? Why must an innocent young Israeli die for something he's too young to understand? Why are my enemy and I so alike, creatures of flesh and blood, love and hate, living on the same planet, a tiny speck of dust in the vast expanse of space?"

"What did you discover?"

"Those questions tormented my mind. At the same time, a subtle feeling grew deep within me. Somehow, I felt at home on this planet, in these mountains, beneath the stars. I couldn't explain it; I just felt it. I sensed there was something I didn't understand, and that this lack of understanding created the disturbance. I was tormented with doubt as to the existence of God, and eventually I came to the realization that what I believed meant nothing at all."

"I don't understand. Why did it mean nothing?"

"I saw that it really didn't matter what I believed."

"But why?"

"Because what I believed didn't have any bearing on the truth or falsity of anything.

"I still don't understand."

"I saw that my belief or lack of belief in God made

absolutely no difference. The truth was that I really didn't know whether God existed or not. At first, I saw that my rejection of the idea of God came from anger and frustration over what I considered to be the injustices of life. Later, I felt I should believe in God, that believing was the right thing to do. I was even afraid not to believe. I lived with these thoughts for some time, until I came to see that the most important thing of all was to know the truth for myself."

"What was the truth?"

"That I didn't know whether God existed or not, that was the truth! That admission was just a beginning. Until then, I'd either believed that God existed or that he didn't. As long as I believed one or the other, I was incapable of finding the truth." Nassir sipped his coffee and thought for a moment.

Hafaz looked at his friend and felt a sense of calmness that hadn't been there in the old days when they'd fought together. His black hair had begun to turn white; dark, imperturbable eyes were set in a dark face. His body seemed lean and strong. Not a trace of bitterness or pain of any kind seemed present in the tranquil expression of his friend's kind eyes. Hafaz wanted to know more about his friend. What had he found? Patiently he waited.

"We believed that by fighting the Israelis, we could force them to leave the land and go back where they came from. That was our belief. It hasn't worked. Even here, our belief had no bearing upon reality. They believed they could destroy us by wiping out our villages, by the sheer destruction they could bring upon us. That belief proved false as well. When people give up their beliefs, reality lies before them. As long as we're locked in our stubborn and self-righteous beliefs, we'll continue to kill each other. That's the futility that you spoke of."

"Yes, it is. So what can be done? We can't convince others of this, can we? We can't stop them?"

"No, we can't. They must realize for themselves, like you and I."

"So what can be done?"

"I don't know."

They talked many times following that meeting. Hafaz wanted to leave the guerrillas, but he was under tremendous pressure to keep the group intact. He was an experienced fighter, and he knew the terrain well. For him to leave would be a great loss.

Nassir remembered the last meeting they'd had. Hafaz had come into the mountains, and they had met at a prearranged spot. Nassir had waited then, as he did now for Kahlil. As usual, they'd talked late into the evening, sharing the bread and cheese Nassir had brought with him. Nassir had heard Hafaz's voice beside him as they gazed at the hills below.

"My brother, you've helped me find a measure of peace. I don't know whether I can leave the group of men I'm with or not. At first I wanted to, and yet I feel a responsibility to those younger and less experienced than myself. I've tried to speak to them about my deepest thoughts. They don't want to hear—they think I'm crazy. In their veins still beats the thrill of war, of living on the edge. As you know, my friend, that edge brings exquisite appreciation to life because we cannot know how long it will last.

"I've outlived all those my own age but you. I feel my time is near. I look out over these hills that I've loved for so long and feel their beauty as never before. I'm thankful to sit beneath the moon and feel that, despite the suffering, I'm part of the earth and part of the stars. My beliefs in God have vanished. In my heart something stirs that I've never wished to speak of before. I mention it now only because I feel you'll understand and be pleased."

Nassir put his arm around his friend's shoulders. "I understand," he said softly, smiling to himself.

"The thought has crossed my mind," Hafaz continued, "that I won't live much longer. Perhaps my destiny is to die doing what

I've been doing. If that happens, I want you to know there's peace in my heart. I feel the events that play across this planet are far beyond my comprehension. I no longer feel I have much choice, if any, in these matters. I feel like an actor playing a part in some great drama, the end of which I cannot know from here."

Nassir sat silently beside Hafaz, a deep compassion welling up inside him. He understood clearly what his friend meant.

Nassir had come to understand that separation, was in reality, illusion. Though he couldn't explain his understanding, he felt one with his friend, with all human beings, with all forms of life. He knew that the illusion of separation was somehow essential to the functioning of life in the world in which they lived. It was something he had no name for. It was something he knew. But it was also something words could not convey.

When the time came for Hafaz to depart, Nassir had walked with him for several miles. They embraced, kissed and parted. Nassir never saw Hafaz again.

....

Months later, a young man called Idries found his way to Nassir's camp. He was tired and hungry when he arrived. Nassir fed him. Over coffee, he had learned that Hafaz was dead, mortally wounded in an Israeli ambush. Some were able to escape. Hafaz had spoken to Idries of Nassir many times. Before he died, Hafaz had asked Idries to find him.

"'Tell my friend I died well because I learned to live well,'" he said. "'I'm tired of the bloodshed and glad to leave at last. Tell him I've cherished our talks and felt the silent stirring in my heart, even in the most terrible of times.'

"Then he said to tell you, 'the heart of the messenger is open, the fruit is ripe. More will come.' He said you'd know what he means."

From that time forth, there were those who sought out Nassir. Some found him, some did not. His reputation spread like a quiet whisper on a gentle breeze. He'd been known as a fierce warrior, a man who one day turned his back on fighting to find peace in the silent mountains tending his family's sheep. For years, those who tired of the bloodshed and hoped for another way came to see him. He talked with them in ones and twos, sometimes more. He met them in the hills, and mountains, in villages and towns and, occasionally, in Beirut.

....

Nassir stood and stretched. The sinking sun cast lengthening shadows, and the rocky peaks of the mountains took on the hue of peach. He turned and looked down over the hills, catching sight of a movement directly below him, two kilometers away. As he watched, two men detached themselves from some trees and turned east, following the ridge and began the long ascent to the grove in which Nassir stood. Kahlil and one of his friends, he thought.

He'd first met Kahlil two years ago. At the time, Kahlil was not in good shape. He'd lost his family. Two younger brothers had been killed fighting the Israelis. An Israeli commando unit had killed his parents, and his eldest brother had been shot in the head in front of him. He and his brother had been recalled to Beirut following an attack on a northern Israeli settlement on the western Golan. There he'd received a bullet wound. His brother had helped him escape. Once across the border of Lebanon, they had been instructed to return to Beirut. Two days later, they had met their cell leaders. Kahlil's wound had still been fresh, and his brother was concerned for his health.

The family had been staunch Muslims, and from an early age the children were indoctrinated. Their duty as Muslims required them to do everything in their power to destroy the infidel. Jews, and the great Satan across the sea, were the enemies. Kahlil and Habish had seen the brutality of the Israeli soldiers and the destruction that their warplanes brought. Eagerly, they awaited the opportunity to slip away from their families and join with other patriots who sought to drive the infidel into the sea. Perhaps if they were lucky, they'd find and kill some of the Americans who were known to work with the Israelis.

Habish and Kahlil wondered why they'd been recalled. It was late afternoon when the old van carrying them pulled in front of a bombed-out building. They were led through the rubble and past several crumbling walls to the back of another building. Entering a doorway, they climbed a set of narrow stairs and found themselves in a dark hall. The guide knocked on a door. It opened, and they were quickly whisked inside. With the heavy sound of a dead bolt, the door closed behind them. There was little light in the room, and Kahlil suddenly felt afraid. He'd never felt afraid around his own people before.

A candle burned on an old crate directly in front of them. Looking around the room, he saw men sitting on chairs and old sagging couches. The smell of stale sweat and tobacco filled the room. A bearded man with short-cropped hair and hard, flat eyes sat directly in front of them. For two hours, they'd been forced to sit side by side and answer questions about the raid led by Habish. As the questioning went on, Kahlil found himself more and more afraid. Something was wrong. Why were they being questioned so harshly? Who were these men who presumed to question them?

For six years, Habish and Kahlil had fought together, even after the loss of their young brothers. No one had ever questioned their patriotism and allegiance to Hizballah before, but now their allegiance seemed to be in doubt. Habish must have felt the same way. He was getting angry. Suddenly he tried to stand, and he was immediately forced back into the chair. Kahlil saw the glint of a 9mm pistol placed at the back of Habish's head. The man in front suddenly moved. As though in a dream, Kahlil heard the muffled report and saw his brother jerk forward. Blood oozed from a dark spot at the back of his skull and formed a small, sinister pool on the floor. The candle guttered in the putrid air. Before he could move, he was yanked from his chair and taken away.

For weeks, Kahlil had been locked in a nearby room. He was informed that his brother was a traitor who'd questioned the orders he'd received from Beirut and could no longer be trusted. Kahlil knew his brother had been unhappy. Habish had talked to him for months about the killing, the raids, and how he thought they were counterproductive. Kahlil hadn't taken him seriously, just listened. Now he thought back to his brother's conversations and realized that perhaps he'd been serious after all.

For many days, Kahlil had been questioned. In the end, he was told to return to his unit in the south. Still in a state of shock, he found himself wondering who these men were and why his brother was a traitor. He'd been told that to fight the enemy was his duty, and to question the orders of his superiors was an act of treachery. Habish, he was told, had questioned his superiors, and it had reached a point it could no longer be tolerated. He was told, "Anyone who so forgets his duty as to question the sacred work in which we're engaged cannot be allowed to continue. If he keeps questioning, he must be eliminated. We cannot risk a man like your brother leading others in this frame of mind. He puts men's lives at risk; that must not be allowed to happen."

Kahlil returned to Tyre, where he rejoined his unit. While his shoulder healed, he remained in town. One evening, while walking slowly along the road fronting the sea, he saw a white-haired shepherd sitting on worn stone steps that led to the beach and the fishing boats. Fishermen sat hunched at their nets, sewing and swapping tales. Old men had come to talk and listen, too. The shepherd drew his attention. There was nothing unusual about him, but Kahlil felt compelled in the old man's direction. As he approached, the old man turned and fixed his eyes on the young fighter. Kahlil realized the shepherd was not as old as he'd first thought. The shepherd suddenly got to his feet and extended a hand in greeting.

"My name's Nassir," he said. "I was sent to talk with you."

Kahlil found his heart beating fast. "I'm sorry," he said. "You must have the wrong person."

"No, you're the one."

"But you don't know me."

"That's what you think."

With a jolt, Kahlil wondered if this was a spy sent from the Beirut cell.

"You need not concern yourself. I'm not a spy," Nassir said with a humorous smile.

Kahlil felt disoriented. How could this man know what he was thinking?

He looked at Nassir and immediately felt at ease. He was surprised; he realized he had nothing to fear from this man.

"Would you join me for coffee?" Nassir asked.

Kahlil agreed, and within a few minutes they were seated at a small table. They were in the very same place Nassir and Hafaz had first sat so many years ago. Nassir put his cup down and looked directly at Kahlil.

"Kahlil, there's a heaviness in your heart and a disturbance in your mind. In such a state, a great opportunity awaits."

"How do you know my name?"

"I don't know. I just do."

Kahlil's mind was swamped with questions. "I don't understand," he said, shaking his head.

"You don't have to."

"What makes you think I have a heavy heart, and that my mind is disturbed?"

"I see it, that's all."

"See what?"

"The violent death of your brother, a death brought about because he questioned what he was doing, as you have now begun to do."

Kahlil found himself shaking. "Who are you?"

"I've told you, I'm Nassir."

"You know what I mean."

"You're right." Nassir paused for a moment and looked at Kahlil, assessing him.

"For as long as I can remember, I've known things about people. At first I thought everyone had the same ability. Only as I grew older did I learn this was not the case. From time to time I find myself drawn to places where I meet certain people. When I see them, I know things about them. All of them are hungry for the truth and weary of deception. I live and work as a shepherd in the mountains with my brother. For years, I fought the Israelis. One day, sickened by the violence and bloodshed, I turned my back on it and went into the mountains to be alone, to think and to find the truth I needed to find."

"You just walked away from it?"

"Yes."

"And you never went back?"

"No."

"Didn't anyone try to track you down and bring you back?"

"No. Our unit was small, and made up of Lebanese who'd suffered at the hands of the Israelis. We were like a family."

"It's not that way anymore," Kahlil said. "Now we have Iranians with us. They speak the truth for all Muslims who are engaged in the struggle against the ungodly. They direct us, and they'll tolerate no doubt in the word of God. My brother's misgivings led them to kill him."

"What makes you think that what they say is the word of God?" Nassir asked.

"They say God doesn't compromise with evil, and that evil

should be destroyed using any means necessary. If the destruction of evil means dying in the process, then it is better to die than to live in such an unholy world. Besides, if we become martyrs for the cause, the members of our families will be ushered into Paradise when the time comes, and we will be looked after by the virgins."

"What do you think?"

Kahlil looked around, suddenly nervous.

"You're safe here," Nassir assured him.

"My brother was a good man. I think he'd begun to question whether the killing was accomplishing anything. He could see it was destroying the young men of our country, while the Israelis seemed to grow in strength and numbers. He also began questioning what he was taught by the Iranians. He asked me once if I had any idea how some men seemed to know so clearly what God wanted when he didn't. I couldn't answer his question. I'd never really thought about such things."

"What do you think now?"

"I'm not sure. I certainly began to think about it after he raised it, but we never spoke of it again. What they did to my brother is no better than what the Israelis have done to the other members of my family. My brother fought and killed for what he believed in. How could anyone doubt him? And yet, these men held a gun to his head and shot him in front of me. That I cannot accept. These last days have been terrible. I used to be glad of the guidance of those who told me what to do, those that quoted the holy Koran and explained it's meaning to me. I was glad I didn't have to think and make up my own mind. Life was easier when I only had to follow instructions."

"And now?"

"Now I'm not sure anymore. Could it be that the enemy we face is not really the enemy of nations and race, but the enemy of hatred, of power and unquestioned allegiance to our religion? Perhaps the enemy lies within us."

Nassir looked at Kahlil and smiled softly."You have said it."

"What do you mean?"

"I mean that your mind has begun to voice the questions that arise in your heart. Your doubt is the stirring of a desire for freedom. When that occurs, there's a turning inward and the true meaning of religion may at last be known."

"I want nothing else to do with religion!"

"I understand your feelings, but don't allocate the meaning of religion to the narrow-minded and bigoted. As you realized for yourself, these people appear to be the most pious of men. Such piety is anathema to the teachings of the masters. These men are in the very hell they speak of, the hell they claim to avoid. They have no idea about what they're doing, no idea about what they are teaching. They are the blind who lead the blind and as such are dangerous."

"Why dangerous?"

"Somewhere deep within them is the knowledge that they're asleep, that they don't understand. That knowledge is the beginning of freedom. Those who are afraid cannot tolerate even the hint of such a thing. So, like sleepwalkers who give the appearance of being awake, they hurt themselves and others. Among them walk the masters who are awake. From time to time, the masters feel the stirring of the sleeper and are drawn to shake him into wakefulness."

"Are you saying that all those involved in religion are asleep?"

"No, but perhaps most are."

"How could that be? What about the mullahs, the holy ones, the wise teachers, those who are there to guide us and interpret the sacred words to us?"

"None are the true masters. There are exceptions, but they are so rare they are almost nonexistent."

"And yet religion is supposed to be where truth is."

"Why should it be?"

"I don't know. It's what I've been told."

"By whom? A thief will try and convince you of his honesty,

but are his words the truth?"

"Of course not."

"So what is your own experience of these men, what they say and how they live?"

"I'm beginning to think that what they profess is not true; their hearts are cold while their words are on fire. Growing up, my brother and I knew some good mullahs who were our teachers."

"I'm sure there are many good religious men. They do the best they can, but most of them are not awake; they're not the masters I'm speaking of."

"I still don't see why."

"When you look carefully, you'll discover the religion of your forefathers is made from beliefs, some of which condone killing, torture and destruction. This should be an indicator that they did not understand what they were talking about. No master would advocate killing and torture, only the misguided and ignorant advocate such things.

"Belief is belief and has nothing to do with reality or the truth. It doesn't matter what those beliefs are and how long they've been held, they are merely beliefs. What master would be interested in living and working within the constraints of an institution that professes to know things, when in fact it does not? For these reasons, the masters go largely unnoticed. They are found by those who are ready to awaken. They remain unknown to the sleepers."

"Wasn't Jesus a master?"

"Probably."

"And Mohammed?"

"Who knows?"

"How can you tell?"

"It's impossible to tell for sure. We have to go by what they say and by their actions, but even then there's no way of knowing for certain. As I see it, truth is simple, not complex. Those who are asleep turn the knowledge of a master into beliefs. The beliefs are handed down through the generations and undergo changes that take them further and further away from the original insights of the master. It could be said that masters know, while sleepwalkers wander lost in their illusions, lost in their beliefs. There's a danger in being a great teacher such as Jesus."

"Why?"

"When a teacher becomes well known, many seek him out. Amongst the sleepwalkers some are destined to awaken, others are not. Those who aren't become afraid of him, afraid of his power, afraid that his light will expose the pettiness they feel in themselves. Sometimes the fear becomes so strong that the most fearful will seek to destroy him. Most masters are not well known. They function best in obscurity, and their teachings are handed down in secret."

"Why in secret?"

"When the master speaks, those who are not close to awakening will not understand the teaching. So it remains hidden, hidden by ignorance.

"The master sees that life has an intrinsic harmony. It's a great dance, perfect in every way. That harmony, however, is not readily apparent to most people. Yet, when the time is right, there are those who go looking for someone who knows. Then, the open heart is rewarded with the guidance it seeks. Awakening, like everything else, is a matter of destiny. Awakening blossoms as the spiritual seeker matures, and then it ripens, ready to be plucked by the hand of the Creator."

"Are you suggesting that the spiritual seeker should make every effort to practice the teachings of a master?"

"No, the teachings are not meant to be followed or practiced at all. They're merely descriptions of an inner process, understood by those who are ready."

"I get the feeling you think beliefs are not useful."

"True. When a master speaks the truth, his words are merely a description of a process. All too often, the words are misinterpreted as instructions to be followed. These instructions become codified into beliefs. The world is then divided between those who believe and those who don't. Belief is a source of conflict and bloodshed. Some of the worst atrocities the world has ever known were perpetrated by those who claim to follow the teachings of a master."

They sat quietly for a few minutes sipping coffee.

"I don't know what to do," Kahlil said. "My brother's dead, and he was the last of my family. I believed in what I did; now I'm not sure anymore. It's hard to keep focused on what's to be done. I feel hatred for those who killed him. For days, I've thought of how I could kill them. At the same time, I feel a strong bond with those in my cell. We've fought together and learned to depend on each other. I feel an allegiance to them. I can't let them down."

Nassir listened quietly; knowing there was nothing he could say. Kahlil would discover for himself what to do.

In the years that passed since that first meeting, they'd met twice in Tyre. Several times Kahlil had sought Nassir in the hills. The young man always came when he had questions. They'd sit and talk for hours and then he'd leave. Once in a while, he would bring friends with him. Nassir watched now as the two men made their way toward him.

Kahlil introduced his friend Tariq. Nassir greeted them then passed them a water skin. With practiced ease, they aimed streams of water into their mouths and slaked their thirst. For a while they sat quietly, the two younger men catching their breath. Nassir sat enveloped in the silence and the approaching darkness. The branches above stirred in the freshening breeze. Kahlil spoke.

"Our unit is moving from Tyre to Bent Jebail. Iranians and Syrians are joining the cells, and we're being divided. With the added numbers, we can launch concerted attacks from many locations at once. They've equipped us with more hand-launched rockets. There's talk of taking hostages and killing those of our own people who favor peace with the Israelis."

"Sounds like an escalation of hostilities," Nassir responded.

"Yes, there's fear that peace negotiations are going on. They intend to make them unsuccessful."

"What makes them think negotiations are going on?"

"The Israelis suddenly stopped their attacks a week ago without achieving an end to the rocket strikes across the border. For them to do so under these circumstances is unheard of."

"What else?"

"There's a lot of pressure on the political cells of South Beirut."

"Where did it come from?"

"We don't know for sure, but some think it's from the Syrian government."

"Why?"

"There's a rumor our rocket attacks have upset something that's under way. What could that be but peace?"

"Why are the Syrians and Iranians getting involved in the local cells?"

"The Iranians are hardliners; they don't want any compromise with Israel or any of its allies. They're afraid we're getting soft, like my brother. By working with us directly in the field, they can keep an eye on us, keep us on track. They're fanatics!"

"It makes us nervous," Tariq said quietly. "They constantly quote the Koran, and we must study with a mullah who travels between the cells on a regular basis."

"I see."

"The Syrians who've joined our cells are also hardliners; they want nothing but the annihilation of Israel. Hizballah, the Party of God, is dependent on Syria for supplies and arms. So it must listen to the Syrian government, which is sometimes more moderate in its approach. Hizballah will not, however, always follow instructions."

"Syria does not have complete control over us," Kahlil added.

"What else?" Nassir asked.

"As I understand it, we've been told to ease up, reorganize, reconnoiter, and get in position to launch hit-and-run rocket attacks. We know very little beyond the activities of our own cell, but we've heard we'll be working more closely with Hamas. They'll work from inside Palestine while we work from outside.

"This gives us time to re-provision with rockets and other supplies. But if there's any truth to the rumors, there may be something else behind Syria's instructions to lay off for a while. There's talk the American President may eventually come to Israel to address the Knesset."

"I see."

Once more they were quiet, each absorbed in his thoughts.

"You've been wondering how much longer you'll stay." Nassir said, voicing the question in Kahlil's mind.

"I don't know what to do. You are my teacher, and what you teach makes sense to me. But I'm not quite ready to give up what I've lived for, for so long."

"If you're meant to leave you will; if not, you won't. No anxiety on your part can change what is to come. The grass does not resist the wind. And I am not a teacher, Kahlil."

"You are to me!"

"No, I merely direct your attention to that which you already know. A teacher is someone who helps others learn something; knowledge is acquired. Look closely at our interactions. Nothing new is learned; nothing is acquired."

"I don't follow."

"You've come here when you felt the need to do so. Usually, a question was present. A question arises in the mind and seeks resolution. There's no resolution when you believe. The tension of the question still exists, while doubt remains at the heart of belief. The question is answered only when understanding dawns. That understanding is the recognition of something that has always been. And that which has always been is truth.

"We've spoken of belief before. When you believe, you mistake words for reality. Truth, which always is, remains forever obscured by the beliefs we hold so firmly. Therefore, the understanding that is truth comes when beliefs fall away. This is the reverse of what teachers do."

"So when you talk with us, you already know what we don't?" Tariq asked.

"You think there's someone over here who knows something. That is not the case. There is no one here, there is only the awareness of truth.

"So a true teacher," Tariq continued, "if I understand you correctly, draws the student to the edge of understanding, and then somehow tickles the awareness into existence."

Nassir chuckled quietly. "As I said, I don't like the term 'teacher' because it has connotations not applicable to what we've been engaged in. Nevertheless, Tariq, you've put it well. We must be aware that words are merely vehicles to convey what lies beyond them, the reality itself. I have no interest in discussions about words, only the understanding to which they point. What you've said, however, is accurate."

They talked for a while longer, then shared the meal Shamir had prepared. Before leaving, Nassir gave instructions on how to find him from Bent Jebail.

☰ 20

Ghost from the past

Jennifer Ramirez?" David was incredulous.

"Yes," Jonathan said

"Are you sure?"

"Yes. She held a press conference in San Francisco an hour ago; it's all over the news. The press is clamoring to hear from you. The switchboard is jammed with calls."

David slowly spun the chair around, leaned back and looked out the window. His mind drifted back to the day he'd first met Jennifer Ramirez, some twenty one years ago. He'd been on holiday in San Francisco. They'd carried on an affair for two years. It had been one of the contributing factors in the demise of his first marriage. David had broken it off with the hope of working out the differences with his wife, but it hadn't helped. That was the last time he'd seen Jennifer. He'd tried to get in touch with her, but had been unsuccessful. Once he had reached her mother, and she had simply told him that Jennifer had gone away. He had no idea that she'd had a child—his child. He was stunned.

"What are you going to do?" asked Jonathan.

David turned to face his friend. "I'll talk to the people through the press," he said quietly. "Let them know. Schedule it for seven this evening." He wanted to talk with Sandra before then. "See if you can get in touch with Jennifer for me, will you? I'd like to speak with her. Let me know what you find."

Jonathan nodded and left the office, closing the door

quietly behind him. David turned back and gazed into the world beyond the window, wondering about the daughter he'd never seen.

....

Two hours later, David and Sandra sat across from each other in the library.

"Have you tried getting in touch with her?" Sandra asked.

"Jonathan couldn't get through to her. All communication is being routed through her lawyer. I want to talk with her and find out what happened. I'd like to help her in any way I can. I don't want to make it difficult for her or her daughter. The press is reporting that she left after our affair because she was pregnant and deeply hurt at the sudden end to our relationship. It was hard to leave her."

"What are you going to do?"

"I'm not sure. I want to talk with her and our daughter if I can. But, we'll have to see whether that's possible."

Sandra took David's hand. "My heart is with you," she said.

"Thank you, Sandra." He lifted her hand to his lips. "I want to know your feelings, any thoughts you might have. I want to be sure you're alright."

"It took place a long time ago," she said thoughtfully. "What happened, happened. Nothing can be done to change it. Besides, who am I to judge anyone? Your relationship with Jennifer was part of your life. She was someone you loved and, it seems, someone who loved you in return. How could I not understand?

....

Jennifer sat on the edge of her seat and watched the television. Her heart was beating fast, and she felt a lump of fear in her throat.

What had she done? She watched as David stepped to the podium and listened as he spoke.

"Twenty one years ago, I had a relationship with a woman named Jennifer Ramirez, a woman I loved. For two years we were lovers and friends. I cared for her deeply. But I was married at the time and my behavior, by the conventions of society, would be considered immoral. My actions hurt my wife deeply and brought suffering to all involved. I left Jennifer to try and restore the relationship with my wife, but that didn't happen. When Jennifer and I parted I didn't know she was pregnant. I didn't know until today. If I had known I would gladly have supported the raising of our daughter. I don't have anything else to say but will take some of your questions."

Yes," Tremaine pointed to a young man in front of him.

"I imagine you have regrets…"

"If I have any regrets," Tremaine interrupted, "it is that I didn't know until now of my daughter's existence and I was not able to be a father to her while she was growing up. Those years are gone and nothing can bring them back. Perhaps now I can help make up for that lost time in some small way."

"Your behavior has brought embarrassment on the government and the people your represent. What do you have to say to the American people?"

"I'm sure there are some who will feel embarrassed by my behavior, but why should they? Think about it. What does my behavior have to do with them? It is certainly not a reflection on them in either a negative or positive manner. They are not somehow less because of what I did, nor are they better for things I've done. They are the way they are, that's all. There are things I've done that some consider immoral. There are others who hold the opposite view. There is no single standard of acceptable behavior that all can agree with.

"What happened with Jennifer happened. It cannot be

changed; it's a fact of life. Life has many twists and turns, we never know what's going to happen and yet through it all, hopefully, we become more relaxed, less judgmental and better able to enjoy life."

"I suppose you think your actions show that you've learned from that experience."

"I would hope so."

"I think your argument is self-serving," a reporter yelled above the shrill of questions.

"You're welcome to think what you wish, but don't be deceived by outward appearances."

Members of the press strained forward, microphones thrust toward the podium, flash bulbs popped. A barrage of questions and shouts filled the pressroom. "Yes." Tremaine pointed to a woman reporter on his left.

"You got this woman pregnant and failed to provide for your daughter. What makes you any different from any other deadbeat father who refused to take care of his kids?"

"Call me what you will. The fact is, until today, I was unaware that Jennifer had a child. I am happy to contribute to the expense and care involved in the raising of my daughter. Had I known, I would have done so earlier."

"Your offer comes a little late, don't you think?" the woman persisted above the shouts around her. "With all due respect to the office you hold and on behalf of single mothers everywhere, this is not acceptable behavior."

"I agree with you. This is an issue of great concern to women and, I would suggest, it is also an issue of concern to men. The fact of the matter is that I did not know of this child, and now that I do I will do everything within my power to make up for all the years that have gone by. This is not an issue that can be resolved with heated emotions or through sound bites, but rather one that deserves whatever time it needs and whatever action required and that, from my part, it will get."

Tremaine pointed to a young man at the back of the room. "Yes?"

"I assume you'll make arrangements for blood tests to determine whether you are the father or not, so my question is, will you make those tests public?"

"Your assumption is incorrect."

"You mean you're not going to have a paternity test done?"

"That's correct."

"Why not? Are you not interested in finding out for sure whether the child is yours or not?"

"If Jennifer says that I'm the father, that's good enough for me."

"And what if you're not?"

"We'll never really know. What I do know is, I loved Jennifer, she was my friend and we were lovers. Why would I not accept her word for it?"

"Will you remain in office, or will you step down, as some are urging?"

"As you suggest, there are those who will urge me to step down. But, how can I do that? I pledged myself to serve the people to the best of my ability through the office of the presidency. I am still the same man I was during the last election. That hasn't changed. The commitment made then remains, and it's what I'll continue to do."

"There are those who will argue that you should step down because you set a bad example to our youth. After all, you are a role model whether you like it or not."

"Yes, a role model, no doubt. But what kind of a role model? Not a role model that fits everyone's picture, that's for certain. If you're suggesting that in order to serve in a position of leadership one must not have had an affair, had a child out of wedlock, used drugs, gotten divorced, or opposed the war in Vietnam and so on then I would disagree with you. The problem is with those who judge, not those who are judged."

"So may I ask what you consider a good role model?"

"As far as I'm concerned a good role model is someone who was dishonest and learns to be honest; someone who was judgmental and learns to let go of it; someone filled with pride who learns first hand the need for humility; someone who knows a lot and learns how little he really knows. These attributes are more important to me than the popular pictures we hold, the conventional wisdom, so to speak."

"There are those who hold strong Christian views who make up a large portion of the electorate and do not agree with what you've done. In their minds to have an affair, a child out of wedlock, all the things you mentioned, would be reason enough for you to step down."

"I would suggest that those who truly understand the teachings of Christ will not have a problem with my behavior. Why? Christ was criticized by the Pharisees for consorting with the impure, those who did not follow the letter of the law, the outcasts of his society. Christ looked on the inside, he went by what was in the heart not by appearances. One of his disciples, Mary Magdalene, is believed to have been a prostitute. What did Christ say to those who tried to stone the woman caught in adultery? 'Let he that is without sin cast the first stone.' No one moved, not a single stone was thrown. Why? Because they knew that they were really no different from the woman they sought to kill."

"Are you not concerned about the next election? You could lose it."

"I'm not concerned. Whether I'm re-elected or not is of no concern to me. My sole interest is to do the best I can to represent the people who elected me, not in their pettiness but in their magnificence as human beings. To me the beauty of a democracy is that it promotes a good exchange of ideas, we can disagree and argue with each other, and in the end it is we the people who express our collective opinion on what transpired. I believe that most people can distinguish between someone who is trying to con them and someone who is telling the truth. That, as far as I can tell, is one of the underlying premises of a democracy. At the next election, the people will render their opinion on how I've done.

"If we do not allow for the fact that human beings learn from mistakes, then we're lost, there is no hope. Not one of you here, not in the entire country for that matter, can claim to have lived a life without mistakes. But there are many who have lived exemplary lives by learning from their mistakes, and it is this that counts more than anything else."

Through the clamor, Tremaine noticed a woman at the back of the room. She appeared to be in her late fifties, neatly dressed and unassuming. He pointed to her.

"I wonder, sir, what you mean by an exemplary life?"

"An exemplary life is a life in which honesty, integrity and accountability exist side by side."

"How can we know whether you live an exemplary life?" she pursued.

"First, I would ask you to think about what I say. Weigh my words with an open mind and an open heart. Second, put yourself in my place. Would you stand in public and admit to the things that you've done, things deemed by some of your fellow citizens to be immoral or wrong? And, if you did, what words would you use? And to those who don't believe what you say, how would you respond? Ask yourself why they don't believe you when you know you've told the truth."

"Your affair with Miss Ramirez brought an end to your marriage. It would appear that learning did not take place."

"My relationship with Jennifer did indeed contribute to the

demise of my marriage. What was learned, and is still being learned from an event like this, cannot be judged from outer appearances. There's no doubt in my mind that the things I experienced as a younger man serve me well today."

....

Jennifer remembered the last meeting with Tremaine. He'd flown down to San Francisco for the weekend.

On that Saturday, they'd they wandered along the beaches looking for shells. It was autumn, and there was frost in the air. They stopped for lunch, their faces burning in the warm air of the little restaurant still open on the strand.

Afterwards they'd walked in the park, stopped for tea and then headed back to the apartment. It was evening when they arrived. They showered and made love. It was wonderful. Afterwards, she'd slept. When she awoke, supper was almost ready, just enough time for a glass of wine. Over dinner, he told her about his wife.

"Jennifer, I don't know how to say this."

Her heart sank. She knew what was coming.

That night had been their last in each other's company. After breakfast, she'd driven him to the airport, wished him well and meant it, even though she was so miserable she wanted to die.

She had walked the beaches all day and in the evening gone to a bar and gotten horribly drunk. She had awakened the following morning in a young man's bed. As she lay there, the memory of the preceding night came back to her. She'd made love to a stranger and had done nothing to prevent pregnancy. Nine months later, Susan was born. Jennifer wished the child was Tremaine's, but knew it wasn't. When her mother and friends jumped to that conclusion, she'd not dissuaded them. She'd almost come to believe it herself. Good God, she thought, what have I done?

....

After the press conference, Tremaine returned to the Oval Office. He sat and looked through the window, listening to the ever-present sound of distant traffic. For fifteen minutes he sat quietly before he turned, picked up the phone and asked for Jonathan.

Jonathan entered quietly. The two men sat across from each other in front of the big desk.

"When you spoke with Jennifer's lawyer, what did he say?"

"He said that she didn't wish to speak with anyone from the White House. All communication was to go through him."

"What else?"

"She wants to be reimbursed for the raising of the child."

"Work it out. Let me know what happens. I will have a letter for her tomorrow, give it to her lawyer but make sure she gets it. Now, on another matter; there's a meeting scheduled with Doug Kersey and Bill Morgan for tomorrow afternoon. See if you can push it back to Friday morning. I'm going to talk with the senators from the Pacific Northwest about the use of recycled paper."

"Ah, yes," said Jonathan, with a knowing look, "I heard the Hill was swamped with lobbyists. They've twisted a lot of arms and marshaled lots of opposition."

"That's the way it sounds, all right. We'll see what they have to say. I'll see you in the morning."

21

In the snake's lair

The Boston Globe
FANCY FOOTWORK
President Seeks to Restore Tarnished Reputation

Presidential aide Jonathan Makarios tried unsuccessfully to arrange for the President to address the National Press Club in New York on May 15. This move was seen by conference organizers as a blatant attempt by the President to restore his tarnished image following the disclosure of his affair with Jennifer Ramirez. Public opinion polls showed a decline in the President's approval rating of thirty points, down to 41%. This equaled the rating he received during the election campaign following the revelation of the use of drugs in his youth.

Senator Cole, the leading Republican spokesman, was quoted as saying, "The President has betrayed the trust of the American people. A man who has admitted to such indiscretions cannot be trusted with the governance of the country. He's an admitted drug user, who avoided the draft during the Vietnam War and counseled other young men to do the same. He is a womanizer and the father of an illegitimate child. Only with the recent revelation was he compelled to assume the financial obligation for his daughter. His interest in addressing the National Press Club in New York can be seen as nothing more than a devious attempt by a desperate man to buy votes."

Cole hinted that there had been talk amongst ranking Republicans concerning impeachment proceedings. Not since the Nixon presidency has government been so badly shaken by such scandalous behavior.

On a related matter, Harvard University President Dr. James Channing confirmed that President Tremaine would address the faculty and students of the university on May 20. When asked if the press would be invited, Dr. Channing responded, "Of course." In light of the refusal by organizers of the National Press Club, Dr. Channing's invitation can only be seen as a slap in the face of ordinary Americans.

Sandra crumpled the newspaper and threw it across the room. "You deceitful, hypocritical bastards!" she muttered.

....

Cole returned to his office following a late breakfast. The day's newspapers lay on his desk. Lighting a cigar, he leaned back and slowly leafed through them. A smile of satisfaction spread across his face when he came to the Boston Globe article.

The phone rang. Tossing the paper on the desk, he leaned forward and picked up the phone. He sat back and made himself comfortable before putting it to his ear.

"Yes... Who?... Sandra Tremaine!... Here, now?... At your desk?.... Yes, I'll see her, but stall her for a few minutes. I'll let you know when I'm ready."

Cole bolted out of his chair, grabbed the newspapers and stuffed them into a drawer. Taking a used handkerchief from his pocket he dusted off the desktop, being careful to sweep the ashes into the garbage pail and empty the ashtray. From the bookshelf he selected three books and placed them strategically on the desk, titles visible: "Political Theory for the 21st Century," "The Role of Contemporary Women in the Modern World," and "Enlightened Self-Government, Its Theory & Application." He placed a pad of paper directly in front of him next to which he placed a pencil.

From the shelf beside the door, he took photos of his wife and children and placed them prominently on the desk. Quickly he surveyed the room, making sure everything was in place. On the coffee table, he spotted the most recent Penthouse. Sifting quickly through the magazines on the table, he found two more and stuffed them in the drawer along with the newspapers. He opened a cupboard and looked in the mirror. He straightened his tie and dragged a greasy comb through his thinning hair. Then, opening his mouth, he rubbed his fingers over his teeth and practiced a smile.

He sat down and spoke into the intercom: "Send her in."

Cole pored over his notes, pencil in hand, and pretended not to hear the door open.

"Senator Cole, Sandra Tremaine is here to see you," his secretary announced.

The senator glanced up with a contrived expression of surprise. He walked around the desk and extended a soiled hand.

"Mrs. Tremaine, Mrs. Tremaine, what a pleasant surprise. Have a seat my dear." He motioned to a large, overstuffed, black leather chair and Sandra sat down.

As Cole walked around the desk to his seat, Sandra's eyes swept the office, taking everything in, including the books on the desk.

"What can I do for you?" Cole asked.

Sandra sat in the high-backed chair and steepled her fingers. Deliberately she crossed her legs, all the while keeping her eyes fixed firmly on Cole. She saw a flicker in his eyes, but he'd caught himself, conscious that she was watching him.

"I see you've been reading," she said quietly.

"I beg your pardon?"

"I see you've been reading," she indicated the books.

"Yes, I like to keep abreast of things." Cole was pleased with his clever use of words. He'd never met Sandra before, and at least part of his surprised look was genuine. She wore a white blouse under a navy blue V-necked sweater and a red tartan kilt. She was an attractive woman, well built and shapely.

Sandra chose to ignore his covert language. "I take it you believe in the equality of men and women?"

"Of course, of course."

"Then why do you hide behind your desk?"

"What do you mean?" Cole was beginning to feel uncertain, like a man in quicksand. What was she talking about? Her dark eyes seemed to bore into him. He wanted to turn away, but she wouldn't let him. He was beginning to sweat.

"Hide behind my desk? What do you mean?"

"Look, Mr. Cole, I'd appreciate it if you'd demonstrate your belief in the equality of human beings by sitting over here, across from me. That wouldn't be too much to ask, would it?"

"No, no, of course not." He waddled from behind the desk and, pulling a chair into place, sat in front of her.

"Thank you. I want to deal directly with you." She let the statement hang for a moment.

Cole sat back in the chair and tried to recover his balance. Sweat dripped under his arms, giving off a sour, pungent odor. He felt self-conscious. "How can I help you?" He had to get something going; the silence was unnerving.

"I read the quote from you in the Boston Globe. I had to see you in person. I had to know what kind of a man would make such statements."

"What do you mean?"

"Senator, you've violated your public trust. By your words, you are doing your best to discredit my husband. You lie; you make him out to be something he is not. In doing so, you make it difficult and maybe impossible for him to give the people of this country what they need."

"And what might that be?" Cole couldn't keep the sarcasm from his voice.

"There was a time when holding public office was a way

for gifted leaders and legislators to provide service to their countrymen. It was a high calling, a calling which no longer receives the respect it once did."

"And what's that got to do with me?"

"It's people like you who give politicians a bad name; it's people like you that undermine the idea of service. You manipulate facts and distort reality, making it appear to be something it's not."

"What makes you think that?" Cole demanded.

"I know my husband. Your comments couldn't have been further from the truth."

"You can't prove that!"

"I don't need to. You and I both know the truth."

"It is men like your husband who do not belong in politics." Cole leaned forward. "I will drive him out if I can."

"What is it about him that fills you with so much animosity? What has he done to make you so angry? This is more than politics, isn't it?"

"Mrs. Tremaine, I don't know what you're talking about," came the syrupy response.

"Oh yes, you do. You know exactly what I'm talking about." Sandra paused, collecting her thoughts. "I had to see you in person. I had to be sure about you."

"Sure of what?" Cole snapped.

She continued, ignoring his question. "I knew that in person you'd not be able to hide from me." Sandra saw the uncertainty in Cole's eyes. "You're afraid of Tremaine, afraid that if he's as good as you think he is there'll be no room in government for the likes of you and others of your ilk. From what I've seen, there'll be no meeting of minds here."

Cole shifted uneasily. "Mrs. Tremaine, you speak in riddles. You don't know anything about me."

"I know more than you think. I know now that you're afraid, although you'll never admit it, even to yourself. Now that I know that, you'll be much easier to deal with."

Before Cole could respond, Sandra stood and looked down at him. "I'm sorry for you, Senator; dishonesty and fear are cruel taskmasters." Turning on her heel, she left the office, closing the door quietly behind her.

22

In the belly of the Great Satan

Miguel and his four top men sat around the table. Armed guards were posted at the doors. The only light in the room came from a hurricane lamp suspended over the table and two others hanging on either side of a large map on the wall. Red, green, blue and yellow pins marked specific areas of the map in such a way as to provide a semicircle inland from the lakefront. It was an area where abandoned warehouses now stood. For four hours, they'd gone over the plans in minute detail. Everything was in place. Six months of planning was now at an end. Miguel looked at his watch. It was eleven thirty. Pushing his chair away from the table, he stood up. The other men did the same.

"Good luck," he said, extending his hand. In a matter of seconds, the room was empty. Miguel lit a cigarette. The light from the match showed the hard face of a man in his mid-sixties. His black, close-cropped hair was streaked with gray; his eyes, unusually dark, had a flat quality about them. He was short and stocky and in excellent physical condition, something he still took pride in. Going to a metal closet, he opened the door and removed an M16. He placed it on the table and broke it apart with practiced ease. Checking each part carefully, he reassembled it with precision and speed. When he was finished, he put it away and, picking up his jacket, slipped out the door and up the stairs to the empty room of the gutted house. Rubble and bricks were strewn about haphazardly, and the cold smell of concrete assailed his nostrils. Spring had come early to Chicago, melting ice, flooding shorelines. The air had been humid, a precursor of things to come. Then suddenly winter returned, taking the city by surprise. The last few days had been the coldest days in April since records had been kept. Miguel shivered, turned his collar up, and stuffed his hands in his pockets.

....

Later, if anyone had noticed, they'd have seen an old derelict shuffling along toward an abandoned pier of shambled warehouses, barely visible in the darkness. A stiff wind came sweeping off the lake, numbing his fingers. Turning his back to it, he hunched over and lit another cigarette before continuing on his way. In a few moments, he came to an old shed at the edge of the pier. A door hung crookedly on one remaining hinge. He stepped inside, into the quiet, where the wind could no longer reach him. Sitting on coils of old rope, he looked out at the dark and restless lake. He was tense, anticipating the events about to take place. He always felt like this before an action. It had always been that way, even in Vietnam.

His mind slipped back to the year of 1966, when he'd first gone to Southeast Asia as part of a unit of Green Berets. He was known as Jack Vincent then. He had operated for a year behind enemy lines. At the end of his tour, he was recruited by the CIA and joined an elite unit that operated beyond the conventions of war. Its activities were top secret and, he learned later, funded completely by opium grown in the highlands of the Iron Triangle.

Their tasks included the assassination of South Vietnamese political and military figures. The purpose? To justify actions of the American military against certain targets in Laos, Cambodia and North Vietnam. "Reprisals," they were called. The unit was the toughest he'd ever known. These men loved killing and most, he was sure, were psychopaths.

He knew why they wanted him. He was a tactician with an uncanny sense of the enemy and an ability to lead men as well as plan an operation. He was completely unpredictable in his actions, and he never asked his men to do anything he wouldn't do himself. For that reason, he was both respected and feared. He was a warrior. Even after all these years, his unit, Medusa, was virtually unknown.

He'd been in charge of one of the most lethal rogue units ever assembled, one that meted out death with dispassionate efficiency. The pay had been good, but he knew his decision to join had more to do with something else, a license to kill. Killing had gotten into his blood; it was an addiction, one he couldn't escape. But even that was only part of it. The other was the risk involved. It was that combination that gave life a richness and intensity of experience he'd not known in civilian life. He liked living on the edge.

By the late seventies, he had left Vietnam and gone to Iraq, where he'd been hired to train commando units of the Republican Guard in the techniques learned in Vietnam. For four years he trained and led small efficient killing units across the border into Iran, where they'd struck with relative impunity. Through it all, his origins remained completely unknown. For all intents and purposes, he was a mercenary from Southeast Asia.

Later he traveled in Syria, where he worked with the Muslim guerrillas operating from Lebanon across the border into Israel. He had no love for the Israelis, but held a grudging respect for their toughness.

Somewhere behind him he heard the sound of a car moving along the deserted street. He listened until the car was gone. Drugs, he thought, a poison eating at the heart of the country he once called home. He found himself reflecting on the events that led him from superpatriot to implacable enemy of the country of his birth.

He despised hypocrisy. His involvement in Medusa, the Middle East and even, for a time, in South America, had given him a new perspective. Now he understood, from behind the scenes, the effects of his nation's policies in its dealings with third world countries. He had no respect for American leadership. It had betrayed one of the principles upon which the nation had been founded, the right to self-determination. Wasn't that the reason they'd kicked out the British and "formed a more perfect union?"

After raids into northern Israel, he had formulated a plan for a new kind of guerrilla warfare. This kind of warfare took place inside the belly of the beast, what the Muslims called "the Great Satan." Convincing those in power had taken some doing.

"You want to use drugs as a weapon of war?"

"Yes."

"How do you propose to do that?"

"The country is corrupt; it's lost its way, and the people no longer have purpose. In this empty state, more and more are turning to drugs, particularly the Blacks and Chicanos."

"Explain."

"These people are second-class citizens. They can't find good employment; opportunities have been scarce, working conditions hard and pay poor. To get away from their suffering, many have turned to drugs."

"I still don't see how you wage war with drugs."

"It's easy. When you attack someone head-on, he resists; it's true of individuals and countries alike. To bring down the Great Satan you must not attack it head-on. Feed the corruption that rots in its belly. Spread drugs into every corner of the nation. Make them cheap and available. Get them into the white communities as well."

One of those present had objected. Turning from Miguel, he'd spoken with his brethren. "How can we provide Miguel with drugs? Surely they are forbidden by the prophet in the Holy Koran!"

"The Great Satan is a monstrous evil, beyond anything the world has ever known. We must not shirk from any method necessary to bring about its destruction. We must act quickly. If this strategy saves the lives of our people, so much the better."

The arrangements were made. One day, he had quietly slipped into the United States across the Mexican border. He'd been in the country now for three years.

Miguel found himself smiling. The process had been easier than he expected. Jack Vincent merely applied for a job as a waiter in one of the better restaurants of Boston. All he needed was his Social Security number. He wondered if the use of the Social Security card might activate inquiries from the authorities, but nothing had happened. Later, he moved to Chicago. He hadn't needed to work; he had enough money. He worked only to maintain a cover and find men.

For more than a year, as Miguel Lopez, he'd devoted himself to the recruitment and training of a small elite corps drawn from a gang called the Scarlatis. From his connections in Southeast Asia, he was able to bring in large quantities of high-grade heroin. He saw none of it, and no link to him could ever be traced.

Miguel looked at his watch; it was time to get things under way. Returning to the basement he prepared for the night's activities. Quickly, he dressed in warm, dark clothing. With the colors he added, he would easily be mistaken for one of the Capones, a rival gang. His men had prepared in similar manner.

At two o'clock, he left and made his way in the direction of the waterfront. He slipped through the darkness, following back alleys and threading his way through the rubble of abandoned cars and garbage. He knew that at this precise moment, three units of seven well-armed men were moving into prearranged positions.

He'd ordered all streetlights within six blocks of their destination taken out. It was three in the morning when he joined the men of his unit. Silently, they took up positions between the houses across from the warehouse. No dogs barked; they'd been poisoned earlier in the week. A small window high in the wall of the old warehouse gave off the only light. Two men leaned against posts that propped a sloping tin roof above a door, one of only two entrances to the building. The second unit covered the rear entrance, and the third lay in wait for the police, who would certainly arrive once the action began.

Lying propped on his elbows behind a low concrete wall, he caught his breath. When he was ready, he slid the M16 into place. With the strap wound tightly around his arm, the weapon became an extension of his deadly intent. Sighting carefully and compensating for the wind, he took aim. The scope, fitted for night vision, brought the targets into easy focus. At precisely three fifteen, the rifle cracked and one of the guards went down. The other followed with a bullet through the heart.

With the first shots, pandemonium erupted. Two of Miguel's men laid down fire from automatic weapons, raking the lower three feet of the warehouse along its length. As expected, men burst out of the door and died. Those that survived lay hidden behind the parked cars. During a brief pause, the sound of gunfire came from the other side of the warehouse. Within minutes, Miguel saw shadowy figures on the roof. His snipers took them out before they could do any damage. Miguel watched, a grim smile on his face. The Capones will be gone this time tomorrow. Most of them in the morgue. The Scarlatis would then control the drug distribution for the whole of Chicago. The attack would look like another war between rival gangs.

And twenty-one well-trained men would slip away, move to another city, and start all over again.

....

It was six in the morning when Tremaine arrived at the office. The news from Chicago was on every radio and television station. Lurid pictures and ugly headlines bannered the morning papers. Twenty-nine gang members dead, four wounded, six civilians killed, including two children. Three police officers had also died, with seven more wounded.

The police who'd tried to intervene had been pinned down and out-gunned. Fire had broken out and, fanned by strong winds, burned out of control. It had already consumed four large warehouses and a block of two-story tenements. Firefighters trying to reach the area were driven back by sniper fire. The cost was five men dead. Only the fireboats along the waterfront had approached, and they'd backed off when one was hit by rocket fire and set ablaze, killing two more men. Governor Mendoza mobilized the Illinois National Guard, which was ordered to cordon off the area.

Tremaine picked up the phone and called Jonathan. "Postpone the meeting with Brock. I'll meet him at four this afternoon. In the meantime, get Travis and the FBI director over here.... Yes, eight o'clock in the Oval Office."

Putting the phone down, he walked across the room and pushed open the French doors. Stepping outside, he made his way through the garden. The early morning sunlight cast long shadows across the lawns. He found a chair beneath the trees in the arbor. Pulling it out, he sat down and closed his eyes. The air was chilly and the sun warm. He heard the sound of a robin in a nearby tree and listened for a while to an exquisite song that welcomed the day.

Sitting quietly, his mind became empty. The time for action had not yet come. Suddenly before him, the smiling face of Avinash filled his mind. The eyes were dark and still, and the familiar smile graced the Master's face.

He felt a deep sense of gratitude for this man. He recalled a morning several years ago in Bombay.

He arrived at the end of the road near the Master's home and, stepping from the taxi, bought a bouquet of red roses from a vendor on the sidewalk. Afterwards, he walked slowly down the hill to the home of the Master. The doorman smiled a greeting as David climbed the entry way and rode the elevator to the top floor. Avinash came to the door and ushered him in. They sat quietly in the empty living room high above the noisy street. David watched the kites through the window as they turned slowly in the hot air rising from the streets below.

"You've been looking for your guru. That search is over, is it not?"

The words had come unexpectedly. David's heart jumped. He'd always wanted to know if Avinash was the one he'd been seeking. For some reason he'd felt constrained, and in time the question had become irrelevant, fading from his mind. The implication of Avinash's words struck him. He looked at the Master through moistened eyes. "How long have you known?" he asked.

"Since our first meeting."

"You knew then?"

"Yes."

"And you never said a word."

"No."

"Why? You must have known how much I wanted to know."

"I did, but you needed to know for yourself. My words have only confirmed this awareness."

It had been true. How long had David known? He couldn't remember, but it had been a while. "What happens now?" He asked.

"Life will continue as it has; nothing will change. The desire for enlightenment that's been with you will slowly fade as the identified consciousness becomes less and less prominent. Difficulties will continue to arise. The conditioning of your upbringing will still function. The drama of life will play out upon the screen of awareness.

"The difference is that you'll see yourself now as merely one of the characters in the drama; your thoughts and reactions will be perceived as if they belong to someone else. It will be like watching a movie. No longer will you mistake yourself for what you are not."

"What is life?" David had asked.

"Life is a divine novel created by Consciousness and played out in Consciousness. And who is David Tremaine? Merely a character in the novel, destined, like all others, to play a part.

"Life would be boring indeed, would it not, if everything always worked out? Who would read a novel that had no problems in it, no difficulties to overcome, no challenges to be met? Who would be interested in a novel where everything always turned out, just as we hoped?"

"Will enlightenment come?" David asked.

"If enlightenment occurs in the body-mind organism known as David, it cannot be until the author of the question, the ego, has vanished, and with it the question with which it was so concerned. When the fruit is ripe, it falls. Not before. Who can say when that is? All is in the hands of destiny. Life is a grand dream. Enlightenment is merely waking from the dream."

David had thought of the Master's words over the years. He found them strangely comforting.

Then one day, something had happened. Quietly and unobtrusively, like the sudden tipping of the scales by a single grain of sand. The personal self had dissolved and everything had become clear.

David heard footsteps and looked up to see Jonathan coming toward him.

"It's arranged," he said. "Travis and Jackson will meet you at eight."

Nodding, David got up and walked with his friend to the office. "See if you can get Morgan in here before eight. I want to talk with both of you before we start."

. . . .

"Come in, gentleman, come in." Tremaine walked across the room to meet them and shook their hands. "I think you both know Morgan and Jonathan Makarios," he said, introducing the Vice President and Chief of Staff. "Have a seat."

As the men seated themselves, Tremaine poured a cup of tea and handed it to Mike Jackson, the director of the FBI. Jackson smiled and nodded appreciation as he took the cup. Tremaine poured coffee for the rest, and Morgan passed it around. "Help yourselves to what you need," he said, indicating milk and sugar with a gesture.

Tremaine looked at the men in the circle. Travis was dressed in civilian clothes. He looked alert, his face freshly scrubbed. Jackson had on a blue suit, well tailored. He was a lanky man well over six feet, with brown eyes and hair to match. He was in his fifties, married, and had three grandchildren. He'd been an agent in the field for thirty years before his appointment by the previous administration. Emerson, impressed with him, had asked him to stay. Jackson had agreed.

"Well, gentlemen," Tremaine began, "we've a fine mess on our hands. I want an up-to-date report on what's happening, and your suggestions on how best to handle it. Jackson?"

"At three fifteen this morning, an attack was launched on a

gang called the Capones at their headquarters in an old warehouse along the lakefront. It was a well-executed attack, led by someone who appears to have considerable training. Whoever was behind it anticipated the moves the police and the guard would make."

"How so?" Tremaine asked.

"When the police arrived, they walked into a trap. They were allowed to get close to the warehouse, but they found themselves surrounded, pinned down by sniper fire. When they tried to break out, they were hit with rounds from automatic weapons."

"Automatic weapons?"

"Yes. When the firing let up, the police tried once more to withdraw, but the same thing happened again.

"Later, when the National Guard arrived and were deployed to cordon off the area, it became quiet; all gunfire ceased. By six o'clock Chicago time, the Guard was in place and considered the area secure. At six thirty, the guard came under sniper fire from behind. Two were killed. We don't know how many were wounded. Police and other guardsmen that came to help were met with sniper fire on arrival. No one seems to know what's going on."

"We've reports that nine police officers were killed and seventeen wounded," interjected Travis.

"What about civilians?" Tremaine asked.

"There are civilian casualties," said Jackson, "but, again, we don't know how many."

"And the fires?"

"There are fierce winds fanning the flames, which now threaten a large industrial area not far away," Jackson answered. "The fire department hasn't been able to do much because of snipers."

"Someone wants this to keep burning," Jonathan said.

"It would seem so," Jackson responded. "Two men on the fireboat that was attacked were killed as well."

"Do any of you know what this is about?" Tremaine asked.

"Not really," said Jackson. "It may have something to do

with rival gangs. We thought maybe the Scarlati gang was behind the attack, but right now that's speculation on our part."

"What can be done?" Tremaine asked, turning to Travis.

"It's a bad situation from the standpoint of civilians trapped in the area. We have to find whoever did this and neutralize them."

"How many men do you think are involved in this action?" Tremaine asked.

"Our best estimate is that there may be as many as sixty armed and well-trained men," said Jackson.

Travis nodded. "What we suggest is to send in small, highly mobile forces, such as two augmented units of Green Berets by land and a unit of Navy SEALS by water. In each of these units there will be two snipers and their spotters. We'll try to pick these guys off. This should minimize the possibility of further civilian casualties and do the least damage. We'll have to see how things develop."

"How soon can they go in?" Tremaine asked.

"They'll be in Chicago by evening. As soon as it's dark, they'll go in."

"Anything else?" Tremaine looked at Jackson.

"The agency is working with local police. We've set up a joint command center from which we're coordinating the operation, including the guard and the units that will go in at dark."

"Who's in charge?" Tremaine wanted to know.

Travis responded. "Brigadier General Clint Duval was chosen. He should be at the command center by now. He's experienced in urban warfare, having spent time in Saigon and Beirut."

"All right," said Tremaine. "We seem to be in good hands. Keep me informed."

23

Change happens all the time

It was a few minutes to four when two men strode purposefully along the corridor leading to the Oval Office. Brock was the senior senator from Oregon, and Prescott was a congressman from Washington. For years they had been staunch supporters of the logging industry. Today was no exception.

Once cleared for entrance, they were ushered into the room. Tremaine stepped from behind the desk to greet them, hand outstretched.

"Thank you for changing your schedules," he said. "With this crisis in Chicago, it was impossible for us to meet this morning."

Both men nodded. Tremaine pointed to seats in front of the fireplace.

"What can I do for you, gentlemen?" From the moment they entered the office, they felt ill at ease. Tremaine as usual was dressed casually. They, in contrast, were dressed in suits, the uniform dictated by custom for men of their station.

"In the Pacific Northwest, there are many who think that recycling paper is not a good idea," Senator Brock said, coming to the point at once.

"Yes, I'm aware of that."

"We agree with them; not personally, you understand," Brock explained, his voice oily. "It's our job to represent our constituents."

"And what about conserving resources?"

"Of course we're interested in that as well," answered Congressmen Prescott. "But we're more interested right now in conserving jobs threatened by this policy."

Tremaine looked at the two men and waited for them to continue. They shifted uneasily.

Prescott continued. "Do you realize that if you implement your policy of using recycled paper, companies such as McClelland will have to downsize and a large number of workers will be laid off?"

"Yes," said Tremaine. "I am most certainly aware of the situation and the changes that will likely take place."

"We don't think you realize how bad the situation will be," responded Brock. "The effect it would have on the primary and secondary industries would be catastrophic. The lumber industry has been hit hard over the last ten years due to environmental issues such as the preservation of the spotted owl."

"You don't approve?" Tremaine asked quietly.

"It's not a matter of approving or not approving," blustered Prescott, "It's a matter of the preservation of human livelihood."

"Let's cut to the real issue, gentlemen, the issue of change. I don't have time for a lengthy conversation today."

"Don't you think this is important?" Brock demanded.

"I didn't say that." Tremaine's voice was steady. "I don't buy your basic premise, that's all. Your view, as I see it, is limited. From where you operate, the problems we face cannot be solved. They'll just get worse."

"How can you say our views are limited?" demanded Brock. "We represent the area. We know first hand the problems of the lumber industries."

"I know you do. What I'm saying to you is that from my perspective, your views are too narrowly defined. They don't address the full scope of the problem."

"But..." Prescott began.

"If you give me a few minutes, I'll explain what I'm driving at," Tremaine said. Something in his tone let the two men know it was time to shut up. "Change is inevitable. It cannot be halted, but for some reason most human beings have a built-in resistance to it. As I see it, we suffer when we resist change. So instead of fighting it, perhaps we're better off embracing it."

"Not all change is for the better," Brock interjected, unable to control himself.

"Let's just say that change is necessary and inevitable. It cannot be stopped. The logging practices in this country have been a sad commentary on the greed, waste and destruction of one of our great resources. We've been poor stewards of these great forests."

"I disagree," Brock protested. "We're the most advanced nation in the world. Our logging practices are far superior to those of Latin American countries. One only has to look at what's going on in the Amazon to know that."

"It seems to me, gentlemen, that you're more interested in hearing yourselves talk than in understanding. I'm not interested in being drawn into a conversation that has no real relevance to what must be done." Tremaine paused and looked steadily at the two men before him. They lowered their eyes. He waited until they looked up before directing a question to Prescott. "Do you have an open mind, or is your mind made up?"

Prescott squirmed. If there was one thing he prided himself on, it was his open mind. "I'm open," he said.

"Good. Now, how about you, Senator?" Tremaine asked, turning to Brock.

Brock leaned forward. His heart was pounding and he was angry. His face flushed and beads of sweat covered his forehead. He disliked being talked to in this way, but a lot of people depended on him. He couldn't allow his personal feelings to override his purpose.

"I'll hear you out," he said.

"Thank you. Going back to your comment comparing our

logging practices with those in the Amazon; we cannot justify our practices by comparing them to those that are worse than ours. What's happening in the Amazon rain forest is disastrous and concerns me a great deal, but it's something I can do little about at the moment. What's happening in *our* forests is my jurisdiction. I intend to do something about that."

"What do you have in mind?" Prescott asked.

"To begin with, I'm sending a signal to the country and the logging industry as a whole that we'll no longer squander our resources. We'll become more efficient and less wasteful."

"If recycling puts men out of work, the government ends up paying for it through workman's compensation or welfare. I, for one, am opposed to the expansion of the welfare state," Brock argued.

"On that point you'll get no argument from me," Tremaine responded. "Everything is interrelated. We must take into account all those interdependent aspects or we'll never move ahead."

"If you go ahead with the idea of using recycled paper in government offices, do you know what effect that single step will have on the pulp and paper industry?" Prescott asked.

"I think so," said Tremaine. "But go ahead and tell me what you think."

"Big companies like McClelland employ thousands of workers. If they cannot maintain their current production levels of pulp, many will be laid off. Crown McClellands in Canada has made financial concessions to end a long strike. They've obligated themselves and wouldn't have done so had they been aware of what you intend to do. The loss of revenue will cripple them. They might not survive."

"Those things I'm aware of. One of the problems we face here, and in Canada, comes from our attitude toward what we've traditionally considered one of our greatest assets, namely, the immensity of our natural resources."

"I don't follow," said Prescott.

"Because of the vast resources, in this case trees, we've been careless and exceptionally wasteful. Millions of acres of land have been stripped. The problems of erosion and the destruction of animal habitat have been largely ignored. Additionally, we take the wood we need and discard the rest. In this way a great deal is wasted that could otherwise be used.

"Only in the last ten or fifteen years have we started to pay attention to these problems. In Norway and Sweden, the lumber resources are considerably less. For that reason, they are generally more careful in preventing erosion and take better care of the land.

One of the dangers of being a member of Congress is that you only see what logging companies want you to see. Unless you're willing to get off the main roads, you'll not see the devastation."

"You still haven't dealt with the problem of unemployment your proposal would cause," Brock interjected.

Tremaine ignored him. "Not long ago I had a conversation with the chairman of Honda Motors concerning the building of more fuel-efficient cars. What he said to me was, 'Tell us what you want, how many miles per gallon and by when. We'll do it.' That's the attitude I like. All the other companies, including our own 'Big Three,' kept telling me it was too costly and therefore not practical. My grandfather said we'd never put men on the moon. He never lived to see it, but it happened."

"Get to the point," growled Brock.

Tremaine went on without acknowledging Brock's irritation. "Requiring the government to use recycled paper creates a demand. That demand, like any other, will be met by industry. The giants may not meet it because it's more difficult for them to make adjustments, but there's no doubt the demand will be met by someone willing to change.

"Those companies more flexible and capable of adapting will rise to the occasion. One of the hallmarks of success in industry is the ability to adapt. For years, industry believed 'bigger is better.' It is not always receptive to change. If those in the industry choose to ignore the need for change, they will fall by the wayside. The idea that bigger is better was always questionable. Although it can have advantages, it has its drawbacks. Change will correct that."

"But what about the big companies?" Prescott persisted.

"What about them? If they try to hold on to the old ways, they'll go down. When creative minds get to work, they'll find ways of diversifying, of being more responsive to the needs that arise. Perhaps they'll get smaller or break into independent subsystems. The point isn't how they'll do it; the point is that they will.

"We are not businessmen; we are not scientists. It's the task of business and science to figure these things out. I've faith that they'll do so. Our task is to keep in mind the public good. To do that, we can't afford to be shortsighted, can't afford to allow segments of our constituency to dictate short-term goals that are not in the best interests of the nation as a whole or of the planet upon which we live."

"We're supposed to represent our constituency. If a large percentage feels a particular policy is no good, then we must say so," said Brock.

"I've no problem with that. You must, however, keep in mind that the interests of Oregon and Washington do not always represent the interests of the nation as a whole. My task is to keep that in mind. All points of view are taken into consideration. That means they'll be considered from the perspective of the whole. No one point of view can be allowed to dictate to others. Now, it's time to develop long-term goals. We must be willing to embrace change and adapt. Above all, we must have confidence in our greatest asset."

"And what the hell is that?" snapped Brock.

"The creativity of the human mind," Tremaine said with a smile. "And we as politicians must be creative, too. I don't mean clever; I mean intelligent. It's obvious to me that one of the tasks of political leaders in a democracy is to educate their constituents. If we fail in this task, then we'll find ourselves reverting to a kind of crisis management. Once that happens, it's difficult to stop."

"How can we hope to educate our constituents when their livelihood is threatened?" demanded Brock.

"We must enable them to see the limits of personal self-interest. We must help them see that their interest is really tied to the whole. As I see it, human beings like challenge. We're bored without it. We have for too long depended on the welfare state. There have been some obvious benefits. Its liabilities, however, have been less readily visible, something political leaders are loath to face."

"And what are the liabilities?" Brock asked.

"We've become dependent on government agencies rather than on the creativity of our minds. In times of crisis, such as war or natural disaster, we pull together; the creative power of our bodies and our minds come into play. The desire to feel useful, to contribute to something larger than our own small needs, is precisely what has caused so many people to enter the Peace Corps. This is the meaning of true service.

"When we lose ourselves in work that we consider worthy, it makes us feel useful and life becomes worthwhile. Of course, service is not for everyone, but it is for many."

"This is getting off the point," Brock interrupted rudely.

"No," Tremaine said sharply, "this is the point. The practical problems will be worked out; but for that to happen, we must have open minds. We must look at things in new ways without being tied to the past, to our traditions. We cannot secure the world by making change stop. Change is inevitable. The only security that exists is in accepting this fact. To refuse to do so is the height of stupidity."

"Are you calling me stupid?" Brock exploded.

"Can you embrace change?" countered Tremaine patiently.

Before Brock could respond, Prescott said, "Coming back to the problem raised by the government's intention to recycle paper, what can the government do to help ease the transition that you point to?"

One thing we're looking at is developing more secondary industries."

"What do you have in mind?" Prescott asked.

"One of the things we'd like to consider is developing several small furniture factories where high quality wooden furniture is produced. We might also consider planting specialized woods that will grow in the climate of the Pacific North West. If we're successful then perhaps we can produce furniture made from these highly prized woods."

"We'd be interested in exploring that further."

"Good we'd like to have your input. Perhaps you'd consider serving on a committee that we're setting up to bring this about? It is our intention to have the factories up and running within the next eighteen months."

"I would like that, how about you, Senator," Prescott asked looking at Brock.

"Its not going to help us in the short term and there's no guarantee it will work in the long run either." Brock was angry.

"Well the opportunity is there and I'd welcome your involvement in the project if your up for it." Tremaine responded. "We'll sit down with anyone who's open to new ideas. Yours and the Senator's ideas are welcome. But don't make the mistake of telling me 'it can't be done.' That is unacceptable."

Brock was boiling. Who does this young upstart think he is?

he wondered. "Some things are impossible to do," he argued, "so don't tell me that it's unacceptable to talk about them."

Tremaine wanted to end the argument. "Look, Senator," he said with an edge to his voice, "I don't have a lot of time to spend with you at the moment. Think about what I've said. I welcome honest ideas and suggestions, but I'll not waste time discussing issues with someone who's already made up his mind, someone unwilling to explore new options."

The room was silent except for the crackling of the fire. In the distance, a horn blared above the hum of traffic. Tremaine stood and the two men followed. He walked to the door ahead of them, opened it and turned, waiting. Prescott extended his hand. Tremaine shook it, his eyes looking into the man. "I appreciate your willingness to be open," he said. "We'll talk further. I'm sorry, but with what's going on in Chicago, I don't have time for a lengthy discussion." Prescott nodded and stepped into the hall.

Brock extended a hand, eyes averted. He wanted to escape before he completely lost control. Tremaine shook the hand and held the grip, refusing to let go, stopping the older man from leaving. Surprised, the senator looked up.

"I hope you'll think about what I've said. I'm open to honest exploration, but I won't be bullied." Tremaine released his hand and Brock strode through the door. The back of his puffy neck was bright red.

....

The two men walked brusquely down the hall, the sound of their shoes echoing off the marble floor. Neither had spoken since arriving at the Capitol. Congressman John Prescott had sat silently in the car on the way from the White House, his mind going over the events that had transpired. Tremaine had shaken him; his usual sense of certainty was in disarray.

Rarely had Prescott seen the old man so steaming mad. Most of Brock's colleagues deferred to the senator, whose white hair and dignified bearing had created an aura of carefully cultivated wisdom and respectability. Prescott knew that when the senior senator felt exposed and vulnerable, he could be a dangerous man to cross.

"Who the hell does that goddamned asshole think he is?" Brock fumed.

Prescott turned and looked at his friend. He'd known Brock for many years and couldn't remember seeing him as rattled as he was now. "He's the President," Prescott found himself saying.

"Don't give me that crap." Brock turned on Prescott, his voice carrying loudly down the hall. People in the corridor turned to see what was going on.

"We were rude to him..." Prescott stopped, cut off by the glare of his angry friend.

Brock turned on his heel and headed for his office.

"We'll talk about this later," he said as he disappeared through the door.

Prescott shook his head and walked slowly down the hall.

24

Intimations of things to come

Miguel shuffled along the pavement. An observer would have seen only an old derelict, scavenging in the gutted ruins of the abandoned buildings. He was dressed in a dirty raincoat and wore a battered, sweat-stained fedora, the brim covering his face. A filthy scarf wrapped his neck and a pair of old woolen gloves covered his hands. It was nine o'clock, Tuesday morning. The area was deserted. He stopped to light a cigarette and, under cover of shielding the match from the wind, made sure no one was around. Suddenly, he stepped between the two buildings and with swift purposeful strides walked fifty meters down the alley.

Empty, ruined houses rose on either side. He ducked into an opening and waited five minutes. Then, in complete silence, he made his way through the rubble to a battered door. He tapped three times and it swung open. He entered and descended the stairs. One man remained at the top while a man at the bottom opened the door and closed it behind him. Not a word passed between them.

Miguel took off his outer clothes and threw them on the back of an old chair. He lit the hurricane lamp, opened the metal cabinet, took out a 9mm pistol and screwed a silencer in place. Taking down the maps, he set them on fire. They burned quickly to a pile of blackened ash he crushed beneath his feet. With a cloth, he carefully cleaned the handles to the cabinet, the door handle, the edges of the table and the old metal chairs. He looked around the room, his eyes covering every inch. Then he went to the door and signaled the men to enter.

"Put your guns on the table," Miguel ordered

The men looked at each other, unholstered their guns and placed them on the table.

"You've done a good job." Miguel smiled. The men visibly relaxed.

"Everything went well." Miguel pulled out a chair and sat down. "There's cash for you in there," he said, indicating the steel cabinet behind them. "There's one bundle for each of you. You'll also find a bottle of wine in the back. Bring it out and we'll drink to a successful operation."

As the two men turned toward the cabinet, Miguel pushed his chair over, sending it crashing to the floor. He jumped to his feet. The two men, startled, spun around. Each received a bullet through the heart. The last thing they saw was the cold look on their killer's face.

Miguel took the two pistols from the table and dropped them into a bag. Once more he cleaned the chair, removing all fingerprints. He lifted down the hurricane lantern and, taking his time, dusted it and left it on the table, still burning.

....

An old man shuffled slowly into a bus station and bought a ticket for Oklahoma City. It was five in the afternoon, two hours before the bus was to leave. Entering the cafeteria, he ordered coffee. The speaker blared a last call for passengers bound for Memphis on platform number four. A few minutes later, a man in his late twenties entered the bus station. He was dressed in a three-piece pinstriped suit of navy blue. In his hand he carried a small briefcase, over his arm a thick coat. He stepped up to the ticket counter and bought a ticket for Oklahoma City. Half an hour later, a young marine stepped up to the window. He too bought a ticket to Oklahoma City. In his hand he carried a newspaper. The headline read, "GANG WAR ERUPTS."

Six well-dressed men entered the train station from different points between ten and eleven the following morning. During the course of an hour they also bought tickets for Oklahoma City. As they boarded the train, each entered a different carriage.

At a U-Haul office that afternoon, two men and a woman rented a small moving van. The wall clock showed two thirty.

"Yes, our main office is in Oklahoma City," the man at the desk responded to the woman's inquiry. "You can leave it there when you finish."

Later that afternoon a priest, in the company of five nuns in habits, rented a large van from Hertz and set out for a convent just outside Oklahoma City.

That evening, three men wearing blue jeans, high-heeled leather boots, warm plaid jackets and Stetsons unlocked the door of a new Ford F250 extended cab. Loading their bags behind the seat, they got in and started the engine. As the truck emerged from the underground parking facility the streetlight reflected off the Oklahoma license plate.

....

"Nothing? You must be shitting me. What the hell are you talking about?" Brigadier General Clint Duval exploded. His chair scraped on the concrete floor as he got to his feet. Before him stood two men. One wore the uniform of an officer in the Green Berets, the other the uniform of an officer in the Navy SEALS.

It was ten o'clock Wednesday morning. Duval had been up for two days. He'd already had reports from the police and the National Guard. Ten police officers dead, eighteen wounded, two firemen dead, fifteen National Guard killed and six wounded. Four civilians had been killed and forty-seven Scarlatis. The police had rounded up fifty Capones for questioning, which was still continuing. No one had a single lead.

....

"Now, what about this thing in Chicago? What's the news? Morgan was telling me seventy-eight people have been killed." Tremaine was in the oval office at the White House with his advisors.

"That's what we understand," said Jonathan. "Travis talked with Clint Duval. They're at a total loss. The special units that went in Tuesday night came across nothing. In fact, there's been no more confirmed gunfire since seven o'clock Tuesday morning.

"The Capones were rounded up and the preliminary questioning has been completed. According to the police department the Capones claim that none of them were involved in the shooting. For some of them the statements check out, but it'll take more time to thoroughly investigate all of them. It's also difficult to know who their members are; they don't keep written records and they don't volunteer information."

"What about the Scarlatis, those still alive?"

"So far as we can tell, only six survived the firefight, and there are another sixteen who weren't there that night. Their reports support what the Capones have said. The six who survived the fight said they didn't see any of the Capones that night. But they're convinced it was them. They may be right, but so far there's no evidence to support what they say."

"I spoke with Mike Jackson late last night," Morgan added. "He mentioned the same thing. He said they'd questioned the Scarlati survivors. One of them insisted that when he got outside, he was surprised to see another Scarlati gang member across the street. He wondered how he got there so fast."

"Are there no other leads?" Tremaine asked.

"No. The Chicago police think that some members of the

Capones' gang have vanished. But it's difficult to confirm this when gang members cover for each other and are so hostile. There's also a report that several dogs in the area were killed the week before. The FBI thinks they were killed deliberately. Poisoned meat may have been used. Anyway, they're still checking. The power company verified that all the lights in the area within six blocks of the Scarlatis headquarters were shot out. Police investigators found air pellets in the vicinity."

"Anything else?" Tremaine asked.

They all shook their heads.

"Then we must wait and see what happens. Is Travis back yet?" Tremaine turned to Jonathan.

"He's due in this afternoon."

"Tell him I want to see him as soon as he gets in."

....

It was six o'clock and Travis sat before the fire, Tremaine to his right.

"What time did you get in?" Tremaine inquired.

"A little after five, I think." Travis looked tired.

"Thanks for coming. Let's make this brief so you can get home to your wife."

Travis smiled his appreciation.

"So what have you got?"

"Not a hell of a lot," Travis responded. "The finger seems to be pointed at the Capones, but I'm not sure that's where it belongs. Jackson won't say either way. He likes to play his cards close to his chest."

"What's your hunch?"

"I don't really know what to say."

"C'mon, Travis, I know that brain of yours must have some thoughts running around in it."

Travis smiled.

"Don't worry, I won't hold you to it, but I want to know what you think."

"Okay. My hunch is that whoever carried this out was highly skilled. There may have been fewer involved than we initially thought but they were exceptionally well trained. Whoever they were, they threw us a curve ball, distracting us by leading us to believe it was a gang war. While we took the time to discover that, they slipped away."

"Any ideas as to who it might be?"

"No, but something about this whole thing has been niggling away at the back of my mind. On the flight back this afternoon, I remembered that when I was in Vietnam, there were rumors of a special unit of mercenaries, funded by the CIA, whose sole function was to operate outside the law."

"What do you mean?"

"Well, I'm not sure whether it really existed or not. This unit's job was to kill selected South Vietnamese politicians and military personnel. Sometimes members of the American support staff at the Embassy in Saigon were targeted. It was always made to look as if it was the Viet Cong. When this happened, it usually precipitated retaliatory strikes that would otherwise not have been justified. Although Cambodia and Laos were not officially in the war, the Viet Cong did operate there. We needed some pretext to set up operations in those countries in order to make certain unspecified strikes where we would otherwise have been prohibited."

"Can this be checked into?"

"I'll do my best. We'll have to see."

"So are you suggesting that a similar kind of operation was mounted?"

"Maybe."

"Anything else?"

"Not for now."

"Thanks, Travis. Keep me informed."

"I will."

Tremaine got up, shook hands with the general, and walked him to the door. "By the way, I'm going to the Middle East June 12th," he said. "I had a call from Levin this morning confirming it."

Travis turned. "Be careful," he said. That's a dangerous part of the world."

"So is Chicago."

≡ 25

Distorted lens, distorted perception

With a bump, Air Force One touched down at Logan International Airport. An hour later, David and Sandra entered the packed hall at Harvard University, accompanied by Dr. Channing. As they walked onto the stage, the hall became quiet. The two men wore the traditional gowns of academia, while Sandra wore a long flowing cotton dress with a floral print of burnished orange. Channing showed the Tremaines to their seats, and then stepped to the podium.

David looked at the sea of young, eager faces that stretched into the darkness at the back of the hall. A section to the left and at the front, below the stage, had been reserved for members of the press. It was full.

Dr. Channing began to speak. "I'm pleased to welcome David and Sandra Tremaine to Harvard. It is my intention to provide Dr. Tremaine with a platform from which to address the nation concerning the role of the press in a free society. In my opinion, the ideal forum for such a conversation would have been at the National Press Club. Since that possibility was blocked, I invited him here to Harvard, where we still value freedom of speech and the exploration of ideas and issues. Without further ado, please welcome Dr. Tremaine."

Tremaine stepped to the podium and as soon as it was quiet, began. "When our forefathers declared the independence of this nation from Britain, they embarked on a great social experiment. That experiment is ongoing; it is a work in progress. Regis Debrés, in his book, *Revolution in the Revolution,* makes the point that when a revolution takes place, it overthrows an existing power structure that no longer takes into account the well-being of the vast majority of its people. But history shows us that, in time, revolutionaries become the new establishment, and are once more out of touch with the people. He argued that in order to prevent this from happening, it was important to create an ongoing revolution, a revolution within the revolution, in order to keep government responsive to the needs of its people.

"In the American system of government, the role of the press is one of the great cornerstones of our democracy. The press is an instrument by which we continue the revolution in the revolution. But when the press itself becomes corrupted, it can no longer do the job it was intended to do. I mean 'corrupted' in a generic sense; that is, it has lost its sense of objectivity and its reliance on facts. The problem is more an internal problem, a problem with the whole system of the press. The idea of a free press as one that functions with integrity and honesty, free from the influence of government and special interest groups, is of great importance in a democracy such as ours. One special interest group, which few thought of, was the special interests of the members of the press themselves and the companies who employ them.

"Increasingly, there is a pervasive skepticism amongst far too many journalists which prevents them from reporting the truth when it's spoken. I would suggest that reporting has become increasingly biased, prejudicial and, at times, inflammatory. The purpose is to create controversy, for it is controversy that drives up ratings and increases profit. Profit has become the focal point of the press rather than the objective reporting of facts, whatever they may be. Controversy, not accuracy, has become the watchword in the world of newspapers, radio and television. When this happens, it's difficult for citizens not to be affected. This all-pervasive negativity offers little hope and fosters a kind of national despair, rendering us almost incapable of extricating ourselves from the morass we find ourselves in. This is a serious problem. It is to this basic issue that I wish to speak this evening.

"It is my hope that it will be an informative evening for all of us. To begin with let me quote from Lao Tzu. 'When the sage encounters difficulties he does not pretend they are not there, he sees things as they are. Difficult or easy, it makes no difference to him, because he knows that by facing facts difficulties are overcome.'

"I'm suggesting that one of our major difficulties concerning the press is the fact that we tend to get opinions masquerading as facts. Unless we know accurately what is going on, the facts, how can we take appropriate action? There are many difficulties and challenges facing our nation today and in order to address these difficulties it's important that we obtain accurate information. It is the role of the press to give us that information, and to ensure it's accuracy.

"I would like us to take a few moments and explore the differences between fact and opinion.

"To begin with, what do we mean by facts? When it rains that is a fact; is it not? When the sun shines, the wind blows or the snow flies, these are also facts. Facts are simply the events themselves, what happens. If I skid my car on ice and end up in the ditch, that is a fact. If I spend more money than I make then I go into debt. That is a fact. When a scientist observes the red and white blood cells through a microscope, the ratio in the sample is a fact.

"Opinions, on the other hand, are not facts. Opinions reflect our biases, how we want things to be. We may believe in the concepts of good and bad, and consequently the events that take place in life are categorized according to our definitions of those concepts. Then of course, we like people we consider good and dislike people we consider bad. Think about it for a moment. In the absence of language, ideas of good or bad no longer exist. If someone is mean or violent we may well avoid him, but we will not project upon him any concept that turns him into a good or bad person. The focus is thus on the action and not the person. When we project concepts onto people we are in a sense judging them, and once that takes place we tend to see all their actions in light of those judgments, interpretations, and opinions. In other words, it becomes personal.

"This tendency to judge people and events takes on another shading as well. It gives rise to the mental action of self-referencing. By self-referencing, I mean the tendency to perceive events and circumstances from the perspective of the ego centered *me*. *My* family, *my* party, *my* religion, *my* country, *my* theory and so on. In this way, the 'me' adds personal meaning to what happens. This personal meaning often causes the human being to feel important, while in reality there's no connection other than the one projected by himself. For example, a distance runner at the Olympics wins the marathon and I'm excited. Why? Because the runner who won was an American. It doesn't matter that I don't know the runner and have had nothing to do with him and might never have seen him before.

"If the same runner loses I might find myself very upset with him or what I consider the unfairness of another runner who rushed by him at the last minute. My elation or disappointment has nothing to do with the facts but with the self-referencing function of the mind. When the self-referencing of events does not occur, facts can be seen for what they are and a great deal of misery is thereby avoided.

"Where does this self-referencing come from? When we look closely at what happens, the self-referencing seems to arise from what we call the personal self, or in psychological terms, the ego. Here's another example. Lets say I'm a basketball player and the night is going well. Our team is winning and I'm in the zone. Every time I go up for a shot, the ball is in the basket, even before it leaves my hand. I can't miss. It so happens that I have a girlfriend who's been away. Suddenly, to my surprise, I hear her cheering and when I look I see her on the sidelines. She waves to me. All of a sudden I can't sink a basket to save my life. I have become self-conscious and that self-consciousness is nothing other than the sudden re-appearance of the ego. In the absence of the ego there is flawless functioning. All of us know this; it is a natural state. It is this state that is present when we become so absorbed in our work that we say, 'time flies.' The writer knows this; the potter, the painter, the mechanic and so on, all have had this experience at times. This is the experience we strive for, or try to recover once lost.

"What this suggests is that in the absence of the ego the detached state of simple awareness comes to the fore and is capable of perceiving exactly what is happening, and, at the same time, responding appropriately without any interference caused by the self-referencing function of the ego.

"Are there any questions so far? Yes, in the front row."

"Are you suggesting that it would be better for us when dealing with whatever problems we face, if we approach them with a kind of detached awareness, and that awareness is present when the personal self is in abeyance?"

"You have stated it well. That is what I'm suggesting."

"Are you also suggesting that when the personal awareness, the ego, as you mentioned, is absent that there is less suffering and less misery?"

"That is correct."

"Are you also suggesting that it is precisely this personal self, the ego, that formulates opinions and uses facts to support its own particular views on life?"

"Again, you have stated it clearly."

"Thank you, Dr. Tremaine."

"Yes, over there."

"I think I have followed your reasoning but I wonder if perhaps this detached awareness you speak of makes us less human, less emotional and less caring of others. When we face facts, as you've said, we will at times see things that seem unfair to those we love, things like accidents or illnesses. I can see we've no choice but to accept these things, because they've happened and, at the same time, I find myself wondering if that acceptance will make us callous and uncaring."

"What's your name?"

"Michael."

"It's a good question, Michael, one that I think points to a prevalent misconception. When we face facts, is there not an awareness of things as they are?"

"There is."

"So what we're talking about is detachment is it not?"

"Yes."

"When we don't accept things as they are, what does it mean? It means that we want things to be different from the way they are. Is that not so?"

"Yes, it is."

"When there's no acceptance of things, as they are, are we more likely to be upset and take offense?"

"I would think so."

"When we are attached to what we want, to our view of things is there not a certain level of anxiety and tension?"

"Yes, I suppose there is because we're afraid that what we want may not happen."

"That's right."

"Now let us take it a step further; when anxiety and tension are present, does it interfere with our ability to be compassionate and loving?"

"I hadn't thought of it before but I think it would tend to

interfere."

"It has been my observation that when detachment is present, there's no disturbance in the mind. When there's no disturbance in the mind, love and compassion are more likely to be present."

"What about sympathy? Is it the same as compassion?"

"No. To me compassion is the antithesis of sympathy."

"In what way?"

"We are using words to point to something, so it is important that we define them carefully. The way I would use the word sympathy is to suggest a sense of hopeless commiseration. For instance, let's suppose that I've experienced a severe loss of some sort. If you have also experienced a severe loss you will know what I'm going through. But, let's say you are still suffering from that loss and have not been able to move beyond it. Your experience will be of your loss and the fact of still being stuck in it. Your heart will go out to me and the expression will be in the form of sympathy. If, on the other hand, you've been able to move beyond your loss you will know from your own experience the possibility that lies before me as well. My suffering will move your heart and the expression will take the form of compassion. That compassion, even in the absence of words, will be uplifting and encouraging. Your very presence will suggest confidence in my ability to work through the difficulties with which I am now faced. In short, compassion is an expression of understanding, respect and confidence in my capacity as a human being. Sympathy, on the other hand, tends to be sticky and hopeless and conveys a lack of faith in my capacity as a human being."

"Thank you, Dr. Tremaine."

"You're welcome. More questions on this point? Yes, over here." Tremaine pointed to a white-haired man with neatly cropped beard and tortoise-shell glasses perched on the end of a long nose.

"It seems to me," the man began, "that this detachment you're speaking of is devoid of emotion and, as Michael mentioned, could make one less caring, less human. Perhaps I've not understood you completely."

"I'll see if I can make it clearer. When detachment occurs, there's a certain equilibrium present, the mind is not disturbed, which in turn allows compassion and understanding to arise; just as the reflection of the moon appears in a pond when the disturbance caused by the wind dies away."

"Are you suggesting that we should be detached in order to achieve compassion and understanding?"

"No, I'm not using the word 'should' at all. I'm simply suggesting that *when* detachment is present, compassion and understanding are more likely to occur. And when this happens, the responses of the person are spontaneous and appropriate to the circumstances in which they find themselves. When this takes place, those responses, whatever they are, are not derived from anxiety, tension, or fear. Does that make sense?"

"It does. Thank you, Dr. Tremaine."

"Perhaps we can move on. As the members of the press lose their objectivity we find ourselves more and more subjected to the interpretations and opinions of the reporter, not the facts of the events themselves. In other words, the personal perspective of the reporter with its attendant biases is selecting the facts and slanting things to support the interpretations and agenda of the reporter, even when the reporter is not aware of it. Such interpretations are usually self-referencing.

"And what form does that interpretation take? Is it not the pitting of one point of view against another, coupled with the belief that one point of view deserves to win, the other to lose? In other words, it is as though the reporter has made up his mind on the matter, and is seeking to gain the support of those who read or watch him.

"The problem with interpretative reporting is that it does not foster understanding. If ten human beings witness a single event, there will be ten different points of view concerning that event. Now, if we were absent when the event took place and wanted to get a comprehensive picture of what happened, we'd have to accept all points of view as perfectly valid. No single point of view would express the whole; no single point of view by itself would be right, and no single point of view would be wrong. In fact, the concept of right and wrong is not present in the event, but as mentioned earlier, it is something we superimpose on it."

A member of the press raised his hand and, without being acknowledged, stood. "Are you suggesting that all points of view are equally valid?"

"That is precisely what I'm saying."

"I'm sorry, but I can't accept that."

"Go on."

"Not all points of view are equally valid."

"Says who?"

"I do."

"That's my point. You have an agenda; you have already determined in your mind those points of view that you think are more important than others. That is precisely the problem I'm talking about."

"But don't you accept that some things are good and some things are bad?"

"Even that is a point of view, isn't it? An elderly friend of mine is fond of saying that from the perspective of the human being, the eradication of the smallpox virus is a good thing, but not from the perspective of the virus itself."

"Aren't some things truly evil and need to be stopped? Hitler is a good example."

"I would say that it is our tendency to interpret things in black and white terms that gives rise to the likes of Hitler in the first place. At the end of the First World War, for instance, the penalties that Germany was subjected to were crippling.

The Treaty of Versailles created a great deal of hardship for the German people. It was in many ways punitive. Given the level of economic hardship at the time, Hitler seemed to offer hope and the restoration of national pride. This is why in certain Asian cultures it is understood that when you defeat an enemy you do not cause him to lose face. In other words he is treated with respect as a human being, regardless of what he's done.

"If we had been more understanding at the conclusion of the First World War, the climate that brought Hitler to power might have been absent. I'm suggesting that a biased, even revengeful, perspective contributes to conflict and suffering rather than the opposite. The problem in short, is personal."

"What do you mean?"

"What I mean is this. Take for example a mechanic. He must correctly identify the problem when he repairs a car. Now if he has a theory that the problem is with the transmission and has invested himself in that position he may well disregard the symptoms that point to the carburetor. After all he doesn't want to be wrong. If he removes the transmission, it will not solve the problem; it will only create an additional one. If we don't identify the problem correctly, how can we solve it? We cannot solve what we do not see.

"Still, the great drama of life goes on; life is the way that it is. And when a Hitler comes to power, there will be those called upon to defeat him. Over time things arise that many will think are terrible, and these things will have to be stopped. Then there will arise those, like Churchill, whose task is to wage war and win it. When that's done, their task is complete, and they'll step off the world stage. Lao Tzu speaks to this when he says, 'When a country falls into chaos, patriots are born.'"

"But what about this problem of good and evil? Surely you agree we must do everything in our power to destroy evil and elevate good."

"Think about it. How can we? Does the idea of good exist in the absence of evil or vice versa? Good and evil are polar opposites on a single continuum. When we think of the concept of beauty for instance, we can have no idea of what it is in the absence of the concept of ugliness. Is it not obvious that good and bad arise together, like the head and tail of a coin? Can you have up without down, the outside of a cup without the inside?"

"I'm not sure, I'll have to give it some thought."

"Good, thank you for your question. Yes, over there, the gentleman with the mustache." Tremaine pointed to the back of the press section. A dignified, elderly man stood up.

"What you're saying is that we should go back to the ideal of reporting the facts. Is that correct?"

"Yes. I don't like to use such words as 'should' because they smack of some kind of moral superiority. I'm not speaking from that perspective, but from the perspective of what actually happens.

"When facts are reported, people will make up their own minds. If the reporter attempts to persuade people by the way he reports, he interferes in that process. What is the reporter saying when he attempts to persuade others? Is it not that he has found the answer and he's afraid others may not arrive at the same conclusions he has? Is this not the same kind of reasoning engaged in by those in religion who try to proselytize?

"As I see it, one of the basic premises of a democracy is that citizens exercise their own judgment about the issues presented to them, and furthermore, they are quite capable of doing so! They may argue and dispute with one another, but the facts will be the facts because the reporter has done his job. Additionally, when facts are presented to us in a dispassionate and objective way concerning our own behavior, for instance, is it not easier to hear? If, on the other hand we are judged and told we are wrong, that we should or should not have done something, is there not a tendency to become defensive and more firmly entrenched in our position?"

"I agree with you, but within the industry it's difficult to implement. For instance I've been disturbed by the direction of televised journalism. The facts are too often shaded to support the hypothesis of the journalist involved. In fact, the journalists are often applauded quietly behind the scenes, so to speak, for their confrontational tactics. I don't think this is helpful. It relegates this powerful medium to the level of tabloids at checkout stands. Despite this fact, the polls show there's more interest in drama and conflict than in knowing the facts. And for those employed in our industry, such as myself, there's pressure to produce what sells. How do we address this problem?"

"Good question. What you are pointing to is a general feeling, perhaps a consensus within the large media corporations, that a reporter must cater to the prurient interests of the human being in order to sell papers or increase ratings."

"That's my point."

" Did you see the movie 'Pay it Forward' or 'Sea Biscuit'?"

"I did."

"Those movies did well, people enjoyed them and went to see them. What was powerful about them was that they presented an alternative to the perpetual emphasis on the negative aspects of human nature. They pointed out that human nature has another side to it as well, and that side has the capability of transmuting the negative and bringing it into balance as depicted visually by the yin yang symbol.

"Since we tend to emphasize the negative aspects of life to the exclusion of the positive, we have distorted reality and created a sense of hopelessness that finds expression in conflict and violence as evidenced in many of our cities."

"What suggestions do you have?"

"What I'm suggesting is that when we start presenting the stories that draw attention to the incomparable beauty, generosity and love of the human spirit we are attracted to them on a very deep level. Why? Because all of us are attracted to that which uplifts and inspires us, as bees are attracted to flowers."

"Can you give an example?"

"When I was in university I worked in a machine shop at night in order to pay my tuition and expenses. The night foreman, Bill, was a man of Italian background, a Catholic with a large family. He was a hard worker. I never had a problem with him but some of the men did. There were stories that he was intensely disliked on the day shift. One story was that he had lost several fingers on one hand when he'd been pushed while working on a large metal press. Bill's missing fingers tended to lend credence to the story and he always refused to talk about what had happened. On the night shift there was a little man with a big rotund belly and skinny legs who perched on a stool and worked one of the presses. He was a timid man in his early sixties and reminded me of Humpty Dumpty. Bill got into the habit of riding this man. He would do this by standing behind him and glaring. This so affected the timid man that he began to shake. His fear became palpable. There was considerable danger for the man too, because he worked a large ten-ton press and those of us who worked such presses always had to be careful lest we make a mistake and lose a finger or hand.

"Bill's behavior came to the attention of the boss and one evening he was called into the boss's office. He was there for about an hour. When he came out he was a changed man. He never engaged in intimidating actions and mental games again. Something happened in that office that completely transformed him. I watched him closely for any signs of resentment toward those who'd reported him. There was none. I worked there for two more years and came to know and respect Bill as a fine human being, as did the rest of the men. The timid man could never bring himself to trust Bill completely, but he certainly no longer suffered from Bill's intimidating behavior. That event showed me what human beings are capable of, the kind of transformation that can take place."

"What you say may be true but there are a lot of bad things happening in the world today, theft, corruption, rape, murder and so on."

"Yes, those things are happening, there's no disagreement on that. My question to you would be, is it all that's happening?"

"Probably not."

"Then why are so few of the other things being reported? They exist as you concede. I remember a woman I knew whose daughter was brutally murdered. The killer was caught and sentenced to life in prison. The stress of this event almost drove her insane. She couldn't sleep, she quit work, was on edge, and easily angered. She suffered from depression and thoughts of death lodged in her mind. It became so bad she and her husband considered separation. This jolted her enough to realize she had to do something about what was going on. She began a process of self-inquiry.

"It didn't take much for her to realize she carried a deep and unforgiving hatred for the man who'd killed her daughter. One day it dawned on her that she and the killer shared an important link. Whereas she'd been present at her daughter's birth the killer had been present at the close of her daughter's life. As time went on she felt more and more the need to get in touch with the young man in question. When she found where he was imprisoned she began writing to him, identifying who she was. Several years passed in which they exchanged correspondence. Eventually she came to peace with what had happened. One day she found herself writing to let him know she could forgive him for what he'd done.

"A year later she went to see him. The prison chaplain was present when they met for the first time. He told me that the woman came into the meeting room first. Then the young man was brought in. When he entered he seemed hesitant, shy and reserved, afraid to look at her. She got up and walking over put her arms around him and gave him a long hug. He broke down sobbing. After that, the chaplain said he was never the same. The transformation that had taken place in her had taken place in him as well."

"That is a powerful story."

"It is, but when it was first reported you can imagine how it was covered by the press. The power is not in the early part of the story but in the conclusion, and the press never reported on that."

"In a way you have highlighted my point. There are good things that take place in life, magnificent and heroic things and yet we are almost compelled by those who own the various press outlets to report those things that cater to the lowest in human nature. What can we do?"

"Perhaps the first thing we need to do is become aware of what we're doing and the effect it is having on us as people. Until we become aware of these things, how can we change them? As awareness increases there'll be those who will put there minds to the task and come up with things that work.

"For instance, my wife told me of a reporter who worked for one of the large newspapers in Vancouver, British Columbia. She became so disenchanted with the negative tone of the paper it affected how she felt about life. She left the paper and formed a small local paper dedicated to the uplifting and transformative aspects of human nature. The paper was so successful she began hosting a radio program on a local station, which broadcast across the border into the states of Washington, Oregon and Idaho. Her programs aired twice a week, as well as over the Internet to a listening audience of over a million people. Here was someone who was revolted by the negativity in her work and did something about it. She presented an alternative that worked and found support amongst a large segment of the population."

"That would have to be an exception don't you think?"

"You sound as if you've given up, resigned yourself to things as they are. Is that true?"

"Perhaps that is the case."

"You have illustrated what I've been pointing to. When we are surrounded and inundated with the negative we begin to forget the other side of us, the creative and ingenious side, the side that loves and cares. Instead we become pessimistic and depressed. In such instances our attachment to the paycheck and the prestige of our position may keep us in positions that no longer feed our well-being. When enough people see the cost of such a trade-off and leave it behind that will be one of the grains of sand that tip the scales."

"What you're suggesting isn't easy."

"You're right. It is not easy and the position in which you find yourself is not easy either."

"Thank you."

"You're welcome. One further point I would like to make on the issue you've raised is this. I have faith in the ability of the human being to overcome adversity and difficulty. I have faith in the creative genius of the human mind, I have faith in the compassion and understanding that resides in the human heart." Tremaine paused for a moment and took several swallows from a glass of water before turning to a tall well-dressed man with dark hair and bright blue eyes. "You have a question?" he asked.

"Yes. I work in the entertainment industry. There has been considerable criticism over the role movies play in our society, in particular with reference to violence and the perpetuation of it. My question is not about that but rather about the role of entertainment in communication. What part do you think entertainment plays in the broadcasting of information? What's behind my question is this. It seems to me that if we can communicate the powerful stories of human lives in an entertaining way then we'll be able to contribute to the kind of transformation you point to. By entertaining I don't mean to slant something or twist something, but rather to present it in a clear and objective way. I have worked as a producer of film documentaries for the past twenty years. I think documentaries have had a tendency to be rather pedantic and not particularly entertaining. As a result they tend not to capture people's attention."

"I think your comments and your question are excellent. I think good storytellers are entertaining. There's no reason why a good reporter cannot be a good storyteller without, as you mention, exaggerating or twisting the facts. Perhaps one of the characteristics of entertainment lies in its ability to capture our attention and activate our imagination. Confrontation, conflict and rudeness certainly get our attention, but they do not enliven the spirit. Such things appeal to the baser side of human nature and I think it does a disservice to us as people. There's no reason why reporters and people like yourself cannot present all the facts along with accompanying perspectives and do so in an entertaining manner. Life itself is hugely entertaining. It has been my observation that most human beings love a good adventure story. But what is it about an adventure story that makes it so intriguing for us?" Silence filled the hall as the producer considered the question.

"Perhaps it is that we never really know what will happen next, so I think that the central characteristic of an adventure is the unknown."

"That's right. And when we stop and think about life we would have to say that when we wake up in the morning we really don't know what is going to happen in the hours ahead. We might have some ideas, even some plans, but the fact of the matter is, we really don't know. The unfolding of each day is an adventure. What could be more entertaining than that? And for someone like yourself, what a great opportunity, what a great contribution you can make."

"Thank you, Dr. Tremaine. I appreciate your comments."

"Yes, the young lady over here," Tremaine addressed a young blond woman in her early thirties.

"I used to listen to the news every day but I found myself getting depressed and on edge. I never noticed it until I spent a couple of weeks in the wilderness where there was no radio, television or newspapers. When we came back to civilization again I switched on the television and immediately felt my stomach knotting. As I listened I realized nothing had really changed. The details were different but the flavor was the same. You'd think nothing good ever happened anymore."

"It's depressing, isn't it?"

"Could we not regulate the press so that it balances the negative and the positive?"

"It is my hope that with greater public awareness and more public forums like this, we'll be able to bring about the changes we want. Perhaps I'm overly optimistic.

"Our society has become increasingly regulated. We have laws that govern just about every aspect of life. When this happens, society becomes rigid and inflexible. This, in turn, inhibits creativity and spontaneity. It reduces internal self-reliance and causes us to depend on external things, other people's ideas of what works and what doesn't.

"Some of you may have heard of Confucius. He was a reformer and believed in developing protocols, rules and regulations that governed every aspect of life in the interest of harmony in society. The sage Lao Tzu, seeing what was happening, went into voluntary exile because he couldn't stand the repression and lack of freedom that resulted. I think we've already gone a long way down the same road. I've no desire to make it worse. I do understand your frustration, however."

A florid middle-aged man at the back of the press section stood up, his face flushed with anger. "You may not wish to regulate the press, but it seems to me that you're interested in bringing social pressure to bear. To my mind, this is just another form of regulation. I think you're afraid reporters will ask questions, but that's our job. The more I listen to you, the more I hear 'press censorship.' I think you want us to stop asking questions because you're afraid of where they might lead, and of the embarrassment they might cause your administration."

"The fear you mention is yours, not mine; the dishonesty you allude to is likewise yours. I have no fear concerning questions you or anyone may ask.

"I think it is essential to a democracy such as ours that the members of the press ask whatever questions they wish, including the questions that might be uncomfortable to ask. I would suggest, however, that those questions are more likely to get a thoughtful response when they are posed with civility and respect born of a genuine interest in the truth, whatever it may be.

"When a reporter poses questions, he selects an aspect of reality to which our attention is drawn. In this instance, you introduced the idea of fear and dishonesty. It was you that drew people's attention to something most had not been thinking of. What you drew people's attention to was simply a reflection of your own mind.

"When Emerson held his first press conference, one of the reporters posed the following question: 'your political party has been denied the White House for twelve years. We know the Republican Party exercised power through questionable means. Now that your party is in power, will you resist the temptation to get even?' By the question he posed, the reporter revealed his own thinking and introduced to public awareness something that was not in Emerson's mind at all: the idea of revenge.

"If you wish to tarnish a man's image, it's easy to do. Arrange a press conference and ask him if he's beaten his wife lately. No matter what he answers, you've introduced this idea into the consciousness of those hearing the question. This is irresponsible journalism, an abuse of the reporter's role and the power of his position in society.

"As a graduate student, I took a course in the philosophy of history. Until then, I had always thought of history as the recording of particular events, facts, occurring in time. It suddenly dawned on me that history is not a factual reality, but rather a complex reflection of the historian's point of view on events taking place around him. One person alone does not record history. Each person that records it does so from a different perspective. After that, I began to see that through the manipulation of news, it was possible to create the illusion of events that actually did not occur.

"I first saw this happen in the sixties; it was a tactic exploited by both anti-war activists and government agencies alike. You might remember a recent example where an illusion was created by the clever use of words. Not long ago, an article appeared in the Boston Globe under the heading "FANCY FOOTWORK." The reporter mentioned in his article that Senator Cole had hinted that key members of the Republican Party were considering impeachment proceedings against the President. For several days following this statement, newspapers all over the country carried articles concerning impeachment, the historical antecedents, the more recent events stemming from Watergate, and the current situation suggested by the Senator.

"Now what was it all about? Nothing. Was there really any talk of impeachment amongst Republicans? As far as I can tell, other than the senator, the answer is no. Senator Cole introduced the idea, knowing it would be picked up by the media, and made into something that really didn't exist. Essentially, he manipulated the press; he got them to do exactly what he wanted.

"Today, the language and images of television weave a reality that is largely unreal. This happens in the reporting of the news, advertising and the programs produced. We've become masters in shading reality so that it conforms to our beliefs. So when the media allows itself to be manipulated, reporters contribute to the problem they're meant to safeguard against. They become purveyors of illusion, making it difficult for the average person to distinguish between fact and fiction. The mind has difficulty distinguishing between the external facts of a situation and the internal story about the facts."

"I wonder if you could explain what you mean?" The question had come from a young student to Tremaine's right.

"When we look at the world around us, our senses perceive the mountains, the trees, the ocean and so on. When we read a book, we receive descriptions of the mountains, the trees and the oceans, which we see in the mind's eye. The mind does not distinguish between the two. As human beings go through life, there is a kind of mental chatter that goes on in the background, which maintains a running commentary on what is going on. This running commentary takes place from the perspective of a well-established story, our personal story; in this story we are the central character, playing both the hero and victim.

"The human being, unaware of this, fails to distinguish between the internal mental story and the external reality. The former is fiction; the latter is fact. It is this to which the Zen master refers when he tells the story about a man who catches a fish. The fish is too small so he throws it back in the water, and for the first time the fish realizes he's been swimming in something. We swim within the mental story that operates in our minds and usually have little awareness of it. In this way, it sets up related thought patterns and the accompanying emotional states.

"It's this kind of thing the courts go to such pains to avoid in legal cases. They have long been aware of the discrepancies between the different perceptions of 'eye witnesses' to a single event. Therefore, such reports are suspect. Why? Because they do not distinguish between the internal dialogue about what happened and the facts themselves."

"Thank you."

"Yes." Tremaine pointed to a young woman in the front row to his left.

"There appears to be an inordinate preoccupation with death and suffering in both the press and society at large. I find it unbalanced and oppressive. Often, I'm left with a feeling of hopelessness. It seems to me that this kind of preoccupation is not healthy. It also seems, as you've pointed out, to be a distortion of what is really going on. Would you please comment on this?"

"I think you said it well. You used the term unbalanced. It's true. What we're subjected to through the media tends to deal with death and suffering. It's another example of what I mean when I talk of illusion. The press tends to focus on the negative aspects of human nature. There's nothing wrong in reporting such things, but the lack of balance creates a negative sense of reality which, taken as a whole, is inaccurate. By drawing attention to one side of human nature, the side that is destructive, vicious and cruel, and failing to report the creative, loving and caring aspects of human nature, we've created despair, cynicism and hopelessness. When this is coupled with the kind of death-dealing programs so prevalent on television, we shouldn't be surprised when our children are drawn to violence and death.

"When a child grows up in the streets of cities engulfed by war, his psychological climate is permeated with death, violence and suffering. Psychologists have known for a long time the effect this kind of environment has upon children.

"Too many of our children are subjected to a similar reality in the ghettos of our cities. Meanwhile, all of our children, the middle and upper-class children as well, are subjected to the virtual reality of television and movies. The reality portrayed consists of an inordinate level of violent and destructive behavior. In time, as our children grow, what they've witnessed on television becomes actualized in the society at large. Actors whose deaths we've witnessed over and over again, only to see them appear in yet another movie, obscure the finality of death. Most parents would not leave their children alone in the presence of psychopathic killers; yet that is precisely what we've done by leaving our children alone with our television sets. Young minds and emotions are being shaped by ugliness and charged with destructiveness.

"The effects of actual reality and virtual reality upon children show many similarities. A major difference, however, is that we evidence more concern for children caught in actual combat than we do for those children caught in the virtual combat portrayed on the screens in our homes and theaters.

"When the young murder each other, as was the case at Columbine, we're shocked and dismayed; we're at a loss as to how such tragedy came about. 'What is wrong with our children?' we ask, wringing our hands. 'Where did these monsters come from?' The answer is simple. They came from us; they cut their teeth on the television and videos *we* created."

"Are you saying that the press is responsible for this?" asked a young man in a wheelchair.

"I'm saying that the press and the movie industry is, yes. The emphasis of reporting is, as the young lady pointed out, on the negative and violent aspects of human nature. This unbalanced perspective is shared by the entertainment industry as a whole. The press, however, is responsible for reporting the events that take place throughout the world. The questions they pose determine the reality upon which we focus. How easy is it for one group of people to dislike another group, based solely on the misinformation and bias of the reporting? Perhaps this is why so many of our countrymen condone the violence of the Israelis and have little comprehension of what it's like for the Arabs living in the squalor of Gaza, or the West Bank."

"It's been said before, violence and negativity sell. People watch it with fascination," responded the man in the wheelchair. "That's why the broadcasting companies program what they do."

"In a circle, there's no beginning and no end. We must start somewhere. Tonight, the point of entry is with the press itself. The press is responsible in matters that pertain to it. Of course, that doesn't mean that we, the population as a whole, are not responsible. We are. We, as well as the media, are responsible for the psychological climate we've created for our children through the medium of television. It's important that we understand what we're doing to our young, and to ourselves.

"Television, perhaps more than any other medium in the history of the world, determines the outlook we have on the world and each other. We must come to terms with it; we must see how it affects our perception of reality. If we fail to see this clearly, we may well lose two important freedoms: the freedom to think and the freedom of direct perception. These are subtle freedoms, not readily apparent. If we lose them, we'll be unaware we've done so."

A slim balding man, his face unshaven, stood in the front row. "Dr. Tremaine, one of the functions of the press is to be a watchdog on behalf of the people. Our job is to ferret out and bring to public awareness corruption, wherever it is found. The press has done a reasonably good job of this when it comes to such things as politics, business and religion. But what of corruption in the press itself, can the press monitor itself? What happens when the lens of communication becomes distorted? Who is left to draw attention to this distortion? Politicians and educators may attempt to do it, but when they're seen as dishonest, how can they be heard or believed when pointing to the dishonesty of the press itself?"

"A very good question. I'm glad you raised it. It's a concern I have, and one for which I don't have an answer. It's something we must think about.

"Many years ago during the Vietnam War, sanctuary was granted to a young soldier by five students. This occurred at Boston University. I was one of the students involved. I was asked to come to the phone to talk to a reporter from the soldier's hometown in Oregon. I spoke briefly with the reporter before being cut off by an operator. When I tried to get the operator to reconnect us, she refused. I asked to speak to the supervisor. She came on the line and also refused. The operators were from the same community as the soldier. They knew the reporter, and were convinced he would give a sympathetic reporting of the soldier's views. They did not want me to talk to the reporter. To them, the young soldier was a traitor. No matter how hard I tried, they would not put me through. I never forgot that experience. I found it frightening. The operators controlled the means of communication and were in a position to prevent it when they so desired. Freedom of the press is of the utmost importance in a society like ours. That freedom must be an internal freedom. The press must take a good look at itself. It must become aware of its biases."

....

It was past ten o'clock when Channing escorted the Tremaines from the back of the hall into the warm evening. A gentle breeze brought with it the smell of the ocean and ruffled the leaves caught in the lamplight. Accompanied by members of the Secret Service, the Tremaines walked along the path that led across the quadrangle to the waiting cars. Students stood on either side and, as they passed, murmured their thanks and good-byes into the hushed night.

26

The enemy within

L evin was ready to give his speech at the rally. Goldstein rode with him in the air-conditioned car through the streets of Tel Aviv.

"This has been a long and difficult process, my friend," said Levin.

"It has. I'm not sure we're there yet."

Earlier in the day, they'd received warning there might be an assassination attempt at the rally.

"We must still attend," Levin had stated flatly. No arguments to the contrary would change his mind. Now, as he sat in the car, he felt a deep sense of quiet. He knew he'd begun the process of moving his people in the direction of peace. The results of their decision was in God's hands.

Half an hour later, Levin stood at the podium under a canvas canopy, shaded from the bright sun's intense heat. He saw before him a vast sea of faces and bright colors stretching in every direction. The square was full, as were the balconies and windows surrounding the square. Loudspeakers had been set up. On the roofs of the buildings Levin saw the IDF sharpshooters. Security was very tight, given the threat.

"I want to welcome you all here today. I am particularly pleased to welcome representatives of the governments of our neighbors, those with whom we are now living in peace. I also wish to welcome Hassan as representative of the Palestinian people.

"We've been in a virtual state of war for half a century. It's time for it to come to an end. There are those amongst the Palestinians and our fellow countrymen who believe that their respective enemies must be destroyed. This kind of thinking has not worked, so it is time for us to move in a new direction, a direction that will lead us to peace with ourselves, our neighbors and our friends.

"I think it is urgent that we address the issue of violence. Violence begets violence. I know this may seem strange coming from a military man like myself. It's because of my military experience that I feel I can say this, knowing first hand that what I have to say is true.

"For many years I believed we must defend our right to exist. I was prepared to do that by the exercise of 'reasonable force.' What I came to see was that 'reasonable force' has a tendency to become more extreme with the passage of time. There's no doubt our use of force has become more deadly. The reasoning behind it was simple but, as it turns out, false. We believed that once sufficient force was used, our enemies would submit. Instead of that happening, our enemies became stronger and more determined. This is not the direction in which we want to go. It is not a way that will bring us the peace we so desperately desire.

"There is a saying that power corrupts. I think the same can be said of the exercise of force. The use of force tends to corrode those who use it and brings out the worst in human nature. As violence has increased all around us, there has also been an increase in violence among our own people. The polarization without is mirrored within. The clash between extremists within our society eats away at our nation's heart and points out that we are not immune from such things. We've set ourselves up as being better than others. We did not consider ourselves subject to the arrogance that afflicts all men. But when we examine ourselves, what do we find? We find the very same arrogance we've been so quick to find in others, an arrogance that blinds us to our own failings, causing us to project on others what we've been unable to see in ourselves. This is dangerous for us and for all who must deal with us.

"It is for this reason I wish to bring this matter to the forefront of awareness. We have within recent history been a people victimized by a horrendous crime, the crime of the holocaust. But just because we've been the victims of such atrocities does not give us the right to inflict similar atrocities on others. If we refuse to consider this, it makes us capable of committing such acts by blinding us to what we're doing.

"All of us are aware of what the Nazis did to our people. But it is important to understand that Nazis are not a nationality but a way of thinking, a way of thinking that says they are better than others. I'm afraid we are guilty of the same thinking.

"By believing ourselves to be the 'Chosen People of Yahweh,' we have set ourselves up as being superior to others whom we regard as inferior. This is not true. To believe that Yahweh, the God of our forefathers, would ever chose between people is a distortion of the truth. There can only be one God and that God, by whatever name, is the God of all human beings, without exception.

"Our beliefs have always given us an air of superiority. That is nothing more than arrogance. In the long run, it makes us a liability to our neighbors and friends. It is one way we insure we have implacable foes for as long as we exist. Instead of dealing with our external foes, let us deal with our internal ones. Perhaps then, if we're lucky, we can turn our enemies into partners for peace.

"This process in which we've engaged cannot go ahead, if it does not have the support of you the people. To that end, a referendum will be held. You will all be able to have your say. This morning I set in motion the dissolving of the government. One month from today, we will go to the polls in order to decide as a people if this is the direction we want to take. For myself, it is the only direction I see. In the coming month, I hope to engage one and all in a national dialogue for peace. Thank you."

A roar of sustained applause answered Levin's remarks. But amongst it, as there had been throughout the speech, sounds of dissent and anger could be heard. Levin knew the next month would not be easy.

Levin and Goldstein left the podium and, surrounded by armed security forces, made their way through the packed throng to the waiting cars. The crowd had pushed toward the Prime Minister, and the security personnel had difficulty keeping the space open for the two men as they approached the motorcade. The area around the cars was cordoned off despite the crush. The noise was deafening. Unexpectedly, one of the security men went down. There was a loud popping. The crowd pulled back, accompanied by hysterical screams.

As Goldstein turned, he saw Levin go down. He felt a burning sensation in his chest, then a bullet severed his spine. He collapsed. He was lying next to Levin, powerless to move. Everything went suddenly quiet, and he sank into the peace of oblivion.

. . . .

Israeli radio and television had carried the news. Levin was dead. Goldstein was severely injured and not expected to recover. A young Israeli rabbinical student had fired the shots. He was a member of an ultra orthodox sect completely opposed to the peace process. He and his family lived in one of the armed settlements that protruded into Palestinian land, an area that, if the peace process continued, would have to be dismantled.

....

David was seated at his desk when Jonathan Makarios pushed the door open. Looking up, David noticed the shocked look on his face. "What's up Jonathan?"

"We just got news that Michael Levin was shot and killed. Joseph Goldstein was severely wounded. They don't know if he'll survive."

"What happened?"

"They were attending a peace rally when a young student stepped up to them and got away several shots. Levin died right away. Goldstein is in critical condition."

"Who was the attacker?"

The door to the office opened and Doug Kersey entered, also visibly shaken.

"You've heard?"

"Yes, I've heard. Is there any word on who was behind it, Doug?"

"It just came in. The assassin was a twenty five year old student, a member of one of the ultra orthodox mystical sects

"What do you know about this sect?"

"They're a group that believes in the absolute superiority of the Jew over non-Jews. They believe that the world was created specifically for them, and that all Gentiles are subhuman."

"That doesn't sound good."

"It's not. They refuse to have anything to do with the Palestinians, believing them to be an inferior race with no right to the land they occupy. Some of them live in the settlements built on Palestinian land."

"And they were behind this killing?"

"Apparently. Levin had just finished giving a speech in Tel Aviv. I haven't read the speech yet, but I heard that he spoke of the need for Israelis to stop looking outside themselves and find the enemy within."

The phone rang and David picked it up. He listened for several moments without comment. Hanging up, he turned to the others. "Joseph Goldstein died about fifteen minutes ago."

27

The end justifies the means

It makes me so angry," Sandra said. She was referring to a program she'd just seen on CBC news.

She and David had been on the west coast and had gone to Victoria to spend a couple of days with her parents. It was a little past seven on a warm autumn evening. Borrowing his father-in-laws truck, he and Sandra had loaded Trapper, the golden lab in the back and set off for the Galloping Goose Trail near Sooke.

"What's that?" David asked.

"They showed something on the CBC news this evening that made my blood boil. They had footage of an olive orchard in Palestine. The local people have harvested the olives in a tradition that goes back several hundred years. One of the Israeli settlements is quite close, and has been expanded into the little valley where the trees are. For several days the Palestinians have been going to pick the olives and the settlers have driven them off. In a period of less than a week, five of them have been shot; two were killed. According to the report, there have been ten deaths in the past three years, all Palestinians."

"And what are the Israelis doing to put a stop to it?"

"That's the point. They're not!"

"No?"

"No. Some Israeli peace activists were aware of what was going on and came to the valley to shield the Palestinians from the attacks so they could harvest the olives. Members of the Israeli army showed up, ostensibly, to keep the two Jewish groups apart.

They escorted the peace activists away, drove the Palestinians out and bulldozed the trees."

"And what was the reasoning behind that?"

"The Israeli officials said the trees presented cover for gunmen to hide and launch attacks on the settlers."

"I see."

"The cameraman caught it all on film. The settlers were carrying rifles and handguns. The cameraman, before being driven off the property, was able to zoom in on the settlers. You could see the hatred in their faces. I just don't understand it, David. How can they get away with it?"

"You don't understand it?"

"Oh I understand it, all right. I'm amazed that human beings can treat each other in such a way. Why do we not see that we're all part of one family?"

They came around a bend. Below them, one of the ocean inlets stretched and twisted inland. Trapper was already out in the water, swimming blissfully. They climbed onto a bluff that jutted out over the inlet and sat down. The sun slipped behind a rocky ridge to the West, and peach colored clouds in the east reflected across the inlet. David put his arm around his wife and they sat watching the colors of the evening slowly merge to a dusky rose.

"Our whole approach to life is wrong." Sandra said quietly.

David looked at her. "What do you mean?"

"Our whole approach to life is one in which we're constantly trying to defend ourselves from some force that's out to do us harm. For Israel it's the Palestinians and for the Palestinians it's the Israelis. Ethnic cleansing and genocide, even terrorism and counter terrorism are also expressions of it as well. But, it's not just in how we address political issues it's far broader than that. Not only do we see ourselves under attack from people, we feel we are under attack from microbes, bacteria, and viruses as well. What is it we're doing in the hospitals, clinics, and doctors offices all over North America? We're *fighting* disease, it's a war in which we try and develop more and more powerful drugs to combat disease. What's the difference between that and developing more and more powerful weapons to combat more and more powerful weapons?"

"That's an interesting perspective."

"It just struck me now while I was sitting here. Western medicine has largely accepted this model of waging war. The result has been the development of diseases that are resistant to the current medical arsenal which has damaged our immune systems."

"You're talking about the development of so called, 'super bugs'?"

"That's right. We've paid so little attention to the development of health in the human organism and have undermined it with poor nutrition, lack of exercise and the over use of drugs. It's evident to me that when the human body is physically and mentally healthy it remains resilient and resistant to disease. The yogis of India and the Taoists of China have known how to maintain health and live long productive lives. I think our over reliance on technology and science has hurt us. In a sense we've tried to use force to solve our medical problems. It's the same approach we've used in trying to resolve external conflicts as well."

His wife's remarks had clarified something for David. It was indeed, as she'd pointed out. "So do you think the recent Avian flu epidemic in the Fraser Valley is an example of our ignorance?"

"Yes. We've talked about this before, disease occurs when animals are kept in crowded quarters, given inadequate exercise and their food has been altered with hormones and antibiotics. The immune systems in these animals can no longer ward off diseases carried by wild animals."

"Perhaps the conflicts we're seeing around the world are a result of similar circumstances; over-crowding, poor diet and so on."

"I think so. I find it fascinating that the microcosm and the macrocosm are essentially the same, reflections of each other."

A cool breeze stirred in the nearby trees and brought with it the salty tang of the Pacific. Rose tinted clouds darkened to a purple hue and evening slipped silently away.

"It seemed so hopeful for Israel and the Palestinians when Levin and Goldstein were still alive," Sandra said. "I find it hard to believe that Israel could so quickly slip into such terrible bloodshed."

In the three months since the funeral, Israel had slid inexorably into a downward spiral of violence and counter violence. They'd elected a new Prime Minister, Samuel Herzog, on the basis of bringing about a "just peace through firmness." He'd started his mandate by visiting a fiercely contested holy site. The Palestinians had taken affront. In the resulting riot, seven Palestinians had been shot and killed. Then came an attack on one of the settlements by Palestinian gunmen, followed by a closing of the Israeli borders to all Palestinians which resulted in a form of economic strangulation. Then had come a wave of suicide bombings that brought counter measures such as the targeting of Palestinian leaders and their families. When this failed, a full-scale invasion of the West Bank had ensued, and Gaza was seized. What Herzog meant by "firmness" was becoming apparent.

"Why can't Hassan do something to stop this process?" Sandra asked.

"He has tried, Sandra."

"Two weeks ago, he called on all Palestinians for a complete stop to the hostilities. He keeps doing that, but it doesn't work. They don't stop. He must have called for a halt at least thirty times in the past nine months."

"That's right, Sandra. But then something like what you saw on CBC happens, and it gives more fuel to those who do not want peace."

"Do you think Herzog really wants peace?"

"According to his words, yes. But when one looks at his actions, it's hard to believe."

Just then, Trapper came bounding up the embankment. They had to scramble out of his way in order to stay dry. The next day, David returned to Washington, leaving Sandra behind to visit with her parents.

....

Travis entered the oval office to find Doug Kersey and Jonathan Makarios already there. Doug Kersey had just returned from Israel. Tremaine was seated in his armchair in front of the fire, and the other two men seated on either side.

"I came as quickly as I could," Travis said as he took off his coat.

Tremaine noticed the tiredness in the chairman. "Travis, help yourself to coffee and then join us. Doug had just begun telling me of his visit to Israel. It doesn't sound too promising."

Tremaine had sent his foreign secretary to convey his concern over the siege of Gaza and Hassan's compound. Israeli bulldozers had been systematically destroying the Palestinian Authority's buildings and had moved on to Hassan's headquarters. They'd sealed him off, along with a dozen of his top aides. They had cut power and water and, on top of that, they'd allowed no food in for a week.

Travis put his coffee on the table and pulled over another armchair.

"The Israelis have refused to lift the siege," David said. "Herzog is demanding a complete end to the suicide bombing and a one month cease-fire before he will even consider resuming peace talks."

"That will never work," Travis responded. "He knows it. What he's doing is ensuring a continuation of the hostilities."

"I agree. I asked Doug to go and talk with Hassan while he was there, but the Israelis refused permission. They have been destroying known Hamas buildings and targeting both Hamas and Palestinian Authority personnel. They've also been destroying the homes of the families of suicide bombers."

"What it does is give more justification to the extremists," Doug interjected. "Not only have they been destroying the water lines to Hassan's compound, but they're also doing the same thing in the areas they've occupied. They seem to be implementing a kind of scorched earth policy. They're denying the Palestinians access to water, enforcing strict curfews and shooting and killing those who violate them. There have been reports that they're not allowing the removal of bodies. So, according to 'Doctors Without Borders,' there is increasing concern over the possible outbreak of disease."

"Are you suggesting the Israelis are deliberately using disease and starvation as a weapon of war?" asked Travis.

"It could be construed that way," replied the foreign secretary.

"And the suicide bombings continue," pointed out Jonathan.

"Yes, they continue," said Tremaine.

"Can we do anything?" asked Travis.

"I've informed the Israelis that we'll no longer guarantee their loans, and that we're stopping all arms shipments and supplies for their military. I've also informed the Security Council at the United Nations that we will no longer veto the UN resolutions concerning Israel. But it seems even that will have no effect. Tell him what Herzog told you." Tremaine said to Doug Kersey.

"He said to convey to the President, and I quote, 'We claim the right as a nation to exist, we claim the right of pre-emptive strikes, and we will defend ourselves by whatever means necessary. As long as our people are being killed, we will not rest. The Palestinians will learn the terrible might of our armed forces, and if they are to survive, they must surrender all weapons and put an end to all terrorist attacks of any kind anywhere and for all time. This bloodshed has been going on for too long. All our overtures toward peace have been rejected. We are left with no alternative but to seize peace on our terms, and it will be peace through strength. And you can tell your President that we will not be blackmailed by financial threats he might make, nor will we be bullied by the United Nations.'"

"He doesn't leave much doubt as to his position does he?" Travis remarked.

"No he doesn't. The trip to Israel has been put off as well."

"So what's next?"

"That's what we're here to discuss."

28

The shadow that we ourselves cast

The Invitation to speak at Lester B. Pearson College of the Pacific had come three months earlier. At the time Tremaine knew only a little of the school but in conversation with Michael Everet, the Dean, he had learned more. "The college, as you probably know is named after the Canadian Prime Minister, Lester Bowles Pearson, a recipient of the Nobel Prize for Peace. We have at any one time about two hundred students in attendance drawn from approximately eighty different countries. These students," Everet explained, "live and study together and are actively involved in community service. Their education is both academic and practical.

"Drawn from a wide variety of backgrounds they're expected to rise above ethnocentric differences and work cooperatively in the accomplishment of specific objectives. By fostering a kind of internationalism the students are taught, by experience, to function beyond the narrow parameters of national views. The students, we attract," he continued, "are those who will likely enter some form of government service within the country of their birth."

"So your purpose is to contribute to greater international understanding by reaching the leaders of tomorrow?" Tremaine suggested.

"Exactly," Everet had agreed.

....

Cleared for takeoff." As the pilot's words came over the loudspeaker system, Michael Reddy settled back in his seat, helped by the thrust of the big engines. Lights flashed by outside as they gained speed. The front of the cabin came up and the rumbling of the wheels went quiet as the big jet lifted into the night sky.

New World Airlines Flight 304 continued to gain altitude as it headed north from New York bound for London. It would achieve cruising altitude over eastern Canada before turning northeast and heading out over the Atlantic.

Michael watched as the lights of the city faded below, followed by occasional clusters of light from smaller population centers. Looking up he could see the stars, like brilliant gems set in the darkness of space. The stewardess came by and handed him a menu; one of the benefits of flying first class was that he could choose his evening meal. When the stewardess returned, he ordered the Thai Chicken dinner and a glass of wine. With only five passengers in the cabin, service was quick. The stewardess served him a White Zinfandel. He took a swallow and settled back in the plush leather seat. He closed his eyes and savored the taste. Before long, he felt the aircraft bank to the right.

There was a rumble, and then a thunderous explosion. A flash of blinding light tore the aircraft apart. Flaming sections of the doomed plane fell toward the ocean several miles off Peggy's Cove.

New York Times
"WHO WISHES US ILL?"

More than 300 Americans and 70 foreign nationals lost their lives in the mysterious explosion of New World Airlines Flight 304 off the east coast of Canada last night. A large number of the passengers on the airline were US diplomats.

Unconfirmed reports suggest the plane, bound for London, was the target of a missile attack or a terrorist bomb. Eyewitnesses on the ground reported a streak of light heading into the night sky followed by a bright flash. These reports, however, are unsubstantiated at this time.

Air traffic controllers said they did not pick up anything unusual on their screens. Military spokesmen stated that there was neither missile testing nor any missions involving Air Force aircraft in the area.

As yet, no terrorist group has claimed responsibility.

Canadian Coast Guard vessels have found no survivors. US coast guard ships are on their way to the scene to help in the recovery process. Seas are high in the area, with winds gusting to 45 knots.

. . . .

Tremaine addressed the nation the day following the tragedy of New World Airlines Flight 304. He could offer little more than condolences for the survivors of the doomed passengers and a promise to report back as soon as information from the investigation was available.

. . . .

The tragedy of this event was on his mind when, a week later he gave a talk at the Lester B. Pearson College of the Pacific.

Tremaine's talk at the college was entitled, *The Shadow That We Ourselves Cast* and was later broadcast over the CBC program, "Ideas," with Alan Daniels.

"Recent events in the Middle East have escalated again. More than a thousand Palestinians have been killed, and three hundred Israelis. Despite considerable pressure to bring the events to a peaceful resolution, things are not improving. Why is that?

"In the Middle East we've not addressed the cause of the problem, and unless we do, how can we bring about a resolution? Those of us who do not live in the Middle East think it is up to the Israelis and Palestinians to resolve their difficulties. It is certainly true that they must approach those events with an eye to understanding the underlying causes, but we must do the same. We as citizens of the nations of the world can look at this for ourselves. The question becomes: how does my country help keep the fires of conflict burning? What is the underlying source of these events? Stephen Mitchell, a contemporary student of Taoism, speaks of a great nation being like a great man. He said something to the effect that:

> *A great nation is like a great man:*
> *When he makes a mistake, he realizes it.*
> *Having realized it, he admits it.*
> *Having admitted it, he corrects it.*
> *He considers those who point out his faults*
> *As his most benevolent teachers.*
> *He thinks of his enemy*
> *As the shadow that he himself casts.*

"Not long ago, New World Airlines Flight 304 suffered a catastrophic explosion over the North Atlantic. All on board were killed. Was this the result of a terrorist attack?

"Recent events give us pause to reflect on the causes of terrorism and what can be done about it. From studies in modern psychology, we know that children from broken homes are more likely to have broken marriages. Children of abuse are more likely to become abusers of their children. In families where spousal abuse takes place, the children who witness it often display the same behavior.

"It is abundantly clear that such behavior is passed down from generation to generation. The implications are there for all to see. If these destructive cycles aren't broken, they'll be repeated. What then is the cycle that must be broken when it comes to terrorism? If we don't find out, we'll continue to suffer. Since we continue to suffer, we haven't found out.

"Perhaps more than at any other time in the history of the world we have large populations of people living in the most hopeless and soul-destroying situations ever devised: refugee camps. Those who live in these camps have been forgotten. They do not show up on our television screens. They've become invisible people, the recipients of benign neglect, a people living under appalling, overcrowded conditions without hope. For many of these people, such conditions are now entering a second generation and, in some cases, even a third. Just as the cycles of abuse and broken marriages get passed from generation to generation, so does the destructiveness of the refugee camps. It is from the camps of the past that the wars of the present are spawned, and it's from the camps of the present that the wars of the future will arise.

"We in North America live in affluence, secure in our geographical and psychological isolation, but I suspect, not for long.

"As those who travel in third-world countries know, through the medium of television, our affluence and lack of concern for others is appallingly obvious. Our nations are largely ignorant of those outside our borders, blind to the poverty and hopelessness that infect so many of our fellow human beings. We're even ignorant of those within our own borders who suffer from poverty, abuse, prejudice and lost opportunities. By that I mean the first Americans, the first Canadians, the aboriginal peoples of North America. They, and those who watch our television programs from beyond our borders, know us well. They do not live with our delusions and denials. We, however, know virtually nothing of them, of the suffering and hardship of their lives.

"What is the question our governments always pose as justification for both our action and inaction? 'Is it in our national interest?' When it is, we act. When it's not, we don't. But such action, or inaction, is selfish and uncaring. We may help end the conflicts in Africa and elsewhere, but as the action of war fades from our screens, we forget about the displaced refugees who've been uprooted from their homes.

"Who are these refugees? Who are they really? Are they not people like you and me, people with hopes and dreams just like us? These refugees are forced into conditions that give rise to new waves of violence. And what of us? We've turned away, become absorbed in our homes, glued to our televisions, lost in the spectacle of the Olympics or our favorite soap opera, once more oblivious to the plight of those around us.

"You may ask, 'Surely this ignorance on our part is not what brings such violence to our shores and our skies?' No, not just that, but something far worse, something rooted in the same ignorance.

"When Hitler's storm troopers surged across Europe, we were slow to react, slow to see what lay behind the words of appeasement and lies. After all, we were half a world away and the fighting was not on our shores. Once we discovered the magnitude of the atrocities, once we entered the concentration camps and beheld the horror of man's inhumanity to man, we were quick to point fingers of blame at the German people for their silence, for letting things get out of hand. Now, forever in our minds, we've associated tyranny with Germany, albeit a Germany of the past. This, along with our Biblically based belief in the 'chosen people,' undoubtedly contributed to the founding of the modern state of Israel.

"Guilt and religious justification are powerful factors in

such matters and cannot be underestimated. This action, and its justification, contributed directly to the displacement of the indigenous people who'd lived in Palestine for so long.

"Let me pose an impertinent question, one that makes us squirm. What is the difference between the hatred of those in the Jewish settlements and the German SS? What is the difference between the hatred that twists Muslims, Christians and Jews alike? There is no difference. To think otherwise is to delude ourselves.

"Tyranny and hatred is not the province of any single group of people. They are states of mind to which all human beings, regardless of nationality, are heir. Terrorism constitutes the violent acts of war and aggression against helpless and innocent civilians. If we truly wish to put an end to this cycle of violence, if we wish to put an end to terrorism, then we must look at what makes us most uncomfortable, our own blindness, our own complicity.

"Just as the bombing of PAN AM 103 over Scotland in 1988 was an act of terrorism, so are the acts of Israeli soldiers against civilian populations in Lebanon, Palestine and the surrounding countries. But because the people who commit these acts of terrorism are Jews, the victims of the Holocaust, the 'chosen of Yahweh,' we remain quiet while governments continue to support these atrocities. And what are our politicians afraid of? Why are they so silent? Money! The money from the Jewish lobby is not something to be ignored; it influences a lot of votes. In addition to that, there are few politicians who have the courage to raise issues such as this for fear of being branded anti-Semites and being voted from office.

"The face of the terrorist is not just an Arab extremist. It is also the face of modern Israel, of Jewish people, descendants and survivors of the Holocaust. The quiet people of Germany have exchanged places with the quiet people of Israel, the quiet people of the Untied States and Canada. We, by either our ignorance or prejudice, lend our silence to the atrocities committed, and thus perpetuate them. We wondered why the German people remained so quiet. Why they did not rise up against the tyranny of Hitler? If we look at ourselves we can know the answer first hand, from our own experience.

"Janis Joplin sang, 'Freedom's just another word for nothing left to lose.' Lao Tzu said, 'When life becomes intolerable death is welcomed and he who has embraced his death lives without fear. A man like that makes a formidable enemy.' Those who live in the refugee camps of the Middle East have nothing left to lose. Under such conditions, death is a welcome release. And since death is welcomed why not make it count for something?

"From such inhuman conditions arises the last and bitterest of hope, the hope of breaking the chains of tyranny by sacrificing one's life for a noble cause. If one has lived for nothing, why not die for something worthy? When death is welcomed, it is a potent weapon against those who fear it. And, as we've recently seen, hundreds of Palestinians have been killed, too many of them children.

"Most of us can recall the story of David, a Jew who defeated the giant Goliath. But the story of David and Goliath is more an archetypal story that depicts the weak overcoming the strong. The Taoist sage understood this well. As Lao Tzu said, 'Nothing in the world is as soft and yielding as water, yet when it comes to dissolving the hard and inflexible nothing can surpass it. The soft overcomes the hard, the gentle the rigid; everyone know this is true yet few put it into practice.' The Vietnamese understood it as well. They did not have the technical superiority to defeat the United States by raw power, so they defeated us by their simplicity; their very weakness became their strength. Rice, foot power and bicycles were key ingredients for defeating a technically superior enemy. The Palestinians are learning this now.

"Those of us who live on this continent live under the illusion that we're safe. War has not come to our shores from outside. But we are not safe. The starving and desperate people outside our shores behold our culture, our social interactions, our life-style and political motives—both national and international—our waste and affluence. We are people who have lived in our homes, absorbed in our television programs, unaware that a village has sprung up around us. Its inhabitants peer through our windows, hungry and desperate, while we are wasteful, satiated and self-absorbed. In the global village in which we now live, such behavior is an invitation to disaster. We ignore it at our peril!

"I remember a man I met in Bombay while I was in India visiting friends. Inundated by beggars, I was pawed at through taxi windows at stoplights, grubby hands pulled on my clothes. I looked into the eyes of hungry children with snot gobbed under their noses, festering sores and flies on their skin. There were so many, I learned not to look. I learned to ignore and pretend I didn't see. One day, on a street in Bombay, a man tugged on my sleeve and begged for a rupee. 'For my family,' he said. I ignored him, continuing on my way. He stayed with me, insistently tugging at my clothes.

"Suddenly, he leaped in front of me and we stood face to face, one human being looking into the eyes of another. 'My family is hungry,' he said, his voice angry and demanding. 'But for an accident of birth that put us in different countries, I am like you, a man of flesh and blood, a man who loves his wife and children. I have no work and I'm desperate. How dare you ignore me and pretend I don't exist. I'm here, and just as real as you. I know you can help. A rupee is nothing for you and everything to me. You would do the same if you were in my shoes. I'm not asking for much, just help for today, just one rupee.'

"He was right. He showed me directly who he was, who I am and the connection between us. And suddenly I saw the connection between myself and the man dead on the street, outside my hotel, food for flies, the victim of starvation, disease and my uncaring.

"Ignorance of the law does not excuse us in the eye of the courts. Ignorance of gravity does not mean we will not suffer its consequences when we step off a cliff. Greed, selfishness and ignorance are seeds that lead to a terrible harvest. Unless we wake up to what is happening, we can expect to reap the whirlwind. Don't think we can escape. Globalization, technology and transportation have shrunk the world. As Marshall McLuhan pointed out, we are all members of one single entity, a 'global village.'

"Just as pain is a warning that all is not well in the body, so is it that social upheaval and violence are nature's attempts to draw attention to the cause. Just as a man who steps on a nail is moved to identify the source of his pain and remove it, so will we be similarly moved by the suffering that comes with social upheaval. But little will happen 'til we suffer ourselves. When that suffering becomes intense enough we'll have to wake up, we'll have to pay attention. Until we do, we'll suffer increasing death on our shores and curtailment of our freedom. We'll be forced to wait in long lines for hours at a time, subjected to X-rays and body searches, wondering why some wish to do us harm and how it came to this.

"It will not just be at our airports that we will experience this, but in our schools and government offices as well, all in the interest of public safety. Is this what we want? I think not. No matter what we do, we cannot protect ourselves. We can purchase all the insurance we want, we can do many things in an attempt to create security. But security is not something that comes with life. Life is dangerous, intrinsically uncertain, and the idea of security is an illusion.

"What's to be done? We can look unflinchingly at the cause of our difficulties and stop blaming others. We can see the inter connectedness of all life and know that we are not separate from anyone. When a fly is caught in the spider's web, the whole web shakes. The more force we use to extricate ourselves, the more tightly bound we become.

"What can we do? If we're lucky, life may cause us to look into our hearts, the only place over which we have any jurisdiction. Searching within we may be fortunate enough to understand the source of our distress: our own self-interest, our own self-delusion. Only by seeing what is, the facts in life, can our eyes apprehend the alternative that is always before us, the alternative found in the joy of living in a selfless manner, the joy of serving and caring for others and our world.

"This great airship hurtling though space is our transportation through time. If we're not careful, the prison it has become for some will extend to all, and, perhaps in our extremity, we may even blow it from the sky. If that should happen, then it will not be several hundred who die, but all of us. If that occurs then perhaps the universe is well rid of us."

....

Two days later Tremaine received an invitation from the Israeli Prime Minister to visit Israel. The visit would take place at the end of December.

䷗ 29

The Master and his disciples

It was evening when Aziz and Shamir arrived above Bent Jebail. Behind them, the great ramparts of the mountains were golden in the setting sun. Through the gloaming, lights twinkled, while streams of smoke from the cooking fires floated on the evening stillness. Shamir heard the sound of dogs barking and watched as people made their way home. She was tired. The walk from Rachaf wasn't long, but the terrain was rugged.

....

Six months had passed since she'd left Nassir's home, the cave she had shared with him after the death of her family.

"Why do we have to go?" she'd asked when he told her they were leaving the following day.

"Because we must," was all he would say.

"I like it here," she'd protested.

"I know."

"Forgive me for asking, Nassir, but can't I stay?"

"No. Your destiny lies elsewhere." Nassir had refused to be drawn into further discussion.

And so, with a sense of sadness, Shamir had left the cave that had been her home. With Nassir, she'd climbed high into the mountains until at last they sat quietly and caught their breath on a rocky outcrop looking east. Below them, the familiar valleys snaked down the side of the mountain to the distant ocean.

After a brief rest they continued along a faint trail that led through the mountains. Several hours had passed when the sound of a shot broke the silence. Nassir reacted instantly. Pulling Shamir off the trail, he raced up the incline and leaped to a ledge. He turned, grabbed her by the hands and pulled her up beside him. Breathing hard, they lay side-by-side, peering down at the trail below. Nothing moved.

From where they were hidden, they had a commanding view of the surrounding area. If anyone came along the trail, they'd see them. Holding his breath, Nassir listened, his ears tuned for the slightest sound. The sighing of the ever-present wind was all he could hear. Half an hour later, they cautiously moved on.

"We'll stay above the trail," Nassir explained.

"What do you think it is?"

"Guerrillas! It's best we not meet them."

The memory of her parent's death made Shamir shudder. For half an hour they moved slowly, keeping the trail below them. Climbing around a rocky promontory, Nassir caught a movement below. Instantly, he froze. Shamir held her breath and watched, trembling. Beneath them, a man had crawled off the trail and sat against the shattered trunk of an old tree. His head fell forward. His hands hung limp at his sides and blood stained his shirt.

"Shamir, stay here. I'm going down to see what's happened."

Before she could respond, Nassir slipped away. Quickly, yet cautiously, he worked his way toward the man, taking care to stay out of sight. The sun was low, and the shadows in the depressions served as hiding places. Nassir checked the surrounding area for signs of life before creeping within ten meters of the wounded man.

Nassir studied the man. The black hair, wet with sweat, was plastered to his forehead. His eyes were closed, his breathing ragged and fast. He wore camouflage pants and a long-sleeved khaki shirt. His feet were bare. A dark stain spread down his shirt from a large, gaping wound in his upper chest. Suddenly, the man's eyes opened. Nassir, with a jolt, recognized Tariq, Kahlil's friend.

Nassir stood. As he did, Tariq's head turned toward him. Recognition spread across his face, and the light returned to the eyes.

"Nassir, is that you?"

"It is." Nassir knelt before the wounded man and examined him.

"I can't survive this, can I?" Tariq whispered.

Nassir looked into Tariq's eyes. "No, my friend, this is the final wound for this body."

Standing, he signaled Shamir to join them. In moments, the young woman was at his side, breathless. While Nassir cradled Tariq in his arms, Shamir unslung her water skin and carefully guided a small stream of water to the man's dry lips. His eyes caught hers and a faint smile crossed his face. "Thank you," he whispered.

"What happened?" Nassir asked.

Tariq shifted his gaze from Shamir and looked out across the desolate slopes. "Iranians joined our unit about a month ago." Nassir and Shamir strained to hear him. "We captured a young Israeli girl two nights ago and brought her across the border. I was ordered to kill her. I refused. The Iranians brought me here today. One of them shot me."

"Was Kahlil with your unit?" Nassir asked.

"He was, but he was sent ahead. We were to rendezvous in Bent Jebail."

"Is that where he is now?"

"Yes," came the hoarse voice.

Shamir raised the water skin to moisten Tariq's lips. His eyes focused on her momentarily. Once more the hint of a smile spread across the ashen face.

Nassir adjusted Tariq's position. "It's almost over, Tariq. Soon you'll leave this place of suffering."

"Will you see my mother for me?"

"Yes." Nassir bent his head to catch the words.

"She's a good mother, please tell her for me." The words had come slowly. The eyes stared, no longer seeing. Nassir knew that in Tariq's mind his mother now stood before him, her arms tenderly encircling the son she loved. "I love you." Nassir heard the dying man's final words.

Shamir watched intently, her heart still pounding. She felt the bond of love between the two men and watched through her tears as consciousness faded from Tariq's body. With a deep rasping shudder, he drew one last breath.

....

Shamir and Nassir had stopped for the night, far from where Tariq had died. It was late and Shamir, exhausted, fell asleep at once. She awoke once during the night and realized Nassir was gone. Long before dawn, he shook her by the arm.

"We must leave at once," he whispered.

In moments she was ready.

"What's going on?" she asked

"There's an Israeli unit nearby. They must be looking for the young girl Tariq mentioned. We must get as far away as possible."

Shamir had trouble keeping up with Nassir. Despite his age, he was agile and strong. They climbed a ridge and descended the other side into what seemed like a shallow valley. Against the stars, she could see ridge lines all around. She could tell from the stars that they were moving east. They stopped only once for a brief rest.

"Where are we going?" Shamir asked when she'd caught her breath. They sat on a low hill. From there they would know if someone were coming. If patrols operated in the region, Nassir did not want to run into them.

"Once we reach the head of the valley, we'll climb back into the high country again. From there it's not far to the village of Rachaf. The Israelis will stay clear of settled areas. I have friends there. We'll find out what's going on."

....

Dawn found them standing before an old wooden door, the entrance to a small and tidy dwelling on the outskirts of the village. In response to Nassir's knock, the sleepy face of an elderly man with a stubble beard and white hair that stood on end had appeared. As he looked into the morning light, his eyes lit up with recognition.

"Come in, come in."

With that, they were welcomed inside. A small oil lamp sat on a wooden table, shedding a warm light in the little room.

"Have a seat."

Nassir and Shamir sat in the chairs at the table.

"Shamir, this is my old friend Aziz. Aziz, this is Shamir."

Aziz gave Shamir a radiant smile. The smile and the disheveled hair struck her as funny. Aziz, understanding the source of the humor, joined in with a chuckle.

Aziz moved quickly to get coffee brewing. Soon the smell filled the room. From an old barrel, he took out dates and placed them in a wooden bowl. Bananas, along with a loaf of bread, a round of cheese and a knife were placed on the table.

"Eat," he said.

....

Shamir awoke. From the slanting rays of the sun, she knew it was late afternoon. Outside she heard the murmur of voices. When she was ready, she opened the door. Aziz sat on the step and patted the space beside him. The warmth of afternoon had peaked and passed. Cool currents of air wafted down from the lofty peaks. Nassir sat on his blanket beneath an old tree, its gnarled, leafless branches twisted at odd angles. In front of him, four men sat cross-legged, engrossed in conversation. A breeze sighed in the branches, providing a soft counterpoint to the melodic sound of voices. The scene bore a dreamlike quality.

One man was speaking in the language of the educated. "I've been searching for truth many years," she heard him say. "I've been told that you are a holy man, a sage, one with whom I can speak concerning matters of the spirit."

"I am merely a shepherd who takes care of his flocks; I have done so since I was a boy," Nassir said.

"Why do you hide from me?" responded the man.

"Why do you hammer on my door?"

"I told you, I seek the truth."

"Would you know the truth if it was before you?"

"Of course."

"What truth do you seek to know?" Nassir asked. "Is it to add to your storehouse of knowledge?"

"To acquire real knowledge, spiritual knowledge, is the only undertaking worthy of a man."

There is arrogance in that educated man, Shamir thought to herself.

Nassir continued. "Real knowledge cannot be acquired; it happens spontaneously, and only to a few. It's a gift of Allah. It's either there or it's not. I'm afraid in your case, it's not."

The man recoiled as though he'd been slapped. "Why do you say such things?"

"Because they're true," came the quiet response. "You said you'd recognize truth when it was before you, so, painful as it is, start with this."

"You insult me."

"No, what takes insult is not real. Who you are lies behind the mask you present to the world."

"What are you talking about?"

"You wanted to know the truth. I've taken you at your word." Nassir paused for a moment as though collecting his thoughts. "When does a mango drop from the tree?"

"When it's ripe, of course."

"The understanding you seek is not something that can be forced. Like the mango, a person cannot fall from the tree of illusion until the necessary ripeness has taken place."

"How can I bring it about?"

"You, cannot; it comes only as a by-product of living."

"I have lived a long life. Maybe not as long as you, but more than this man beside me."

"Wisdom, the ripeness of which we speak, is not a matter of age in the way that you understand it. Who can measure the unfathomable experiences of the ancient soul? How many times has it dressed to enter this vast hall of life for the feast of the senses?

"Your time will come, my brother. Never fear. Walk abroad in the world. And, no matter what you do, pay attention. Find the happiness that does not disappear. That search will turn your life into a great adventure. One day, when the time is right, you'll sit before the one who will shake you into wakefulness. Then you will know the truth you seek."

"It was a mistake coming here today."

"No mistake. From deep in the dream you heard the voice of the Divine and responded. It is reassurance that is needed by the sleeper enmeshed in life's dream. Now you may go your way, relieved. Go back into life. Forget about the search for now. Live life to its fullest. After all, is life not the greatest story ever told?" Nassir stood, reached down for the man's hand, and helped him to his feet.

"Aziz, give him dates, bread and cheese for his journey;

make sure his skin is filled with water." Nassir embraced the man, who suddenly seemed uncertain. Shamir watched the man walk slowly up the road and disappear. She wondered, was it sorrow she sensed in those stooped shoulders?

"I'm so sorry for bringing him," Shamir heard one of the men saying.

"It was something you had to see for yourself," Nassir responded. "These teachings have nothing to do with making converts to Islam. Who can improve on the handiwork of the Divine? Any attempt to convert anyone is the antithesis of truth."

"I'd heard him say many times how much he wanted to know the truth. He's always reading. He's a learned man, while I am not. I was sure he'd love to meet you. When I told him of you, he was excited. I didn't know where you were, so it was coincidence that brought us to Aziz's house. I thought he might know when you'd be back, and there you were."

"Timur, I know that in your heart is generosity and love, but you must understand what I said about the mango. Until the human being is ripe, the presence of a Master does no good. Those who are compelled to seek the Divine cannot help themselves. The seeker does not choose to be a seeker. How could he? It is the action of destiny, the love of the Divine for Itself that brings about the sacred search."

"But what about the mullahs who teach that the only way is the way of the prophet?" one of the young men asked.

"A wagon wheel has many spokes, surrounded by a wooden and steel hoop. At the center is the hub, where the spokes are attached. In the center of the hub is a hole around which everything else revolves. The spokes come from the four corners of the world and arrive at the center. The center is the nameless and formless.

"Out of necessity, we have given it the name of Allah. The spokes represent the many paths that lead there. The farther they are from the center, the more distinct and separate they appear to be. At the outer limits, beliefs are rigid. Those found there believe that their particular spoke represents the 'one and only true way.' Those close to the hub already sense that all spokes lead to the same place; their beliefs are less rigid. Those who have arrived at the hub have discarded belief altogether. They know that all the spokes, though coming from different places, arrive at the same place. When this is known, it's not long before each one dissolves into the formless center. This is the end of the journey, the union with the Holy One that words cannot describe."

"Why is there so much conflict at the outer edges of the spokes?"

"Because the world is divided into right and wrong. This division is a kind of mistake, a misunderstanding, something superimposed upon creation by the mind of man himself."

"I don't understand."

"What we see around us can only be seen in the combination of presence and absence. The tree can only be distinguished when seen against that which is not tree. This is known as duality. Everything has two aspects to it; inside goes with outside, beauty with ugliness, good with bad. As two banks define a river, so duality gives rise to the perception of the world. Believers in religions the world over have not understood the nature of reality. They have sought the good without the bad. They struggle and strive, prisoners of their own beliefs, unable to see the obvious truth."

"How foolish we are."

"Yes, in a way. On the other hand, nothing is out of place. All is as it is and so brings about the Divine dance known as life. This is the way it is. This is life; it could be no other way, nor should it be."

"Then why are we here?"

"Because the fruit is ripe."

Later, Nassir, Aziz and Shamir sat eating around the table in
Aziz's home.

"Where are you going, Master?" asked Aziz.

Shamir had never heard Nassir called "Master," yet she
realized she felt the same way toward him.

"I'm going to Bent Jebail tomorrow. I'm leaving in the
afternoon."

"Are you going by road? Maybe I can find someone to take you."

"No, I think I'll stay off the road. It's not far."

"Can you see Tariq's mother in the morning? She heard you
were here and sent word this evening, asking to come and see you."

"Yes, let her come."

"Karima wants to see you as well. She came by yesterday,
asking for you."

"How is she?"

"As well as can be expected. Ibn-Saud wants to marry her,
but she confided that she couldn't go to another man's bed. She's
heard the reports of her husband's death, but even after three
years, she's still convinced he's alive. If he's dead, she says she
wants no other man. One loss like that is enough for a lifetime."

In the morning, Durri, Tariq's mother, knocked on the door.
She immediately reminded Shamir of her own mother. Once more,
the sorrow in Shamir's heart stirred and tears came to her eyes.

Nassir embraced the woman, then held her at arm's length
and looked her over. "It's good to see you again, Mother."

"It's good to see you again," came the response in soft
mellow tones.

Shamir's heart went out to the woman; she knew what was
to come.

"Durri, this is Shamir."

The two women acknowledged each other.

"Let's sit under the tree. Aziz, come and join us."

Durri sat on the carpet that Nassir had spread beneath the

tree. Her long black dress covered her crossed legs. "Have you any news of Tariq?" she asked.

"I have," Nassir said. "Shamir and I saw him yesterday."

"Was he well?" came the eager inquiry.

Nassir, sitting directly in front of Durri, took her hands in his. "Beloved Mother, your son is dead."

Shamir felt the shock like a blow. She watched the woman's eyes moisten as she bowed her head.

Nassir kissed Durri's hands and watched as silent tears fell into her lap. Aziz knelt behind her and placed his hands on her shoulders for support. Suddenly, like the bursting of a dam, huge, racking sobs shook Durri's frame. From the depths of her sorrow came a long, mournful cry.

....

It was late in the morning when Nassir accompanied Durri home. When he returned to Aziz' little house, it was mid-afternoon. Shamir and Aziz joined Nassir beneath the tree, the sunlight warm in the cool air.

"Shamir, I want you to stay with Durri. I've made the arrangements. You'll take care of her for a little while. She's a good woman, and you'll be good for each other. If you need any help with anything, you can speak with Aziz. He will help you."

"Where are you going?" Shamir asked.

"To Bent Jebail. I have business there."

"Will I see you again?" she asked, suddenly, inexplicably afraid. She sensed something in Nassir she hadn't felt before.

"Yes, you'll see me again."

"What's happening? Something's changed. Tell me." Suddenly chilled, she shuddered involuntarily. "You know, don't you?" she demanded.

Nassir looked directly at her. His eyes no longer danced with humor; they were clear and tranquil.

"My dear Shamir, you are precious to me. You are like my own daughter. Destiny decreed that in this lifetime I would not have children of my own. My family has always been very important to me. And now only you and my brother remain."

Shamir found herself crying. Yes, she thought, you and your brother are my family too.

"What do you mean?" she said through her tears. "You frighten me."

"I am merely a bridge to help you along your way. Your life stretches where mine cannot go. My time is short."

"Nassir, this kind of talk frightens me. I don't want to lose you. What's happening?"

"Life is so vast that no one can ever know the whole of it. Each of us must play our appointed part. We have no say over where we are born, to whom, or the gifts we are born with. Most people live out their destiny, not knowing what is to happen. There are some, however, who have the gift of seeing. They know ahead of time what is to take place. Time is an illusion, part of the great dance we call life. The seers are not subject to time, so they know things others do not. This gift was instrumental in saving your parents' lives many years ago. It brought me to the well where we met. Through this gift, I knew to bring you here."

"Are you going to die?"

"Yes."

"When?"

"Within a year, this body will return to the earth."

"Oh, Nassir, I can't stand to lose you. Everyone I've loved is gone. You're the only one left."

"Beloved daughter, I do understand. That is why you must stay with Aziz and Durri. They are your family now." Leaning over, he took Shamir's hands in his. Tears streamed down her face. "Though I'll be gone in form, the love we shared will always remain. When the time is ripe and wisdom matures, the honey of that love will drip from the hive. Then, you will feed the spirits of those whom Allah sends your way."

"Why does this have to happen?" Shamir sobbed, despair in her voice.

"So much sorrow for someone so young." Nassir said quietly, as though to himself. "It takes a hot fire to melt the ore and release the imprisoned gold. Nothing is wasted in life; all is essential. There are some, however, who look upon their lives with sorrow and despair. That attitude alone makes sorrow unbearable. Your destiny is to bring healing. It is Allah who has set in motion the preparation of his holy vessel, Shamir." Nassir took her in his arms and held her as she cried.

"Is there a way out?" she finally asked.

"No. Even the Master Jesus in the Garden of Gethsemane asked if the cup of suffering could pass from him, knowing there was no other way. Life is not as it seems, little one. In the West, people go to watch movies. The movies are life stories projected on a screen and as such they are not real. But they can become so involving that those who watch them feel all the love, hatred and sorrow as if it were their own. Although it may not seem so at the time, life is much like a movie. It's real in a certain sense, unreal in another."

"I don't understand."

"You dream, don't you?"

"Yes, of course."

"In your dreams, do you experience love and sorrow, happiness and joy? Do you see babies being born, old people dying, people making love and people making war?"

"Yes."

"And what happens to them when you wake up?"

"They vanish."

"And what happens to the joy, sorrow and pain?"

"It is no more."

"Was it real?"

Shamir was crying softly. "Why, Nassir, why are you telling me this? I can't stand it! Let me die with you."

"It's not your time."

"I don't care," she sobbed. "I can't stand the thought of losing you."

"Your task right now is to help Durri. There is a deep connection between you. You need her for a mother; she needs you for a daughter. Such unions as this are not made from flesh and blood. This union is born of the heart. Sorrow has prepared the ground. Love will flourish here. This will be. You sensed it when you heard Durri's voice; it reminded you of your own beloved mother. Durri, for her part, felt a strange stirring in her heart when she first saw you. It was as though she'd been waiting for you."

"But I don't want to lose you."

"You can't lose me, Shamir. I am love, and love is without form even though it takes form. Don't be attached to the form, little one. Feel instead the love that is here, in Aziz; feel the love in Durri and know that it is me that you feel. I will never leave you. I am with you always, to the very end."

"Oh, Nassir," Shamir sobbed.

"Shamir, this world is a dream; it's not real because it doesn't last. When you wake up, the sorrow and the pain will vanish. You will remember it, but it will no longer affect you. Then you will understand that you have always been home. You have never gone away, you have just been sleeping."

They went into the house and, sitting around the table, ate in silence. The silence soothed Shamir. When they finished, Nassir gathered together what he needed.

"Aziz," he embraced his friend, "take care of my daughter."

Aziz nodded, tears obscuring his sight.

"Daughter, take care of this father."

Shamir was on the verge of tears again.

Nassir held her tight and then, pushing her away, took her hands. "I will see you one more time before I leave. Never forget, my beloved daughter, that this body cannot contain the love I am. When the time comes to leave it behind, do what is before you. Enjoy the dream until the time comes and you awaken."

....

Months later, as she looked down at Bent Jebail, she wondered if Nassir was somewhere in the town. Would this be the time of which he'd spoken?

30

Kidnapped

Jonathan Makarios and Doug Kersey arrived at the White House early Wednesday morning. It was still dark. Morgan was already present when they entered. The three men sat in the comfortable chairs;

David stood with his back to the fire. "Let's get down to business," he said. "This could be a long day. Let's start with the Middle East trip. Where do we stand?"

"The arrangements have been finalized," Doug Kersey began. "You leave December twelfth. You'll go to Jordan first and meet with the King. You'll have two days there before going on to Syria for two more days, at which time you'll meet with President Bashar. Following that, you'll have two more days in Lebanon before returning to Washington, with a three-day stopover in Tel Aviv. You'll be back just in time for Christmas. Samuel Herzog has agreed to let you address the Knesset."

"He has?"

"Yes, but reluctantly."

"How so?"

"Both Levin and Goldstein's widows insisted. Herzog is speaking of it as a chance for you to explain your policies in the light of the new reality."

"New reality?"

"Yes, he considers himself and his country in a state of open, if undeclared, war. I don't think you will be made too welcome. You and Sandra will stay over with Levin's wife Rebecca, at her request."

....

It was December twenty-first. The trip had been productive. His meetings with the Jordanians, Syrians and Lebanese had been fruitful, creating a greater understanding on the part of all involved. Tremaine had discussed with them ways in which they might be able to move toward defusing the conflict by methods other than resorting to violence. In Jordan, he had found considerable receptivity from the king and his ministers. In Syria and Lebanon there had been more of a "wait and see" attitude.

The Israelis had been another matter altogether. Tremaine had addressed the Knesset, stating his case clearly and concisely. Accorded a measure of politeness, he had been aware that much of what he had to say didn't go down well. The give-and-take following his speech might have opened a breach in the wall of closed minds, but even that was uncertain. Following the speech, which had been broadcast nationwide, Tremaine had received calls for further radio and television interviews, which he accepted. The polite hostility that initially greeted him had given way to a more thoughtful consideration of what he had to say.

In Samuel Herzog, the Prime Minister, Tremaine had found the strongest opponent of peace. The diminutive man had been tough, antagonistic but straightforward, with a keen mind and a pessimistic assessment of human nature. Tremaine recognized in Herzog a man who believed that peace came as the result of superior force.

"We'll talk more when you visit again. I'll be curious to know if your views have changed by then," Herzog had said when they parted. Tremaine recognized the not so subtle statement as indicative of a man rigidly locked in his position.

....

Sitting in the hotel room in Tel Aviv, David and Sandra watched the evening news. The announcer was saying that the American President and his wife had left aboard Air Force One for the return trip to Washington after their trip to the Middle East. On the screen, the Israeli Prime Minister and his foreign secretary shook hands with Tremaine and his wife, who ascended the ramp to the waiting plane. At the top, they had turned and waved before disappearing inside.

The idea to stay had been David's. For all intents and purposes, they'd returned to Washington. But in fact, they remained behind to take a brief vacation. Four Secret Service agents remained with them, two unobtrusively accompanying them wherever they went. Sandra colored her hair for the first time in her life, as did David. Additionally, David hadn't shaved. The stubble on his face was already visible.

David had spoken with Phillips, the chief of the Secret Service. He had exploded. David listened patiently, then quietly informed Phillips as to what he was going to do.

"I'll keep two agents with me," he heard David say.

Phillips balked. "Four!" he snapped.

David, in the end had acquiesced. "All right, four; two men and two women."

David reasoned that if they created the illusion that the President and his wife had returned to Washington, he and Sandra would be relatively safe. Only the Prime Minister and the head of Internal Security were privy to the facts, albeit not too happily.

The three couples were now on holiday. To all appearances, they were American Jews visiting the Holy Land for the first time.

The day after Christmas, Sandra and David finished an early breakfast and left the restaurant with two of the agents. They walked leisurely along the street as the city came to life. Above the mountains, a fiery sun burned in a cloudless sky. The street, cast in the shadow of the tall buildings, was a hive of activity. Local merchants opened their stores, sliding back the iron grates, removing shutters and wheeling out display carts loaded with produce. Along the street, traffic was becoming heavy, impeded by trucks unloading fruit and fresh vegetables from the kibbutz.

Sandra put her arm though David's, giving it a squeeze. He looked at her and smiled. He was happy to have privacy and anonymity. His eye caught sight of bright red hair blowing in the open window of a passing bus. A young girl of about ten looked out. Their eyes met, and they exchanged a smile. David waved, and the girl waved back. The bus continued down the street, disappearing from sight behind two large trucks unloading produce from the kibbutz, several hundred meters away.

Suddenly there was a blinding flash and a thunderous roar. Sandra, David and the two secret service agents were knocked to the ground by the force of the explosion. Sandra was the first to regain her wits. Getting up, she checked David and the agents. Realizing they were fine, she turned and ran in the direction of the explosion. She saw at once what had happened. The bus was a twisted shell of metal and shattered glass. Lurid yellow flames flickered in the wreckage, giving off a black pungent smoke. Without thinking, she'd rushed to help, her training as a nurse immediately coming into play.

David and the two agents had run after her. When she had climbed into the bus they were right behind. Looking around the smoking remains, they quickly assessed the situation. Sandra looked for survivors and checked the seriousness of their injuries. The red-haired girl lay pinned beneath the twisted seats, a shard of metal protruding from a bloody shoulder beneath a shattered collarbone. The two agents carefully lifted the twisted seat. David bent down and together he and Sandra eased the girl off the metal spike. She groaned and passed out. Then, carefully, they lifted her over the side to waiting hands and safety.

Climbing out of the bus, Sandra knelt beside the injured girl. Blood was pumping from the wound and she knew it would have to be stopped. Ripping pieces from his shirt, David, on the other side of the girl handed them to Sandra. She glanced up and found herself looking into the green eyes of her husband. Bunching up the pieces of shirt, she stuffed them into the bloody wound and quickly bound them tight. In the distance, sirens wailed. Once the girl was taken care of Sandra looked around to see where else she could be of help.

A woman lay on her back nearby. Black powder covered her face and blood dribbled from her mouth. Her clothes were in shreds. She moaned as though in sleep. Sandra felt her pulse; it was strong. The sound of sirens filled the air. People were rushing in every direction. Someone had put a coat under the woman's head. Sandra adjusted it to give her greater comfort. As she stood, she felt a blow to the back of her neck. At the same time, someone charged into her side, knocking her over. As she fell, strong hands grabbed her arms and pulled her back on her feet. A pair of intense, dark eyes stared at her through a black ski mask. The man held a gun against her belly. On either side of her, men similarly attired held her by the arms.

"You're coming with us," said a heavily accented voice from behind her.

Before she realized what was happening, she was being pushed along the sidewalk. The gun had disappeared. Then she heard a grunt, as though someone had the wind knocked out of him. She felt something heavy fall against the back of her legs, tripping her. The men on either side of her had spun around. Both of them drew guns. She saw David step into the man on her left. With his right hand, he grasped the wrist behind the gun and thrust it into the air. At the same time, she saw him twist, strike the man's exposed side and send him sprawling, the gun flying harmlessly through the air. The two Secret Service agents struck the other man and, knocking him down, twisted the gun out of his grip.

She watched, mesmerized. Six more attackers, each with a ski mask over his head, materialized. One of the agents went down under a fierce attack from two of the gunmen. A third had drawn a knife and lunged at David. She screamed a warning.

David stepped toward the man, letting the knife pass a fraction of an inch from his face. With a fierce yank, he pulled the wrist down. Simultaneously, he drove his shoulder under the armpit of his attacker. With a quick rotation of his hips, he sent the man flying through the air.

Before her husband could recover, Sandra watched as one of the attackers put a gun to the back of his head. She saw the hammer click back. David had begun to turn and, sensing what was happening, jerked his head down. At the same time, she heard the crack of the gun. David dropped to the ground and lay still, blood already forming a pool. With a vicious jerk, she found herself being propelled toward an alley. She struggled with all her might, her screams no longer audible above the din of approaching sirens. Before they reached the alley, the man at her right staggered from a heavy blow to the side of his head. From the corner of her eye, she saw the Secret Service agent drive his heel into the man's knee and heard the cracking of the bones. At the same time, she saw a dark red stain suddenly appear on the agents chest. A look of surprise crossed his face as he fell heavily to the ground.

Quickly she was rushed down an alley and emerged on the other side, propelled by the men holding her arms. Two men were in front, three behind. A small black panel-van stood nearby. As they approached, the doors opened and she was shoved roughly inside. In a matter of moments, they were speeding down a narrow street. A scarf was tied around her eyes and rough hands secured her wrists behind her back.

....

At the precise moment David felt the gun at the back of his head, he knew what it was. As he jerked his head down, he heard a roar in his ears. Everything went black and silent. When he came to, he was in a hospital bed. Janet Merril, one of the agents, was beside him. A nurse stood nearby. To the right, a doctor was standing, a stethoscope around his neck; he peered at his watch while his fingers felt David's pulse. David noticed the armed guards at the door.

"Where's Sandra?"

"They got away with her," Janet responded.

"Who were they?"

"We don't know."

"Where's Robert?" David asked, referring to the other agent who'd been with them when the attack came.

"He's in critical condition with a chest wound. The doctors think he'll pull through."

....

Morgan was in his office when Travis knocked on the door. Jonathan Makarios accompanied him. He hadn't called ahead. The smile on Morgan's face faded when Travis walked in. Travis was pale and shaken.

"Have a seat." Morgan motioned to a chair.

"Have you heard the news?" Travis asked.

"What news?"

"Sandra has been captured by Hamas, and David is in a hospital in Tel Aviv with a gunshot wound to the head. One of the agents who was with them is in critical condition."

"Good God." Morgan's face had turned pale. He sat in his chair, stunned.

"I had a phone call from Samuel Herzog. He thinks the group that captured Sandra may not know who they have."

"What happened?"

"Apparently a bus was blown up by a suicide bomber in Tel Aviv. David and Sandra were in the vicinity and went to help. During the commotion, she was captured. When David and the agents tried to rescue her, one of the agents was shot in the chest. David suffered a bullet crease to his skull. It was superficial, but he lost a lot of blood."

"What's being done?"

"I spoke with David just before coming here. He said the Israelis are following every lead. They've mounted a massive search, but they are trying to make it as unobtrusive as possible."

"What can we do?"

"David has asked that you take over in his absence. Jonathan is to be your assistant. He'll be able to help you. I'm going to Israel. I'm leaving in an hour."

31

Rescued

Samuel Herzog and his foreign minister, Yosef Sarid, met Travis and his two companions at the Israeli airport. After the introductions, they were on their way to the control center. It took the better part of three hours to bring him up to date. After the briefing, Travis and his two companions were driven to the U.S. Embassy.

Upon arriving, Travis showered and changed. In less than an hour he was on his way to the hospital.

Travis slipped quietly into the room. David looked up in surprise, and then smiled.

"What are you doing here?"

"What do you think?"

David didn't respond; he knew why Travis was here. He also knew the man would not be dissuaded. The truth was, David was glad to see the Chairman of the Joint Chiefs. He knew that Travis, being who he was, would do everything in his power to find Sandra. Travis was skilled and highly capable. The two men talked for an hour. After he left, David, weak from loss of blood fell into an exhausted sleep.

When he awoke, he lay quietly, listening to the sounds of the city coming through the hospital window. He found his mind going back to a day ten years ago. He'd been sitting with Avinash in the front room of his light airy apartment in Bombay. Sandra had been with him.

The sounds of traffic and the cries of those selling their wares floated through the open windows. He sat watching the Master as he spoke, answering the questions of two guests who leaned toward him eagerly listening. He found himself crying silently, filled with a love that overflowed. The Master looked at him and with a knowing smile said, "It's like the love of the lover for the beloved, isn't it?" Then he continued the conversation with the two men, never losing a beat.

David had been too choked with emotion to respond with words, but Avinash had accurately captured the feeling.

....

Sandra lay on a rusty cot in a darkened room that smelled of rats and urine. A chain fastened her ankle to the wall. Her head pounded, and she was stiff all over. There was enough room to stand and, when she needed to, she could relieve herself in an old bucket against the wall. But at night she was so cold, she shivered uncontrollably and curled in a ball to keep warm. She was not dressed for the cold, and her captors had provided nothing for warmth.

All she had eaten since her abduction were dried crusts of bread and a little water. She had no idea where she was. Days passed, but she was uncertain how many.

After she was put in the van, they had traveled for three days, changing vehicles several times. They hid during the day and at night had traveled with great caution. On the third morning, they'd continued driving. It was slow going along seldom-used trails. By late afternoon they stopped near some foothills leading into the mountains. Sandra was pulled out of the car. She watched four men unload and cover the vehicle with camouflage. As soon as it was dark they set out on foot. Her hands had been untied. They walked in single file, two men in front of her, two behind. It was late when they stopped.

Above and to her left, a sea of stars shone through the limbs of overhanging trees. Moonlight revealed shadowy shapes on the uneven ground.

"Try to escape and you'll be shot!"

She turned and stared at the short stocky man who'd spoken. In the light of the moon, she saw he was clad in army fatigues and a short jacket. Unshaven and smelling of cigarettes and sweat, his eyes were hidden in shadow and conveyed no emotion. At his waist, a holstered pistol was barely visible while in his hands he held what she guessed was a high-powered rifle. Within half an hour, five more men joined them. The men sat in a circle and a discussion ensued, carried on in a language unfamiliar to her. From time to time the men looked at her, some with curiosity, all with hostility.

They traveled on foot for two nights more. Before dawn of the second night, she was blindfolded. She felt herself being led down a steep and uneven path. She slipped several times, and each time rough hands jerked her upright. She heard the cry of a rooster in the distance and detected the smell of smoke. About an hour had passed before they reached even ground. She guessed they were close to a village. Her captors walked on either side of her now. It was another fifteen minutes before they stopped and she heard subdued voices and the sound of a door creaking on a hinge.

....

Hours later Sandra awoke. She felt as though she'd been chained for days. The blindfold had been removed, and a gag was forced between her lips and tied behind her neck. There was nothing to see. The room was dark and empty, and the only light came from tiny pinholes in the wall during the day. At night she was fed by a guard, one of the men who'd traveled with her. Whatever she didn't eat or drink when the gag was removed was taken away.

Alone in the dark, dingy room, she'd been enveloped by sorrow. She found her mind going back to the last glimpse she'd had of David before the walls of the alley had blocked her view. He had been on his side, unmoving. Blood from the head wound had obscured his face and formed a frightening pool on the pavement beneath him.

In the intervening days, as she lay cold and shivering on the cot, the sorrow over the death of her husband crested, then receded, leaving her suspended in a profound emptiness.

At the peak of her sorrow, she found herself recalling the words of Avinash. While visiting the island of Maui, he'd gone sightseeing with friends in a helicopter. They had flown into one of the valleys with steep walls that had risen several thousand feet on either side. Rivers disgorged into space, and it seemed the rotors would hit the sides. Avinash mentioned later that as they flew further into the valley it became even narrower. The thought crossed his mind that death could come easily. He said he suddenly felt a rush of emotion, a deep and abiding joy at the thought of going home. She wondered about that comment. Avinash had welcomed death. He was not afraid. She questioned him about it.

"Your observation is correct, Sandra. I'm not afraid of death. Why would I be afraid?"

"What is it like? What is it that you know that makes you so unafraid?"

"Have you ever been to a theater?"

"Yes."

"When you see the actors on the stage, they appear to be sitting in a room talking with each other. The room seems real, as does the conversation of those in the room, doesn't it?"

"Yes."

"Have you ever been backstage?"

"Yes."

"When you're backstage, you can see that the room the audience sees is really just an illusion. The actors are really not who they appear to be either. Knowing that, one can hardly take what is being said with the same seriousness as someone who is convinced that what he sees is real. Death in life is no more real than death on the stage. It simply means the play is over and it's time to go home. Are you not glad to go home when the time comes?"

"Yes, I am."

Sandra found herself remembering a similar conversation with David. They were discussing the dangers inherent in his position, dangers for him and for her. The conversation had taken place several days before they left for the Middle East.

"Sandra, if something should happen to either one of us, rest easy. Know that whatever happens is purely the play of destiny. Nothing can be done to avert it; whatever is to happen will happen. "

....

Lying on the bed, Sandra was awakened by a strange noise. She listened silently, trying to identify it. She had no idea how long she'd slept. Then she heard the bar being removed from the door. Light from a lantern flooded the room as the door was pushed open. A man unfamiliar to her entered. His hair was white, his skin dark, and he wore a shepherd's clothing. At first glance he gave the appearance of being elderly, but the ease to his movements suggested otherwise.

Sandra found herself looking into eyes she would never forget. In the lantern's light they were completely peaceful, yet alert, not missing a thing. For the first time in days, she didn't feel afraid.

The thought crossed her mind that she was dreaming. She sat up and put her feet over the side of the bed, shivering. The man set the lantern down and, producing a small key, knelt down and unlocked the chain that held her foot. Looking down at the man, she saw he was dressed in soft but coarse woolen clothing. He straightened up and looked into her eyes.

"You must be very quiet," he said, his voice low.

She nodded.

Then, reaching behind her neck, he untied the gag and then her wrists. She could smell the lanolin of raw wool from his clothes.

"Are you all right?" he asked.

"Yes," she said, her voice a hoarse whisper.

"Then follow me. We don't have time to waste."

With that he stood and, taking her by the hand, helped her to her feet.

"My name is Nassir," he whispered, his head inclined toward her ear, "and yours, I think, is Sandra."

She nodded.

Picking up the lantern, Nassir went into the other room. The guard lay slumped on the floor facing the wall, his hands tied behind his back. As she looked up, she saw a man standing against the wall, almost hidden in the shadows. He held the door open and they slipped outside, but not before Nassir had extinguished the light.

Outside the building, Sandra could barely make out the form of small houses in the darkness. Nassir and the other man guided her away from the dwellings and into the open desert hills.

Once they were clear of the habitation, Nassir stopped. "This is Kahlil," he said. In the light from the stars Sandra saw the young man bow, inclining his head in her direction.

"We've a long way to go before dawn," Nassir said. Sandra noticed his voice had a melodic tone, and an accented English she was unfamiliar with.

"Who are you?" Sandra whispered.

"We can talk more later. We need to get as far away from here as possible," Nassir responded.

Kahlil removed his jacket and handed it to Sandra. Then he set off at a good pace. She followed, and Nassir brought up the rear. They traveled hard for hours, when, just before dawn, Kahlil knocked quietly on the small wooden door of a tiny house. Quickly they were ushered inside.

....

"Where is she?" Abdullah asked.

"El Quozah," Harith responded.

"Is she safe?"

"Of course. Why did you call me here?"

Harith had been rushed to Beirut from Bent Jebail after the abduction. He'd had little chance to rest and was feeling in no mood for idle talk. What he wanted was sleep. He looked around the hot, stuffy little room. Although it was midday, very little light entered from outside. An oil lamp flickered on a packing crate, casting an uneasy light, barely keeping the darkness at bay. Harith and six other men sat in a circle on old crates and broken chairs.

"Where did you capture the woman?" continued his interrogator.

"She was on the street, helping the wounded in the bus that was bombed. We knew she was American from her accent. She must be quite wealthy, because it looked to us as if she had two servants accompanying her, as well as a man we think is her husband."

"We lost four men in that action of yours. Hardly worth it for the life of some wealthy American." Abu spit the words out, his hatred spilling forth.

"Abu, hold your tongue."

Harith looked up at the powerfully built Abdullah, who'd suddenly gotten to his feet.

"Whoever this woman is, she must be very important. In less than an hour, my sources told me, the Israelis launched a massive manhunt. It is unlike anything we've ever seen before. There are even rumors that the American Chairman of the Joint Chiefs arrived in Tel Aviv the day after the kidnapping. Nothing has been reported in the press. That makes me suspicious; they don't want us to know who we've captured. We must find out, and quickly." Abdullah looked slowly at each man. "We'll meet tomorrow. Harith, get some sleep; we'll see you in the morning."

....

"Travis, we've reason to believe she's been taken across the border into Lebanon."

"What makes you think so?"

"We managed to trace the vehicles. They used three. The last one was found ten kilometers from Bar'am, right on the border. Hamas seems to be coordinating their activities with Hizballah. There's been a lot of guerrilla activity in this area the past year. The Lebanese security forces have been unable to control it, if they ever really wanted to in the first place," Rotstein ended cynically.

Travis looked at Rotstein. "You must have more than that."

"We've word from informants that a small group of men crossed the border and were headed toward Bent Jebail. They had a captive with them. It was night, so my sources couldn't be sure if it was a woman."

"Do you think they'll go to Bent Jebail? It seems to me they would avoid the populated areas, don't you think?"

"Yes, I think they would, but the guerrillas who operate in the area seem to have an excellent network. They're considered heroes by many of the locals."

"Do you have people up there?"

"Yes, we've inserted two commando units in the area. We'll be in touch with them regularly."

"Let me know what develops."

"Will do."

. . . .

Travis left for the Embassy, frustrated at having to sit around and wait. But he could do nothing until he was sure of Sandra's whereabouts. He was convinced it was Sandra the guerrillas had when they crossed the border.

He was familiar with the area. In 1974, he'd spent time in Israel, working with Special Forces. The Israeli government had hired him to train highly skilled units in techniques of counter-guerrilla warfare. For six months they'd worked in a section that stretched some twenty miles into Lebanon along the border. It was a rugged area, ideally suited for guerrilla warfare.

It had been a clandestine operation. During that time they'd mapped the area and become familiar with the mountains and valleys, all the places where small mobile units could hide. They became familiar with the trails used by the guerrillas, their caves and hiding places, and the most likely areas from which they would launch their attacks.

That information had been invaluable when Israel crossed the border and later launched their own attacks.

Back at the Embassy, Travis opened a map and spread it on the table. Peter Nevis and Kevin McCloud watched.

"This is where they think she is," Travis pointed at the map.

"That's rugged country," Nevis whistled.

"We'd never find her without a lead," McCloud added

"Maybe we should go in anyway," Travis interjected, "see what we can find, in disguise, of course."

The two younger men looked at Travis, shaking their heads.

"No sense, General. Without a better lead than we've got, we'd be at a complete loss; they could be anywhere in those mountains," McCloud responded.

"We could stay in touch with the Embassy," Travis continued. "We could be kept informed of developments. Who knows? We might get lucky." Travis knew he was grasping at straws, but he couldn't stand the waiting. He was a man of action. He knew his impatience was clouding his judgment. "It's late; we'll see what the morning brings. Let's get some sleep," he said.

The two younger men, looking relieved, wished him good night and left.

Travis had difficulty sleeping. He lay on the bed between sleep and wakefulness. He'd brought with him the two ex-Green Berets because of their training, because they were masters of disguise, and because they were fluent in Arabic. He'd known them for years and trusted them implicitly. They'd jumped at the chance to come with him and only learned the purpose of their mission once they were airborne.

When he'd received word of what happened, Travis had begun to make preparations to leave for Israel. The decision to go had just happened; it had never occurred to him to stay.

He'd become close to the President and his wife; he liked them very much and held them in the highest regard. Tremaine had impacted him like no other man in his life, and Travis had only known him a short time.

Over breakfast, Travis told his wife he'd be out of the

country for a few days, maybe a week or so. She knew enough not to question him.

It was a long time before Travis finally drifted to sleep.

The sound of the phone jolted him awake. For a moment, he couldn't remember where he was. The loud ring came again and he grabbed for the phone.

"Yes.... I'll be right down.... Yes."

Grabbing his clothes, he pulled them on. Quickly he strode down the hall and knocked on one of the doors.

"Nevis and McCloud, get down to the conference room. I'll meet you there."

....

"It came in this morning?" Travis asked, looking at the clock. It was zero three hundred hours.

"Yes, about fifteen minutes ago."

"And you recorded it?"

"Yes, we record all incoming calls."

"Let's hear it again."

There was the sound of static on the line and then the voice of the Embassy operator. "U.S. Embassy, can I help you?"

"Listen carefully," came the response. The voice was accented. "Sandra Tremaine was abducted. She's been freed and, for the time being, is safe. We will bring her to you."

"Who is this?"

"It's better that I don't give you my name for now."

"How can we be sure we can trust you?" asked the Embassy operator.

"You can't. But please listen carefully. Send some of your people to Bent Jebail; two or three are enough. More will only attract unwanted attention. They must look like merchants traveling in the area. Go to the shop of Jabil and arrange to purchase thirty pounds of dates from him. We'll take it from there."

With a click the line went dead.

....

"The President's wife?" Harith was stunned. "No, it couldn't be. I saw them boarding the jet for the return flight. I saw it on television."

"I don't care what you saw Harith, the woman you abducted is the American President's wife."

"Now we can break the will of the great Satan." Abu's voice cut through the silence like a whip.

"If we play our cards right. We must get her out of the country at once."

"Why?" demanded Harith.

"The Israelis and the Americans will turn the country upside down looking for the woman. No hiding place will be safe."

"Where do you suggest?" interrupted Abu. "The leaders of Jordan, Syria and Lebanon were impressed by the hard line the American President has taken with the Israelis. They were even more impressed by him when they met him. None of those countries will help us; they'll expose us if they find out."

"That's right, so we have to get her out of the country and into Iraq. I'll make the arrangements. Harith, bring the woman to Ar Rutbah."

They'd spent the morning hastily planning a strategy, knowing that if they were going to pull it off, they had very little time.

....

"She's gone?" exploded Harith. "How can that be?"

"We don't know what happened," Ali responded, afraid of Harith's anger.

"What do you mean, you don't know?" Harith demanded.

"When we got there in the morning to relieve Bayazid, we found him tied up and lying on the floor. The inner door was open and the woman was gone. We've scoured the area all day. We even got old Tambal to see if he could track them. It seems there were two men besides the woman. Tambal was able to follow the tracks for several kilometers, but then he lost them."

"Which direction did they go?"

"South toward the border."

"Bring Tambal here. I want to talk to him," ordered Harith. "In the meantime, get me some food."

Harith had traveled hard all day without eating and it had been late when he arrived in El Quozah.

He had just finished eating when there was a knock on the door and Tambal was ushered in.

"Sit," ordered Harith.

The old man sat down and looked at Harith. "What do you want?" Tambal despised the Iranian.

"Tell me all you can about the escape and where you think the woman is," Harith ordered.

"I'm not a seer, Harith, I'm a tracker."

"Don't fool with me, old man." Harith's patience was getting thin. "Tell me what you know."

"Two people got her out. They were headed toward Ramiye when I lost their tracks."

"Do you think they were heading for the border?"

"That's what it looks like, but that could also be what they want you to believe."

"What do you think, old man?"

"I think they were trying to lead you astray."

"What makes you think so?"

"Whoever was leading them left only a hint of a trail, not obvious to the inexperienced eye. I followed it for five or six kilometers before the trail led up into some rocks along a ridge. Then it vanished completely. I followed the ridge for several kilometers in either direction, and checked both sides, looking for the trail to start again. It didn't. This makes me think the people involved knew exactly what they were doing. They wanted you to follow the tracks in one direction. They're very familiar with the terrain."

"Who might it be?" Harith was from Iran and not familiar with the area. "Who, besides you, knows this area well?" he demanded. "Think!"

"The people who live around here know it well."

"Who else?"

Tambal thought for a moment.

"There's an old shepherd who lives in these hills. His brother is retarded. They move their flocks from place to place. Often he picks up supplies in Bent Jebail," Ali suggested.

"What do you think, Tambal?"

"I've heard about him. I've even seen him from time to time. He keeps to himself, seems to be a hermit."

"I've heard it said he's a Sufi, not really a shepherd." Barat spoke for the first time. He was one of the older men in the cell. For twenty-five years he'd fought the Israelis.

Harith turned toward Barat. "Tell me what you know."

"I don't know anything for sure, but over the years some of the men disappeared into the mountains. They'd come back after two or three days. I heard rumors they'd gone to see the old Sufi. He seemed to have a strange effect on them. They'd lose their will to fight, would become soft. I think Kahlil and Tariq were two of the most recent ones to visit him."

"Kahlil?" Harith snapped. "Where is Kahlil?"

Ali looked at the others, suddenly frightened. "He left for

Bent Jebail two days ago. He was supposed to be back tonight."

"He and that traitor Tariq were friends, you say?"

"Yes," responded Barat. "He and Kahlil were from the same village."

"Where's that?"

"Rachaf."

....

It was mid-morning when Nassir returned. Aziz was sitting on the steps. Kahlil came out of the house and joined them.

"I got through to the American Embassy. They'll send someone into Bent Jebail either tonight or tomorrow night. They'll contact Jabil to buy dates. That's how we'll know them."

"So we're going to meet them there?"

"Yes."

"How are you going to get the woman there?"

"You and I will leave at sundown and meet whoever comes. Sandra will remain with Shamir and Durri. She can rest. Once we meet the Americans or their representatives, we'll go from there."

....

Travis and his two companions entered Bent Jebail from the east. It was late afternoon. Their disguise was impeccable, allowing them to mingle easily with those entering the town. Like merchants passing through, they attracted no attention. They made discreet inquiries, and then made their way to Jabil's small shop. Pushing the door open, they entered and were greeted by a short, potbellied merchant.

"What can I do for you?" he asked politely.

"We'd like to buy some dates, thirty pounds," Travis said.

"Good, good. Please, have a seat. Can I get you some coffee?"

"Yes, that would be good," Travis, responded.

For an hour they drank coffee and haggled over prices, seemingly enjoying the exercise.

"You must come for a meal at my humble home," Jabil insisted when they were finished.

After he'd closed the shop, Travis and his companions walked leisurely up the road with Jabil. It was dark when they arrived at his home.

Jabil's wife, a short, stout lady with graying hair, had prepared a meal. Her face was hidden behind a veil. Making sure her guests were taken care of, she placed food on the table and, with averted eyes and a slight bow to the men, excused herself and disappeared.

....

They'd just finished their meal when Travis heard a light tap on the door. Jabil opened it. Travis heard the whispers of greeting and watched as two men were ushered into the room.

Jabil made the introductions.

"Coffee?" he asked.

"Yes," answered the older of the new arrivals.

While Jabil made the coffee, Nassir and Kahlil sat across from the three Americans.

Looking at Travis, Nassir spoke in his accented English.

"Sandra Tremaine is safe and well."

Travis recognized the voice on the tape.

"Where is she?"

"We'll take you to her. She's not far away."

....

It was past midnight when Kahlil, Nassir and the three Americans approached Rachaf. They'd traveled quickly, but slowed their pace as they approached the populated area. As they rounded a bend, Nassir stopped, listening intently. The night was dark and moonless. High clouds hid the stars. They listened, holding their breath. There it was, the sound of small stones being dislodged above them. The sound carried easily in the cold air. Quickly, the men melted off the road and waited.

Nassir and Kahlil knew that the trail from El Quozah entered Rachaf just in front of them. No one but guerrillas would be using it at this time of night.

"Nassir, take the men to Durri's. I'll meet you there," Kahlil whispered. "I'm going ahead to see what's happening. If I'm not there within an hour, get the Americans away." Before Nassir could respond, Kahlil vanished in the darkness.

He made his way to where the trail met the road and waited in concealment. Fifteen minutes later, he heard the distinct sounds of men traveling at night. They moved cautiously, but the weight of their equipment and the darkness made it difficult for them to be completely quiet. As the men left the trail and entered the road, Kahlil could make out ten of them altogether, all well armed. Once they were on the road, they put down their equipment and stopped for a few moments to rest. Kahlil listened carefully. He heard whispering and, with great caution, moved closer.

"Which way is Tariq's home?"

"About three kilometers down this road there's a small trail which enters from the east. It's at the end of that trail, about five kilometers altogether," came the whispered response.

Kahlil recognized the voices of Harith and Barat. This was his cell. He knew at once why they were here. Turning away from the voices, Kahlil moved back silently along the road. He'd take a shortcut to Durri's home and get everyone out. Suddenly, he froze. He sensed someone directly in front of him, almost within arm's length. He held his breath, listening. A light flashed in his eyes, blinding him.

"So, Kahlil, what are you doing here?"

....

Nassir and the three Americans arrived at Durri's home and knocked on the door. Durri let them in. An oil lamp burned in front of an old picture of Tariq.

"Durri, this is Travis, McCloud and Nevis. They've come for Sandra."

Durri, eyes averted, welcomed the men to her home.

"Sandra's sleeping," she said.

"You must wake her at once."

"Nassir."

Nassir turned to see Shamir standing just inside the door. Sandra, hidden in the shadow, stood beside her, holding her hand. The two women had been sleeping. "You've come at last," Shamir said.

"Yes."

"This is what you spoke of, isn't it?" Tears glistened in her eyes.

"Yes. Shamir, you and Durri must go with Sandra and these men. They'll take you safely away from here. I told you once that one day you'd go far away across the sea to another land. Now is the time for that to happen. You must help Sandra and Durri. There's not much time so you must get ready at once."

Shamir and Durri left the room.

Sandra had watched the interaction between Nassir and Shamir. She sensed something momentous was happening; but, unfamiliar with Arabic, she didn't know what it was.

Travis had watched as well. Shifting his gaze, he saw Sandra looking at him. At first he didn't recognize her. She'd lost weight, and her hair had been cut. She wore long pants and a loose-fitting shirt. In the subdued light, Travis had at first mistaken her for a man.

"Sandra, is that you?" Travis stepped forward.

Sandra was shocked. "Travis?" She stared at him in disbelief. Suddenly she was in his arms. Like a giant bear, Travis held her. "Is it really you?" she said looking up into the big man's face.

"Yes, it is. We've come to take you home."

"Tell me about David," she said, almost choking on the words.

"He's in a hospital in Tel Aviv."

"He's alive?"

"Yes, he'll be fine."

Sandra stood transfixed. Her mind had difficulty adjusting, but her heart leapt with joy at the news. Her legs suddenly weak, she sank onto a nearby chair and sobbed in relief.

Moments later, Shamir and Durri came back into the room, dressed and ready to travel.

"You must hurry," Nassir said. "You and Durri must guide them to Bent Jebail. Can you do it?"

"Yes," she answered.

"We're familiar with the area, too," Travis added.

"You're not coming, are you?" Shamir directed her question to Nassir.

"No, daughter, I'm not. You must hurry. There's not much time; danger is approaching."

Sandra, sensing the agony in Shamir, took her hand and gave it a squeeze. With all her heart she wanted Shamir to know that she would do her best to take care of her.

"Durri, when you leave here, take the trail from behind Aziz's house and head south. Do you know where I mean?"

"Yes," Durri responded.

"Are you ready?"

"Yes."

"Then you must leave at once. Under no circumstances are you to return, no matter what happens. Understood?"

Durri nodded. Then she knelt in front of him and kissed his feet. "Master, I will ever remember you."

Nassir gently reached down and, taking her by the hand, helped her to her feet. His eyes looked long and deep into Durri's, and she returned the gaze. "Good-bye, Mother. Take care of this daughter of ours."

Nassir turned and placed his hands on Sandra's shoulders. "Shamir will need your friendship and guidance when you return to your country," he said in English.

"You need not worry," Sandra responded. "I'll take care of her." Impulsively she hugged Nassir, kissing him on the cheek. "Thank you," she said.

Nassir smiled at her then turned and shook hands with the three Americans. "Take care of them," he said.

"They're in safe hands," Travis said in Arabic.

Nassir smiled. "God be with you."

Shamir stood in front of Nassir, wiping away the tears. He took her in his arms and held her. Then, he gently pushed her away. "You must go. Remember I will always be with you. God speed, my dearest Shamir. Now go." Nassir gently turned her around and, kissing the top of her head, guided her out the door.

Once outside, it took a few moments for their eyes to adjust to the dark. Shamir looked back and saw Nassir silhouetted in the light from the door, hand raised in a gesture of parting.

32

"You will not defile the temple of Allah"

Nassir traveled hard all night, just far enough ahead to keep the guerrillas following, never close enough for them to catch up to him. As he climbed, a light snow began to fall, making travel more difficult.

At first light, Nassir entered a stand of ancient cedar, the glade carpeted with the droppings of the great trees, the snow absent. The scent of cedar filled the cold air.

Nassir had moved rapidly ahead of the advancing guerrillas for several kilometers now, knowing they could easily follow his trail in the snow when revealed by the light of dawn.

The stand of trees grew against the side of the mountains that rose in giant ramparts seven hundred meters above and to the west. Before him, the land fell away in great rifts and canyons that opened to the valleys beneath them. Snow covered the peaks; silence reigned.

Nassir jumped onto a low ledge against the rock face, four feet off the floor of the glade. With the blanket around his shoulders, he sat quietly with his back to the mountain and waited. For the last time, he watched the soft colors of the rising sun bathe the surroundings in purple and gold.

Savoring the beauty of this remote place, Nassir bid a silent farewell to the mountains and the life he'd loved, glad at last to be going home.

He heard the sounds of approaching men long before they arrived. Unmoved, he watched as they slipped into the glade along the length of its curved perimeter, rifles at the ready, searching him out. It took only a few moments for their eyes to adjust to the subdued light in the grove. Then they saw him. Quickly they advanced and surrounded him, not more than five meters away.

"You led us on a merry chase," Harith hissed. He was furious.

Nassir said nothing.

Earlier, on the trail, Harith had raged. With the coming light, he saw at once they'd been following only one man. Nassir had led them away from their quarry; he'd outsmarted them.

Harith knew the President's wife would now be far away. This round in the battle with the great Satan was lost; opportunity had slipped through his hands. He was bitter. He, of all people, had failed to do the bidding of Allah. Now he'd have to return to Iran in disgrace, his promising career in ruins.

Harith's men were unsettled. There was something strange about the man before them. He sat unmoving, seemingly unafraid, his eyes alert, taking everything in.

The fury in Harith suddenly burst. In three swift strides he stood before Nassir, his fist drawn back ready to strike. The only thing in his mind was smashing the face of his enemy with his bare hands.

As Harith moved toward him, Nassir's eyes glittered. Harith stopped. Something in the gaze of the man before him caused Harith's mind to suddenly go blank. Harith lowered his hands.

"It's over," Nassir said quietly, as though to himself.

"What did you say?" Harith demanded.

Just then, a shaft of light from the rising sun struck the rock face above the trees to the west. The reflected light suffused the glade beneath it in soft golden light.

"It's time to leave," Nassir said, his voice barely audible.

"You'll never leave here alive," Harith screamed. Spittle flew from his twisted mouth, rage once more taking hold. Jerking his pistol from its holster, Harith leveled it at Nassir's head and cocked the trigger.

Looking past the gun, Nassir fixed his eyes on the would-be killer. Raising his hand, Nassir pushed the gun aside. "You will not defile the temple of Allah this day," he said quietly. Then, shifting his gaze, Nassir looked into each man who stood before him. He felt their fear, anger and frustration; he saw in it the never ending disturbance of the wind over the vast silent depths of the ocean.

The boundaries of normal consciousness melted away and, as the men looked on, Nassir closed his eyes, a slight smile playing across his lips. His breathing slowed, becoming shallow until at last it stopped. The men stood waiting and wondering, lost in their own private thoughts, eyes fixed on the figure before them. Then, one by one, they lowered their rifles and bowed their heads.

☰ 33

Birth of a terrorist

It had been a hot evening, but was now beginning to cool. Everyone in the little coffee shop became silent as they stared at the television. Some of those passing by stopped and, realizing what was going on, pushed their way into the tiny space to catch the most recent news. Flames flickered across the screen, and the sound of sirens set everyone's nerves on edge. A suicide bomber had entered a crowded nightclub in Tel Aviv and blown himself up. Thirty-two Israelis had died, and more than a hundred had been injured.

The Israelis won't let this pass, Ismael thought. There will be reprisals, and they'll come fast. Over the past nine months, there had been thirty bombings that had claimed the lives of one hundred and fifty Israelis. The loss of Palestinian life in the reprisals stemming from the bombings was approaching six hundred.

Ismael pushed through the crowd to where his son was standing. "Mohammed, go upstairs and let your mother know what's going on. Then I want you and your brothers to go and get water," he told him.

"At this time of night?" Mohammed asked.

"Go," he said, and pushed his son out the door.

Mohammed bounded up the stairs at the side of the building to the cramped quarters where he lived with his parents, his grandmother, his two brothers, Mustafa and Mahmoud, and his little sister, Sarah. Sarah was three, Mahmoud was eleven, and

Mustafa was fifteen, a year younger than Mohammed himself.

"There's been another bombing," he announced to all as he burst into the room. Nada, his mother, was seated at the table with his grandmother, Hanah. Both of them had been engrossed in mending clothes by the light from two candles. "We've got to get water," he told his mother. He went to wake up his brothers, who were already asleep on their cot.

Nada got up from the table. "How bad is it?" she asked as she emptied the water bottles.

"It looks pretty bad. I think father expects a curfew again," Mohammed responded.

Hanah continued sewing, but took everything in. She was a slight frail woman with gnarled fingers that seemed to work the needle without effort or thought.

Mahmoud and Mustafa stood by the door, yawning and rubbing the sleep from their eyes. They picked up the water containers, handing two to Mohammed.

"Be careful," Nada said as she opened the door for them. "Don't take any chances. Get back as quickly as you can." Pushing the door shut, she listened as the boys hurried down the stairs.

The room was stifling hot. Nada removed her shawl. She was short, about five foot two, with a solid, stocky build. She went and checked on Sarah, who was asleep in the corner on one of the sleeping mats. Nada, though she loved her boys, felt a deep affection for her daughter, who even at this tender age bore a marked resemblance to her husband.

Nada returned to her seat and resumed her sewing. Her dark hair, tied up during the day, now hung about her shoulders. The unsteady light from the candles revealed streaks of white. She was a comely woman, but hard work and the raising of four children had taken its toll on her. Yet, despite the hardships of her life, the wrinkles around her eyes and mouth suggested an irrepressible sense of humor. It was something her family appreciated, because it made even the most difficult times better.

Hanah reached over and turned on a small battery operated radio. The announcer was saying that Israeli troops, accompanied by tanks, had mobilized and were preparing to enter Palestinian controlled areas. The Prime Minister of Israel had delivered a brief statement, which the station now played.

"Tonight's killing of innocent Israelis is an act of barbarism that will not go unavenged. Since those behind the attacks target civilians and show no respect for the conventions of war, they cannot expect us to do so either. To that end, we now assert the right to take whatever means necessary to defend the sovereignty of Israel and to safeguard her people. We will root out this cancer of terrorism, wherever it may be found. We serve notice to all those nations who have lent support to terrorism that we hold them responsible for this bloodshed. When we find who you are, you will suffer the consequences. The time for this endless talking is over. Action is all we have left. We will not waver in bringing about the safety and security of the State of Israel."

Hanah turned off the radio. The two women looked at each other, knowing that what was coming wouldn't be good.

Mohammed and his brothers picked their way over the uneven ground in the darkness, and then ducked down a narrow alley. The Israelis had cut the water lines in the neighborhood. For six months, they'd had to fetch water from a well in a small market square half a kilometer away.

Five minutes later, they emerged from the alley into the square. People had already gathered, waiting to fill up their water containers. Most of those present were women and young boys. An elderly man pumped furiously at the squeaking pump.

"Hurry," hissed a woman behind them.

The boys could feel the fear and tension all about them. While they waited, they caught snippets of subdued conversation, none of which was reassuring. Then, in the distance, over the sound of the pump, came the dreaded sound of helicopters.

"Hush," someone said. Everyone listened to see if the sounds were coming closer. They weren't, not for the moment, at least.

It was the boys' turn. Mohammed worked the arm of the pump as hard as he could. He had just finished filling the containers when the night sky to the west lit up. The sound of the explosion shook the night air.

Walking fast, arms straining, Mohammed and his brothers headed for home. Twice they stopped to rest their aching arms before turning back onto the street where they lived. As they rounded the corner, more flashes, followed by the deep booming sound of high explosives, lit the night sky to the north.

When they arrived at the shop, they could see by the flashes of light that their father was boarding up the windows. Mahmoud and Mustafa carried the water up the stairs while Mohammed went to help his father. Neither said a word. They worked in unison, aware of the gathering storm, but unaware of what it would mean this time.

Throughout the night, the sound of helicopters could be heard in the distance, the volume steadily increasing. Suddenly, the little apartment was illuminated by a high intensity light from a helicopter hovering above the buildings across the street. The noise from its motor was deafening, and the downdraft from its rotors tore through the open windows and filled the house with dust and debris. Plates rattled on the shelves and came crashing to the floor.

Nada and Hanah held Sarah between them, trying to shield

her from the fierce winds and deafening sounds that raged all around them. The boys cowered beneath one of the windows on their sleeping mats and covered their heads.

Ismael saw the danger they were in. The wall was flimsy and provided scant protection. Crawling on his hands and knees, he grabbed them and in the intense light moved them to the sides of the room and away from the windows.

Heavy caliber machine gun bullets tore through the front of the building, sending splinters flying in every direction. Ismael watched as the wall disintegrated, leaving them completely exposed. He was struck in the chest with such force it threw him against the far wall. Then, as suddenly as it began, it was over. The light shifted, and the sound of the helicopter receded into the night.

....

Mohammed would never forget that night for as long as he lived, which wouldn't be much longer. In a few hours, he'd be united with his family again. Soon, the sorrow that had sapped his life and the hatred that had replaced it over the past nine months would be exchanged in the miracle of death. Once more he would see his beloved mother's face and hear the melodic tones of her voice. His father would be there too, his siblings, and his grandmother with her comforting wisdom. This time they wouldn't be separated. This time, they'd be together and enjoy the blessings the prophet spoke of, blessings the Israelis could not understand and could never take away.

Mohammed had gone to the olive grove just before dawn. He could see the settlements above him; it was well lit and well guarded. He'd said his good byes earlier to those who'd trained him, those who'd nurtured and molded the hatred in his heart and turned it into an unstoppable weapon.

He sat in a depression, hidden from the light, his back against one of the trees. At last, the sun pushed back the stars and a pink glow lit the eastern horizon. He was at peace again. He felt possessed of a strange lucidity, something he'd never known before.

Mohammed was tall for his age, and slim. The stubble of his beard was dark and made him look older than he was. He was dressed in an oversized uniform of the Israeli Defense Forces. By the time the sun slipped above the horizon, he was in position.

The Jerusalem Post
BOMBER STRIKES AGAIN, NINE DEAD, THIRTY WOUNDED.

Early this morning, a suicide bomber attacked a bus filled with passengers from one of the outer settlements in the West Bank. According to reports from the scene, the bombing took place as the bus was leaving the settlement. One of the survivors said a young man jumped out of a ditch and ran at the passing bus. The resulting explosion was so powerful it blew the bus on its side and tore a hole in the road.

At press time, the number of dead stood at nine and was expected to climb, as several passengers appear to have suffered severe injuries. Thirty passengers were taken to a nearby hospital for treatment. The Al-Aqua Martyrs Brigade claimed responsibility, stating their attacks are a direct result of Israeli brutality. They will continue for as long as Israeli occupation makes Palestinians prisoners in their own homes.

The Israeli Prime Minister stated at a mid-morning news conference, "We will not tolerate these acts of terrorism and will take whatever steps necessary to bring it to an end. We will do whatever we have to. If it means enclosing the Palestinian areas in a ring of steel and fire, we will. If it means we must root them out and kill them one by one, we will do so. If it means we must lay siege to them and starve them into submission, we will do that as well. We will destroy the nests of these terrorist rats and anyone who supports them."

34

Reaping the whirlwind

David and Sandra had gone to British Columbia to visit Sandra's parents and to check on Shamir and Durri. Sandra's parents had a small cottage on their property just outside Victoria. When it became vacant in the spring an invitation had been extended to the women to come and live there. They had accepted and were currently going through the immigration process in Canada.

David and Sandra left Victoria airport at midnight and were scheduled to arrive in Washington a little after nine, local time. Once Air Force One was airborne David and Sandra had gone to bed and quickly fallen asleep.

....

Tremaine was up at seven thirty and went to the galley to put on coffee. He showered and dressed and was just sitting down when the phone rang. Picking it up he listened intently to the voice on the other end.

"I'm sorry to disturb you," Travis apologized, "but we just got word that all communication has been lost between the ground and four commercial airliners, two originating from Boston, one from Newark and one from Washington."

"Is it a technical malfunction?"

"It's hard to tell, they're running tests and everything seems to be working from the ground."

"Any idea what's going on?"

"Not at the moment."

"Alright. Let me know when things change."

"Will do."

Tremaine put the phone down, puzzled. He looked at his watch. It was eight twenty five.

Sandra pushed the door open and came into the galley, yawning.

"Tea or coffee?" David asked.

"Coffee." she said, smiling. She came over and put her arms around him, then taking her coffee sat down in one of the soft leather chairs, pulling her legs up beneath her. David sat opposite and sipped his tea.

"We'll be landing in about an hour, so do you want breakfast then?"

She nodded. "It was good to see Shamir and Durri again," she said. "They seem to have settled in well. Dad was saying they've been taking English language classes for a month."

"I'm impressed with how much they've learned already. I was concerned about them being so far away, but as you said they seem to be settling in."

"Do you know when…?"

Suddenly the phone rang, the sound startling them. David picked it up. "Tremaine, here."

Travis was on the other end. "We still haven't been able to contact the four aircraft. They simply do not respond to the ground and their transponders are no longer working. The one from Boston is off course and heading toward New York instead of Los Angeles, its destination…hold on a second…I've just been informed that the second flight from Boston is also off course and heading toward New York as well. I'll call you back. Something's not right." David replaced the phone.

Sandra knew by the look on her husband's face that something was wrong. "What's going on?" she asked.

"We don't know," he replied. "There are four commercial airliners and none of them are responding to air traffic control. Two of them originating from Boston are off course."

"That is strange." Again the phone rang.

Tremaine picked it up. It was Travis. He could tell by the sound of his voice, the General was shaken ."The first airliner just crashed into the North Tower at the World Trade Center."

"What?" Tremaine was shocked. "What about casualties?"

"We don't know at the moment."

"And the other airliners, where are they?"

"The second one from Boston is still airborne and holding a course for the New York area."

"Thanks Travis. We should be on the ground shortly."

Tremaine cleared the line and then spoke into it. "Jonathan, meet me in the lounge." He turned to Sandra, "One of the planes just crashed into the World Trade Center."

"No." Sandra jumped up and followed Tremaine into the lounge. He flipped on the television just as Jonathan entered. The three of them stood transfixed.

....

It had been a long day. Tremaine diverted Air Force One to New York after the second plane had struck the South Tower of the World Trade Center. On the way he ordered American airspace closed; nothing was allowed in or out. Planes that could not return to their point of origin were diverted to Canada. Shortly afterward the Pentagon was hit and fifteen minutes later news came of the final plane crash south east of Pittsburgh. Air Force One had landed in New York shortly after the collapse of the second tower.

By helicopter they had gone to the site of the World

Trade Center where they had been appalled at the extent of the destruction. Smoke and dust covered the area and through it all they could see the crowds of people filling the streets. Tremaine had ordered the helicopter to land and despite the urging of his staff he and Sandra had made their way through the crowd toward the site. People were in a state of shock. Those they passed were covered with dust and looked like white powdered ghosts. It was difficult to see and breathe.

On the way back to Washington Tremaine had been in touch with Travis and watched events on the television. Now he sat quietly with Sandra and Jonathan in the lounge. All of them were covered in dust.

"This is what I've been afraid of," he said quietly as if to himself. "I had hoped we could move fast enough to avert catastrophe but we didn't. Now we have reaped the whirlwind. Perhaps if we're lucky we can avert a similar harvest, but it will take action not words."

....

At seven o'clock in the evening Tremaine addressed the nation and the world.

"Today, Tuesday, September 11th is a day that will go down in history as one of the darkest. Today, we were forced to reap the whirlwind. Today, thousands died in the worst attack on our nation since Pearl Harbor. Unlike the attack on Pearl Harbor, however, those who attacked us are, as yet, unknown. This attack was the work of terrorists, men willing to sacrifice their lives to do us great harm.

"In the light of these events, we must ask ourselves this question: Why were they willing to make such a sacrifice?

"The Chinese sage Lao Tzu, reflected on this point some

twenty five hundred years ago. 'Why,' he said, 'do people care so little about death? When life becomes intolerable, death is welcomed. And he who has embraced his death lives without fear. A man like this makes a formidable enemy.' We must understand what he said; for if we don't we will find ourselves engaged with an enemy that cannot be defeated by force of arms.

"When an event of this magnitude happens, the first impulse is to strike back, to use force against our attackers. But this we must not do, we must instead, show restraint. Again, the sage understood this well. He cautioned those who would listen, 'Repay bitterness with kindness and force with softness.' Christ when he stated, 'Resist not evil,' and 'love your enemies, do good to those who despitefully use you,' made the same point.

"History shows that we have lived by the dictum of 'an eye for an eye and a tooth for a tooth,' and the events of today have shown us where it leads. In the past our actions have contradicted our words. We Americans have not practiced what we preached. And what has it brought us, other than the perpetuation of conflict all over the world? It is this to which the historian George Santayana was referring when he said, 'Those who fail to learn from history are condemned to repeat it.'

"I do not believe anyone wishes to repeat the events of this morning; no one in their right mind wishes to continue this cycle of violence. For that reason I say, let this be the end of it. Let those who died in the attacks earlier today be the last to die. What more fitting memorial could we make than to remove the causes that led to such destruction and death? What more fitting memorial than to have their sacrifice bring us to our senses so that we find a way to live in peace with one another.

"For that reason, I direct my remarks to those who wish us ill, to those who have attacked us. You have our undivided attention. As the representative of this nation, I am prepared to meet with you or your emissaries without pre–conditions at a place of your choosing. Our purpose is simple. To listen, to hear what you have to say, to find out what caused you to engage in these acts, to uncover the underlying causes, whatever they may be, and then to do all we can to eradicate them. To this I give my word.

"My heart is heavy with shock and sadness. What happened this morning is hard to comprehend. To those of you who've lost loved ones, know that our hearts go out to you and we'll do everything in our power to ease your suffering.

"Life is always uncertain, we never know when it may end. It is our love for those who've gone that fills our hearts with grief and loss. But, human beings are resilient, capable of rising from times of terrible suffering, capable of bypassing bitterness and the desire for revenge. I say to you, let these events bring us a deeper appreciation for our brothers and sisters, from every corner of the earth, who've lost loved ones through starvation, genocide, war and terror.

"We've lived in this land, largely removed from the troubles of the world, and within our borders we've increasingly become strangers in a land of strangers. Since this morning we've become brothers and sisters again, deeply moved by the plight of those who are suffering. In the rubble of the World Trade Center and the Pentagon, we've witnessed, as happens at times like this, the rebirth of compassion where strangers reach out to strangers. For in the face of our common mortality, we recover the brotherhood of our humanity.

"Let us not poison the springs of human compassion with hatred . Perhaps one day, the world will look at us and say that the United States, like South Africa, demonstrated that human beings can break the cycle of violence, can rise in spirit from the dust and ashes of great suffering.

"Citizens of the world, I say to you that in this crisis, in this unspeakable suffering lies the potential to transform our world if we have the wisdom to see it and the strength to take the necessary steps. At this time of tragedy we must recognize, once and for all, that all human beings, regardless of their color, their creed or nationality, have the right to earn a living and the right to raise their family in relative safety. We, the wealthy nations of the West, cannot expect to enjoy these rights while others do not. We live in a global village and as the events of today demonstrate, no one is safe unless all of us are.

"Let us find a way to end terror in all its forms, let us put an end to war and bring about peace, permanent peace. I believe this is what the vast majority of Earth's inhabitant's desire

"There are no maps or plans on how this is to be done. The only guideposts, so to speak, are those offered by the wise ones, the sages, who saw beyond violence and understood the importance of yielding. They knew it was not the mark of a coward to forego revenge, but was instead an act of courage and faith.

"Some will argue that we must protect ourselves, that we use our technology and military might to make ourselves impregnable from outside attack. I say it cannot be done. We can increase security and develop greater technology but no matter what we do, there will always be someone who'll find a way to penetrate our guard. In the process of trying to protect ourselves, we'll be forced to abridge the freedoms we enjoy and we'll live in a state of perpetual fear. We'll be prisoners in our own land; prisoners in a continental fortress and this would demonstrate the fact that terrorism had accomplished its objective.

"It is time for us to make a radical departure from the actions that have perpetuated this cycle of suffering. If we truly desire lasting peace, then what alternative do we have but to identify the roots of terrorism? We need to understand how we have contributed, wittingly and unwittingly, to these terrible events. This, if we have the will, we can accomplish. It will neither be an easy task, nor one that can happen quickly. It will take patience and persistence. But if we persevere, I believe we will, in the end, prevail." *

....

The following morning Tremaine and Sandra went to the Pentagon. Over the next three days they'd returned to New York each day at sunrise. They moved from place to place, serving soup and sandwiches, talking with the people they met, hearing the stories and offering encouragement. They returned to Washington each day by two. Afternoons and late into the night were spent in dealing with the results of the attack. Travis and Morgan stayed in Washington and kept abreast of events. On Saturday evening Tremaine had agreed to be interviewed by James G. Whitfield the chief BBC foreign correspondent based in Washington. The interview was broadcast live by all the major broadcasting companies worldwide. **

JGW: "Dr. Tremaine we've recently witnessed the worst terrorist attack ever on American soil. There are those in this country who believe you should respond with all the force at your disposal, setting aside for the time being that we still don't know who is responsible. Others argue that if you retaliate against those who were behind the attacks it will only precipitate further attacks. Would you comment please?"

DT: "I agree with the latter perspective. It is time we engage in a worldwide conversation concerning the issue of terrorism and what to do about it. What is needed is an exploration of the major underlying causes that lead to such events.

"My heart goes out to all the people affected by this attack, to all those who've lost loved ones and all those who still don't know if their loved ones are coming home. For that reason we owe it to them to put an end to this madness and not use their deaths as justification for further bloodshed. Retaliation and revenge make an unfitting memorial to those who have died."

JGW: "There are those who will argue that the perpetrators of these acts were evil misguided men. What's your view on this?"

DT: "That depends on one's perspective. Men and women we consider terrorists might be considered patriots and martyrs by our enemy and vice versa. To England, George Washington and the Fathers of Confederation were traitors but to the new nation they were heroes. So, it is one's perspective that determines who is called a traitor, who a patriot, who a terrorist, and who a martyr."

JGW: "Some may construe your remarks as condoning violence."

DT: "I do not condone violence. It is important that the events of Tuesday signal an end to the violence, not the next step in it. I want those who died to be remembered as the last to die in this cycle of violence. As far as I can tell violence of this sort is an act of last resort, engaged in by those who are desperate, those for whom all other avenues are blocked.

JGW: "It's been suggested that these events have traumatized the psyche of your nation and that life will never be the same. Until now you've lived in a country that, other than Pearl Harbor, has never been subject to a major attack from beyond its borders. In the continental United States you've never been subject to an attack of any kind at all.

"The morning after the attack I happened to go for a walk in some fields near where I was staying in Virginia. The sun had not yet risen and from my vantage point there were mists in the valleys and the nearby mountains were pink in the light of approaching dawn. It was beautiful and peaceful. Yet, despite that, I found myself thinking of the terrible events that took place the day before. I realized that this planet I love is not safe from destruction. Such thoughts had never crossed my mind with such immediacy before. It made me realize how precious life is and that, for the fist time, the life I've loved so much can no longer be taken for granted."

DT: "What has happened is having a profound effect on all of us and on the national psyche as you put it. The evening after the attack there was an interview on television. The interviewer asked a psychologist what were the effects of such violence in human lives? The psychologist went on to describe some of the effects that people go through. As I listened I found myself thinking that he was describing the daily experiences of many people in the world. Palestinians and Israelis have certainly had to deal with this, as have others; the people of Iraq, Iran, Chechnia, Ireland and so on. This kind of violence has been the daily experience of all too many and yet we've been removed from it, separated by two vast oceans. Now we must deal with it first hand. It is now here on our doorstep."

JGW: "There are those who suggest that your nation has had a tendency to practice your foreign policy in a naive and unrealistic manner and have attempted to enforce it through economic pressures, and failing that, through the use of force, and long range weapons of war. There's no doubt this act of terrorism has in many ways united the American people and stiffened their resolve. But, I wonder if the connection has been made, that your recent history of long range impersonal attacks has also stiffened the resolve of those who've had to deal first hand with your bombs and missiles."

DT: "This has been my concern as well. I'm not sure we have."

JGW: "One thing that's quite clear is that there are some people who are very angry with you, so angry they're prepared to give their lives in order to hurt large numbers of your people and thereby make a very strong point. How can you fight against such violence, such fanaticism?"

DT: "I don't believe we can fight against this in a conventional way. As long as we try to meet force with force the cycle of death and destruction will only continue and get worse. In the body, pain serves as a warning that all is not well. It draws attention to the problem and causes us to take whatever action is necessary to eliminate the cause of the pain. The same is true in the body politic. We must address the underlying causes of our collective pain."

JGW: "But do you really know what that pain is?"

DT: "We know what the pain is because we experience it, but we must come to understand the underlying cause of that pain. There is really only one certain way to find out and that is to ask those who wish to do us harm. They are obviously trying to say something to us and we better be sure we hear them accurately. But, to hear what they have to say requires an open mind on our part. If we have an open mind then perhaps we'll hear what, until now, we've been unwilling to hear."

JGW: "When someone is willing to sacrifice his own life in order to achieve his ends, how can you counteract that kind of dedication? Will he listen to what you have to say?"

DT: "First of all I'm not suggesting we say anything. *We* need to listen. That must be our first priority. We can respond after we hear what needs to be said."

JGW: "How do you counteract those who are willing to sacrifice their lives for what they see as a just cause?"

DT: "As I've mentioned, we need to listen and find out the underlying causes that motivate them."

JGW: "That may be true but while you try to find that out you could well be killed. These are not peaceful men, they are quite prepared to take life to further their objectives."

DT: "Part of what has riveted our attention about these attacks is the fact that the men involved were willing to give their lives for a cause they believe in. Are we prepared to do the same? Are we prepared to risk our lives and if needs be lose them for something we believe in? And by that I mean, finding a resolution to this conflict."

JGW: "Well if we listen to some of the leaders in Congress it seems clear that there are those who are eager to take on the terrorists. I would imagine there are also those who'd be prepared to die if necessary in order to destroy the perpetrators."

DT: "But the question I've raised comes from another place. Are we prepared to risk *our* lives, not to destroy other lives, but to spare further killing. That is an important distinction. As you mentioned these are dangerous men and one might be killed in the process of dealing with them. As I said in my address on Tuesday, I'm willing to meet whoever is behind these attacks at a place of their choosing and with no pre-conditions. I'm willing to do this knowing the risks, and if in the process my life is forfeit, it will be in the interest of putting a stop to the bloodshed."

JGW: "When I heard you say this it reminded me of a dog that yields to another by baring its throat. The attacking dog then leaves it alone."

DT: "Most of the time that's what happens, but with human beings that is not always the case. So my question again is, are we prepared to make ourselves vulnerable and possibly give our lives in the interest of putting a stop to this madness? The history of mankind is replete with warfare that resulted when leaders did not communicate effectively with each other, when someone didn't listen, for whatever reason, and as a result they were unable to resolve their differences. What followed upon these failures was the launching of one army against another in order to cause one point of view to prevail over another. To what end? Was it not to prove one leader right and the other wrong? This does not put an end to conflict. It's how we perpetuate it. It's how we keep it going from generation to generation."

JGW: "Some have argued that this enemy is a coward made up of madmen unwilling to make themselves known, men who operate in the shadows and thus are not worthy of respect. Consequently, it is argued that you should not offer them any consideration whatsoever."

DT: "Well, they've proved otherwise, haven't they? The men who hijacked those planes, though we may despise what they did, were certainly not cowards. They carried out something that led to their deaths. I think we may well find that they reached across the ocean to attack us in the sanctuary of our own home, to bring the war to us, so to speak. Such an enemy is certainly a worthy opponent. If we attack him I would say we do so at our peril. We cannot risk another attack like this."

JGW: "There are those who will disagree with your use of the term, 'worthy opponent.'"

DT: "When I speak of a worthy opponent I'm talking of one who makes us sit up and take notice, someone capable of doing us great harm, someone who can inflict the same kind of damage we can on him. Tuesday definitely proved this. That's why I said they have our undivided attention. Now, if we don't listen to what they have to say, and we haven't 'till now, then we'll suffer the consequences. In other words, someone is willing to bring the battle to us; they're prepared to sacrifice themselves in order to do so. A person such as this is certainly a worthy opponent, in Lao Tzu's words, 'he makes a formidable enemy.'"

JGW: "As I mentioned earlier there are those who are calling upon you to retaliate. There argument is that you have a great deal of sophisticated weapons at hand. I wonder if anyone can stand against such power?"

DT: "If we were to unleash this power it would make everyone

wonder just who the terrorist really is. Perhaps this might be the
purpose of the attack on September 11th?"

JGW: "You mean that they may wish to provoke a response
from you that would lend further credence to their position and
thereby play into their hands?"

DT: "It wouldn't surprise me. This enemy is not as
unsophisticated as we might think. Concerning technology and
weapons at the disposal of the American government; whatever
technology it develops, others can utilize as well. In addition the
proliferation of modern weapons is largely the result of a strong
interest in profit on behalf of the munitions companies in the
United States and elsewhere. This must be stopped.

"Keep in mind that we lost the war in Vietnam despite
our sophisticated technology and the supposed superiority
of our military forces. We could not defeat an enemy who
transported goods by bicycle and lived on rice. This is the
principle pointed out by the Taoists in which softness is used
to overcome force."

JGW: "It will be argued that you simply cannot do nothing.
So if you cannot do nothing what can you do, particularly when
you don't, at this time, know who the enemy is?"

DT: "I would say we do know who the enemy is. He is closer
than we ever imagined."

JGW: "What do you mean by that?"

DT: "The enemy is within, within us. We are the enemy we
need to deal with. The enemy is our selfishness, our greed, our
lack of concern for others, and our self-absorption as a people.
You and I have lived in relative safety and considerable affluence.
The United States and countries like Canada and those in Western
Europe comprise a small proportion of the planet's population and
utilize the vast majority of its wealth and resources. We the people
of the United States are a people of unprecedented wealth in a land
of incomparable beauty, albeit a land we stole from others and

now call our own. To indulge ourselves as we do at the expense of others on the planet makes us the real enemy, does it not? Is it not we, more than anyone else, who jeopardize the well being of the people on this planet?

"Huge segments of the population have been uprooted from the countries of their birth and driven into refugee camps. In those camps what hope is there? People in such conditions go largely unnoticed and unrecognized. They are treated in all too many ways like vermin, like rats. When there's a catastrophe and people die in a plane crash our interest is not in how many died but in how many Americans died. That is the kind of self-absorption I'm talking about. Who are we really interested in? Is it not ourselves to the exclusion of others?

"We can no longer ignore these situations. In order to make the world safe for us we have to do our part to make it safe for all of us, regardless of where we live, our nationality, our cultural views, our political views or our religious views. No longer do we have the luxury of human rights for ourselves while denying them to others. And by human rights what I mean is the right to make a living, to have a place to live, a roof over one's head and the freedom and resources to raise a family in relative safety.

"But we have not used our influence and power to help bring this about. When a man has nothing left to live for he may be prepared to give his life in a cause he considers worthwhile, such as doing what he can to ensure that his children do not have to suffer in the kind of world he did. After all, who in their right mind would want to live under the conditions in the refugee camps? Would you? Would any of us? The answer is pretty obvious, is it not? And if we did live under them, might we not be moved to do the same thing?"

JGW: "You mention our greed and selfishness. Has it not always been the case that those nations who come to power operate from that perspective? "

DT: "It's always been this way and it will continue to be this way until we find a way to share, until we realize the joy that comes in giving rather than in taking. And if we don't learn this we'll go the way of all other nations who have been in the same position. There is, however, one important difference at this time. In the past those nations who took their brief turn at the top were eventually overcome without too much effect on the world. Now, however, with the kinds of weapons we have, the communication systems and everything that follows upon globalization, we are now faced with the world as a whole being divided between the wealthy and the poor. We no longer operate in isolation. So with so much potential for destruction there is an equal opportunity for resolution and the introduction to the world of a new way of being."

JGW: "What do you mean?"

DT: "Life is always in balance although we may not always be aware of it. This balance is depicted by the Taoist Yin Yang symbol.

"As the discrepancy between the rich and poor increases, so does the potential for global destruction. This gives rise to the possibility—perhaps necessity is a better word for it—of moving beyond destruction to a world that works for everyone. For this to happen the wealth of the planet must be shared amongst the inhabitants.

"In as much as we now have the potential for global destruction we also have the potential for making a global resolution of issues that have plagued us since the beginning of human history. The idea of imminent death might, if we're lucky, cause our minds to become clear, open to the awesome possibilities in both directions."

JGW: "That at least seems hopeful, in fact exciting, in light of recent events."

DT: "The union of complementary opposites has, as far as we know, always existed and so there is no need to be discouraged. It is in a sense a signal of the next chapter in this divine novel we call life."

JGW: "Some argue that what's going on is a gigantic struggle between two opposing religions, the Muslims on the one hand and the Christians on the other. Do you have some thoughts on this?"

DT: "To digress for a moment; I find it interesting to note that most of the Christian clergy I've heard on the radio or seen on television since the terrorist attacks are talking about the book of Revelations and preaching about the Apocalypse, the day of doom. I've yet to hear them quote Christ. What did Christ have to say about such things? He certainly lived in a time of great conflict. Israel was an unruly country, subjugated and controlled by the Romans. Yet, despite its apparent defeat certain factions managed to wage a guerrilla war against their overlords.

"Perhaps the most famous were known as the Siccari or Zealots. At the time many Jews were looking for the return of the Messiah, the second coming of David, at which time the Romans would be overthrown and the Kingdom of Israel restored. There were many who hoped Christ was this person. But Christ refused over and over again to accept that mantle. When asked if he was the Messiah they'd been looking for, he said, no. He knew they were looking for a warrior king who would restore the kingdom of Israel. Christ made a point of saying that the only kingdom he was interested in was the 'kingdom of heaven.' When asked where that kingdom was, he replied that it was within us. In fact, Christ's teachings were antithetical to any outer kingdom, antithetical to the idea of taking up arms to establish such a kingdom. What Christ taught was a radical departure from the ancient Babylonian principle to which his fellow countrymen subscribed, and still do."

JGW: "What was that?"

DT: "It is best summed up by the words, 'an eye for an eye and a tooth for a tooth.' Christ said repeatedly that what he taught was a new code or as he put it, 'new covenant.' And that new covenant was very different from the old one. Its central theme can be found in his statements; 'Resist not evil,' 'Love your enemies and do good to those who despitefully use you,' 'Turn the other cheek,' and 'Give even the shirt off your back to your brother who is in need.'"

JGW: "There are those who will argue that this idea has never been proven to work and will point to the state we find ourselves in today as proof. They argue that with the rise of Christianity there has been more blood shed than ever."

DT: "I would say that it has never been proven not to work. It has rarely been practiced and when it was it did work. Ghandi employed those principles in the move for Indian independence. Martin Luther King did the same during the Civil Rights movement and so also did Desmond Tutu and Nelson Mandela in South Africa following the end of apartheid.

"There's a basic principle in Tai Chi that expresses the same idea, in fact it is one of the central themes of Taoism. Anyway, from the perspective of Tai Chi, the practitioner knows not to counter a hard blow with an equally hard blow. The understanding is; that which is soft absorbs that which is hard. Lao Tzu, the Chinese sage speaks to this when he says, 'Sometimes it's better to retreat a mile than advance a yard. This is known as going forward without advancing, rolling up one's sleeves without showing an arm, capturing an enemy without an attack, neutralizing an opponent without resort to weapons.' Then, just in case we might have misunderstood him he says, 'When you underestimate an enemy, however, you could well lose your life.' He concludes with the statement, 'when well matched opponents face each other, victory goes to he who yields.'

"But to come back to your point concerning the potential global conflict between the Christians and the Muslims. Generally speaking I would suggest this is a reflection of the growing disparity between the wealthy and the poor. By and large it is the Christian West that is wealthy with high living standards when compared to the rest of the world. The Muslim nations by and large have been poor. In those cases where they are wealthy, the wealth has not filtered down to the people themselves.

"On the other hand when things become increasingly difficult even desperate, people turn and look for answers they can understand and many such answers are derived from religion. The idea being that if they gave up their wayward ways, and returned to the fold, God would bless them again."

JGW. "What you're suggesting is the idea of a return to a more fundamental or literal interpretation of the Koran or the Bible.

DT. "That's right. And my concern is that as long as the basic needs of people are not being met, the world over, then there will be a rise in fundamentalist thinking, of right and wrong, people of the one true God against the infidel and so on.

JGW. "What you are suggesting is a radical departure from the way your nation has functioned since the Second World War. It will perhaps be a radical departure from the way even the world has functioned. It will require a complete shift in your foreign policy. I wonder if that is being realistic?"

DT. "I would point out that what is not realistic is to expect that the poor and the powerless people of the world will stand by while the wealthy and powerful become more wealthy and more powerful at their expense. As long as we think this way we will continue deluding ourselves and the events that took place Tuesday will serve only as the opening salvo in a global war unlike anything we've ever seen before."

JGW. "What do you mean?"

DT. "If we fail to reverse this kind of thinking we will be at war. But in this war there will be no clearly defined armies and nation states. The enemies we face can come from anywhere and strike at any time. In the past armies have fought armies but in this war those opposing us will not be visible. The United States and other Western nations have developed nuclear, chemical and biological weapons. In fact our arms manufacturers have contributed to the proliferation of them in the interest of profit. It will only be a matter of time before these or similar weapons fall into the hands of those bent on our destruction. If that happens who knows if the planet will survive?"

JGW. "The approach you're advocating involves a complete shift in thinking. You want to take us in a direction, which, as far as I know, has never been taken before. What guarantees are there that this approach will be any more successful?"

DT. "There are no guarantees in life. All we can do is examine realistically and factually the difficulties that face us and trust that all concerned have the wisdom and will to proceed on a global basis. To my mind this will only come about following a change in perspective, in attitude, and thinking. What we've tried in the past has not worked; we know that, we have the evidence before us. So let us embark on a road not traveled and let us employ the wisdom of the sages and those who share a similar vision for all. It is my fervent hope that we have enough time to avert another catastrophic event. But, this will only be possible through concerted action and good will. Words are inadequate when it comes to matters such as this."

JGW. Thank you Dr. Tremaine. Is there anything else you would like to say?"

DT. Mr. Whitfield I appreciate you taking the time to conduct this interview. Your questions, I'm sure, are those that have been on the minds of many the world over. I would like to leave all of you with a story I heard from a friend of mine called Shamir. She heard it from her teacher a man by the name of Nassir who was a Sufi sage. It comes from the Sufi tradition and points in the direction I think we must go.

"Many years ago, two kings ruled neighboring countries. One of the kings died, and his son Kabir came to the throne. He was a relatively young man of thirty-five. Abdullah, the king in the neighboring country, was greedy and power hungry. When he attended the coronation of Kabir, he saw how prosperous the country was, and how vulnerable. It wouldn't be difficult to invade and seize power; Kabir was young and inexperienced and definitely no match for the wily Abdullah.

"Six months after the coronation, Abdullah sent a message to Kabir. When the messenger arrived, he was shown into the king's presence. The message was delivered as follows: 'you will hand over the reins of government to me, Abdullah. If you refuse, I will cross the border with my army and take your country by force. However, if you will peacefully pass over the reins of power, I will assume the throne and there will be no bloodshed.'

"Kabir sent the messenger away and told him to return in an hour. Then the king convened his advisors and presented them with the demands of King Abdullah. The advisors urged him to resist the predatory actions of their neighbor. Kabir listened carefully and then asked them, 'what difference does it make who rules? What difference does it make if I step down and let Abdullah take over? Surely he's right in thinking it will save much suffering, death and bloodshed.'

"'That's true,' they countered. 'But you are our king and he has no right to take over our country.'

"'That may be so, but Abdullah has done a good job of governing his own country, and there's no reason to think he'd do any differently here. Besides, whether I am king or not makes no difference to me.

"When the messenger returned, he was told that Kabir had accepted Abdullah's demand and would step down in order to avoid bloodshed. By the time Abdullah entered the capital city as its new king, Kabir had vanished. Stripped of his wealth, he lived among the people in relative anonymity.

"As the years passed, Abdullah realized that he did not have the allegiance of the people. They still revered and respected Kabir above him. Abdullah realized he would not have the allegiance of the people as long as Kabir was alive. So he put a price on the young king's head. 'One hundred pieces of gold will be given to the man or woman who turns him in,' Abdullah proclaimed. He then sent his soldiers out to spread the word. Years passed and still the young king remained hidden, free, and more highly regarded than ever. Abdullah increased the price on Kabir's head to five hundred pieces of gold.

"One evening, Kabir was traveling through the forest high in the mountains when he saw a fire and heard voices. As he was about to enter the clearing he heard his name mentioned. He paused and listened. Peering through the branches, he saw an old man and his young wife sitting around a campfire over which the evening meal was being prepared. The old man said to his wife, 'I'm getting old and may not be able to take care of you much longer. Today when I was in the village buying food, I heard that a huge reward is offered for turning in our king, Kabir. I was thinking that perhaps I should look for him. The reward would be more than enough to take care of you after I'm gone.'

"'No, you couldn't do that,' exclaimed the young wife in horror. 'The king has done nothing to hurt you and has done so much to make sure that none of his people are hurt. How could you think about such a terrible thing?'

"'I know what you're saying. But we're close to starving, and

I'm worried what will become of you when I die.'

"The argument went back and forth until the king stepped into the firelight. Not letting on that he'd heard the conversation, he asked if he could spend the night with them. They agreed and shared with him their meager meal. Later that night, Kabir revealed himself to the couple and said that he'd overheard the conversation. 'In order to help you in your predicament, I'm surrendering myself to you. Take me into town, turn me over to Abdullah's men and receive your reward.'

"Suddenly faced with the situation, the old man refused. Kabir insisted. 'If you don't take me in, I'll say you hid me and that will bring about your execution.' With that, the old man capitulated.

"The next day they went into the capital. On the way, some of the people recognized the king and followed along to see what would happen. By the time they reached the palace there was a large crowd. Stopped by a sentry, the crowd was asked who had captured the young king. Two of those who'd followed along claimed to be the one. Kabir interrupted them and pointing to the old man said, 'He's the one who brought me in, it is he who should get the reward.' Kabir was taken and thrown in the dungeon to await his fate while the king called in the old man to give him his reward.

"'What really happened?" Abdullah asked. The old man then recounted what had taken place. Abdullah realized he'd never command the allegiance of Kabir's people in the way that the young king did. He also realized that he'd seriously underestimated the wisdom and courage of the young man. Calling Kabir before him, Abdullah bowed at his feet and asked forgiveness. The next day Abdullah withdrew to his own country and Kabir once more resumed the throne. The two kings became good friends, and their countries prospered under such benevolent and enlightened leadership. That story illustrates my point."

JGW. Thank you again, Dr. Tremaine.

THE ANCIENT MASTERS

The ancient masters were subtle,
mysterious and profound
Their wisdom unfathomable.

How can they be described?

By their appearance.
As careful as a man crossing an icy stream
As alert as a warrior behind enemy lines
As courteous as a visiting guest
As fluid as melting ice
As easily shaped as a carver's block of wood
As receptive as a valley
And as invisible as clear water

Lao Tzu

TAOIST I CHING HEXAGRAM
#48. CHING (THE WELL)
WATER ABOVE,
WIND, WOOD BELOW

THE IMAGE -
WATER OVER WOOD: THE IMAGE OF THE WELL.
THE ENLIGHTENED MAN ENCOURAGES THE PEOPLE
AT THEIR WORK AND EXHORTS THEM TO HELP ONE ANOTHER.

SUFI SYMBOL

THIS SYMBOL REPRESENTS THE IDEA THAT THE PHENOMENAL
WORLD, THE WORLD OF MANIFESTATION, IS NOTHING
OTHER THAN THE EXPRESSION OF ALLAH, OR THE DIVINE. A
PHILOSOPHICAL EXPRESSION OF THE SAME IDEA STATES: THE
WORLD OF PHENOMENA IS NOTHING OTHER THAN THE
EXPRESSION OF THE NOUMENAL. IT CAN ALSO BE STATED AS:
CONSCIOUSNESS IS ALL THERE IS.

Notes:

* Tremaine's speech was written the afternoon of September 11th several hours before President Bush addressed the American people and the world. It shows a divergent view and approach to the catastrophe of that day.

** Tremaine's interview was written two days after the events of September 11th.

Both articles first appeared on September 18th 2001 in a special edition of *The Mountain Stream, A Journal of Perennial Philosophy.*

Chapter 28 consists largely of the fictitious speech Tremaine gives to the Lester B. Pearson College of the Pacific. It was written in 1997 and first appeared as an article in Vision magazine, San Diego. At the time the author felt strongly that unless something was done to eradicate the underlying causes of terrorism, it would be just a matter of time before terrorism was brought to the shores of North America.

The events depicted in this book are factual and reported by the press in Canada, India, and the United States between 1968 and 2004. The characters and their response to these events are fictitious.

Colin D. Mallard, Ph.D.

World War II and Vietnam were pivotal events in Colin Mallard's life, drawing him into the study of psychology, social action and philosophy. Witness to a brutal event during the peace struggle of the sixties, he was determined to understand what leads a man to violence and beyond it to peace and harmony. His search led him to India where he met and studied with the Advaita sage, Ramesh S. Balsekar.

ALL QUOTES
OF
LAO TZU
ARE TAKEN FROM THE BOOK,

"SOMETHING TO PONDER."
BY
COLIN D. MALLARD

BOOKS CAN BE PURCHASED

FROM YOUR BOOKSTORE

OR FROM THE WEBSITES:

booksurge.com

amazon.ca

amazon.com